STARVING THINGS

A Story of Horror

Andrew Herold

COPYRIGHT

This is a work of fiction. All of the characters, organizations, and events portrayed in this novel are products of the author imagination.

ISBN: 979-8-9924120-0-0

Cover by Antoine Mainguy

www.starvingthings.com
www.andrewheroldbooks.com

To Mark and Ann, who taught me not to care

PART 1
THEN AND NOW
2014-2026

CHAPTER 1
A TOUR

Willow Hall stood tucked amongst the trees atop a stone precipice eighty feet above the river like a vulture looming over a dying creature; its sagging roof, a pair of slumped, eager shoulders, its peaked arches staring eyes, the crack in the heavy stone wall made by a falling pine tree, a corrupt sneer. For a hundred and twenty years it had stood poised to strike, but now its time of waiting was over. Willow Hall was a starving thing. And it hunted.

-Nan Wickwyre, *Haunting Willow Hall*

-1-

2014

As Nan looked up at the big old house in awe, these words from her first novel came to her. The photos in the online listing beneath the description—*Historic 'House on the Bluff' With River Frontage!*—hadn't come close to capturing its true face. But cresting the small hill in the driveway and having it suddenly appear before her like an act of prestidigitation had taken her breath away and solidified the connection instantly. It was all she could do to bring the car to a full stop before scrambling out into the driveway to look at it.

The house in front of her *was* Willow Hall: the tower in the northeast corner with the conical slate roof was the same one where her hero, Keaton Blackburn, had first spied the ghost of Lady Boyle; beneath the bluestone arches along the veranda was where Keaton and his wife Maisy had kissed passionately after discovering they were going to have their first child; the overgrown great lawn, which seemed to flow down the side of the stone cliff to the Hudson River, was where Keaton had killed that no good Vincent Shelton after Vincent had tried to kill Maisy the same way he had poor Lady Boyle… even the five stone chimneys, which stuck up through the roof like the pleading hand of Lady Boyle's corpse from the old well, were exactly as she had described them in her book.

The house wasn't just similar to Willow Hall, it was *identical*. Standing in the shade of its impossible creeping rooms with their oddly slanted walls was like standing beside a mythical creature. *Haunting Willow Hall* had been published more than twenty years ago, and she had never laid eyes on this house in her life. It was as if she'd seen it so clearly in her mind that somehow she had written it into existence.

"It hurts my brain," her husband, Nick, said. "There's nowhere for the eye to rest. It just keeps going and going, and none of it seems to mesh with the rest." He wrinkled his nose. "Sorta feels like it's looking at us, too."

Although Nan had used the trope in her own writing, windows acting as a house's eyes had never made much sense. None had ever looked very much like eyes to her. That wasn't to say a house couldn't feel *watchful*, as this one did, but it was never the windows that felt like they were doing the watching. She peered into the dark tangle of trees and weeds that grew up in the neglected flowerbeds and could almost feel something looking back.

"It's un-be-goddamn-leivable," she said and blinked hard. "It's exactly like Willow Hall."

"What are you talking about? It looks nothing like it," Nick said.

Nan wasn't paying attention to him. *I made it. It's mine,* she thought with wonder and pulled a flask from inside her jacket.

Nick watched without comment as she drank deeply, his eyes ringed with raccoon circles.

The fight they'd had before leaving the house still clung to them like a bad smell, and neither of them was yet willing to break the indifferent peace that had been forged on the long car ride.

It had started with Lizzie. It *always* started with Lizzie.

Nick checked his phone and, finding no reception, shoved it back into his coat pocket. "He's late."

"He'll be here. I texted him when we left." She spoke absently, exhaling scotch fumes, her attention commanded by the house.

Despite just ridding himself of it, Nick took out his phone and checked it again. It wasn't the realtor, Bobby Buckland, he was anxiously awaiting news from, but the babysitter who was at home with Lizzie.

Nan sighed, perhaps a little more theatrically than necessary, and pulled her flask back out. *Let him glare,* she thought. *Dammit, I've earned this.* When even the magic of the house couldn't stand against the rising tide of reality, magic needed a helping hand. "Can you just cool it? You heard Doctor Osborne. Lizzie is in remission. She'll be just fine playing with the neighbor girl for a few hours."

"She's been in remission before. I don't know why we couldn't have found a better sitter. An adult. What if something happened, and she's trying to get ahold of us right now?"

"Could you be any more dramatic? It's not like we left her with some kid off the street. Maddie's seventeen. We watched her grow up, for God's sake. Besides, her parents are right next door if something goes wrong." Nan rubbed her temples. A headache was gnawing at the back of her eyes and it was going to be a bad one. Even her teeth hurt. "She's perfectly capable of keeping an eye on Lizzie. Just... I don't know, try to enjoy this. How often do we get to do anything, just the two of us?"

Neither one of them needed to supply an answer to this question. *Never* was an easy statistic to remember.

Before she could wander down this well-worn trail and get lost in the familiar yet shifting thickets it contained, they both raised their heads at the sound of a squealing, knocking engine slowing down at the head of the driveway, where it spilled out onto Little Church Road.

"Finally," Nick said. "Almost twenty minutes late." He gave his phone one last regretful glance and shoved it back into his pocket.

"God, why don't you just wait in the car? You're obviously already annoyed, and your negativity has a way of spreading. I just want to enjoy this one—*one*—afternoon of freedom." Her words were too harsh, but she was just so tired; of Lizzie, of Nick, their crappy house in town... all of it.

He snorted softly, shook his head, and crossed his arms.

They watched as the gray Buick materialized over the small hill in the driveway, wheezed to its peak, and started to roll back down. The man behind the wheel eased the gargantuan rolling chunk of Detroit steel into the turnaround and put the car out of its rattling, knocking misery.

Bobby Buckland was a large man. Nan had been able to tell this from the photo on the website, despite it being only a headshot, and a heavily retouched one at that. But seeing him through the windshield now was like comparing a photo of a mountain to the *actual* mountain. Standing just over five and a half feet tall and weighing in at a solid 260 (maybe closer to 270 if he was really being honest, or if he'd had more than one helping of supper), Bobby was pretty well packed into the Buick's front seat. Nan didn't see how he would be able to get out. Even with her and Nick helping, she didn't believe he would manage. So, when the door screamed open and Bobby leveraged his ungainly mass up and out of the seat with one hand on the post and one hand on the door, she was relieved. Despite a little wobble that made it look like he was going to faceplant into the gravel, he somehow stayed upright. When he turned and reached back into the car for his lemon-yellow blazer, which proclaimed UNDERHILL REALTY in purple stitching on the breast above a heavily stylized house, Nan could see there were already dark circles beneath his arms despite the mild October afternoon. There was no way he would be able to keep up with them as they toured the immense, metastatic estate.

And as ridiculous as it sounded, Nan didn't want Bobby in her house. There really was magic here—somehow, implausibly, there was—and Bobby's presence would spoil it.

He lumbered toward them with that same duck-footed plodding gait used by all obese men over thirty, the one that said they'd rather be doing *anything* but walking, leaving long scuff marks in the gravel behind him. He clutched a brown folder in his hand with the company name on the front, which was already turning damp in his fist. He arrived, breathless, at the bottom of the veranda steps, which he eyed with tired venom.

"Afternoon, folks." His voice was high, squeaky, and not what Nan had imagined. He dragged his fingers back through his thinning hair, wiped the greasy sweat off on his blazer sleeve, and held out his hand. Nick, ever the people pleaser, took it and shook it. Nan offered a little wave. "Beautiful old place, isn't it? Good bones. Lots of room." Bobby had been glancing at the sales pages in his folder while he spoke, and when he finally raised his head and looked at Nan and Nick, he did a double take. His mouth fell open stupidly. "Holy *shit*, you're that writer lady, arentcha?"

Nan nodded.

"Holy shit, you are! *Shit*! Um, excuse my language and all, but I just didn't think you were *that* Nan Warwick when you got in touch."

"Wickwyre."

"Oh, sorry, 'course, *Wickwyre*." Bobby brushed his blazer back, placed his hands on his hips, and stared at her like she was some sort of exhibit in a museum. "Shit," he said again. "Yeah, I saw you on that talk show a while back when they were interviewing you about that book you wrote. Willow something... or something Willow."

Rather than help him, Nan just grinned her crooked grin (the one Nick called her Nixon smile) and nodded.

"Yeah... I never read the book, but the movie was pretty okay. Not enough blood and guts for me, but still pretty okay."

"Gee, *thanks*," Nan said, not even trying to hide her irritation. She knew from experience it wouldn't matter if she did or not. Men like Bobby Buckland wouldn't pick up on it anyway.

A queer look passed over Bobby's face then; his brow furrowed, and his right eyebrow arched as he swallowed hard and exhaled with a little gasp. It was as if he was trying to think of something important while holding in a gut-busting fart.

Nick put his hand on Bobby's shoulder. "You okay?"

A moment passed while Bobby's unfocused, bovine eyes started blankly at nothing, before he blinked rapidly, swallowed, and finally seemed to come back to himself. "Um... yeah, sorry. Warm today, isn't it?" He armed a film of sweat from his rapidly receding hairline, darkening his jacket from lemon to butterscotch.

"You sure you're all right?" Nick asked, patting Bobby's arm. "You want to sit down for a second?"

Instead of answering, Bobby fumbled a set of antique keys from his blazer pocket and held them up in embarrassed triumph. "Let me just get the doors open for you guys, and you can see what your new dream home looks like inside." He ambled up the steps one at a time and began the apparently arduous task of unlocking the cathedral-style doors. They were each eight feet tall, made of some thick burnished wood, and came together to a point. The wood was warped, and the latch plates rusted, which could have accounted for some of Bobby's difficulty, but Nan knew better; the handicap was all him. She'd known men similar to him throughout her career: frumpy and dumpy, dour and frowsy, and especially inept when it came to the simplest of tasks.

Perched above the door on a small stone ledge, a gargoyle with widespread wings and a grinning bulldog face looked down at Bobby as if mocking his ineptitude. It even looked a little like him. Just around the jowls.

"Come on, you whore," he grumbled under his breath and kicked the bottom of the door. When that proved fruitless, he began to wring the key back and forth in the lock.

"Maybe that's not—" Nan started, but a sharp, metallic snap rendered the rest of what she was about to say pointless.

"Shit. That happens sometimes with these old places. A good locksmith will be able to take care of that for you, no problem. Actually, here." He dug a voluminous wallet from the shiny seat of his pants and pulled a business card from it, which read:

Bobby Buckland
Underhill Realty
A Whiz in the Biz!

On the back, he scribbled *John Duckworth*, followed by a phone number. "Ducky's a handyman and contractor. The best around. He'll take care of you. Just tell him I sent ya, and he'll treat you good."

Nick took the card when Nan just glared at Bobby in disbelief and tucked it into his own wallet. "So, what now?" she said, barely keeping her annoyance in check. "Can we still get in, or do we have to go through a window?"

"Well, maybe that did it anyway," Bobby said. He twisted the handle and kicked the bottom of the door again, harder this time, and it shuddered open, dragging along the warped floor of the foyer. It made a wooden chuckling sound. Cool, damp air that smelled like old stones and river water wafted from the opening.

He cleared his throat of what sounded like a pint of phlegm, mopped the sweat from his face with a grimy handkerchief he had produced from his pocket, and led them over the threshold.

-2-

October in the Hudson Valley is an incredible time of year, Nan thought. The air was crisp and heavily perfumed by fallen leaves and the sweet, cidery smell of apples that hadn't made the cut during the last picking season rotting on the ground. The trees seemed to glow with almost neon colors, like the whole world was a photograph that had been oversaturated. She had forgotten how amazing it could be. Between Lizzie's first diagnosis at the age of three to her most recent remission, life had been little more than doctor appointments, worry, fighting, and, when time permitted, writing. Even those rare escapes when she was on tour were so tainted by guilt and regret that she couldn't fully enjoy them.

She was enjoying herself now, though. Despite Nick mechanically checking his phone every few minutes and Bobby Buckland (*A Whiz in the Biz!*) droning on in that high-pitched voice of his about the history of Holt House (which he was reading word for word from the listing), she had somehow still been able to tap into the magic of this place. Normally, admitting that something felt magical would have made her feel stupid, but that didn't seem to matter here.

"Just needs a little love, is all," Bobby was telling Nick. "The dampness has a way of creeping into things this close to the river, but you can't put a price on all the original wood moldings and the hardwood floors."

Nan wandered off. Through the door on the left side of the hallway, she entered a long room with high ceilings and boarded-up windows. Decaying velvet curtains framed each of them like forgotten victims of the hangman's noose, and sparkling shards of glass lay beneath them like breadcrumbs for the birds that came to pick the corpses clean. The room wasn't totally dark, though. Set in the far wall, one window remained, having somehow escaped the delinquents' rocks. It was filmy and speckled like dirty ice, but clear enough to let the afternoon light through to dribble across the floor and bring into sharp relief a table covered by a threadbare tarp. *A billiard table,* Nan thought. It stood to reason, then, that an age ago, this had been the billiard room. She went to the window, her nose almost touching the glass, and looked down the great lawn toward the tree line and, just beyond that, winking blue through leaves that shimmered orange and red like a crackling fire, the Hudson.

Bobby plodded over and stood beside her, his breathing labored and wheezy. She wrinkled her nose—his natural body odor was powerful this close—and stepped to the side. "How much frontage comes with it?" she asked, mostly to say *something* to cut through the awkwardness.

After a rustle of paperwork that seemed to go on forever, he said, "Four hundred feet and change. But you could probably get more if you wanted to. The properties to the south and the east have been coming on and off the market for a coupla years now. They're too steep to build on. In fact..."

And then he was off, droning on about something else

(Nan heard the words *formal garden* before just tuning him out entirely).

Instead, she watched Lizzie running and playing croquet with Nick on the manicured great lawn (mostly they were bashing the balls as hard as they could and laughing like loons). And over there, on the wide bluestone patio, Lizzie was carving pumpkins and giggling at how cold and squishy the guts were between her fingers. And down a little farther than that, just entering the shade of the full, green trees, the three of them were tramping down to the rocky sliver of beach, carrying a wicker basket stuffed with sandwiches, sodas, and chips. Lizzie was healthy. They were *all* thriving.

That these visions of health and peace could come true here was too much to hope for and *believe*, but Nan believed anyway. The magic in this place had resurrected the little girl she had been once upon a time; a girl who had believed in Santa Claus and the tooth fairy. That little girl had no doubt in her mind that as the house was restored and repaired, Lizzie would be too.

She had been so lost in these beautiful thoughts that she hadn't noticed Bobby had edged closer until she turned and saw him leaning toward her with that unnerving detached look in his eyes. His skin had taken on a grayish tinge that might just have been the gloom of the room, but Nan knew better. She backed away quickly.

"Empty a *looooong* time. Too long." Bobby's voice was hardly a whisper, but she heard it clearly. Sweat sprang up on his large forehead and coursed greasily down to his sagging jowls. "Those kids that come up here... come like rats, to gnaw and shit and fuck and break the goddamn windows."

"*What* did you say?" It wasn't the swearing that shocked her (she'd begun her third novel, *The Gunners*, with the line "Hey, cunt!" and hadn't the critics just loved *that*), but rather the strange and sinister mush that had just tumbled from his mouth.

He grinned, and his misaligned eyes seemed to float farther

apart when he did. "I'm getting used to my chicken feet," he said in a harsh whisper much deeper than his normal voice.

Nan had never seen a stroke before, and though it was the first thought that popped into her head, she didn't think this was one. His strange, simple words sent a shiver up her spine, and she felt a prickle at the back of her head, as if someone were standing behind her staring. The feeling was so real that she quickly turned and checked. The space was empty, but—and call her crazy if you must—it felt like someone *had* been there. And there was a smell in the air, the same one she had smelled when Bobby had first stood beside her, but she no longer thought it was his B.O. Or not *just* that.

And still, he grinned with his mouth slightly agape and his lower teeth pooched out like a llama's, leaning toward her in a way that seemed hungry. Nan reached out to tap his shoulder, terrified that when she did, Bobby would fall toward her in a series of quick, jerky movements, but no such thing happened. She patted his shoulder, unyielding as stone, encased in that awful yellow blazer. His expression did not vary. She was reaching out to do it again—and a little rougher this time— when Nick came into the room, phone in hand, and loudly proclaimed in an annoyed voice, "You need to see how bad the dining room is. It's packed to the rafters with shit, and the ceiling is leaking."

Bobby's eyes swam slowly back to true, and he swallowed wetly. "The kitchen is down the main stairs in the basement," he said as if they had just been discussing this. "These big old places had wood-fired stoves back in the day, and building the kitchen below ground level kept the house cooler in the summer." He turned on his heel, walked out into the hallway, and hung a left, moving deeper into the house.

"There's something wrong with him," Nan said. "Like medically wrong."

"Seems fine to me." The simple statement was loaded with subtext that Nan didn't have to be a detective to parse. *You're worried about the realtor? Really? Why don't you take some of that concern and point it your daughter's way?*

"Okay. Fine." She started to follow Bobby down the hallway before he became lost in the maze of rooms, but Nick's fingers closed firmly around her bicep.

"Nan, what are we doing here, really?"

"Let go of me."

He released her and turned with his arms raised in disbelief, pointing out a giant spray-painted phallus on the wall behind them. "You're not seriously considering buying this place."

"What do you care if I am? I can afford it."

"Yeah, but... I mean, it's falling apart. Half the house is too far gone and will probably have to be torn down, and the other half is going to take hundreds of thousands of dollars to make it livable. Not to mention there's probably mold and asbestos and bat shit and radon... even the tap water will probably cause cancer. Do you really think this is the best place for Lizzie?"

And there it is, she thought. *Not is it the best place for you or for* us, *but for Lizzie.*

"I'm going to find Bobby before he gets lost or falls through the floor or something." Before she made it a few feet her temper got the better of her, and she came back to deliver a parting shot she knew would get under his skin. "I told you that you could wait in the car, you know. That I didn't need you here with me. You should have just stayed at the house with Lizzie. It's where you want to be anyway." Then she turned, fuming, and went down the hall before Nick could respond. A few moments later, he followed her. Neither of them saw the two violently red drops of blood on the floor that had fallen from Bobby's nose and stained the wood where he'd been standing.

-3-

Most of the northern end of the house, the end facing the Hudson, was dominated by the dining room and serving pantry. Unlike the other rooms they'd toured so far, this one was stuffed with junk: bent and tarnished cutlery (including an imposing looking meat cleaver with rust blooms along the blade), old boxy televisions with kicked-in screens, piles of fallen lath and plaster, broken electronics, empty dime bags, smashed gas lanterns, a broken bong, crumpled beer cans, castoff condoms, greasy potato chip bags, and, of course, used needles. It was a time capsule of filth, yet somehow, that was the least interesting thing about it.

Along the wall beside the boarded-up bay window, which would have an incredible view when the glass was replaced, was a hastily cobbled-together shrine.

Nan leaned closer to inspect it. "What the hell is this?"

Bobby tsked rather prissily, and said, "Just at the end of the Second World War, this place was used as a nun... house... a nunnery. You know."

"Convent," Nan supplied distractedly.

"Yeah, a *comment*. They were a cloistered sect. After the last of the old gals died out, the place sat vacant until after '62 when it became a women's boarding school, but that lasted maybe only ten years. Most of this stuff is probably left over from the nuns. Historical society might want it, or you could prolly burn most of it. Pay some kids five bucks an hour to haul it to the dump or whatever. Out here, kids still consider that a lot of money. You want my opinion, though, even that's too much, considering the little shits are probably the ones who put it here in the first place."

Nick entered the room quietly, his phone no longer in sight, arms crossed. "Jesus," he said.

Hanging above the shrine by rusted twists of barbed wire was a wooden figure of Christ half as big as Nan was, its face

13

turned up to heaven, its mouth pulled down in an agonized grimace. Someone (probably those elusive kids to whom Bobby kept referring) had painted the eyes a shiny black, so when the light changed, they seemed to roll toward her. They'd also smeared something red around the mouth, into which they had carefully inserted thirty or forty rusted needles.

It was fascinating. She may have even dubbed it genius if the figure had been hanging in an art museum in the city. Hanging in this abandoned house by rusted wire though, it was only disturbing.

"Kids come up here and get into all sorts of trouble," Bobby said slowly. He frowned, shook his head as if clearing it, and took Nick's arm, leading him a little distance from Nan. "Between you and me, this place isn't the best one on the market. I don't know why you'd want to buy it, really. You'll probably still get the occasional trespasser, you know. I can show you some other properties with frontage if that's what you're looking for. *Good* ones."

If this was his idea of salesmanship, it wasn't any wonder that his shoes were sprung and broken down and looked as if he'd stolen them off a dead man. But neither his ineptitude nor his bad shoes were the reasons Nan suddenly wanted to sock him in the gut. It was how he'd taken Nick by the arm and spoken to him in that hushed *let's-not-worry-the-little-lady* tone of voice; a tone with which she was, unfortunately, intimately familiar despite her accomplished career and B-list celebrity. But here, in this place, *her* place, the slight was all the more egregious. *Sacrilegious* was actually the first word to spring to mind. Nick wasn't paying for the goddamn house, *she* was. When she was certain Bobby and Nick were distracted by one another, she pretended to be looking at something in the corner, snuck her flask out, and swallowed as much scotch as she could.

Like all others like him, Bobby stayed true to form and barreled ahead, blissfully oblivious. "Not just kids, either," he told Nick. "People traipse across other people's land all the time, especially to get down to the river. They just don't care. No respect for anything. Prolly oughta put up post-it signs first thing."

The notion that someone could be in the house with them right now, listening to their conversation, staying just out of sight, and stalking them from room to room probably would have frightened most people, but Nan wasn't the least bit concerned. The house felt empty. There was no way she could possibly know that it was, yet she did. Call it a byproduct of her magic connection with the aging wood, glass, and stone.

Besides, she was more concerned with what Bobby had just said than with trespassers. "You mean *posted* signs?" she asked.

He nodded. "Yuh-huh."

He wasn't exactly what Nan would have dubbed a wordsmith, but surely, as a realtor, he knew it was supposed to be *posted* signs. And what was the other word he'd flubbed? *Across*, that was it. He'd said *acrosst*, the way a little kid would have.

It's almost like he's drunk, she thought, then shrugged to herself. *So what if he is? He's not my responsibility. If that's what he needs to get through his day, I'm the last one to judge.*

She left Nick to handle Bobby and went to study the figure of Christ, which was even more loathsome up close. Where wood grain should have shown through the paint, it was hideously smooth and flesh-like. Still, she couldn't resist poking it. It boinked and squoinked in its barbed wire restraints, sending shivers racing up to where it was anchored to the walls.

Bobby's head whipped toward the sound as if he'd been called by name. "Probably shouldn't do that," he chided, speaking to her like a little girl. "That wire'll give you tetanus. Or something worse."

Part of her wanted to reach out and touch it again out of spite, but doing so would only justify Bobby's parental scolding, and she wouldn't give him the satisfaction.

"I should just take it down anyway. Boss wouldn't like it if I left it up there. That sorta thing puts most people off from buying a place. Gives *me* the creeps, that's for sure. I don't think I could stand to live in a place like this." He clomped over, took ahold of the figure with one big fist that closed around it like dough, and yanked down with as much force as he could muster, as if doing so could magically snap the wire. It twanged in protest but held.

"That won't work. You need to unwind it," Nan said. "See there where it's looped around the neck? And again around the arms?"

Nick came over to add his two cents to the mix with an offer to help, but Bobby wasn't hearing it.

"Best not," he said, and Nan noticed his eyes had started to do that strange floating thing again. And again, her scalp prickled at the back of her head, and the skin of her face seemed to tighten. "Insurance-wise, if something happens, I'm covered. Be done in a spiffy." He frowned. "A *spiffy*." He chuckled humorlessly and shook his head. "A *jiffy*. That's it. Yeah, I'll be done in a spiffy." He grabbed the figure with both hands and yanked it harder, making the wires shriek and tremble and causing a fine mist of plaster powder to filter down and land on his head and shoulders like dandruff. "Oh, come on, you fucker."

"Bobby, just leave it there," Nan said. She'd already decided she was going to buy the house, and didn't care if Jesus wanted to hang around for a little while, but Bobby continued to pull as if he either didn't hear her or couldn't understand what she was saying. He was wheezing again, his skin ashen and his hands bleeding where the wood cut into them, yet he continued to pull, almost to the point it seemed the wires *must* break. There was no way they could withstand this assault much longer.

Then he stopped. He cocked his head suddenly to the side as if he could hear something Nick and Nan could not. "Yep," he said quietly as a fat drop of blood pushed out of his nose and ran down his lips.

Nan stepped back, her whole body shivering, her eyes watering.

"Bobby, you all right?" Nick asked. Bobby turned slowly to him and stared with his off-kilter eyes.

"Obviously he's not," Nan said. "No, this is fucked. Nick, go up the road until you get reception and call 911."

"No. Absolutely not, no. I'm not leaving you here with him like this."

"Goddamnit, can't you just for once in your life do what I say? There's something really wrong with him. Just go!" She knew Nick well enough to know he would have stayed and argued the point until he got his way, if the barbed wire that tethered Christ's figure to the ceiling hadn't chosen that exact moment to let go. One moment, Bobby was straining and wheezing while the wires screamed bloody murder, the next there was a *TWANG* followed by a whistling brown blur and a sound like a whip striking a side of beef. Nan flinched as if she had been struck, shuddered, and covered her mouth with her hand.

The room was silent for a moment except for the *clang-twang* of the Christ figure bobbling up and down on the wires still holding it, and she had a moment to hope that maybe Bobby hadn't been hit after all.

Then his hand flew up and covered his eye.

As a horror writer, she'd written innumerable scenes in her books in which a character shrieked in pain, but to hear it in reality sounded nothing as she had described it. When Bobby inhaled sharply and started to shriek, her first thought was that there was no intelligence in it, no controlled nuance or dignity; it was a wavering, inarticulate, *insane* sound, sort of like a sentient teakettle. In the sound, she could hear the baby that Bobby Buckland had been, squalling in fear in his bassinet.

"Nick, go now! Call an ambulance!" Nan screamed, and for a wonder, he did it without further argument, pounding down the hallway toward the front door.

Being the mother of a girl prone to dizzy spells, nosebleeds, and infections, Nan carried a small pharmacy in her purse that was probably better stocked than most people's first aid kits at home. She tugged on Bobby's arm, trying to get him to lower his hand away from his eye so she could survey what kind of damage had been done, but he was surprisingly strong, as was his caterwauling.

"Goddamnit, Bobby, let me take a look," she said. The adrenaline dump to her system was making her hands shake and causing her to feel nauseated. Bobby's screeching wasn't helping matters. Finally, fed up, she jerked his arm down as hard as she could. "Oh, Jesus fucking *Christ.*"

The wire had struck him high on the cheek and carved through it like the blade of a deli slicer. If it had stopped there, she might have been able to help him, but the wire had smacked him with such force that it had continued on through the meat, had torn through the tear trough just below his right eye, and shredded the eye itself, leaving behind a weeping, ragged hole flecked with rust.

She stumbled away from him until the back of her legs hit something solid and sat down hard as all the strength ran out of her legs. Her purse spilled onto the floor, but that didn't matter. There was nothing in it that could help Bobby now.

"Dammit, Nick, hurry the hell up," she muttered. She couldn't hear the returning rumble of the car engine, but then, perhaps she wouldn't; Bobby's screaming had reached an unbearable pitch. Any higher and it would only be heard by dogs. *How much breath can one man have in him?*

And that's when the noise stopped. For a split second, she thought maybe he actually *had* raised in pitch to a level unable to be heard by the human ear—his mouth still hung open as if he was screaming—but then she realized she *could* hear something. It sounded like a low voice speaking from somewhere in the room. Bobby's one eye turned toward the sound, and he took a shaky breath. His skin, which a moment ago had been a hectic and splotchy reddish-purple, was now almost entirely white, and his mouth hung open, dribbling blood, his lips quivering.

Nan tried to stand and go to him, but she couldn't. It wasn't that she was frightened and her muscles had frozen in fear, she just was physically unable to stand.

Bobby collapsed in stages. First, he landed on his left knee, which sent tremors through the floor and caused some of the more precarious piles of junk to cascade down in a jangling mess. Then came his right knee, which cracked as if the bone had splintered. He squeaked, then gurgled. "Fucking... the shitting... *spiffy!*" he said, but his words had almost no air to carry them.

He clutched his left arm tightly, his mouth pulling down into a grimace, not unlike the Christ figure's mouth (a terrifying thing to see on the face of a man missing an eye), and croaked, "Rot."

Nan was oddly calm. A handful of times in her life, usually after receiving bad news from the doctor about Lizzie or when one of her books was critically panned, she had taken a Xanax to help take the edge off of the sting. She felt as though she'd just taken one. Observing Bobby Buckland struggle for his every breath, she watched with an almost clinical detachment as if he were a character in one of her books. The fact that she couldn't stand had become inconsequential. *What could I possibly do to help him now anyway?* His story had led him here; she had no control over whatever was about to happen. *I'm nothing more than a reader along for the ride.*

She took the flask from her jacket, drained the last of the scotch from it, then spun the cap back on with a practiced flick of her fingers and secreted it away again.

Bobby's arms went rigid and fell to his sides; his single eye opened wide, and his whole body quaked. He fell forward from his knees to the floor, gasped, and died with a face full of splinters.

The figure of Christ bobbling on the wires behind him fell to the floor then and broke open as if it had only been waiting for him to give up. Termite larvae boiled out of the punky wood, writhing together in a ball before scattering for parts unknown. A few of them made their way onto his face, but he didn't seem to mind.

Not even cold and already covered in worms.

One of his shoes had skittered off across the floor, and Nan watched as a termite wriggled up the side of it and then down inside, where it was dark.

Nick's feet thundered hollowly down the hallway, and he ran into the room, his phone still in hand. "Ambulance is coming."

"Too late," Nan said, and stood. Her legs worked just fine now.

Nick slung his arm around her waist, and pulled her into him.

He whispered sorrowful, reassuring things into her ear, things she'd heard him say to Lizzie when she awoke scared in the middle of the night, but Nan wasn't listening. Her mind had turned to the voice she had heard right before Bobby stopped screaming and collapsed. It was the strangest thing. At the time, she hadn't really heard what it had said, but reflecting on it now, she would have sworn it had spoken the same words that her poor murdered dowager, Lady Boyle, said to Keaton Blackburn during the séance scene in *Haunting Willow Hall*:

"I rot in the well, Mr. Blackburn. Deeeeep down in the blackness, where the water is cold, and slimy things slither in and out. I rot alone in the dark."

CHAPTER 2
THE INTERVIEW

The spirit's words sent shivers up Keaton Blackburn's spine, and his hand felt unnaturally cold where the spectral hand of Lady Boyle had gripped it with her bony fingers. She was gone now, but the room was still uncommonly damp. *Take heart and forge on*, he told himself. *You're doing this for your poor darling Maisy, still confined to bed, trapped in her strange fugue state.*

"What did she say?" Vincent asked, leaning forward with greedy eyes. "Did she tell you where her money is?"

Keaton nodded slowly. *Let him believe the lie*, he thought. Lady Boyle had not said anything about her money, but she had revealed where her body had been squirreled away by the man who had murdered her. The same man who sat at this very table now between Keaton and the medium.

-Nan Wickwyre, Haunting Willow Hall

-1-

2026

Time is a strange and muddled thing. One moment may bleed into the next as quickly and as easily as ink into water. And then, if you're not careful, those two will bleed into a third, and then a fourth, and so on, until an entire day has passed in an instant.

And then there are other moments that become indelibly etched into our memories and grow large there, nurtured by our imaginations, and go on to balloon into fifteen minutes or even full hours, and before you know it, they've overtaken an entire day.

Over the decade or so following Bobby Buckland's tragic (though perhaps not untimely) death, Nan had lived through roughly eighty-seven thousand hours. Looking back on them now, only fifty or so stood out in stark relief, like a handful of color photos in a sea of indecipherable black and white snapshots.

But even most of those fifty were inconsequential. The moments that mattered, the ones containing the memory she continued to return to unbidden and against her will, amounted to only three minutes. That's all. In a whole decade, just three lousy minutes, during which her real life had ended.

In those three minutes, the family car, loaded with gifts for their friends, had hit a patch of black ice and skidded off the road on Christmas Day. It had smashed into a guardrail before finally fetching up against an old pine tree with a metallic crunch that still sometimes haunted her dreams. Nan limped away from the car with a broken foot and a fractured wrist (both of which still pained her when it rained heavily like it was now). Nick and Lizzie hadn't walked away at all.

Usually, Nan thought about those three minutes during her darker moments, when the horrible thoughts started to seep in like water through the walls of a stone foundation. If she had still been able to silence these thoughts with booze, she might have been okay, but her rotten sobriety denied her this solace. All she could do was wait for them to leave.

Thankfully, she wasn't in a dark time now. The only reason she was thinking about the accident was that it would have been Lizzie's birthday in a week. Her sixteenth. Even when Lizzie was just a chapped-ass newborn, Nan had been looking forward to celebrating the big one-six with her the same way her own mother had. She would have woken up early in the morning, made Lizzie pancakes out of yellow cake mix, and frosted them with vanilla frosting (her favorite). Then there would have been a huge party on the lawn with all of her friends (with a little bit of beer, just enough for each kid to have a drink apiece), and when everyone had eaten their fill of whatever junk food Lizzie had decided on, Nan would have given Lizzie her gift. A new car. Nan's parents had thrown her a version of this party, but instead of getting to pick the junk food, they had roasted a whole pig on a spit, and instead of a new car, she'd gotten her dad's old farm truck. And there had definitely been more than one beer apiece for the kids.

But Lizzie was dead, and the party wouldn't be happening. It only existed in Nan's mind, the last remaining shred of a life she might have had. Instead of her family, Nan was alone. Fifty-one years old, fatter than she was ten years ago, filled with regrets... and sober. Instead of scotch to comfort her, she had tea.

She poured herself another mug of the barely flavored piss-water and took a sip. Coffee would have been better, but since hitting fifty, it made her too jittery and, more often than not, sent her running for the bathroom. Soda was likewise out; it had been a big part of the reason she'd packed on thirty-five pounds after rehab. But she needed something while she wrote; *especially* while she wrote. Something she could mindlessly suck down her throat the way she used to suck down scotch.

She was writing now, hidden away in her office in the attic, but it wasn't going very well. Thinking about Nick and Lizzie had slowed her flow to a trickle as it usually did, though incredibly not immediately following their deaths. Others may have found that strange, but she'd been in the middle of a project when it happened, and the spigot had stayed open. Somehow, the work always remained.

Some people had a muse; Nan had a plump, hairy Brooklynite named Vito, who smoked cheap cigars and wore shiny suits. *He* was the one in charge of the flow of words from his office in some strip mall, and she had absolutely no control over when that asshole would give the order. When Vito decreed, his crew turned the knob, and when he'd had enough, he bellowed for them to shut it down. When she'd first begun writing, he had been in charge of a fire hydrant; now, he had domain over a garden hose. But it could still put out an unholy amount when it was turned on at full bore.

Even while in rehab, where she spent most of her time wanting a drink and dreading that moment when she would return home to that huge house that looked empty but was really chock-full of beautiful and painful memories, she had been able to put pen to paper. Sometimes, it was only a few disjointed sentences, sometimes the words that came were actually good, but even when they came out like spoiled milk from a cow's teat, the joy of *doing* was still there.

And after all that, when the worst of it was behind her, and she found herself with nothing but time stretching out before her all the way to the horizon of old age and death, it was still a comfort to come back to the pulsing cursor and spill the horrors from her head onto the gently glowing page and know that eventually they would be buried between the covers of a book.

The windows in the northwest corner of her office were shuttered to keep out the view and, with it, distraction. Nan closed her laptop (Vito had fucked off for the day down to the corner bar, probably to break someone's legs in the back alley behind it) and opened the windows, letting in the damp air.

The wet soil smell that reached even up here was rich and inviting. In another month, maybe a little less, the snow would start to fly, and she would have to pull her little mower out of the garage, take it to Henderson's to have them fit it with chains and put its plow blade back on it, and begin stocking up on salt. But right now, the world was damp and fragrant and perfect.

Far below, the Hudson was muddy brown and churning with runoff from the fall rains, which had knocked most of the leaves from the trees, leaving behind skeletal things standing stark against the gray sky. She breathed in deeply, inhaling the intoxicating scent of the water, then lit a cigarette. It was the one thing that really seemed to help the cravings, even though before giving up the booze, she had never been much of a smoker. Just the occasional hit off a joint if others were partaking. But then, desperation did make strange bedfellows. The cigarettes tasted awful (like the tea), but at least they gave her that slight sense of euphoria when the first rush of smoke hit her lungs and lit up her neurons like fireworks. It was as close as a teetotaler like her could get to tipsy.

But thinking this way wasn't helping anything. Now, on top of being unable to finish the day's writing, she wanted a drink.

Just one.

A big one.

Her phone chimed, momentarily driving from her mind the image of a sleek highball glass sweating crystalline beads of water, filled almost to the brim with dark brown, oily-looking scotch. Mostly. Clamping the cigarette between her teeth and squinting her eye against the rising smoke, she dug her phone out of her hip pocket. About three years ago, a cell tower had gone up a couple of miles away, and she had crystal clear reception. The years hadn't been all bad.

It was a text from her assistant, Lauren.

Don't forget interview at 1PM. Claudia McKinnon interviewer. Will check in 2-3PM to see how it went. Trev has another ear infection, so taking him to get meds. Luck!

And now this shit. Nan had conveniently put this appointment out of her mind, hoping it would just go away. Claudia McKinnon was a local news "anchor" (and yes, she thought of it in air quotes), with a personality so plastic and bubbly, Nan could have cheerfully rammed a spike through her head. If that had been all, she might have been able to stomach her, but Claudia also had this air of desperation about her, like she thought she should be headlining some major network instead of telling viewers what days Connie the Cow would be taking center stage at the state fair.

Given her way, Nan never would have agreed to do this in the first place, but her agent, Tim Rossiter, had specifically requested it. Considering it would be her first interview in ten years and her first published book in that time as well (despite writing like her life depended on it, she had not published one blessed thing since the accident), she didn't really have a choice. Tim had been all sympathy and understanding in the beginning and had waited a full month and a half after the funeral before hounding her for the book she'd promised him. But his patience had worn thin. If she hadn't been such a major player before the excrement hit the fan, she would have been dropped like a sack of flaming dog shit years ago.

Oh, and speak of the devil, look who's calling. Her cigarette was down to the filter, so she pitched it out the window and lit another.

"What's up, Tim?" In the background, she could hear the clink of glasses and drunken, good-natured cheer.

"Hey, doll face, how's tricks?" The same opening volley as

always, even though she'd talked to him about calling her doll face more than once.

"They don't pay enough. How've you been?"

"Fine, fine. I'd complain, but who'd listen, you know?"

"Yeah, I hear that." The shelves over her desk were filled with various knickknacks that didn't fit anywhere else in the house. Nan picked up the ceramic frog wearing a sombrero that Nick had gotten from some relative who had traveled to Mexico when Nick was still in elementary school and examined it while she spoke. "So, listen, Tim, I'm kinda in the middle of something. What do you need?"

"Foreplay's all done, huh?" he said, slurring a bit and laughing stupidly. "Well, fine, I was never very good at that. With women, anyway. You know why I'm calling. Don't forget the interview, she should be there soon. Whatsername, you know."

"Claudia. Lauren texted to remind me."

"Glad she's staying on top of you. You ready for this?"

Nan laughed. She set the frog down and picked up a pink pinecone blasted with glitter that Lizzie had made as a Christmas ornament when she was five. The glitter rubbed off on her hands. "What's to prepare for? The woman gives farm reports three days a week, and she's only here to ask about the new book." There was silence on the other end of the line, followed by a wet gulp. "Tim, where'd you go? See something cute?"

"Yeah, maybe."

"This one at least old enough to be your son?" The last one of Tim's boys she'd met had just turned twenty. *He's my gift to myself for my forty-fifth*, he'd said. *Since no one else was gonna get me one.* After that, Nan had stopped accepting party invitations from him.

Tim laughed humorlessly and belched softly into the phone. "Just be nice to her when she gets there, okay? I need this new book to sell. *We* need it to sell. So smile pretty for the cameras and keep the claws in your paws, *capisce*? I wasn't the one who decided to become freaking Garbo after the accident, not publishing new stuff or doing signings or interviews or anything, so suck it up, honey."

There were a few more seconds of silence in which Nan heard a chorus of voices drunkenly singing a Troye Sivan song over the relentless beeping of a cash register as Tim's brain hurried to catch up with his mouth. "Fuck, doll face, I'm sorry. You know I didn't mean it that way, right?"

"Sure." Of course he had. People like Tim *always* meant it that way. They just didn't want you to know what a piece of shit they really were. Nan's mouth was full of saliva and more than anything, she wanted an ice-cold beer.

"I'm forgiven?"

"Nothing to forgive."

"Splendid. You're all class, y'know that?"

"I've been told. By you, actually. Hey, by the way, does she want anything signed? I don't have many copies at the house right now. I've got a couple of *Willow Hall*..."

"Oh, she's never read anything of yours," Tim said. "I'd be surprised if she can read a menu without help. But she'll play along and pretend she has."

Nan snorted.

"Come on, don't put on your bitch pants for *that*. You know the deal."

She did. And though Tim probably wouldn't have believed her if she'd told him, she genuinely thought it was funny.

"And now, if you don't mind, I've got something that requires my immediate attention, so I'm gonna hafta jump." Over coffee about a year ago, Tim had, unsolicited, given her the rundown on all the hot, young performers he liked (and not just for their music), which was how Nan knew that the Troye Sivan song had given way to one by Omar Rudberg. The drunken songbirds sang along to this new one with equal gusto.

It was a bittersweet sound. She needed to get off this call before she decided to just drive to the liquor store and buy a bottle.

"Just make sure this one doesn't steal your wallet *and* your computer before he sneaks out in the morning," she said and hung up before she had to hear the disgusting bon mot she knew he'd already thought up in response.

She looked down at the mangled pink pinecone in her hand. She didn't recall crushing it, but the proof sat in pieces on her palm.

The thing that pissed her off the most was that Tim was right. That obnoxious, predatory scumbag was one hundred percent right. She had been the one to pull back from the public eye and refused to publish anything. She couldn't remember why anymore, but it had seemed like the right thing to do at the time. Of course, at the time, immediately following the accident, she was still drinking heavily. Maybe if she'd been less rigid, things would have gone differently.

Oh well. Can't put the shit back in the horse.

The garbage can beneath her desk was empty of anything but a few old teabags and a candy bar wrapper, so she dumped the remains of the decoration into it and dusted her hands off.

It was just about 12:30 now. Claudia would be arriving in about a half hour. That gave her time to tidy up and eat something sugary; not the same as a belt of scotch, but not the worst substitute. *Good god, if I can make it through this fucking afternoon without a drink, I can make it through anything*, she thought. She pitched her second cigarette butt out the window —made a mental note to pick them up before her housekeeper, Ava, came later in the week—latched the shutters, and went downstairs.

-2-

Nan had chosen to do the interview in the library. It was both comfortable and impressive with its large marble fireplace, which had cost a king's ransom to restore (now roaring cheerily along to drive out the chill out of the day), and its collection of over ten thousand books. From the time she was a child, she had dreamed of having a library like this and had stocked it with the classics, rare prints, a few signed books (a Shirley Jackson was floating around somewhere), and leather-bound editions that looked nice when photographed for a magazine—which this room had been, twice. The books she actually read were somewhat less impressive, usually just paperbacks from *Second Story*, the used book place in New Paltz, which she kept stacked in a pile on the floor beside her bed.

Despite its grandeur, the room didn't seem to impress Claudia McKinnon. She marched in wearing her pink pumps and matching headscarf as if she owned it, lowered her oversized sunglasses (which she wore despite the rain, and which made her look vaguely alien), and arched an overplucked eyebrow. When she spoke, she used the same ridiculous affected Southern accent Nan had heard her use on air (even though she had been born and raised on Long Island), which turned Connie the Cow into Connie the *Caow*. "It's really cute. How many rooms y'all got here?"

"About eighty-six." Out of all the questions people liked to ask Nan, this one was the most common, even more so than *where do you get your ideas*? To her, it was a pointless question —what could anyone possibly do with the answer to it except ooh and aah and move on with their life?—but she supposed there was a certain fascination that came from this type of excess. Still, it was bizarre. "I lost some to a fire a few years back, and there's still a part of the house I haven't gotten around to renovating, so that's still closed off. There are probably fifteen or twenty rooms I use regularly." In truth, most of the remaining sixty or so were collapsing and likely beyond redemption, but that wasn't quite as impressive.

"Mmm, okay," Claudia said. She set a briefcase on the coffee table in front of the sofa and a large black plastic box on the floor in front of it. "You live out here all alone?"

"Just me and my attack dog." Said dog, Peanut, was a four-hundred-year-old dachshund with two milky eyes and about eight teeth, who contented himself with sleeping the day away in front of whichever fireplace happened to be lit and farting himself awake every so often. He'd been Nick's dog way back when, and somehow just kept on living.

Claudia removed an old-fashioned video camera and collapsible tripod from the black plastic box and started to set them up with practiced ease. Plastered on the side of it was a huge circle decal with *Details News* written in big blue letters.

"So, no cameraman then?"

"Oh no, not for small stories like this one, hon. This is a simple one-on-one interview, no fancy panning or zooming or nothing. This camera dunt even link up over satellite. I gotta record it all on these little bitty SD cards here." She continued to plug things in, connect wires, and lay out papers on the coffee table, all while wearing her sunglasses. It wasn't until she was completely ready that she sat down and removed them, along with her headscarf. Her hair was somehow still perfectly coiffed and looked hurricane-proof.

There was something about her that Nan didn't like. She'd met plenty of divas in her line of work (hell, even her agent was a bit of a diva himself), and had never had trouble handling them. Divas were easy. Appeal to their ego, don't argue with them no matter what, and keep your cool. Simple. Claudia wasn't a diva, though (or not *just* a diva), but she sure seemed to want to make Nan think she was. There was something sly there, not to be trusted.

Calm down. She's just the first person who isn't Lauren or Ava in your personal space, that's all. Don't get crazy.

Nan poured a cup of white plum tea and gave it to Claudia —it was the one she kept for the houseguests she truly despised because it tasted like hot water and nothing more—and lit a cigarette while she watched Claudia set up the *mise en place.*

"Prolly don't wanna be smokin' on camera, sends the wrong sorta message nowadays, dontcha think?"

Nan shrugged and flicked the butt into the fireplace. She didn't really care what sort of message she was sending, but Tim would, and the last thing she needed was a scolding.

"Alrighty, looks like we are set to go. Now I know you've done these sorta things before, so just try to act as natural as possible and answer as clearly as you can. And if y'all need a break, just let me know, and we'll stop rolling, 'kay? Should be fun."

"I can hardly wait."

The camera was set up equidistant between the wingback chairs, roughly ten feet away. Once running, it would provide a nicely framed shot of the two of them and the heavy slab coffee table (on which Claudia had set an advance copy of Nan's new book to show the viewers, along with a manila folder), a section of the bookshelves in the background, and a sliver of the view going down the great lawn toward the woods. Claudia checked that everything looked exactly like she wanted, then depressed the record button. A red light on top of the camera glowed angrily like a bloody eye, making Nan think of Bobby Buckland for the first time in forever. She put that thought out of her mind and took a deep breath. A half hour, maybe a little longer, and this would be over, and she could have a whole pack of cigarettes if she wanted to.

And don't worry. If you come across as an asshole, they'll edit it to make you look like something vaguely resembling human. It's one of the perks of being a minor celebrity.

Claudia sat, smoothed her navy blue dress, and cleared her throat.

And then they were off to the races.

-3-

"Howdy folks, I'm Claudia McKinnon, and I'm here talking to the Queen of Horror, our very own local legend, Nan Wickwyre, about her upcoming book, *Dead Stories*. Sounds spooky, dunnit? And y'all, Halloween *is* right around the corner. If you don't know her already, you need to crawl out from under that rock you been living under! Nan is the winner of multiple awards, including the Hudson Valley Voices Medal, and is the author of such books as *Haunting Willow Hall*, *The Gunners*, and *The Boneyard*. And that last one is a personal favorite of mine. Nan, thanks for welcoming me here to your beautiful home."

"Thanks, Claudia, pleasure to have you here."

"So now, let's get the big question out of the way. I know it's the one I'm most curious about, and it's the question the largest percentage of our viewers wanted to know... how many rooms do y'all have here?"

"Um, about eighty-six or so total. There's quite a few."

"You ever get lost?"

"A few times, actually. People don't realize how these old places are laid out. There's not always a sense to it."

"And which one is your favorite room? Let me guess, y'all have a mausoleum here?"

"No, no mausoleum, but there is a little cemetery out back. Actually, I'd have to say *this* is my favorite room at the moment. I read a lot, of course, and this room is just so... *cute*. Don't you think?"

"Why sure, cute as a bug. Now is this where you do all your writing?"

"Sometimes. Mostly, I just stick to my office. Keeps me focused. Here, it would be too tempting just to pick up a book and start reading."

"I can sense that it might be distractin'. That's one heck of a view out there. I could spend the whole day just looking out the window."

"Sure, it's very peaceful."

"Now, I gotta ask because Halloween is just around the corner. Is this house haunted just like the house in your book *Willow Hall*?"

"Well, Claudia, if you remember, Willow Hall was not haunted at all. Spoiler alert, by the way, for those who haven't read it."

"Why 'course I remember that. I just didn't want to give away the ending! I'm trying to drum up some new sales for y'all, seeing as how that book is thirty years old now."

"Well, I appreciate that. Hopefully, they'll want to pick up the new one, though."

"But have you ever seen a ghost?"

"Nope, never."

"What about the Holt curse?"

"I mean... I know it's bad for business, being a horror writer and all, but I don't believe this place is cursed. That's just local legend. Every town has theirs. Some true bits of history get twisted over time, and these legends grow out of them. But there's nothing more to it."

"But in this case, it seems like the history and the legend go hand in hand, dunnit? I mean, look what happened to the Holts back in 1860. Someone killed them poor kids, Persephone, Jeremiah, and Cora, and then their parents, Percy and Gretchen went missing. And then, in the sixties, Thomas and Valerie Price bought the place and moved in with their little boy, Ricky, and were gonna turn it into a resort, but Thomas and Ricky wound up dead, and Valerie wound up missing just like the Holts. And that was their first year here."

"Look, I've heard the stories, but none of that stuff happened because of a curse. Look into the history of any old house, and there are bound to be a couple of tragedies. And that's what those were, just tragedies. This house is over a hundred and fifty years old. A couple of horrible things happening in that time is nothing in the grand scheme of things. I say let the dead rest."

"So did any of this stuff make it into your new book, then?"

"No. All writers draw from real life to a degree, but the horrors in my stories are all made up. Communities like this one are close-knit, you know? And there's a difference between retelling local stories within the community and exploiting them for fame and fortune with outsiders. Especially when you're an outsider yourself, even after ten years."

"But this book *is* full of all sorts of scary stuff, right?"

"I mean, *I* think it is, and hopefully, it will scare the readers, too. It gave me the creeps while I was writing, and that's usually a pretty good indication of whether or not people will respond to it. *Dead Stories* is a collection of ten shorts dealing with death, so that's a pretty fertile area when you want to scare someone. I guess if you want to know more, you'll have to read it."

"And are all these new stories, or have you been writing all along over the last ten years?"

"I've been keeping busy. That's the thing about being a writer, I guess. The ideas and words come when they come."

"But you haven't published anything?"

"No, this will be my first book since *Darker than Night*."

"Mmmhmm, mmhmm, now is that because of the accident when you lost your daughter and husband, or was rehab the reason?"

"..."

"..."

"... We need to stop."

Claudia turned the camera off. Nan waited for the red light to wink out before she spoke.

"What the *fuck* was that about? Why would you bring that up?"

"Which one, the accident or rehab?"

Nan stared, dumbfounded. "Are you trying to be smart? You were told that was all off-limits. And it's *recovery*, not rehab."

Claudia smiled, and Nan could see now what she hadn't been able to see earlier. Claudia McKinnon hated her. She took her seat across the coffee table from Nan, opened the manila folder, and took a sheaf of stapled papers from it. She slid them across the tabletop.

At first, Nan considered just not picking them up, but curiosity got the better of her. She scanned the first page, numb. "What is this?"

"*That* is Muriel Duckworth's statement to me yesterday about how you murdered her husband, John 'Ducky' Duckworth, when he was up here working on this house for you in 2016."

Nan threw the papers back at Claudia. "You can't be serious."

"Oh, as a heart attack, hon. Go on. Read through it if you wanna. I corroborated most of that already by talking to the people on his crew and asking 'round town. Miss Kitteridge down at the library told me you'd been running a little writer's workshop there for some of the local high schoolers, but when Ducky disappeared, you were nowhere to be found for two weeks."

"Oh, for the love of God... I was out in Marin County visiting a friend!" Linnie Kitteridge saying anything against her was a shock; she'd always been incredibly sweet, but then Nan *was* from away, and Muriel wasn't. People who had never lived in a small town like this wouldn't have understood, but being *from* a place carried a lot of weight in these tiny, insular communities.

"Well, Muriel and Miss Kitteridge think that ain't the whole truth."

"Look. I don't know what Linnie's issue is, but Muriel is *nuts*. Like, actually, legitimately certifiable. You can't trust a word that comes out of her mouth. Her husband went missing —*missing*—he hasn't been declared dead even though it's been more than three years, and she started blaming me for no reason at all, except that maybe I'm the rich lady who isn't from here. Talk to people who aren't a part of her inner circle, and you'll find just as many people in town who tell you that she and John fought all the time and that he was going to divorce her. Dig a little further, and you'll probably find out he took off for the Caribbean or somewhere to get away from her without having to pay alimony."

"So, then your story is that he decided to run away and leave the country, am I gettin' that right?"

Nan shook her head in disbelief. "I have no *story*. I don't know what the hell happened to him! How are you not getting this? Muriel Duckworth's mental instability is pretty well known to the people of this town. You can't believe a damn thing she says. And by the way, I think it's incredibly unprofessional of you to come into my house and attack me with these baseless accusations. I'm going to call your station manager when you leave and get your ass fired. What do you think about that? *Hon*?" Claudia was still smiling, though, and Nan didn't care for that one little bit. "You know what, on second thought, get the fuck out. Right now. We're done here. And just a heads-up, I'm going to call my lawyer when you leave, and if you run one word of this interview, I'll sue you and your station into the ground."

"Ain't no call to get mad at me. I'm just doin' my job, is all. B'sides, I can't leave without showing you this." She took another sheaf of photocopied papers and tossed them across the table. "How do y'all think people are gonna start lookin' at you after I release this, hmm?"

Nan almost slid them back without looking at them, but what would have been the point? This was the textbook definition of gotcha journalism. Claudia was just trying to drum up a controversy to increase her viewership and maybe use that as leverage for a ticket out of the podunk station where she'd stagnated for years. It was as plain as the nose job on her face. But it was always better to know which way the storm was coming from, so Nan scanned the top page, her eyes jumping from word to word until her hands began to shake and her face went tomato red. "This is the police report from the night of the accident. Where did you get this?"

Claudia leaned forward and glanced furtively at the camera. Nan would have seen it, but she was still scanning the paperwork as if disbelieving it was actually in her hands. "Did you know that state law says any traffic accident resultin' in a death requires a field breathalyzer test? Imagine my surprise when I found out *yours* ain't listed there. Or anywhere, for that matter. Now, why do ya think that is?"

Nan couldn't speak. There were about a million things she would have liked to have said, but the connection between her brain and her mouth seemed to have been temporarily severed.

"What *was* your blood alcohol level that night?"

"..."

"One of my sources said y'all paid off the local sheriff to keep it under wraps. Care to comment on that?" When Nan still didn't respond, Claudia barreled ahead. "I mean, everyone knows the story you released to the press. You were driving, and it was a little icy out, and it was just one of those tragic things. But you checked yourself into rehab just after that, didn't you? Is that why you been hiding out up here all by yourself? Afraid the truth might get out?"

"Get out," Nan finally managed to say, but Claudia

pretended she hadn't heard. Her lips felt dry, but she didn't dare lick them. She wanted a drink more than anything in the world.

"And when you stand *that* little tidbit of information up next to Muriel Duckworth's accusations, well, dun't that sorta seem like there might be something more to the story? I mean, maybe y'all were drunk when you killed Ducky, too."

Nan clenched her fists so hard her palms spasmed painfully. When she looked at them later, she saw faint purple bruising along both of them from where her nails had dug in. That was when everything got a little... hazy. If she had been sitting where Claudia was, she would have seen her eyes soften and begin to unfocus. Nan was still there, but it was as if she'd taken a back seat in her own mind, and her body was on autopilot.

Claudia furrowed her brow unsure of what, exactly, she was looking at... and then it all clicked into place. She smiled nastily. "Oh my dear sweet Jesus, are you actually drunk right now? During your interview?" Her eyes danced maliciously, and darted once more to the video camera. Beneath the black piece of plastic she had taped on the top of it, the little red light remained steady.

She was thinking about how, when she sent this footage into one of the larger news outlets down in Manhattan, she would finally be able to get the hell out of this dump of a town and afford a nice apartment in the East Village (maybe the Upper West Side), when Nan stood abruptly, knocking the table with her knees and sending Claudia's teacup crashing into her lap. Tea spilled down the front of Claudia's navy blue dress, and she crowed with indignation. "Hey, watch it!"

When Nan advanced on her, a blank look on her face and her eyes disconcertingly off-kilter, Claudia forgot all about her dress and her stupid accent. "Don't you touch me," she warned. "I'll sue you back to the Stone Age if you touch one hair on my head. You never should've agreed to a real interview if you couldn't handle it. You think anyone even gives a shit about you anymore? You've been off the front page since before you got your family killed, so why don't you just—" But that was as far as she got.

Nan was plump, but her arms were more muscular than they appeared. Whenever she wanted a drink badly enough that she thought she might take one, or when the memories of Nick and Lizzie became too loud, and she couldn't sleep, she lifted weights. It was the best way to tire herself out. So when she reached out and yanked Claudia's head down by her hair into the slab wood coffee table, she did so with a speed and force Claudia hadn't expected, flattening her nose down with a crunch and mashing her lips back into her teeth. Impossibly red blood exploded out of her face.

Nan wrenched Claudia's head back up with cool detachment.

"You goddamn bitch, you broge by fuggin *DOSE!*"

Of course it's broken, Nan thought. *Just look at how it leans, haha!*

Claudia's hands went to Nan's, and she tried to untangle them from her hair, but Nan held on with ease. She still wasn't seeing the look on Claudia's face that she wanted to see. The reporter's eyes were filled with anger and hate. Nan wanted to see fear in them. She slammed Claudia's head down again, and once more, it connected with the heavy table with a flat, declamatory *WHUNK.*

Claudia screamed as best she could, producing a piercing sort of burbling-gurgling sound as two of her front teeth slipped from between her lips on a runnel of blood and clattered to the table. "Stop!" she tried to scream, but in for a penny, in for a pound, as Nan's grandmother used to say.

WHUNK!

When she lifted Claudia's head this time, one of the teeth she had lost on the last go-round was embedded in her cheek. Claudia vomited without warning, splashing it all down Nan's shirt. Her eyes were dazed and terrified. Nan leaned close to her,

her own eyes still hazy and far away, and said in a dead voice, "You should have left when I told you to."

Claudia screamed and cried out (which by now was starting to get old), so when Nan jerked her head down this time, she aimed for the edge of the table instead of the center. There was no scream following the meaty crunch. When Nan pried Claudia's head off the table edge, having to muscle it more than she thought, she could see why. The entire center of her face, from her nose to her bottom lip, had caved inward from the force, the way a rotten jack-o-lantern will when you kick it. Nan dropped Claudia indifferently onto the rug. In a strange moment of déjà vu, she saw the reporter's shoe had fallen off, just as Bobby's had all those years ago.

She sat and lit a cigarette. When she was about halfway through, her eyes started to refocus, and by the time she was done, she felt more like herself again. She pulled her phone out and glanced at the time. 2:10. Christ, where had the time gone?

She tapped Tim's name in her recent calls, and he picked up on the second ring. "Kinda in the middle of someone here, Nan. What's wrong?"

"Charming. Look, I thought you said that reporter was supposed to be out here around one. It's ten after two, and she's still not here. Did we get the date wrong?" She didn't even have to manufacture the perturbance in her voice. The rest of the day was shot to hell now, and she *was* perturbed.

On the other end of the line, she heard someone say something too low for her to make out. "Just relax," Tim said, before returning his attention to her. "She didn't show up? It's definitely supposed to be today." She could hear the relief in his voice that she wasn't calling to tell him she'd fucked everything up.

"No, she didn't show. I was in the middle of working, and I stopped for this." If anything would get to Tim, that would. Now that the golden goose was laying again, he wouldn't let anyone mess with it.

"For fuck's sake. Just..." More sounds on the other end of the line. When he spoke again, he wasn't talking to her. "Don't bother getting dressed. I'll be two minutes. Nan, you there?"

"Yup."

"I'll call you back." Without waiting for a response, he hung up. Claudia's station manager, Earl something or other, would be getting a hot little earful in a few moments. Not only had his reporter screwed over Tim's client, but she'd taken him away from more pressing matters.

The clock in the corner ticked off two minutes. She smoked and watched Claudia's chest to see if it moved. It didn't. She was dead as dog shit. When Claudia's phone started chiming a few seconds later, it startled Nan so badly she jumped.

Have to remember to turn that off. They probably won't be able to pinpoint her location to the house, but better safe than sorry. She didn't like much of the new technology; didn't trust it.

Her own phone rang in her hand, and she answered it. Tim didn't bother wasting time with a greeting. "They said she checked in just outside of Newburgh when she left home, but no one's heard from her since. They tried calling her, but no answer. They're not really too surprised, though."

"What do you mean? This happen often?"

"Look... this is on the down low, okay?"

"Yes, Tim, I'm a vault."

"Earl—that's her station manager—said she's been battling her own addictions lately. Mostly coke. And since her divorce, it's been becoming more and more of a problem. She's flaked on a handful of interviews in the last couple of months. Told everyone she was getting clean, but... well, you know how that goes."

"Better than most." She moved her foot away from the pool of blood spreading toward her. The area rug was absolutely ruined. *Shame. I liked that rug.*

"Anyway, if she shows up now and she's coked up, obviously don't let her in. Don't call the cops, either. Let me know. Earl wants to deal with it himself rather than have her face splashed all over his competitors' stations. But there's a chance she just got lost or had car trouble or something."

Nan allowed how that might have happened, said her good-byes, and let Tim get back to who he'd been doing with a promise to call him if she needed anything (but not for another couple of hours at least).

She lit another cigarette and called Lauren. Normally, Nan wouldn't have bothered checking in, but Lauren might consider it odd that she hadn't when she found out Claudia had been a no-show. Besides, she should check and see how Trevor was doing.

"It *can't* be over already," Lauren said when she picked up. "Be honest. Did you yell at her and make her cry? Ooh, does her spray tan look as fake in person as it does on TV?"

Nan laughed. "Didn't get the chance to find out. Never showed up, the son of a bitch. I've been waiting since I got your text—thanks for that by the way—and just called Tim to find out what's going on."

"Well damn, that sucks. I'm sorry. I know this was impor-tant. They'll reschedule it, won't they?"

"I guess there's still a chance she'll show, but if she doesn't, yeah, they'll reschedule."

"Maybe she had a flat tire or something. Did they say what happened?"

Nan relayed the information Tim had given her (Lauren particularly enjoyed the bit about Claudia's affinity for powdering her nose), and then asked how Trevor had made out at the doctor's.

"Oh, he's fine. Back on amoxicillin for now. They're talking about putting tubes in his ears if this keeps happening. More of the same. You know how it goes. What's another co-pay, right?"

"Poor little bug. How's he holding up?"

"He's thrilled he gets to stay home from school the rest of

the week. And he's been asking to come and visit his Aunt Nanny. You up for a little company this afternoon?"

A fly landed on Claudia's open eye, walked in a quick circle, and rubbed its front feet together like a villain about to commit some dastardly act.

"Claudia might still show up, and even if she doesn't, I think I'll get back to writing. How about we plan for this weekend instead? We could make a day of it on Saturday, have a picnic down on the beach, the whole nine yards."

"Sounds perfect, he'll love that. You working on something hot?"

Lauren never asked Nan directly how the work was going or what she was working on. Instead, she talked around the edges and didn't pry. Nan liked that about her. "Could be. If I'm right, I'll be working on it late. Oh hey, and listen, before you go, I was wondering if you could do me a favor?"

"Yeah, sure, what do you need?"

This was probably a bad idea, all things considered, but Nan knew she wouldn't sleep through the night if she didn't ask. Something Claudia had said was bugging her. "You know Linnie Kitteridge down at the library?"

"Yeah, sure, her kid Melanie is in Trev's class. Nice enough lady."

Nice my goddamn ass.

"Do you think she likes me?"

There were a few seconds of silence before Lauren sort of laughed. "Of course she likes you, why wouldn't she? Did she say something?"

Not to me.

"No, nothing like that. I just haven't heard from her in a while about the summer writer's program for the high school kids, and then the other day, I saw her in town when I was coming out of the post office, and I waved, and she didn't wave back. I don't know, maybe she just didn't see me..."

"Oh, I'm sure that's it. Linnie likes you just fine. The one you have to worry about is Muriel Duckworth."

"Do they know each other?"

"I'm sure they must, at least by sight. They both grew up here. But I don't think they're really friends or anything."

"You're right. I'm just overthinking this. But... and I feel so stupid asking this, but—"

"Next time Trev and I are in the library for story hour, I'll see what I can find out," Lauren said. Even though Nan could hear the smile in her voice, she knew Lauren would take this just as seriously as she did everything else. "On the down low, of course."

"Of course," Nan said.

They chitchatted for a few more minutes. Lauren admonished her not to smoke too much or let the reporter not showing up get under her skin and then hung up.

Nan sat in the chair and stared straight ahead for a few minutes, thinking. The interview with Claudia had been, if nothing else, very informative. The revelation that Linnie and Muriel might be in cahoots with one another was particularly troubling. Muriel had been a thorn in her side for a long time, and if she was successfully swaying other people—especially people like that mouse, Linnie Kitteridge—into her camp, there could be problems down the road. Why couldn't the old bat have a heart attack or get hit by a bus or something? Nan would have loved to step in and help fate along, but Muriel wasn't exactly discreet regarding her theory about what had happened to her husband. If tragedy were to befall her, the cops would show up on Nan's doorstep within the hour, so unfortunately, there wasn't too much she could do but keep an eye on the situation.

And there was still the copy of the police accident report that Claudia had thrown in her face to think about. Someone had given it to her and told her about the blood alcohol content law and it sure as hell hadn't been Sheriff Lambert. He had reasons to keep that to himself; about a hundred thousand of them. But the other one, Deputy Sanders? If she was drowning, he would have thrown rocks at her. Elections were coming up, and Nan had been seeing his signs cropping up all over town the last six months or so. Lambert was retiring and moving in with his sister in Florida, and Sanders was gunning for the top spot. If he won, that would spell trouble for her.

Maybe I should pay Lambert a visit. See if I can get a read on him. Maybe convince him to hang around for a couple more years, give me a little breathing room.

Yes, there was lots to consider.

The somnolent drone of flies brought her back to the present moment, and she looked down at Claudia's body. Whatever else had to be done, this is where she had to start.

Begin at the beginning, her grandmother had been fond of saying. It was good advice for writing and good advice for life.

Chapter 3
Compulsions

Keaton's hands shook as he pulled Vincent's lifeless body along the rocky ground through the mist. The churchyard was abandoned at this time of night. Even Reverend Gibson, known to enjoy his drink and cards a little too much, was long in his bed.

Lady Henry had been buried earlier in the day and Keaton spied her plot now. It was the only one with the fresh turned soil. The shovel he hauled along with Vincent's corpse clanked against the stony ground, a knell alerting everyone to this night's dark deeds. Vincent's eyes were open and staring but didn't look alive. They had clouded over like old glass.

Keaton couldn't stand how they seemed to look at him, but it wasn't something he would have to worry about for much longer. Vincent would disappear very nicely into Lady Henry's grave, and when people asked what had become of him, he would tell them the truth. That he was probably off with some woman.

—Nan Wickwyre, *Haunting Willow Hall*

-1-
2026

The little maroon roadster parked in the driveway started right up with a shudder and a rumble. Nan didn't know what she would have done if it had chosen to be persnickety (as old sports cars sometimes did). Her knowledge of cars spanned changing tires, the oil, and a few of the easy-to-reach filters, and that was about it.

Instead of turning it off and chancing having it not start up again, she left it running in the rain and went back to the library to gather up Claudia's things; her sunglasses, headscarf, and shoes (which kept falling off of her dead feet), as well as the camera and tripod. Nan turned off Claudia's phone in its idiotic pink case and put it in her pocket to deal with later (*stupid things won't let you just pull the batteries anymore*, she thought). The manila folder with Muriel's statement and the police accident report went into the fireplace. Nan watched with vicious satisfaction as they turned to ash.

She threw Claudia's crap into the car's backseat and drove down the gravel drive heading away from the main road. The house had been listed for sale with just over ninety acres, but Nan had taken Bobby's advice and purchased the adjoining plots to the south and the east, which brought the grand total up to two hundred and eight. The plot to the east included the original carriage house that used to sit along Carey Farm Road, which had been the only way in and out of the property until it had fallen into disuse. The Holts had Little Church Road built to the south, which connected to Route 9, making it easier to get to their property. No longer traveled at all, Carey's Farm Road grew over and was swallowed by the forest and the carriage house with it.

Nan had discovered it while walking the property to get away from Nick that first year (neither moving in, nor the news of Lizzie's remission had stanched their fighting), and had asked

Ducky to extend the driveway to it. The plan was to have him restore it along with the rest of the property and turn it into her office so she would have a place all her own to work in complete solitude, but he'd disappeared before that could happen. Although it was still standing, it might not be in a couple of years. It was just another rotting ruin slowly being reclaimed by nature.

She opened the flaky green doors wide and drove the roadster into the first bay through a wall of thick summer weeds that didn't seem to know it was fall.

The first bay connected to the second where she and Nick had stored furniture they had planned to refinish, and other bric-a-brac they hadn't gotten around to tossing (and now probably never would). This was covered with a large canvas tarp. Nan pulled it off and used it to cover the roadster. It wasn't a permanent solution, but it got the damn thing out from in front of the house. She paused and cast a cursory eye over the scene to see if anything looked out of place. It *looked* fine, but there was a sound coming from the back seat of the car. She would have sworn to it.

Just check. You know you won't be able to rest until you do.

The bay lit up in a stutter flash of light as thunder crashed overhead.

Pulling the tarp back and opening the side door, she could hear the sound more clearly. It was an electronic sort of whirring sound.

The camera. It has to be.

It had fallen off the back seat and rolled under the front, so it took a moment to fish it out. The small piece of plastic Claudia had taped to the top of it had fallen off, and the red light glowed steadily in the afternoon gloom.

"You sneaky fuck." Nan pulled the SD card out (it would go into the fireplace the second she got back to the house) and dropped the camera back to the floor to run its battery down. With that done, she re-covered the car with the tarp and took one last look at her handiwork. Not seeing or hearing anything amiss, she closed the big green doors and padlocked them shut. Later, when things calmed down, she would figure out what to do with the car, but more pressing issues needed to be dealt with first. That didn't mean she had to hurry back, though. She took her time, enjoying the cool October rain, humming a little song to herself that she used to sing to Lizzie when she was little.

-2-

The smell of blood in the library was overpowering, especially after the earthy smells of the forest. The fireplace continued roaring along, which didn't help, and cluster flies crawled all over Claudia's pale skin. Usually, by this time of year, they had found some dark crevice in which to pass the winter, but it had been a warm, wet fall.

On the way back from the carriage house, Nan had grabbed a new blue tarp from the garage. She dropped it to the floor and spread it out beside Claudia's body, keeping an eye on what was left of her face the whole time. There was something creepy about how her eyes were half-lidded, as if while Nan had been in the woods taking care of the car, Claudia had tried to wake up. It was ridiculous, of course, but she couldn't shake the feeling. When Claudia disappeared into the tarp and was wrapped as tightly as a home-rolled cigarette, Nan found breathing a little easier. Before dragging the body from the room, Nan also rolled up the rug and moved it out onto the back patio beneath the overhang. Her weather app said the rain would be ending in an hour or so, and she could burn the rug then. At least for now, it was out of the house.

The library smelled a little better when she went back into it, but the odor of death's various bodily fluids was still noticeable. Ava Bakker, the local woman who came in a few times a week to give the rooms Nan used a once-over, would be here the day after tomorrow. A stern woman whose family had lived in town since its founding, Ava would certainly notice something amiss and wouldn't think twice about leading the mob with their torches and pitchforks right up to the front door.

At least with Claudia rolled up in the tarp, she would be easier to move and wouldn't leave behind a trail of blood (or anything else) for the eagle-eyed Ava to pounce on.

Nan dragged the corpse into the hallway and toward the north end of the house, where the staircase led to the lower level. When they'd first moved in, Nick had floated the idea of installing an elevator, but Nan had shot him down quickly, saying an elevator would ruin the lines of the hall and stand out gaudily against the rest of the original woodwork. This was part of it, sure, but truthfully, she'd said no because Nick had wanted it. Simple as that. He was already thinking ahead and worrying what would happen if Lizzie wasn't able to take the stairs instead of focusing on her improving health. Nan hadn't done it to be petty. At least, that's what she told herself then. With the benefit of time on her side, though, she could admit pettiness played a heavy role in it.

And now, muscling Claudia McKinnon's dead weight down the stairs, she could have kicked herself for not relenting. This part would have taken half the time and wouldn't have left her as sore the next morning. And yet, with each meaty *whack* Claudia's head made hitting riser after riser, she thought maybe she'd made the right decision after all. Sure, this way was more work, but it was like listening to vinyl instead of digital. Digital may be cleaner with a deeper range of sound, but vinyl was fucking *vinyl*.

The final crack Claudia's head made on the stone of the downstairs floor would have knocked her unconscious if she had still been alive to feel it. After that, pulling was much easier.

Nan navigated toward the southern end of the house where

there was an old coal cellar beside a stone-walled root cellar that had been dug into the hillside. It had been a while since she'd had reason to come to this part of the house, and the October rains had swelled the doorjamb. She had to drop Claudia and yank the handle with both hands, her sore muscles quaking in protest until, finally, the door squalled open. The musty-smelling room beyond was long and dirt-floored, illuminated by a string of bare bulbs hanging from the ceiling like spider egg sacs. Nan maneuvered the tarp inside and pulled the door shut.

At the far end of the room stood an empty wine rack on which Nan used to store special bottles (but when you're an alcoholic, aren't they all special? It's like having a bunch of kids, you're not supposed to pick favorites). Back in the day, she had been a firm believer in the *take a bottle, leave a bottle* philosophy, so there was rarely space available on the rack. After rehab, though, she'd emptied it totally, and it had stood that way ever since, sad and forlorn-looking under the yellowish lights. It was actually while emptying it of its precious cargo, which she would soon have to dump down the drain, that Nan had discovered a secret.

When they had been looking at the house, Bobby had mentioned a local rumor that there was a crypt somewhere on the property where the nuns had been laid to rest when they died (being a cloistered sect, that made sense), but no one had ever located it. There wasn't even a record of its construction filed with the town. But when Nan pulled the last bottle of Russian River Pinot Noir from the rack, she saw something that the bottle had been hiding. Way at the back of the storage cubby, something glinted metallically.

She pulled her phone out and shined the flashlight back into the gloom. Beyond the spiderwebs and accumulated dust was an old-fashioned door latch. Her heart had been pounding even while her brain was trying to mitigate her expectations. *It'll be nothing. An old storage closet, or else the handle isn't actually connected to anything. At best, it was probably a hiding spot for illegal booze that had been used during Prohibition and then shuttered up when the law was repealed.*

But when she clicked the latch down and pulled, the whole wine rack swung slowly outward, revealing a set of wide stone steps.

Nan pulled Claudia's body down these steps now, using the same care she had while bringing her down to the lower level of the house. She had installed a series of extension cords and used these to hang a string of bulbs along the wall to illuminate the never-ending vault below, but her first time coming down the stairs, not knowing what she might encounter in the dark, she'd needed to use her phone's light to make her way through the pitch black.

According to the local history section of the library, there had been twenty nuns living here when it was Sacred Haven, and as Nan had picked her way along using her cellphone as a flashlight, she'd counted exactly nineteen caskets. Each was made of ornately carved stone and rested on a raised platform in its own cubby beneath an arched ceiling.

Why only nineteen? she'd wondered at the time. It seemed odd until she thought about it in the sunshine and fresh air. One of the nuns had been buried in a family plot elsewhere, or had been cremated, or maybe even had decided the cloistered life wasn't for her and had run off to Vegas. Simple as that.

Claudia smacked onto the dirt floor, and when Nan started to pull again, the tarp came away, but the body stayed where it was. Claudia's cloudy eyes peered sightlessly at her surroundings, her hair now matted with blood and looking oddly flattened. "Oh, you miserable whore."

Well, who cares anyway? She's where she needs to be, so let her bleed all over the dirt if she wants to. It's not like anyone would even notice a little blood down here, even if they were able to find the place.

They *would* notice it in the library, however.

So far, she'd been lucky. If this had been one of her novels, a neighbor would have dropped by to say hello or borrow a cup of sugar, or someone would need to use the phone because their car had broken down right out front, forcing Nan to play hostess with Claudia's blood drying to a tacky mess behind the closed library door. But this was real life, and that sort of thing rarely happened.

She maneuvered Claudia's body, which was now almost entirely out of the tarp, over next to a stone plinth in the center of the room and dropped it unceremoniously. She would muscle it up onto the platform when she had time.

With the ease of a practiced pickpocket, she bent and combed through Claudia's dress until she found what she was looking for. A plastic baggie filled with white powder, tied at the top in a knot.

"Getting clean, huh?" she said, slipping the bag into her back pocket.

She started to climb the steps, her legs tired and rubbery, her arms hanging like limp noodles at her sides, yet for all of that, she felt pretty good. She could have used a belt of scotch and a cigarette, but otherwise, things were hunky dory. But the day's work wasn't done. It had really just started.

From the corner behind a stone pillar, something stood unseen, watching her.

-3-

2016

The *compulsion*, as she thought of it, started very near the time of Nick and Lizzie's funeral in January of 2016.

Nick's family had shown up a few days before the services, ostensibly to gather a few mementos from the house that Nan had agreed to let them have and to attend the funeral (funeral singular, Nan couldn't bear the thought of having to sit through the same thing twice, so had consolidated them like credit card debt). She'd been drunk most of that visit, so she had not really noticed how cold his family had been toward her. They'd always been somewhat cold, but it wasn't until after they'd gone back home that she learned Nick's mother had spoken to the sheriff and asked him if Nan had been drunk when she'd crashed the car. Of course, Sheriff Lambert had reassured her it was the ice that had taken her son and granddaughter away, not alcohol, but it was a question she shouldn't have known to ask.

And it was really that realization which had pushed Nan toward recovery. Until then, she wasn't so delusional as to think she was hiding her drinking perfectly, but she really had believed it wasn't all that serious. Not even after the accident that had killed her family. She told herself it had been a mistake, a miscalculation, a one-time thing, and she'd believed that wholeheartedly. But if Nick's mother, whom she saw once or twice a year at most, knew enough to ask that question, others would, too. (Nick must have told her about the flask and the bottles that disappeared with some regularity, though he had never mentioned it to Nan.)

Rehab was really the only option.

After rehab, when she got back home and the big quiet house seemed even bigger and quieter than usual, thoughts crept into her mind.

Night was the toughest time. It was when she most wanted a drink, and it was when the loneliness and quiet of the house seemed to grow overwhelming. Before, if she'd had trouble sleeping, she could have had a whole glassful of scotch and woken Nick up to play cards or just keep her company. Now, she was allowed neither of those comforts. So when sleep wouldn't come, there was nothing to do but sit in bed, stare at the ceiling wishing for a drink, and think.

And after a while, thinking became more dangerous than drinking.

It was a month after returning from recovery and, wonder of wonders, she was actually drifting in and out of a light sleep when an idea came to her as if it had been whispered in her ear. Her eyes flew open, and she sat straight up in bed, peering into the darkness. She was expecting to see someone stooped over her, but there was no one there. Sitting in the dark, not daring to move or even to breathe loudly, she recalled the day Bobby Buckland had died and the voice both of them had heard in the dining room right before it happened:

I rot in the well. Deeeeep down in the blackness, where the water is cold, and slimy things slither in and out. I rot alone in the dark.

The voice she had just heard had been sort of like that one, only closer... close enough to tickle the cusp of her ear.

It said, *Bring me decay.*

As the moments passed, nothing else moved or made a sound. Even Peanut had fallen back to sleep without concern, and Nan started to believe she had dreamed it. It wasn't such a crazy leap. She had been sleeping (or close enough to), yet what the voice had told her seemed to still linger in the air, not made of the diaphanous flotsam of dreams but very much real.

And there was a slight smell in the room.

But it wasn't possible. She switched on her bedside lamp, throwing a pool of light around the bed that she had thought would be comforting but only made her feel exposed and isolated, and shook her head as if this could dislodge the words.

The books she had been reading before the accident were still piled up beside the bed, untouched, but those weren't the ones she wanted. On the dresser across the room was a copy of *Haunting Willow Hall*. She ran to get it, then ran back, closing the final few feet with a leap because she was convinced that something beneath the bed would grab at her feet when she got close enough.

This woke Peanut again, who raised his head, sneezed,

glared at her with his creepy milk eyes, and laid back down. Nan flipped through the pages rapidly.

And there, at the bottom of page 227, where the ghost of Lady Boyle spoke to the comatose Maisy Blackburn, paralyzed in her bed but able to see and feel everything going on around her (including the old crone who leaned over her at night and whispered things in her ears) were the words that filled her with equal measures of fear and excitement:

"Bring me decay," Lady Boyle said, *her festering skin mere inches from Maisy's young cream-white cheeks. "Fill Willow Hall with screams, turn it into a charnel house. Unhallow this ground. Make the earth of the cellar foul with rot!*

Nan closed the book with a snap and set it on the comforter beside her.

A moment later, she started to laugh. A moment after that, she was almost screaming with laughter. She must have been thinking about Lady Boyle as she drifted in and out of sleep and had somehow transposed herself into Maisy's sick bed for just a moment, long enough for the thought to come to her the same way it had come to poor Maisy.

And it made sense. As she trudged her way through her recovery program, *Willow Hall* had been forever on her mind. There had been something comforting about taking walks through Lady Boyle's rose garden (in her mind, of course), while Helen P. was bellyaching about being fired for the umpteenth time, and of strolling the corridors of Willow Hall, opening doors and seeing what was behind them while Mike F. talked about losing his license after he hit that kid in the crosswalk, and staring out endlessly at the Hyde River just as Lady Boyle had done in her story, while in the real world the brain-dead alcoholics droned endlessly about their petty little problems. In a way, by walking the grounds of Willow Hall, she was walking around her own home. Both it and Holt House seemed to be a part of her and equally real.

But now that she was actually in her home, able to stroll,

meander, and enjoy to her heart's content, Willow Hall had been relegated back to the land of fiction.

Funny. Maybe *that* was the reason for the dream.

But over the next two months, rather than fade into the background static of life as any dream would have, Lady Boyle's admonition to "bring her decay" only seemed to grow. Nan found herself hearing it even during her waking hours, while writing, washing the dishes, or watching a movie, as if someone were crouched just out of sight, softly muttering the words to her.

In her book, it hadn't been Lady Boyle whispering to Maisy at all, but rather the maid, Temple Humphry, who had lost her mind and was imitating her voice. She was trying to get Maisy to kill Keaton and then herself so that Willow Hall would revert to her, the house's once heir and rightful owner.

But there was no Temple Humphry on which Nan could blame the phantom words. And what started as bemusement quickly turned to fear, as they started to come with greater and greater frequency and intensity.

I'm going crazy, she thought one morning, staring at her face in the bathroom mirror. *Not in a fictional heroine sort of way, and not in a melodramatic TV movie kind of way, but in a psych ward, straight-jacket, chlorpromazine kind of way.* The words had been coming from behind her to the left of the bedroom doorway for the last two minutes, though she could clearly see the space from which they issued was unoccupied.

She stared into her eyes reflected by the mirror until they didn't look like hers anymore. They seemed to drift away from one another in opposite directions. Her nose seemed like someone else's, too. And her cheeks... the ones she could see in the mirror were higher and sharper than her own, she was certain of it... until eventually none of her face seemed to be hers. She glanced away quickly and then back, thinking that would spoil the illusion and return things to normal, but it didn't.

As she watched what might be her reflection and what might not, she didn't notice that the light in the room changed and grew brighter, and then dimmer and dimmer until the image reflected in the mirror was almost too dark to see. She could hear it speaking to her, though, and only now, in the low light, could she make out the way mirror Nan's mouth moved.

She looked away quickly, her whole body gooseflesh, and left the bathroom, closing the door behind her so her reflection couldn't get out. It was only then that she noticed it was 4:30 PM. The entire day was gone, spent in front of the mirror watching... well, she wasn't entirely sure what.

Back in college, Nick had been interested in the occult (mostly because he was interested in a *girl* who was interested in the occult) and had gone to Floyd's, the local department store, to purchase a spirit board. He and Nan had used it a handful of times back before Lizzie was born, usually while drunk. When they'd bought their first house, they'd sat for hours trying to see if the place was haunted, but when the spirits were less than talkative, they ended up having sex on the bedroom floor instead.

She ran down into the billiard room where they kept all the board games in a gigantic armoire that had come with the house and dug through the boxes until she found it.

As she pulled it from its slot, she broke out in goosebumps again and suddenly wanted nothing to do with the armoire. It was just a shallow cupboard, packed tight with old game boxes, but there was something unnerving about standing so close to it while its doors were opened that she slammed them shut and spun the key in the front to lock it.

Calm down, you're just freaking yourself out. There's nothing in the armoire to be afraid of; you just worked yourself up, and you're losing the plot a little. You're not really going crazy. Crazy people don't think to even question their sanity. But if she wasn't going nuts, it could only mean something was in the house with her.

She dumped the box's contents onto the floor, weeded out the bits from other games, and settled the board and planchette in front of her. For the next twenty minutes, she focused with all her might on getting the hunk of plastic to move. When nothing happened, she sat statue still for thirty more until her eyes softened and started to lose focus... but the spirit board wouldn't speak to her.

But something did. It actually had been for a while; she just hadn't noticed it.

The voice came from behind her, from within the armoire. The right-side door was cracked open, revealing a wedge of darkness.

The air around her seemed to go wavy as her eyes watered, and her breath caught in her throat. And when the voice spoke again, it seemed to howl like an animal.

BRING ME DECAY! BRING ME ROT!

And that was all Nan remembered of that day. When she awoke, it was just after midnight and she was still on the billiard room floor. The spirit board was not in front of her. Her book, *Haunting Willow Hall*, was, and the pages had all been folded over in a fastidious way. The armoire doors stood wide open. She recalled coming down to get the spirit board but nothing that came afterward. There was a slight stench in the air, like unwashed skin and rot.

That was the one and only time since recovery that she had a drink. And it *was* just one—Nick's last IPA that lingered in the back of the fridge—but she knew had there been more in the house, she wouldn't have stopped there.

She didn't care for the taste of it, though. She had tossed back her fair share of beers with Nick over the years (although it wasn't her drink of choice, any port in a storm, as the saying goes), but this one was skunked or something. Still, she choked it down, as any respectable alcoholic would have, and tossed the bottle in the returns bin. After that, it was easier to think.

It was getting dry that started all this shit. How had she not realized that before? *Of course* it was. Going through detox was known to cause hallucinations, and she had been through one hell of a detox. *I'm not drinking, but I'm still blacking out. I'm probably the one who opened the armoire doors without even realizing I was doing it, just like I folded the pages of my book for some reason.*

Before going to bed that night (well, morning, technically), she promised to herself she would drive into Kingston the following day, where no one local was apt to turn up and attend the 4 PM meeting at the Treatment Center. There, she'd confess to her slipup and move on.

But life (as it so often does) had other plans.

-4-

2026

Her phone rang just as she was finishing mopping Claudia's blood off the library floor. Thankfully for her poor twitching muscles, the wood had been coated with some sort of glossy sealant Ducky had talked her into, so in addition to not staining, it was easy to clean. Shaking herself partway out of her memories and performing an exhaustive visual search for any blood she may have missed, she dug her phone out of her pocket. It wasn't Lauren, as she'd expected.

"Tim, what can I do for you?"

"What are you doing? You sound winded."

"Damn dog shit on the rug. I was trying to clean it, but I think it's a goner." There, another thing off her list. When Ava asked what had happened to the rug (and she would), Nan would have an excuse locked and loaded.

"I take it Claudia never showed then?"

"Oh no, she did. I've got her on her hands and knees in her pretty pink pantsuit, scrubbing dog shit out of my carpet while she does the interview. Two birds, one stone, and all that." Rather than snipe back with something bitchy and witty (at least to him), Tim made a sound in his throat that Nan didn't really care for. He sounded perplexed. "What is it, Tim?"

"I just heard back from Earl... the cops will probably pay you a visit either later tonight or tomorrow. I'd guess tomorrow. Just the local boys."

"I thought you said he didn't want to involve the cops unless he had to."

There's no need to worry yet, she told herself when her heart started to pound. The worst of the mess had been cleaned up, and if they were sending the local smokeys instead of the staties that meant Lambert...maybe Sanders, too. Nothing she couldn't handle.

"*He* didn't. Claudia's ex-husband did. She was supposed to swing by and pick her daughter up from school after leaving your place, but she never showed."

"Well, if she's off on a bender, she wouldn't have, right?"

"The ex doesn't think that's the case. He's the one who talked her into going into rehab. Told her if she didn't go, then he was suing her for full custody of their daughter. According to him, she'd do anything for that kid."

Nan laughed bitterly and fingered the baggie in her back pocket.

"Care to share with the rest of the class?" Tim said.

"No, just take it from an old booze bag. Sometimes that shit is easier agreed to than done. If I were her ex, I'd start checking the local bars in Newburgh where she was last seen. Like as not, she's passed out in a booth somewhere with a nose full of powder. Or else shacking up with some degenerate."

"You're probably right. Oh well, it's not my problem anymore. All these interruptions drove off my house guest, so now I've gotta head back to the bar tonight."

"Tough being you."

"Don't I know it. Anyway, I told Earl to reschedule the

interview and to send the other guy they've got to do it. If Claudia shows up, I figured you probably didn't want to have to deal with that shitshow."

"Just send the info to Lauren and have her put it on my schedule."

"Will do. Oh, before I forget, you want me to put in a call to Ed Hunt? He's still your lawyer, right? Probably ought to have him on standby for when the local po-po shows up."

Ed Hunt was her literary lawyer and not a bad egg as far as lawyers went, but a potential criminal investigation would be a bit out of his depth. He could probably recommend someone ruthless (as he himself was), and for a moment, she considered it. "If it gets to the point I need one, I'll give him a call and get a recommendation. I've run into both the sheriff and deputy out here more than once. They're a pain in the ass, but they're not exactly rocket scientists. I can handle them."

Nan hung up, and Peanut trotted up the hall and sat in the doorway watching her (or at least looking in her general direction through a film of cataract). He was a funny little thing. Almost seemed like he was looking past her.

"Sorry, bub, you had to take one for the team today. But I promise you'll get a nice treat tonight for playing along. Deal?" Peanut wandered over toward the sound of her voice, ramming his head into three separate table legs before making it, then sat splay-legged on the floor in front of her, panting. His tail thumped twice, then fell still.

"Yeah, you're a good little dingbat, aren't ya? At least you love me." She scratched him behind the ears for a few minutes, deep in thought.

If Lambert and Sanders did make it out here tonight, things could go off the rails quickly, despite the cleanup. Lambert alone wouldn't have been a problem, but Sanders was almost as sharp-eyed as Ava and would be looking for anything amiss. And there was still work to be done down in the crypt. If they showed up while she was down there...

The gate at the end of the driveway stood wide open as usual (it was easier than keeping it closed and having to run up every time she was expecting someone). Sanders would take that as an invitation to come down and snoop, which made locking it up her top priority.

Right after changing out of those blood spattered, vomit covered clothes, of course.

Yes, of course, right after that.

For the interview, she had dressed in an off-white cable knit sweater and a pair of gray slacks. The pants showed no blood, but the sweater looked like a red and brown homage to Jackson Pollock. She took both off carefully to avoid getting any of the drying fluids on her skin, stuffed them in a garbage bag, and then pulled on one of Nick's old college sweatshirts and a pair of jeans. She left the bag by the front door on her way out so she would remember to take it out later and burn it along with the rug.

Seven minutes later, she pulled the rusted gate closed and secured it with a padlock, and seven minutes after that, she was back in her foyer. Easy as falling off a log. Now, she could put the police out of her mind for a little while, and focus on the task at hand.

She grabbed the mop and bucket from the hallway where she had left them (both dyed a lurid pink) and carried them down toward the servant's pantry off the dining room. The mop would also need to be burned, but the bucket would live to fight another day. After emptying it down the sink, she chased the pink water with a gallon of bleach, opened another bottle, and used it to swamp out the bucket. The library floor needed just one more pass, and it would be as good as she could get it.

On the way back, Nan gasped and dropped the mop bucket, sending its soapy-bleach water slopping over the lip and onto the hallway flagstone.

A person stood outside the library doors, staring at her with dark, empty eyes. They were impossibly tall with hands stretching down to their knees and a gaunt white face. Their mouth hung open, revealing blackened teeth which all seemed to reach out toward her, driving their lips back into a startled O.

The hair on Nan's arms and the back of her neck stood straight up as goosebumps spread across her body like poison ivy, and her mouth opened and closed like a fish's.

She stepped back and skidded in the bleach water, almost going ass over teakettle onto the floor, but she managed to catch herself before she did. That little shift of perspective was all it took to spoil the illusion. When she looked back up, the person by the door was gone, turned back into what they had been the whole time; a conglomeration of junk which just happened to line up from that one angle. The coatrack in the foyer holding her fall jacket supplied most of the frame, the boots she'd just worn up to the road made up the feet, and a photo Nick had taken of a total solar eclipse they'd driven to Maine see in '98 had turned into the horrible reaching mouth. Light and shadow had helped her brain to fill in the gaps.

She moved her head this way and that, trying to make the person come back into focus, but the bunch of junk stayed a bunch of junk.

Just like knowing how a magician does a trick ruins it after that. It made sense. And yet... *Let's go, get a move on,* she scolded herself. There would be plenty of time to ruminate on this later. But now, there was still work to be done.

She cleaned up the water she'd spilled on the floor, then carefully lifted the bucket and carried it into the library, making sure as she passed through the doorway to stay as far to the left as she could. Her eyes never left the spot where the person had appeared. Once inside, she closed the doors and locked them before she started to mop.

-5-
2016

The day after the spirit board experiment, Nan awoke just before noon, not because she was rested but because she was sick. Her head throbbed like an appendix ready to burst, and her stomach was sour. It felt remarkably similar to the hangovers she used to get.

I only had the one beer last night, though, she thought.

Immediately, her mouth flooded with saliva, and her throat started to constrict.

Thankfully, the bathroom door was wide open, and the toilet lid was raised, or she wouldn't have made it.

Once she was emptied out, she lay back with her head against the tiled wall, liking the cool feeling on her sweaty scalp, and tried to remember if she might have eaten anything suspect yesterday.

Bring me decay, the voice whispered from across the room. Nan looked up, her eyes like two heavy marbles tethered by an optic nerve that felt bruised, and stared at the shower curtain. It rippled lazily as if caught in a light breeze, but the air in the bathroom was still and stagnant.

Nan's eyes unfocused and seemed to grow heavier. When the putrefying hand came shaking around the edge of the curtain to grasp it, she didn't see it. Nor did she hear the meat slurry laughter that followed. But she heard the words just fine.

Make the earth of the cellar foul with rot.

Nan scrambled to her knees and vomited again, only this time, all that came out was beer. The yeasty smell seemed to fill the bathroom. Sweat rolled down her forehead in fat beads, and it felt like her brain was cooking in her skull. A wave of vertigo swept her up like an invisible, drunken dance partner, swirled her messily around, and dropped her back to the floor. It was that smell. That godawful *stink*. She struggled for the toilet handle and flushed it down. The nausea retreated almost at once.

Her legs shook when she stood and her head swam so badly that she needed to sit on the now closed toilet lid to avoid falling. Something was becoming very clear to her in the way a fever dream can bring with it an insane sort of lucidity to the sleeping mind.

"I'll do it," she croaked. "Just stop this, please, and I'll do it, I swear. I swear to God I will. Just let me sleep, and I *promise* I'll do it for you. I promise... I..."

It was dark. Something cold and hard pressed into her back. Swinging upward into a seated position, she noticed her headache was completely gone, and so was the day. She'd slept it away on the bathroom floor, with her face pressed into the cool tiles, which had left a geometric imprint on her cheek.

She thought that the events of the afternoon would seem crazy (or maybe even funny, the way time can soften a tense situation and reveal its hidden humor), but they didn't. They still felt very real (what she remembered of them, that was), and if that wasn't enough to convince her, the voice was. It still whispered from somewhere close by.

Nan stood slowly, giving her body a chance to collapse while she was still close enough to the floor that it wouldn't hurt so badly, but her legs didn't feel weak anymore. They felt strong. And she was ravenously hungry.

The bedroom light was on, casting a pale glow across the floor and into the bathroom. It was enough to see by, and she made her way into the room without barking her shins on anything.

She opened the closet, grabbed her old gardening clothes from the back, and dressed quickly. The voice wanted decay, and she would bring it decay. But not in her good clothes, which she had fallen asleep in, and not on an empty stomach.

Making her way down through the darkened house to the kitchen, Nan realized she no longer felt that little tug of fear she had been feeling so often since returning from rehab, despite the nagging voice that seemed to keep step with her through the darkness, muttering ceaselessly.

She fixed herself two ham and Swiss cheese sandwiches with extra mayo and gobbled them down, then chased them with yesterday morning's leftover coffee, which she drank staring out the windows at the lights across the Hudson.

I wonder what it would be like to live over there in one of those cozily lit houses.

The dishes went into the sink for Ava to deal with later, and Nan went out the kitchen door onto the patio and took a deep breath of the cool night air. It hadn't snowed in almost a month. Spring was just around the corner, and the ground was soft, which would make the night's task easier.

About a week after they'd moved in, Nick had talked her into buying a little ATV to haul gardening tools out to the formal garden, which was across the great lawn and down a narrow trail through the woods. The orange and black machine was still parked right where he'd left it last in the garage. Nan had meant to winterize it, but it had fallen through the cracks in all the hubbub, so it took a little coaxing to get it running.

Like all the rest of Nick's projects, started but rarely finished, his tools were still in the back: shovels, a pickaxe, a hoe. To these, Nan added a battery-powered light on a tripod and a few old canvas tarpaulins, which they had discovered in the coal cellar covering moldering furniture.

The ATV's motor had smoothed out and was running fine now. Nan backed it out into the driveway and drove past the front of the house, lit up like a piece of a Christmas village, and continued on down the laneway. Instead of taking a right and ending up at the carriage house, she took a left and headed toward the river and the Holt family cemetery. When the Holt children had been buried, the view of the Hudson would have been incredible, but over the intervening years, the underbrush and pines had grown so high and thick that the river was obscured. Not that the Holt children would mind. She parked the ATV in front of the gate, killed the engine, and got out. It was dark and quiet down here, sort of peaceful, but the crowding trees made it seem like people were standing around watching.

Graveside mourners, she thought with a shudder. *Get to work then. Soonest begun, soonest done.*

A wrought iron fence with sharp spindles hemmed in the three headstones, which leaned and sagged, giving Nan just enough room to swing the pickaxe to bust through the tree roots and bluestone. To her credit, there was a flickering moment of pellucidity before she started digging in which her mind screamed, *WHAT ARE YOU DOING?* but that went by the wayside when her head throbbed again. She felt a little like her hero, Keaton Blackburn, digging up Lady Henry's grave to bury the body of the dastardly Vincent Shelton. Thinking this made her task easier.

She started with the oldest, Persephone, who'd been fifteen when she was killed. Nan dug until her shovel struck something solid, then switched to the hoe and scooped the mud up and out of the hole. The casket was little more than pulpy splinters in a vaguely rectangular shape, and the girl's remains just bones in a tattered dress. While cleaning out the attic during their first year, Nan had come across a few old tintype photos of the children. Persephone was fair-haired and slim, with a thin, cunning face and humor in her eyes, even as young as she was.

She stared down in morbid wonder at the crumbling bones that belonged to the girl in the photo and noticed something didn't look right about them. Laying on her stomach and leaning down into the pit, Nan used the tips of her fingers to pull up the ratty, soiled hem of the dress. Where there should have been two sets of bones sticking out from the hip sockets—femur, tibia, fibula—there was only one.

"That's weird," she muttered, frightened by how loud her voice sounded in the still night. None of the stories she had been told (or the official report that had been provided to the paper at the time) mentioned the eldest girl was missing a leg. According to Caroline Lewis at the Historical Society, the children had been butchered with a hatchet, which would explain *why* the limb was missing but not *where* it was. Surely, it would have been buried with her.

What does it matter? How much longer do you need to be out here? Just get the bones and get a move on!

Using the shovel, Nan lifted as much of Persephone's body onto one of the tarpaulins as she could before donning thick leather gloves and grabbing the few stragglers, and shoving the whole lot into the bed of the ATV. Nan took baby Cora next because she figured it would be less to muscle out of the ground, and she was right. In addition to making a very small bundle that weighed almost nothing, Cora was also missing some pieces. Persephone's right leg was gone; with Cora, it was the left. And she had no head. It was perplexing, but nothing that impacted the night's work, so Cora was wrapped up and bundled in beside her big sister. Nan then turned her attention to the final grave.

The male heir was not in a pine box like his sisters, but rather a metal casket with some intricate scrollwork along the top of it, with his name "Jeremiah" etched into the surface. Just below that was the word "Son." It must have cost a pretty penny when it had been buried, but now it was nothing more than a rusted hunk of junk.

"Guess they loved you best," Nan said breathlessly.

The lid proved more stubborn than she would have thought, but in the end, the pickaxe made short work of it. When she opened it, Nan had to stifle a little yelp. Jeremiah lay on a stained bed of what at one time had been white satin, his arms crossed lovingly over his sunken chest. But that wasn't what had given her a fright.

Whether from the metal casket or because he'd been buried slightly higher compared to his sisters and, therefore, out of the groundwater, Jeremiah's body had fared much better than either Persephone's or Cora's; almost as if he'd been mummified. His brittle skin was pulled taut over his bones, reminding her of onionskin paper, and his hair still held the stylish wave in it the undertaker had brushed over a hundred and fifty years ago. Once her fright died, she noticed Jeremiah still had all his limbs. It was an odd thing that she could puzzle over later, but now all she wanted was to get him into the back of the ATV and up to the main house.

The girls' bones had made Nan a little squeamish, but the boy's body was something she was unable to bring herself to touch, even with gloves on. The thought of supporting the weight of that desiccated *thing* was too much to bear, so she laid a tarp alongside the hole and, using the hoe and the pickaxe as pincers, leveraged him up and out in stages. Alive, he couldn't have weighed more than 55 pounds, but hauling him out now made her lower back and forearms throb. When he finally rolled in a clattery heap onto the tarp, she breathed a sigh of relief and covered him up so his empty eyes could no longer stare at her.

She didn't come down this way often (and Lauren and Ava never did), so she filled the holes in haphazardly, telling herself she'd do a better job during the day when she could see. Right now, she wanted to get the fuck out of here. The night seemed to be growing larger and darker around her.

For one horrible moment, she thought the ATV wouldn't start. It sputtered and gurgled but then finally caught. Nan drove as fast as she dared up the laneway, avoiding the deepest ruts and boggy areas, goosing the speed up as she brought the machine sliding out onto the gravel lane.

She went to bed that night, hoping that now the voice would leave her alone. With the Holt children's bodies re-interred down in the soft floor of the crypt, Nan had brought decay and rot as she had been bidden, and things could now get back to normal.

But they didn't.

The quiet lasted a couple of days, just about enough time for her sprung muscles to heal, and then the voice returned.

She was making a cup of coffee when she heard it. It was only a whisper, a pathetic pleading thing, but if she turned a blind eye to it now, it would soon become a full-throated howl.

She set her cup on the counter, wandered into the hallway, and listened. It was coming from the direction of the root cellar.

With the onset of the voice came the return of her headache as well; like the voice, it started out quiet. Nan massaged her temples and swallowed drily. The walk to the root cellar door felt like a mile, and the trip to the wine rack felt like two more. She hadn't gotten around to installing the lights for the crypt yet, but had fortuitously left the gardening tools, along with the big barreled flashlight, on the floor beside the door. She grabbed the light and pulled the secret latch in the wine rack.

The air around her turned humid and cool as she descended, and the voice grew stronger the deeper she went.

Across the room, next to the platform which, according to the placard on the front of it, held the remains of Sister Louisa, was a six-foot by three-foot patch of freshly turned earth where Nan had buried the Holt kids.

Something had been digging there. Before she had left for the night, she'd tamped the soil down pat, level with the dirt around it. Something had dug that soil back out and left behind a hole in the floor. She scrambled over to it, fell on her knees, and pawed at the dirt.

There was nothing there. Not one bone or strand of corpse hair.

Maybe they're deeper than you remember.

She dug deeper, using her hands as scoops. After excavating a hole at least five feet deep and still finding nothing, she fell back on her legs and sat, staring and afraid.

Rot, the voice said from behind her.

She spun around and saw another platform in the middle of the room (what she was pretty sure was called a plinth), which did not hold a casket as the rest of them did. The bones of the Holt children sat atop it and were scattered and smashed as if something had taken out its rage on them. (And when she came down later that night, the bones had disappeared entirely.)

Oh Jesus, no, Nan thought. *Please, no, I can't.*

A stabbing pain accompanied by a bright flash of light rocketed through her head.

Decay, the voice demanded.

She gasped.

And knew that, yes, she could.

-6-
2016

Her first thought was to use a dog. Something old and sick that no one would ever miss. As a child, she'd helped her parents take care of about fifty head of beef cows and about a million free-range chickens, so she was familiar with the cruelty of farm life. Even though she hated it, one of Nan's jobs was to help her father cull the newborn chicks.

And it always started the same way. "Stop that crying right now, Nannette," her father would say sternly. "What we're doing fer 'em, it's a mercy. They'd languish and die slow if we didn't." And then he'd toss a handful of chicks into the grinder. She, in turn, would bawl her eyes out. As she grew older, her feelings never changed, but the tears stopped. It was around this time she decided she had to get away from the farm, or she would end up just like her father.

And now look at me, she thought, cradling her head. *Ready to sacrifice a dog to this insanity.* She knew just the dog she'd use, too. Its name was Duke. It was about a hundred years old and was left outside chained to a stake year 'round. It would be a mercy.

But even as she started to form her plan, she knew it wouldn't work. It wasn't the headache, which persisted, or the ever-growing voice demanding rot and decay like a broken record, but a sort of intuition that told her this. She'd tried to cop out once by using the Holt children even though they'd been dead over a century. Using a dog or a cat now would be the same thing. The voice didn't want an animal, and it didn't want bones. It wanted something *fresh*.

Yet she procrastinated.

A week went by, and her headache became steadily worse until even the small moments of reprieve she had experienced no longer came. She was swallowing ibuprofen by the handful, and although it helped a little, it still didn't come close to touching the rotten throb in her temples and behind her eyes.

The morning she found the surprise Nick had hidden for her, she had woken with her entire face feeling swollen and hot and went to grab another handful of pills, only to find the bottle was empty. It had still been half-full when she'd gone to bed the night before.

You probably got up in the middle of the night and took some more without realizing it.

Maybe, but she didn't think so.

Maybe you have a brain tumor.

That thought was coming to her more and more often as the headaches grew angrier, but she didn't really believe it. "No, I just need some more ibuprofen, that's all," she told her reflection in the mirror. "I'll get some this morning and then figure the rest out when I get home." She took a few swallows of water from her hand, dressed quickly, put on dark sunglasses, and drove into town.

It was a Wednesday morning, and Cutler's Food and Pharmacy was nearly deserted. Only a few old people wandered around pushing their carts, blocking the aisles when they stopped to talk to someone they knew. Nan grabbed three of the big bottles of ibuprofen, considered, added three more, then headed toward the checkout via the refrigerated aisle, where the cooler air made her feel slightly better. She was about halfway to the front, the comforting beeping of the cash registers getting tantalizingly close, when she happened to turn her head and catch sight of what was in the next aisle over.

A wall of beer, a couple of hundred bottles at least, all different brands and varieties lined up on shelves like fat, happy soldiers. Without thinking, she headed toward it, mesmerized.

For some reason, her head felt even better standing here than in the frozen food section. She ran her fingertips over the dark brown glass, enjoying its cool, slippery feel. She picked one up. The label was yellowed, but the bottle sparkled like it was fresh off the line. It read: HOLT HOUSE IPA. Below the name was a drawing of her house as it was now, complete with the weathervane on the garage roof in the shape of a raven that Ducky had just put up last week. In the upper attic window where her office was, just below the roof, was a dark splotch that looked a bit like a woman seated at a computer.

That's me, she thought. But the longer she looked, the less it resembled her, just like when she stared at her reflection in the mirror. *Oh, this is just stupid. It isn't real. Either someone put it here as a joke, or else I'm hallucinating, but it's not real.*

A small boy of maybe ten rounded the corner and slowly walked down the aisle. He moved as if in a dream, his body seeming to creep along unhurriedly, his eyes fixed on her. Nan's attention was taken entirely by the bottle of beer in her hand, so she didn't see him until he was almost on top of her.

She jumped and spun guiltily away from the beer, her head throbbing like an infected tooth.

The boy was dressed in overalls with a white button-down shirt and a straw hat. His face was angular and cunning like a fox's, and his eyes seemed to hold a smile that wasn't very pleasant.

Nan took a step back, not wanting him that close to her. "Um, do you need something?"

The boy grinned and removed his hat, revealing a head full of blond hair that was swept into a stylish wave on his forehead.

"Sorry to bother you, ma'am, but are you that writer who lives up to Holt House?" His tone, while mostly friendly, had a hint of mocking. It was the *ma'am.* It made him sound much older than he looked.

To be recognized in public was not uncommon in Nan's world (though perhaps a bit more uncommon now than before the accident), but it still threw her for a moment. "Yeah, that's me. Aren't you a little young to read my books? Some of them are pretty scary."

"My mom don't care. I like scary stuff." He picked up a bottle of beer and started to shake it lazily back and forth.

"You probably shouldn't do that, it might explode."

"You probably shouldn't do that, it might explode," the boy mimicked, but he stopped shaking it. "Did you like scary stuff when you were my age?"

"I guess so, sure." Her head was pounding. It was all she could do not to rip the lid off the bottle of pills and swallow a handful right now. "Where's your mom? You should get back to her. She's probably worried about you."

"Will you help me find her? She was up by the registers, but we got separated, and now I'm lost." He didn't sound like a lost kid. He spoke emotionlessly as if merely stating a fact.

"Um, sure, what does she look like?"

The boy's hand crept into hers, and they started to make their way to the front of the store. He shrugged. "Oh, just like any old mom. You know. She's tall, I guess."

"No, I *don't* know. If you want my help you need to stop playing games. Now tell me, what does she look like?"

The boy's head turned to the side, a weird smile on his face. He was enjoying this. "If you don't wanna help me, I'll just go find her myself. She's gotta be close by now. But she's gonna be mad at you."

Nan stopped and grabbed his shoulder, spinning him to

face her. She had done this same thing to Lizzie on the rare occasion she talked back. "Why are you screwing with me, huh? Did you even really lose your mom?"

"No." The boy giggled.

"Well, what the hell do you want then?"

His mouth fell open like a marionette's, his eyes went dark, and from his lips issued one word in a voice that wasn't his: *Rot.*

Nan shoved him back violently as pain exploded in her head, accompanied by flashing lights. She heard his little body hit the shelf behind him, jingling the glass bottles together before they started to fall and shatter. The yeasty smell rising from them made her gag.

He was crying, his face splotchy and red through his tears. "Why did you do that for?"

"No, I..." The boy on the floor surrounded by beer and broken bottles was maybe six, not ten, and had dark brown hair, not blond. And he wasn't dressed like a turn-of-the-century gondolier, either. He wore a t-shirt with some cartoon characters on it Nan didn't recognize, and a pair of jeans. His nose was caked in snot.

"You're scaring me!" he wailed. "You're mean. Go away!"

She saw the boy's shirt was ripped on the shoulder where she had grabbed him and felt deep shame fill her body.

Get out of here, now.

The maternal part of her, which hadn't been too near the surface recently, wanted to pick him up, dust him off, and take him to the front of the store where someone else could help him find his mother (she was pretty sure that part of her recollection was true). But the louder part of her agreed with that voice in her mind. She needed to leave before anyone came to see what all the commotion was.

Nan picked up her grocery basket from the floor, saw the bottle of IPA in it (*when did I put that in there?*), and took it out. The label read: Emerald Dreams, and beneath that was a picture of a green genie giving a thumbs-up. She dropped it on the floor next to the wailing child and walked as calmly as she could to the registers.

And when the cashier, a girl she'd seen in here before with two-tone hair and an earful of piercings, asked what was going on back there, Nan just shrugged and said she didn't know, but it sounded like something had broken.

Sitting in the driver's seat of her car, she ripped the foil off the bottle of ibuprofen, dumped some out into her shaking hand and swallowed them.

Get out of here before they call the cops!

"I'm going," she moaned, starting the car.

The whole way through town, she didn't let her speed drop below fifty even though the speed limit was thirty, and then once she was out on the country roads, she kept it at seventy-five.

Her hands wouldn't stop shaking until she was back home in her own kitchen, slurping down her second cup of tea and trying to wrap her mind around what had just happened.

What happened is I'm losing my goddamn mind.

But as easy as it would be to blame it on that, she knew she wasn't. The pain from the headaches was very real. And that very real pain had stopped (at least for a little while) when she had given in to what the voice had demanded of her. It stood to reason, then, if she gave it what it wanted now, the headaches would go away again, maybe even for good.

But where could she get an actual body to put down in the crypt? A human one?

"No," she said aloud and stood, slopping tea over the rim of the cup. "No, this is just *insane*. I can't."

But she could.

And she would.

Nan began opening cupboard doors, searching through each one all the way to the back, convinced if she looked long enough, she would find a bottle of alcohol squirreled away somewhere, even though she had cleared the booze from the house herself.

Why didn't I buy that beer I had in the store?

She dragged plastic mixing bowls out and let them clatter to the countertop. Then, she did the same thing with Lizzie's plastic cartoon character plates and cups.

"Come on, *come on.*"

And finally, in the small cabinet to the left of the refrigerator, she found what she was looking for. Hidden in the back behind an orange silicone baking sheet shaped like a pumpkin were two bottles: a half-full bottle of peppermint liquor and a full bottle of scotch.

Nan pulled them both out and set them on the kitchen table, then sat in front of them, steepling her hands beneath her chin.

She picked up the bottle of peppermint, unscrewed the lid, and inhaled, then put the cap back on when her head started to swim unpleasantly.

Then she picked up the scotch. About a million years before her career had taken off, Nan had worked front desk at a hotel, writing at night whenever she got the chance. Nick had been a high school math teacher. It had taken them six months to save enough for their wedding (a small affair attended by six people) and their honeymoon in the Scottish Highlands. While there, Nick had secretly purchased an extravagant gift for them at the time: a bottle of expensive scotch. On their first anniversary, he surprised her with it after dinner.

"We'll have a toast every year on our anniversary," he'd told her, pouring a healthy slug into the monogrammed glasses her parents had given them as a wedding gift. "And while we have our drink, we'll talk about everything we did together over the last year and everything we're going to do over the next."

"What do we do when the bottle's gone?"

Nick shrugged. "Get a divorce, I suppose. It's the only respectable thing to do in that situation, don't you think?"

That bottle hadn't even lasted the night. The two of them sat up into the wee hours of the morning, talking and laughing and drinking (her more than him, but not by much, back then, he could keep up), and then they screwed right there on the kitchen table in their crappy apartment like a couple of college kids.

The next year, he'd given her another bottle and wrote on the label: OPEN IN CASE OF ANNIVERSARY OR APOCALYPSE.

Now, sitting at her kitchen table in a house that would have fit about a hundred and fifty of that first apartment within its walls, Nan traced the writing on the scotch label with her finger. Only it wasn't the same *open in case of anniversary or apocalypse* message it used to be. On this one, Nick had written, *I love you still. I hope you love me, too.*

She pulled the cork, and the whole kitchen seemed to fill with the intoxicating smell. "I miss you," she said as bitter saliva squirted into her mouth and her scalp prickled.

Something behind her moved. She saw it reflected in the neck of the bottle. At first, it looked only like the changing sun dragging shadows across the room, but as she watched in a state of disconnect, the shadows seemed to melt together and resolve into something else.

A man. He was dressed in a white button-down shirt with a red and white bowtie.

That's what Nick was wearing the night of the crash. She would have sworn it *was* Nick, only she couldn't see his face. Where it should be, only a shifting black stain seemed to bleed into the air around it.

It's because his face was liquified when I hit the tree. It doesn't have a face because he doesn't.

She didn't scream; there wasn't enough air in the room for that, but the bottle of scotch slipped from her hands and landed with the base flat on the table, sending a gout of liquor shooting up through the neck, splashing her face and shirt. That snapped her out of the stupor she was in, and she stood, whirling around, trying to see in every direction at once. The kitchen was empty. She broke out in a cold sweat, suddenly aware of just how many doors there were in here; one that led to what used to be the bedroom of the cook and her apprentice but was now a large walk-in pantry; one on the western wall which led out onto the sunken patio beneath the back porch; one to the old walk-in pantry where the dishware and more cumbersome kitchen appliances were stored; one for the dumbwaiter; and one which led out into the downstairs hallway. Every single one of them hung still and silent.

Oh god, no, that's not true.

The sliding door to the dumbwaiter was open just a crack, revealing a line of darkness within. Nan never used the thing. There was something about it that gave her the creeps, so the door was always kept closed. When they had first moved in, Lizzie had begged to take just one ride in it from the kitchen up to the dining room, but the idea had filled Nan with inexplicable horror and she'd put the kibosh on that notion quickly.

"Nick, is that you?" Her throat tightened as she stepped toward it, keeping her eyes on it like she would have a venomous snake. "Nick? Lizzie?"

What are you even doing? You probably look crazy right now, do you know that?

She didn't care. She didn't feel crazy. Her head throbbed, and her eyes hurt so much every time she moved them, yet even that pain took a back seat to the terror coursing through her body.

Just go over there and push the door down and make sure it's shut.

Yes, that was exactly what she would do. And then she'd go and find Ducky (his crew was working in the east wing, converting the nuns' cells into guest bedrooms) and have him rip the whole goddamn thing out. Still, she found it very hard to just walk across the floor and *do* it.

Instead, she inched forward a little at a time, the gap beneath the door growing larger and larger in her mind as she did, until she stood beside it.

Something smelled foul over here, like garbage left in the sun.

Hurry up then, just close the damn thing!

She reached out to do just that when she saw something that made her whole body feel like she had just plunged through the ice into a frozen river.

Three fingers stuck out from beneath the door. They began to waggle as if waving hello, and a bright spike of pain pounded into her head.

She stumbled backward, and the door fell with a shriek like a dying seagull. At the same time, the swinging door that led into the downstairs hallway started to flap frantically back and forth as if someone had just run through it. She considered not following whatever had been in the kitchen with her out into the hall... but only for a moment.

Nan pushed through the double doors like a madwoman, afraid that if she didn't just barrel through, she would be too afraid to ever leave, and nearly collided with a man waiting outside for her.

That time, she did scream. But it wasn't the faceless specter of her dead husband or whatever had been hiding in the dumbwaiter. It was Ducky: short, squat, balding (but hiding it with his dirty Greek fisherman's cap) Ducky. Sentient mashed potatoes. He stared at her with eyes so big it was a shock they didn't just tumble out of his head.

Nan's hand flew to her chest. "Ducky, what the hell are you doing down here?"

Ducky peered at Nan's wet shirt and sniffed. He didn't say anything then, but Nan knew that by tomorrow, the whole town will have heard this story. He would tell his wife, Muriel, and she would, in turn, tell everyone else.

Oh well, not much you can do about that, is there?

"Sorry, Miss Wickwyre, I got turned around, I guess. This place is a maze, and I'm still getting lost in it, even after all this time." Usually a very direct man, he was now acting cagey.

"Where were you trying to go?"

He glanced behind her at the kitchen door. "Oh, don't worry, I can find my way from here. I just needed a landmark, and now I got one. Sorry to put a scare into you like that. Everything okay? You don't look so hot. Kinda pale."

Ha! Everything's so far from okay, I can't even see it in my rearview mirror.

"It's just a headache. I was going to go lie down for a while." Not that sleeping would touch the sick throbbing in her head. If anything, it would only be worse when she woke up.

As if to punctuate this, from behind Ducky, Nan heard the voice whisper *decay and rot.* If Ducky heard it, he made no indication.

It was at that moment she knew what she had to do. The headache wouldn't get better until she gave the voice what it wanted.

I can't do it. There's no coming back from this. This isn't like digging up and moving some old bones. This is murder.

But oddly, even that wasn't enough to make her reconsider. The pain was just too great. Who knew how much worse it would be in another week? Or two? She shivered at the idea of it. Besides, Ducky was up to something sneaking around in this part of the house. He might be looking for something to steal, or maybe just something juicy to sell to the tabloids... either way, she didn't like it.

"Ducky, I was wondering if you could take a look at the old dumbwaiter in the kitchen. I'm thinking about ripping it out, but I'd like your opinion."

His response was quick, almost panicked, making her wonder again what sort of things he had heard about her. "I should be getting back to the guys. If I'm not there to stay on top of 'em, they just fart around all day long, and then you end up paying more." As he spoke, he absently scratched his scalp beneath his fisherman's cap.

"Oh, it'll just be a second. I'm sure they'll be fine. Besides, I wanted to talk to you about a bonus. I'm loving the work you've done so far."

She pushed through the door into the kitchen without waiting for his response.

"Well... sure, I guess. So long as it's quick. I've got another job up to the college I gotta check in on later this afternoon once I get the boys squared away here."

Ducky looked the dumbwaiter over, yanked the door up with a scream of metal on metal (it was all Nan could do not to scream herself when he stuck his fingers beneath the door for leverage), and then told her if she wanted to add it to the job he could work up a price over the weekend.

"Any way you could figure it out now? I was hoping to have an idea today."

"I guess I got the time."

"That's great, thanks."

He cleared his throat. "So about this bonus then... what didja have in mind with that?"

Nan turned the gas back on under the teakettle. "You like tea? Have some with me. You can figure out the cost, and we can go over the bonus stuff at the same time. I think I've got some cookies here, too."

"I really oughta be getting a move on."

"Oh, come on, it's one cup. I know I'm from away, but no one's going to take away your 'local card' because you had one cup of tea with me, will they?"

"No, it's nothing like that..." He looked at the open bottle and puddled scotch on the tablecloth.

"I'm not drinking again."

"Sure. 'Course not."

"I'm really not."

"Well, why you got the bottle then?"

"I just found it today. See the little note on the label? That's from Nick. A gift. I went through the cupboards looking for something and found both bottles." She sighed. "You're almost right anyway. I *was* going to drink. I'm not proud of it, but things have been tough lately, and... just forget it. I know you don't want to hear all my problems. I'm just trying to tell you why it was opened when I dropped it, and why it splashed all over me."

"Look, Miss Wickwyre—"

"You can call me Nan."

"Well, anyway, you don't gotta explain anything to me. Hell, I get it. I usedta have a little more than I should on Friday nights after work. Drove my pickemup into a parked car one night. That's what scared me away from the drink. Figured it was only a matter of time before..." He fell silent, his cheeks red.

"I was going to dump it down the drain, but it's the last gift he ever got me. I don't know what to do."

"Want my advice? Dump it. That way, when you're tempted again, it's not there to grab. You can always keep the empty bottle."

"That's true."

The teakettle started its warbling screech, and Nan got up to fix their drinks and then rummaged through the pantry until she found a half-eaten box of chocolate chip cookies, which she dumped on a plate and set on the table in front of Ducky. "There, isn't this civilized?"

He grabbed one, took a bite, and then washed it down with a sip of tea. "Never could get usedta this stuff. My wife drinks it like it's going outta style, though."

"How is Muriel?"

Ducky talked for ten minutes or so in the manner any of the people from town would have with someone from away. They had a habit of talking *around* a situation instead of meeting it head-on like they would have with someone who was born and raised locally. For instance, he didn't mention Muriel's spending or her medical issues, both of which had worsened over the last couple of years (as a writer, Nan was adept at listening and picking things up), but rather he talked about her growing ceramic cat collection, and how the new wing on the hospital in Poughkeepsie was coming along.

Toward the end of his rambling, he started to cough and took a big gulp of tea to wash the tickle from his throat. When he spoke again, his voice was broken, and the coughing became more persistent.

"You okay? Can I get you some water?"

Ducky shook his head and waved her away while his face deepened to a brick-red color, and the broken capillaries in his nose turned purple. Then, all at once, the color drained from his face, leaving only two bruised, brown smudges beneath his eyes. He sucked in a whistling breath and his hands went to his throat as if they would be able to clear whatever was causing the unbearable tickle.

"I'm going to get you some water," Nan said (watching this was worse than she had imagined), and as she stood, Ducky opened his mouth to protest, but instead of words, a fine spray of blood spattered first his lips, then the enamel tabletop. Nan leaped back to avoid it. Ducky tried to take another breath but only succeeded in making a high-pitched keening sound that she worried the others might hear even so far away in the east wing.

Quickly, she locked the patio door and the door leading to the hallway. Ducky watched her do this with confusion and, she thought, growing fear. His face was deepening in color from brick-red to the purple of a ripe plum, and a thin, foamy trickle of vomit started to leak from the corner of his puffed lips. On account of the broken blood vessels from coughing so hard, his eyes took on the appearance of a zombie's, like in the movies they were always playing nowadays. His mouth clacked open and closed. No sound came out.

Nan's eyes became soft and unfocused, and she leaned in

close to Ducky's face. "You shouldn't have been snooping in my house. Did you find what you wanted?" She hadn't known she was going to say that, and the voice she spoke in didn't sound like her own, but neither of these things bothered her.

A horrible dawning realization came into Ducky's face, and he tried to grab the front of her shirt with his calloused hand. She stepped back easily out of his reach, and he wound up grabbing ahold of the tablecloth instead. As he slid to the side, no longer able to support his own weight sitting upright, he dragged the cloth and their afternoon tea down to the floor with him. Little hooked shards of broken porcelain exploded everywhere.

Blood and vomit surged from between his lips with greater force onto the stone floor, the pool beneath him growing so large it surrounded him, leaving him an island in the center of it. Still, it came.

Nan watched, horrified, sickened, and excited. When Ducky finally fell silent, his fingers no longer curling and relaxing, curling and relaxing, his work boots no longer tapping out S.O.S on the floor, she counted to sixty, waited, counted to sixty again, and figured it was all over.

Her headache was entirely gone.

She thought she would have felt *something* more than she did once the deed was done. Ducky was dead. She'd liked him well enough, but she'd killed him without much thought.

No time for that now. Get a move on before someone else comes snooping around where they don't belong.

Somehow, Ducky's cup had landed upright and still held some of the drink she had mixed for him containing tea and a healthy spoonful of the E-Rat-Icator rat poison she'd bought at the grocery store that morning. She dumped this down the drain, ran the water to flush it, then put the cup in the dishwasher and turned it on. The teapot and her cup had shattered when they hit the floor, so these went into the garbage, and the garbage bag went on the floor beside Ducky so she could dispose of the pieces.

Bob, the painter, had left a large roll of heavy-duty plastic when he'd finished up in the old servant's room at the southern end of the hallway, and she ran to it, her bare feet slapping on the cold stone floors. The sounds of hammers and chop saws came from far in the distance as Ducky's crew worked diligently in their boss's absence.

If this had been one of her novels, upon reentering the kitchen, she would have found that Ducky had only been playing possum and was gone, leaving behind him a trail of blood and vomit as he crawled toward freedom. But he was right where she'd left him and just as dead.

A lifetime of working in construction had left Ducky more solid than he appeared at first glance. What she had mistaken for flab was actually all muscle, so it took a great deal more effort than she had anticipated to roll him out of the puddle of bodily fluids and onto the plastic sheet. There was no way she would be able to move him down the hallway by dragging him on the plastic, as had been her initial idea. She also hadn't anticipated the Old Faithful reenactment that he had performed and couldn't very well have a trail of blood and vomit leading from the kitchen right to the secret doorway of the crypt.

She was at a loss until she remembered that when she went to grab the roll of plastic Bob had left, she had seen a flatbed furniture dolly in the corner of the room.

Once he was on that, the rest was a piece of cake. She ferried him down the hall and into the root cellar, the whole time certain that someone would come at that exact moment, see her, and alert the rest of the crew to what she had done, but no one did.

It took a little finagling to get the dolly and its load down the stone steps into the crypt without incident, yet she managed. (She would end up leaving it down there. It was just too heavy to bring back up. It still sat where she had left it, rusting in the dark.)

Later, when it was quieter, she would haul Ducky's body off the dolly and up onto the plinth (it had to be on the plinth; she was fairly certain of that, though she didn't know why), but until then, the most important thing was cleaning up the kitchen before anyone saw it.

Luckily no one bothered her as she scooped, sopped, mopped, and bleached every surface. The paper towels went into the garbage bag with the broken tea set, and when her hands were raw and bleeding from the bleach and hot water, and the kitchen sparkled like new, Nan took the garbage bag and tossed it down the steps into the crypt.

It was on her way back to the kitchen for the second time, sore, tired, and starving that she remembered Ducky's truck. It was one of those huge jacked-up asshole pickups with his company name emblazoned on the side of it, and it was parked in the front driveway beside her own more sensible car.

"Shit," she muttered. If she left it there, the cops would know he'd gone missing while at her house. If she tried to move it, someone could see her. How would she explain that?

Maybe the best thing to do is call attention to it now.

If they believed the story she concocted, things would probably be okay, even if the cops did have to come and search the house. If they didn't, she could be shooting herself in the foot. Still, it felt like less of a gamble than doing nothing.

Ducky's second-in-command was a man named Ramirez, who always seemed to be smiling. Usually, he caught a ride to work with a heavyset man named Blake because they lived on the same street, but not always. Nan had seen the men arrive in the same vehicle this morning, which was another stroke of luck.

After giving herself a once-over in the mirror to make sure there was no blood on her clothing or skin (she looked fine, if a little harried), she made her way to the east wing where the guys were laying floor and found Ramirez.

"Hey, Ramirez, how's it going?"

"Hey Mrs. Wickwyre. How do you like the new floor? Classy, isn't it?" He was always calling things classy. It tickled her.

"Classy as shit," she replied, which never failed to make him laugh. "Listen, I've got to talk to you really quick. Out in the hall."

He looked puzzled but went along with her. A few of the other guys started teasing him, saying "Uh-oh, you're in trouble now," like a bunch of high schoolers picking on someone called down to the principal's office. Ramirez grinned. "Just keep working, *tontos*."

Once they were out in the hall, the usual worksite chatter resumed. When Nan was certain no one was listening in, she said, "Look, I didn't want to say anything in front of the guys, but I was just talking to Ducky, and he got a phone call and said he had to leave."

"Oh... okay, well, we're almost done for the day anyway, so that's no problem. I can—"

Nan was shaking her head. "No, it's not that. Someone came and got him."

"I don't follow you. Is everything okay?"

"I don't know. He didn't really say much. A guy in a blue truck just picked him up out front. He asked if I would have you drive his truck to his house tonight and leave it there for him because it might be late when he gets back, and he doesn't want to leave it here all weekend."

Ramirez frowned but didn't seem too put out by this news. "Huh. It's a little weird, but I'd be lying if I said it was the first time something like this happened. Never off a job site, though, usually just from the bar."

"I know his wife has some sort of medical problem. Maybe something happened to her?"

Ramirez nodded but didn't elect to fill her in on the specifics. "You're probably right. I don't know why he just wouldn't drive himself, though."

Nan hadn't been able to come up with a reason for that, so it seemed safer not to try to explain it. Ramirez didn't seem put out by this, either. He just shrugged and said, "I rode in with Blake today, so I can do it no problem. Did he say if he left his keys in the cab?"

"Yeah, up in the visor." She'd checked this out before coming up. Wouldn't that have been a fine thing if his keys were still in his pocket?

"Cool. If he calls, tell him I'll take care of it."

"Sounds like a plan. And do me a favor, too. If you hear from him first or see him when you drop his truck off, tell him to call me if there's anything wrong. Now that I'm thinking about it, I guess he *did* look a little bit worried when he left. I hope everything's okay."

Ramirez grinned. "Ducky's bulletproof. He'll be okay."

Nan left Ramirez to get back to work. She walked on shaking legs back down to the kitchen and fixed herself a bowl of ice cream with chocolate sauce and peanuts. She deserved a treat. Her headache was gone, and the Ducky situation was tied up as neatly as she could get it for now.

As far as alibis went, this one wouldn't keep her out of the electric chair, but she thought the cops would buy it if it came down to that.

And they did. Not Sheriff Lambert and Deputy Sanders, but two stone-faced state boys from Poughkeepsie who didn't know how to smile and had identical creases in their pants. She was questioned twice, once in her home and once in a drab little room at the station that smelled like a dentist's office. Nan had hired a local rent-a-lawyer so as not to appear too concerned about the investigation, and both times, she told her story exactly as she had told it to Ramirez. By the time she was done with the second interrogation, she actually believed her own version of the events, and so did the troopers. Enough of it, anyway. Writers are nothing if not professional liars.

With Ducky MIA, Ramirez took over as interim lead on the job, and though he still smiled and chatted pleasantly with her, something had changed about him. He was colder, as if some part of him knew she had made him a party to something unsavory the day Ducky disappeared.

There'd been a big search of all of Ducky's haunts; his fishing hole and favorite hunting spots, the state parks where he liked to walk on weekends, and all up and down the shores of the Hudson. He was well-liked in the local community, so there were hundreds of volunteers during those first two weeks. But as time went on with no trace of him and no new leads, interest started to wane, and rumors started to fly. Most people thought the pressure of dealing with Muriel's health concerns (and increasingly fragile mental state), had gotten to be too much for him, so he'd taken off for St. Barts, where he always talked of retiring to. Some people thought he'd been kidnapped by whoever had picked him up from Nan's that day, the illusive driver of the blue truck who had never been identified despite Nan's spartan description of him.

And then there was the fringe contingent led by Muriel Duckworth, who thought Nan had something to do with Ducky's disappearance. Sundays after mass at Saint Anthony's, Muriel would hold her own little sermon on the front steps and preach her theories. Because of her history, few people listened to her at first, but as weeks turned into months and Muriel became more insistent on her version of events, her little band of followers began to grow.

For the most part, Nan could ignore them, but as their numbers swelled to include more reputable community members, this task became increasingly difficult. Unable to stand the staring and whispering anymore, she decided to just do her shopping and run errands in Rhinebeck, New Paltz, and Wappingers Falls. She pulled out of the local community entirely and started living as a recluse, but even this didn't satisfy Muriel Duckworth. She started showing up in front of the gates of Holt House to shout at traffic (of which there was thankfully very little) about how Nan had killed her husband.

When this happened, Nan called Sheriff Lambert, who came out with a tired sort of patience to haul Muriel back into town and advise her to stop harassing the nice writer lady who had nothing to do with Ducky. This usually worked for a day or two before she would be back out there raving like a loon—snow, rain, or shine.

Nan considered just inviting Muriel into the house and telling her to search to her heart's content (Ducky's body wasn't there anymore; just like the bones of Persephone, Jeremiah, and Cora Holt, it had disappeared from the plinth). If this would have put an end to it, she'd have done it, but finding nothing would have only further fueled Muriel's insanity.

In a way, she admired the old woman.

-7-

Ducky had been the first but not the last. Every six months, almost to the day, over the next nine years, Nan's headache would return. And like that first time, it would continue to grow more severe the longer she did nothing about it until it felt like her head was being split in two from the crown down by some agonizingly slow-moving crusher. The first couple of times, she denied what the headache meant and put off what she knew had to be done to alleviate it, telling herself Ducky had been a fluke, a momentary mania, and no sane person could even *begin* to consider what she was considering. But when the pain continued to grow to the point it left her crippled and limping from room to room, pulling the heavy drapes closed against the sun like a character in an old gothic romance novel, it was easier to forego her scruples. After all, it was a fool who didn't learn from their own mistakes. Nan Wickwyre may have been a lot of things, but she was certainly no fool.

In time, taking lives became as inconsequential as taking ibuprofen to stop a hangover. During her good times between the pain, life would go on much as it always had before. Mornings were for writing, afternoons for napping, reading, and editing, or taking in the occasional movie over in Red Hook when the mood struck her. At night, she slept like a baby. It was easy to forget what happened twice a year when the voice started demanding rot and decay... until it happened again with the same inevitability of death and taxes. One morning, she would awaken to the sick beat in her temples and the inhuman voice whispering from the closet or from beneath the bed, and know it had started again.

Nineteen people had gone onto the plinth down in the crypt and disappeared in those nine years; like the couple from Oregon who had hitchhiked across the country and, on a whim, decided to jump the fence bordering her property to snap a few candid photos of her house. She'd locked them up down there in the dark, and they'd starved to death, their fingers bloody and worn to the bones from trying to dig through the stone walls. Or the tourist from Ireland who had made a wrong turn down her driveway one spring morning. She'd served him a cup of tea laced with roofies, then buried him alive. When she was quite certain he was dead, she dug him up and put him on the plinth. After a while, though, most of them just blended together. She never considered or plotted the method of their deaths in advance. It was as if one moment she was in charge, and the next someone else was at the controls, pulling switches and pushing buttons... a little like being drunk. Looking back on it afterward (in those rare moments when she did), the acts she committed while in that "drunk" place didn't always make sense, but in the moment, they seemed to.

For nine years, things progressed in this predictable, some

might say boring, manner, until one day, suddenly, everything changed. That was almost a year ago. Sometimes, she still cried about it even now.

It started when someone rang her doorbell.

-8-

2025

It was December 15th. Snow had finally come to the Hudson Valley, and it looked like it was fixing to unpack its things and stick around for a little while, which was sort of a Devil's blessing; on the one hand, there was something comforting about the quiet and isolation it provided. And it *did* contain a certain beauty that took Nan back to when she was a child looking out her upstairs window at the Christmas Morning snow... how it sparkled like chips of diamonds. But on the other hand, those beautiful days were few and far between. Most were gray and slushy and cold, which her interior weather tended to reflect no matter how hard she tried to overcome it.

By the morning of the 15th, Nan's headache had gotten so bad that she woke with a rotten throbbing in her face that made her teeth seem to vibrate in time with her heartbeats. Even gently touching her cheeks made her feel like screaming.

If that had been the only problem, she might have been able to handle it, but there were others. Before the cold snap arrived the night before, nearly two weeks of constant rain had dampened her spirits as the world turned drab, muddy, and uninviting. This, in turn, caused her writing to suffer more than it already was; before the headache started, she'd been having difficulty with her current story. More and more it seemed like she was forcing the words, and they just fell flat on the page. By the end of each session, she would often delete the day's output and slam the laptop closed with petulant rage. Then, as her headache worsened, it became painful to sit upright and look at the glowing screen even when she turned the brightness all the way down. But all of this paled in comparison to her real problem that December.

Muriel Duckworth. It had been roughly nine years since Ducky had gone missing, yet instead of becoming less fixated on Nan, her obsession only seemed to grow. Not steadily as one might expect; it came in fits and spurts. Sometimes Muriel would forget about her entirely for weeks or months, and then one day, she would seemingly be everywhere, following Nan when she went out of town to run errands and camping out in front of the gates across Little Church Road watching Nan's comings and goings and jotting things down in a notebook.

Nan would have had her removed by Sheriff Lambert, but the property across the road was owned by Lyle Cooper, one of Muriel's newest converts, who had given her permission to be there, providing she did not yell at cars or cause a ruckus. In short, she wasn't doing anything Nan could have her hauled away for.

Which meant Nan couldn't do a damn thing about her headache. She knew she needed to deal with her head if there was any hope of getting back on track, but with Constable Muriel staking out her house, that wasn't an option. So she spent most of her days on the sofa with a blanket pulled over her and the curtains drawn, trying to sleep.

A gnawing worry about what would happen to her if she couldn't procure a sacrifice had started to plague her as much as the voice did. What had started as a raspy whispering plea was now a full-throated, gravelly demand.

Worse than just hearing it, Nan was starting to see the voice's owner out of the corner of her eyes. It moved quickly and seemed to hide in the shadows just far enough away so she couldn't make out what it was. She had the sneaking suspicion that if she couldn't find a body for it, this thing would come for her. But as time wore on and the pain got worse, even this didn't worry her anymore.

She had just started to drift off on the sofa, her belly full of painkillers that didn't do one goddamn bit of good, when her doorbell rang. The sound was like a shish kebab skewer shoved through her ear, and she cried out in pain, leaking gummy tears from her eyes.

"Goddamn you, go away!"

As big as the house was, though, her voice wasn't carrying to the front door. A few seconds later, this was confirmed when the bell rang again. She threw the blanket back, pulled herself into a seated position using the coffee table, and started a fast shuffling hobble down the hall before the sadist outside her door could ring the bell a third time.

It would be Muriel. *Of course,* it would be her. Who else? Muriel come to yell and scream and gibber like a lunatic demon, her words sounding more like hoots and hollers than actual words.

But when she checked the security camera feed on her phone as she lurched brokenly toward the door, she saw that it wasn't Muriel who had rung the bell. It was a kid. Nan swiped to a different camera feed that showed the front gates and saw that Muriel wasn't even at the end of the driveway today.

She yanked the door open, startling the boy on the stoop. He was maybe ten or twelve. It was hard to tell because he was wearing a puffy red and blue snowsuit and a matching hat with a tasseled pom-pom on top. In his hands, he carried a snow shovel that was almost taller than he was. Nan saw that a fresh three inches of snow had fallen while she was drifting in and out of consciousness.

"Didn't you see the signs?" she snapped. The boy blinked and stepped back, his footsteps squeaking in the snow. "Can't you read? They say *posted* and *private property*. You know what that means?"

The boy nodded fast, his eyes big and afraid.

"Well, then you know that means you're trespassing, and I can have you arrested. So what do you want, huh? What's so important that you came all the way down here to bother me while I'm working?"

"I... um, I..."

"Come on, spit it out."

From the living room came the dry sounds of something scrabbling against the stone floor, and then the voice shouted at her *DECAY AND ROT!* Her eyes went unfocused as the dark, slouching thing crept up the hall behind her, and her mouth fell slightly in a crocodile grin.

She fetched a deep, theatrical sigh, pulled her blanket closed around her, and lowered herself to her haunches so she and the boy would be eye to eye. It made her look vulturine. The owner of the voice behind Nan crouched too as it shuffled silently closer. The boy didn't seem to see it at all.

"Look, I'm sorry I shouted at you, okay?"

The boy nodded rapidly, his pom-pom flouncing back and forth.

Maybe he's not even twelve, she thought. *Just tall for his age. He's certainly reacting as if he's much younger.*

"I wasn't expecting anyone today, and you surprised me. But that's no excuse. I shouldn't have yelled at you, no matter what. Do you forgive me?"

The boy nodded, the material of his snowsuit swishing. It was the only sound in the still morning except for a few especially chatty birds. His eyes were still full of distrust, though. The urge to take a drink suddenly roared to life, and for a moment, Nan considered just slamming the door in his face and taking one. The bottle of scotch was still hidden away in the cupboard by the fridge. Maybe it would even get rid of the rotten pounding in her face.

But the urge passed.

"Okay," she said, her voice not quite steady, "let's start again, then. My name's Nan. What's yours?"

"Caleb. Caleb Montgomery," he said cautiously.

Nan stuck her hand out. "Hi, Caleb. What brings you all the way out here by yourself?"

He looked at her hand suspiciously but still took it. Kids were trusting like that. When she didn't grab him and gobble him down like some fairytale ogre, Caleb seemed a little more at ease.

Behind him, the sky was spitting down snow at a heavy clip. Another fifteen minutes or so and his footprints would be totally erased.

"Um, I'm, um, going around and shoveling snow out of peoples' driveways for 'em, and then they pay me for it. It's five dollars for the whole thing, but if it takes more than a hour, it's five *more* dollars." He cast a dubious eye at the length of her driveway. "I think yours might take longer."

The temperature had been dropping steadily throughout the day, and if the snow kept on at this rate, by nightfall, there would be at least two more feet of fresh powder covering the ground. The kid could use a snowblower and still be unable to keep up with it. Probably hadn't gotten a nibble all day.

"I think it might take you a whole year if you were going to try to shovel my driveway by yourself, Caleb. Have you got someone to help you?"

"No, my friend Mikey was 'sposed to help, but he's home sick. I think he's faking 'cause he doesn't like shoveling, and my mom says he's lazy."

Nan laughed. "Well, I've got a little tractor I use to plow the driveway, so I'm not really in the market for someone to shovel it. What about the big white house down the road? Have you tried there?"

Caleb looked disappointed and shook his head. "No, that's where I live. Me 'n my mom. She said I'm not 'sposed to go out onto the main road because people drive like idiots in the snow."

Nan suddenly recognized the little face staring back at her.

She'd waved to the young woman and her son while driving past the white house more than once. They were usually out front late during the summer, swinging on the rusted, sagging swing set or playing tag on the shaggy lawn. The house was maybe a mile and a half away. This kid must have struggled to make it this far. "Your mom sounds like a smart lady."

He shrugged. "I guess so."

Nan's right eye suddenly squinched shut when a needle of agony pierced it, and she struggled back up onto her feet. The dark, stooped figure was nearer now, not shouting anymore, but Nan could still feel the greedy *want* coming from it as it waited impatiently. It was hungry.

"Are you okay?"

She nodded and tried to smile. When she opened her right eye, fresh suffering flowed into it. "I've just got a little headache. Actually, do you think you could help me get back inside? I'm feeling... a little tired right now. And a little sick." This was all true. It felt as if the dark thing she couldn't see had somehow reached into her brain and twisted some dial that had sent her internal balance out of whack.

Caleb tugged his hat up and down, scratching his head. "My mom tole me not to go into anyone's house."

"That's good advice. What if I paid you to help me? Would that be okay?"

He looked uncertain. "I dunno. How much?"

"How about twenty bucks? That's like four *whole* hours of shoveling. And all you have to do is help me down the hallway to the couch."

"Wow," the boy said. "You're telling the truth? Twenty dollars just for that?"

"Yup, cross my heart." *Hope to die.* And right then, she really did. "I could even make us some hot cocoa if you want. Something warm on a cold day."

"Well... I guess that would be okay. Mom says I'm 'sposed to help people who need help. She said it's what good people do."

"You're a good boy, Caleb. Your mom would be proud."

He came up onto the porch. Now that he'd decided to help (and with the promise of such a financial windfall in his immediate future), his caution was gone. He stepped to her side and allowed her to put an arm around his shoulder. Putting her weight on him, they crossed the threshold together, the dark thing retreating along the hallway in the shadows as they approached, and Nan swore she could sense it drooling.

As with Ducky and all the others, once the decision had been made, the pain in her head retreated almost completely. She still hobbled along, allowing Caleb to help her, but she no longer needed the support.

"The kitchen is downstairs if you want some cocoa." They steered away from the living room doorway and descended the stairs slower than necessary, the blanket trailing behind her softly.

If Caleb sensed any change within her, he didn't show it. "This place sure is big," he said.

"Sure is."

Stop this now! God and Jesus, please fucking stop this!

Once he was seated at the enamel-topped table under the windows in the same seat Ducky had sat in, and his hat and gloves had been removed, Nan set a big mug of cocoa in front of him. Caleb took a sip and wrinkled his nose. "This tastes funny."

"Oh, I'm sorry. I put some peppermint in it to make it more Christmassy. Don't you like it? I should have asked you first."

"No, I like it okay. Now that I'm expecting it. Do you have some in yours, too?"

Nan sipped her own, watching as Caleb sucked down a great deal of peppermint liquor and E-Rat-Icator. "I can't have any. I'm allergic."

"Why do you got it then?"

"Well, my... my little girl used to like it in her cocoa."

"She doesn't like it anymore?"

"No, not anymore. Drink up." She was having second thoughts, even though it was much too late for that. By this point with the others, she had been moving along in a mechanical sort of way, completing each step of the process without much thought or emotion. But with Caleb, it was different. The owner of the voice wasn't taking over. It was still nearby—she could feel it watching hungrily from the darkness of the hall—but it was almost like it was afraid to take control and finish what it started. For the first time, Nan despised it.

Caleb considered what she had said with a shrug and drank more. They talked a little about Christmas and about Mikey, the faker who was supposed to be shoveling driveways with him, and after a while, she saw Caleb's eyes begin to droop and sag. A few minutes after that, his speech started to slur. "Idonfeeltoogood."

"Finish your cocoa, then. The peppermint will help to settle your stomach." Her voice was barely a whisper as her mind rebelled.

"I don't think I can. I feel like I'm gonna puke."

"You can do it. And if you're still not feeling well when it's all gone, I'll take you somewhere nice and dark to lie down and rest. How would that be?"

"Are you still gonna... pay me my... twenty..." His head sunk down to the tabletop with a light thud.

"You'll get it, I promise." Her voice broke.

Nan drank the rest of her cocoa, but her hands weren't steady, and the mug chattered against her teeth.

You can't do this. You can't do this! He's just a kid, for God's sake! Take him to the hospital and drop him off in front of it if you have to! Just wait another couple of days and find someone else!

"There isn't anyone. There's no more time. It's too late." She didn't really know if she believed that, though. There might be time, but that didn't really matter. It was the goddamn *compulsion* driving her. She had to follow through.

"Whuuh?"

And that was the last thing Caleb Montgomery said on this earth.

He died quietly, much more so than Ducky had, and with much less curdy vomit to clean up, which she set to work doing immediately, while Caleb's tiny body waited on the heavy plastic in the hall. When the kitchen was sparkling again, Nan bleached her mop and pail, replaced them in the closet where they belonged, and then pulled on her heavy coat and winter boots. There were tears on her cheeks.

"You don't get this one," she said, peering through the kitchen door into the darkened hallway as she spoke. Whatever was out there watched her with big, lidless eyes. She could feel its confusion, but that was just a fleeting blip before it was overrun by white-hot rage.

GIVE ME DECAY! it bellowed in a voice so hoarse it distorted. *GIVE IT TO ME, IT'S MINE!*

Cradling the crinkling plastic in her arms, Nan turned and walked to the kitchen door, which led her out onto the lower patio. "I'll bring you someone else, but you can't have this one. And if you bring my headache back, I'll kill myself. I swear to God I will. And then, who will you get to bring you what you need?" She meant it, too. When faced with the reality of what she had done here in this house, it wasn't a difficult threat to follow through on. The voice must have sensed that because, although Nan waited for the headache to return, it didn't.

Satisfied, she carried the boy outside and set him on the picnic table still littered with citronella candles from last summer.

If you knew you wouldn't give this one to that thing, why did you do this?

The answer was unsatisfying, but it was the truth. "I had to."

Nick's ATV was up in the garage, but the tires wouldn't make it through the thickening snow, and the chains would take forever to put on. Luckily, the tools she'd used to exhume the Holt kids were still in the back, and the rains had softened the ground considerably, so digging would be a snap. It would still be a long night, dragging poor Caleb all the way out to the Holt family plot and putting his body in Jeremiah's casket, but she was going to do it anyway. Knowing he was resting beneath the intricate scrollwork and the word *Son* made her feel better. And then, after getting a good night's sleep, she could find someone else to take his place down in the crypt.

Nan grabbed her trusty flashlight from beneath the kitchen sink and set off into the darkness.

The rest of that night and the following day she remembered only in bits and pieces. The way the dead tree branches seemed to grab at her as she passed like pleading skeletal fingers. How each shovelful of snowy mud weighed about a thousand pounds, and how her hands blistered and bled by the time she was done (it had taken almost two weeks for them to heal). How she had slipped a folded twenty-dollar bill into the boy's pocket, as promised. And how, afterward when the mud had been smoothed down, and a fresh half inch of snow had fallen on the grave, she'd stood in the backyard looking up at the lighted windows of Holt House, afraid to go back inside. Her headache hadn't returned, but she could sense fury from within the bluestone walls. And maybe fear, too.

She'd fixed herself spaghetti and meatballs from a can that night, followed by a few handfuls of chips and then some ice cream with nuts and chocolate sauce for dessert, before falling into bed with her clothes on and sleeping uninterrupted through the night.

Early the next morning, before the sun was up, she picked up a dirty, scrawny twenty-year-old kid named Keith from Poughkeepsie, whom she'd found nodding on heroin under an overpass, brought him home, and fed enough junk into his veins to kill ten of him (after watching how he did it). When he finally lay still, and the foamy vomit stopped, and his lips and fingernails had turned a deep shade of blue, she planted him down in the dark on the plinth like some weird, deformed bulb.

Keith's body had remained for two full days before disappearing, something which had never happened before, and when the voice finally left her in peace, it felt like an uneasy one. Its anger was everywhere.

Around this time, two other things happened, which seemed out of the blue. The first was that she ended her contract with the builder she'd brought up from the city to finish off the house (Ramirez, who had inherited Ducky's business, would no longer work for her), leaving about four thousand square feet of rooms unfinished. She didn't recall making a conscious decision to do this. One day, she called Kevin, the project manager, and pulled the plug. And when he told her she still had to pay off the remainder of the contract, she'd done so without argument, leaving Kevin annoyed and puzzled. Nan had locked the big double doors leading into the unfinished section of the house and washed her hands of the whole thing. She'd contemplated razing the crumbling rooms but, for some reason, couldn't quite bring herself to do it. It was like cutting off a finger because you had a hangnail.

The other thing that happened was she started writing again, scrapping what she had been working on and starting something new. That weird creative logjam formed in the months leading up to the Caleb Montgomery incident had finally cleared. When she'd written her first novel, *Haunting Willow Hall*, it had been mostly done at night, due in part to her schedule at the hotel but also because that's when the story seemed to flow the best. Her muse, Vito (he of the Brooklyn accent, cheap cigars, and shiny suits) had been suffering a bout of insomnia at the time. And now, history was repeating itself. In the mornings, usually her most productive time, she was met with creative constipation, but after sunset, she couldn't hold it in any longer, and the floodgates burst open. She didn't think at all, just wrote. And, unlike her usual process, she didn't begin by reading the previous day's output but instead soldiered ahead, believing everything was taking care of itself. It was a sequel to her first novel, which she had provisionally titled *Return to Willow Hall*, but strangely, if pressed, she wouldn't have been able to say what had happened so far or even who the characters were. But it felt *good*.

Just keep going and don't look back, she told herself. *Before you know it, the headache will rear its ugly head, and everything will come to a crashing halt.*

But six months or so later, when the first twinges of pain should have started, heralding the beginning of a new cycle of torment and agony, there was nothing. She waited, certain it was just around the corner.

And a month after that, when there was *still* nothing, she waited some more. But there was only silence in the house, unbroken by phantom voices or headaches.

The funny thing was, this scared her more.

-9-
2026

Wetness on her cheeks. This strange sensation dragged her up out of the jumbled mix of memories and sleep, and she sat up with a start at the kitchen table, causing her back to shudder with pain. She'd wrenched something dragging Claudia's body downstairs, she was sure of it.

Peanut slept on the floor beside the plate she had fed him his treat on for taking one for the team; a rare porter-house mixed with steak sauce and potatoes, which she had pureed in the blender so he could actually eat it. His tiny tongue stuck out from between what was left of his front teeth as he snored softly.

In front of Nan on the table sat a glass of scotch poured almost to the brim, just the way she used to like it back when she was drinking. Although the evidence sat right in front of her, she had no recollection of doing this. Beside the scotch was the baggie of white powder she'd taken off Claudia, still tied up in a neat little twist.

She picked up the glass. "Well, hello there. Been a while since I've seen you around." The light caught the bronze liquid, so it looked like it was winking at her.

You should have dumped that bottle years ago, you know that.

Some things were easier said than done. You never knew when you'd need a bottle to break in case of emergency. She couldn't taste scotch in her mouth, so at least she hadn't been drinking while in her weird fugue state.

This was all Claudia McKinnon's fault; she'd dragged all of this shit back out into the open when she started squawking about Ducky.

Nan carried the glass carefully over to the sink. At the sound of her approach, Peanut opened his milky eyes but didn't pick his head up off the floor. For one crazy instant, she wanted to toss the scotch back and let it warm her throat as it worked its way down to her belly to soften these horrible memories that seemed so near the surface today... but of course, she couldn't do that. Not now, not after all these years. Not with Peanut's watchful gaze settled on her.

"Sorry, it's gotta be this way," she said, and with a pang of sadness and regret, dumped the glass, sending that beautiful liquid down the drain to gurgle in the sink's throat on its way to the dark chamber of the septic tank.

If it bothers you that much, why didn't you pour it back into the bottle?

A good thought, but at the moment, she lacked the

willpower and the steady hands to accomplish that Herculean feat. No, down the drain was better.

Then dump the rest of the bottle, too.

"Oh, shut up and mind your own business." The bottle would keep just fine where it was usually stored, in that little cupboard beside the refrigerator behind the baking sheets. One of the greatest lies she told herself (and she'd told some whoppers over the years) was that when all of this was over and done, she would be able to dump it without a second thought.

But not tonight. She tucked it in where it belonged, along with the baggie of cocaine, and closed the cupboard door.

The house watched intently as she made her way upstairs, feeling very much like an amoeba in the body of a giant, spinning its way endlessly through a pitch-black maze. She crawled into bed, feeling eyes all over her body, and then did something she hadn't done since she was a little girl. She pulled the covers over her head so the monsters couldn't see her. But even the thick winter comforter didn't seem to be able to keep them out, and it was a long time before sleep came and alleviated her of her memories.

-10-

A hunched figure clattered softly across the thick-pile carpet on two sharp, bony legs over to the hump beneath the covers. The woman's breathing had slowed and steadied. She was asleep.

The figure stood at its full height, its dark head nearly touching the ceiling, its large, lidless eyes at the same height as the crown molding. All at once, it bent at the waist with a soft series of cracking sounds, staggered its spiked bone legs to steady itself, and draped its clotted hair over the woman's sleeping form. She shifted and moaned beneath the blankets but stayed asleep.

The thing pulled shaky air through its ancient lips, producing a wheezing, clicking sound. And when it was certain the woman wouldn't awaken, it grinned a horrible grin that split the taut skin around its mouth, showing its overlarge rodent teeth... and it started to whisper.

PART 2
REPRISAL
FALL & WINTER
2026

CHAPTER 4
VISITORS

Constable Bell pounded on the door for so long that Keaton thought the wood would splinter and crack. He was a large man, a planet stuffed into a blue uniform, but his eyes were sharp and shrewd despite his body's porcine appearance.

"What can I do for you, Constable?" Keaton asked. Vincent's blood was still drying beneath his fingernails, mixed with the cemetery dirt from Lady Henry's grave. He hid his hands behind his back, had second thoughts, and instead stuffed them into his pockets.

"Blackburn." The nod was curt and unfriendly. "Got a question or two for you."

"Now?" Vincent Shelton's blood still stained the dirt floor of the cellar. If the rotund constable searched the house, there was no way he would miss it. "My wife, Maisy, needs her medications, and the nurse isn't here yet. Could this wait until this afternoon?"

"Fraid not," Bell said, bellying his way through the door and into the foyer. "Things have gone a bit too far for courtesy."

Keaton closed the door quickly behind them, throwing the room into darkness, and invited the constable down the hall into the kitchen. In his mind, he tried to decide if he would plead self-

defense or if perhaps Bell might also disappear and with him any suspicions. After all, there were other graves in the churchyard besides Lady Henry's.

-Nan Wickwyre, *Haunting Willow Hall*

-1-

Sheriff Chester Lambert and Undersheriff Pete Sanders stood on Nan's front porch. Lambert slouched, his potbelly riding out prominently in front of him, his gray shirt rucked up, exposing a triangle of hairy, pink belly. A toothpick that had been chewed nearly to splinters stuck out of the corner of his mouth. Sanders, on the other hand, stood with his legs spread slightly apart, his arms straight down at his sides, eyes forward, as if he was about to receive a medal from the mayor.

"Christ, will ya relax, Sanders? You look like you got hemorrhoids." Lambert rang the bell.

Nan watched them arrive on the camera feed, and then listened to their chitchat for a moment before opening the door with a nod of recognition.

"Sheriff. Deputy."

"Actually, it's *Undersheriff* Sanders, now." There was a look of spite on his face as he said this. He'd had a hard-on for her ever since the accident and was letting her know that soon he would be able to do something about it.

She didn't let it bother her. "Well, I'm sure the county's residents are sleeping better knowing that. Who'd you leave in charge back at HQ today? Answering machine?"

Sanders' face turned red, and he frowned. She had intended for it to sound glib (mostly, anyway), but the slight headache she'd woken with, coupled with the bad night's sleep, had put her into a funk this morning. It wasn't one of her *special* headaches—at least, she didn't think so; over the years, she had become adept at recognizing them and distinguishing them from the normal ones—but it was frustrating nonetheless. And, as if that wasn't enough, Claudia was *still* down in the crypt and starting to stink as she bloated like a parade float. There was a bucket of lime in the root cellar for just such an eventuality, but this morning was the first time Nan had ever had to use it. She wasn't worried, though. Not *yet*. It had taken two days for Keith, that junkie kid, to disappear, so there was still time.

"Nan," Lambert said with a nod. "Gotta ask ya some questions. Can we come in? You can call your lawyer if you wanna, but then we gotta take this downtown."

Downtown, Nan thought while inwardly rolling her eyes. *The whole of downtown is hardly a wide spot in the road.*

"If you're not planning to arrest me, just come in. But clean your shoes off first. Your feet are all caked in mud. Ava's coming tomorrow, and I don't want her to have to scrub the floors. The arthritis in her hands and knees gets bad this time of year."

Lambert scraped his boots perfunctorily on the welcome mat and stepped over the threshold. Sanders prissily scraped each side of his patent leather shoes and then the bottoms until no mud showed.

"Coffee? I was just sitting down to my morning cup."

"Love one."

"No, thank you. We're here on business. This isn't a social call."

Instead of taking the boys in dark blue down into the kitchen as she would have any other morning, Nan took them to the living room where she had already laid out coffee service for three and some amaretto breakfast cookies. They wouldn't yet be able to smell Claudia downstairs, but it seemed like tempting fate to take them so close to where she was hidden.

"You were expecting us," Sanders said. The disappointment on his face was obvious and gratifying.

"My agent mentioned you might drop in."

"Hell of a view right there," Lambert said, plopping down onto the sofa with an old man grunt. He took one of the cookies. Within seconds, there were crumbs all down the front of his uniform. "Jesus wept, Sanders will you pull that dick outta your ass and siddown?"

"If you don't like coffee, I've got hot chocolate. Or tea?"

Sanders sat like he stood, ramrod straight, and said nothing. His hair was still in that same 1950s crew cut he'd had ten years back, but it was a bit grayer at the temples now and had lost some of its boyish charm. Nan thought that it was, perhaps, more Sheriff Lambert than the job that had caused the change. He produced a small red notebook from his shirt pocket and flipped it open. "We need to ask you some questions about Claudia McKinnon, the reporter from Details News over in Poughkeepsie."

"Okay, but I'm not really sure what I can tell you about all that. I don't really know what's going on."

"What do you mean you don't know? She's *missing*."

Nan frowned and shrugged. "I wasn't aware of that."

Sanders' smile was still as she remembered. Crafty. His lips, thin but reddish and oddly sexual, slid up on one side of his face while remaining still on the other. "No one told you she was missing?"

"Not in so many words, no. She never showed up here for the interview and I heard she didn't pick her daughter up from school, but beyond that, no one's really kept me in the loop."

Sanders' smile drooped, and his face hardened. "You had an interview scheduled with her yesterday, didn't you?"

"Sure."

"What time?"

"I don't remember exactly, but I think it was around one-thirty. You'd have to check with my agent to be sure. That's Tim Rossiter. He'll know."

"And she never showed up."

"Like I said, no, she never showed up. I called Tim to let

him know. Not sure what time, you'll have to ask him that, too."

Lambert's hands were laced over his belly, and he chewed on his toothpick contentedly, watching a sailboat go by.

"What happened then?"

"I'm not sure why you're asking me this stuff. All the information I have is secondhand from Tim. You'd be better off getting it straight from the source."

"Please just answer the question."

"Basically, he said that he called the station, and they said that they hadn't heard from her and to sit tight while they checked it out."

"And they didn't seem worried at all," Lambert mused. "Doesn't seem like her to blow off work like that. 'Course, all I know of her is what I seen on TV. Pretty little thing."

He had perfected this act over the years; not, she suspected, because he was especially clever, but because it made his job easier. Lambert was lazy with a capital L. To the casual observer, he would seem like a dim bulb (and there *was* a little bit of that mixed in, sure), incapable of following what was going on... the big belly with the shirt that didn't quite cover it, the toothpick, the cookie crumbs... all of this made it seem as if he was incapable of even directing traffic. Most people, wanting to believe they were smarter than him, let their guard down.

Nan wasn't most people. She was used to picking up on nuance when people spoke and had been able to see through his ruse quite handily the first time she'd met him.

"Did your agent, Rossiter, mention anything else that Miss McKinnon's station manager might have said? That would be..." Sanders consulted his notebook. "Earl Burroughs."

Nan narrowed her eyes and glared at him. "Why does it feel like you already know the answers to these questions, and you're just trying to see if you can catch me in a lie?"

"Now, Nan, no one's accusing you of nothing," Lambert said.

"That isn't what I asked," she replied, looking not at Lambert but at Sanders.

The crafty smile was back. "Just a few more questions."

"Jesus, fine. Yes, Earl told Tim something else, which he told me, but I was told not to spread it around. I'm not sure Tim was even supposed to tell *me* about it."

Sanders was twirling his pen, telling her to go on.

"He said Claudia has been battling a substance abuse problem. That this wasn't the first job she'd missed. Earl thought she might be off on a bender somewhere, and he was worried about getting the police involved and ruining the station's reputation. And that's *really* all the information I have about her. If you want more, go talk to her ex-husband."

"We did," Sanders said. "He told us he'd talked her into going into rehab and that she'd already attended a handful of NA meetings. Seems like she was trying to get her act together. Doesn't sound... *believable* to me that she would have gone off on a bender."

Nan thought of the baggie full of white powder in the cupboard by the fridge. "Anyone can relapse," she said. "Especially right after deciding to get clean. But it doesn't matter if you've been clean for a day, a week, a year, or ten years."

"Have *you* relapsed, Mrs. Wickwyre?" There was pure hatred in his eyes, and for a second, Nan felt the old anger flare up in her. If Lambert hadn't been there as a witness, she would have driven a spike through Sanders' priggish mouth and pinned him to the floor like the cockroach he was. A cold, dull spike.

Lambert sat up, his face flamed red (anger or guilt? Nan wondered), upsetting his second cookie and the crumbs he'd already collected all down his front. "Sanders, back off this, it's not why we're here."

How much Sanders knew or had guessed about her little arrangement with the sheriff was something worth considering.

Lambert never would have spilled the beans about that—he had just as much to lose as she did—but Sanders was the hypervigilant type. He knew *something,* or thought he did.

Nan leaned forward, her face carefully blank. "I'm not ashamed of who I used to be. And for your information, no, I haven't relapsed. Come close to it a few times, but so far... no. You sit there all holier than thou. I hope to God you never have to find out what addiction is really like."

"Nan, you don't hafta—"

Nan steamrolled over Lambert, and he fell silent, watching. "It's not that I just *want* a drink, okay? It's like some primal *need* for one, a pulse that keeps beating in your brain like a drum until that's all you can hear and feel. It becomes life and death, and it's all you can think about. So if Claudia McKinnon fell off the wagon so soon after climbing up into it, no one who's been through it could blame her one bit." Was she laying it on a little thick? Sure. But that's what writers do. She thought Sanders might look chastened, but if anything, he looked more smug.

"So your story then is that you didn't see her at all, correct?"

"Oh, for the love of God, yes, that is my *statement,* Sanders. She was supposed to come, she didn't come, the end."

Sanders spoke softly, then. "We have a witness who places Claudia McKinnon's car at the intersection of Little Church and Black Pond Roads, about a half-mile from your house, at five minutes of one. Earl Burroughs at Details News confirms the appointment was at one PM, and she checked in last from Newburgh just after leaving home, at about quarter after twelve. Times line up."

The car, Nan thought. *That idiotic little roadster of hers stands out. Of course, someone would have noticed it. How could I have not thought about that?* The answer to that was easy. It was because, over the years of getting away with murder, she'd become complacent. Claudia had gotten under her skin, and she'd let her anger get the better of her and overwhelm her common sense, and as a result, she'd done something stupid.

Sanders stared at her like a wolf would a lamb, and Lambert watched curiously. She had to say something.

"Okay. So?"

Sanders' lip curled into a snarl. "What do you mean, *so?* We have someone who saw her on this road five minutes before she was supposed to be here. We've traced her cell phone signal to the tower in Hyde Park before it went dark, and you're sitting there with a straight face telling me she didn't show up?"

"That's what I'm telling you, yes."

"Don't you think that's all just a little coincidental?"

"It means nothing at all," Nan said. "Unless you have a witness who places her at my house or puts the two of us together, you've got nothing."

When Sanders spoke again, his voice rose in anger, which helped to steady Nan's nerves more than anything else. "You're telling me she never came here, never knocked on your door, called, texted, anything?"

"Yes, Sanders, that's what I'm saying."

His face was so red she fancied she could feel the heat baking out of his skin. "How do you account for all of this, then?"

Lambert sat up straighter. "Now Sanders—"

"I don't have to account for it," Nan said. "It's up to you to find her. But fine, let me do your job for you. Maybe she got an emergency call and had to turn around. Have you thought of that?"

"Her phone records don't—"

"Okay, maybe not a phone call then. It wouldn't account for her current whereabouts. So then, what about her finances? I *know* you haven't had time to check into those yet. I've interviewed cops for books a bunch of times, I know the process and the legal hoops you need to jump through, and there's just no way you could know anything less than twenty-four hours after she went missing. If she really is a cokehead, she might owe some dealer a lot of money. Someone who wouldn't let the debt slide." She looked at Lambert as she said this. He turned away and watched the same sailboat still cutting its way across the water.

"Her husband indicated—"

"*Ex*-husband, have to make sure we keep the facts straight in a case like this, don't we Sanders? Now, have you considered that maybe she was abducted by some sort of crazed fan? I've had a handful of those over the years, and let me tell you, they aren't the easiest bunch to dissuade. I imagine it would be easy enough to figure out her schedule and trail her to this remote location, don't you think so? Probably be worth talking to Earl and seeing if she's had any complaints against stalkers recently. I'm willing to bet there's at least one of them. After all, as Sheriff Lambert said, she is a *pretty* little thing."

Sanders watched her sharply, and oh boy, he wanted to hit her.

"Actually, I'd be interested to know who this eyewitness is, too. Because I'd bet a literal million bucks that it's Muriel Duckworth." The look on Sanders' face told her she got it on the first guess. "Sheriff Lambert here can fill you in on her background of harassment and mental problems. Maybe you should go to the end of my driveway where I'm sure she's sitting, and ask her if she might have any reason to try to smear my name."

Sanders leaned forward, his notebook gone, back into his breast pocket, Nan assumed, though she hadn't seen it disappear. "I see you've got security cameras out at the road and by your front door," he said.

Shit. Shit, shit, shit.

She did her best to try to keep her voice even. "I do. I *had* to get them because of Muriel."

"And I don't suppose you'd want to share the footage from yesterday with us, do you?"

"I wouldn't mind at all. Come back with a warrant, and it's all yours. I still have a right to privacy." She made a mental note to get rid of it once they left. With the paltry amount they had on her, no judge in the state would grant them a warrant, but better safe than sorry. "And now I've answered all of your questions and suffered your badgering long enough. I've got work to do so I'd like you to please leave. If you've got any more questions, you can direct them to my attorney."

"Don't suppose I could use your facilities?" Lambert asked. Nan glared at him. "Yeah, didn't think so."

She accompanied them out onto the veranda. Sanders immediately went down the steps to the only cruiser the sheriff's department owned (which had seen better days), leaning against it like a sulky child.

Lambert hung back for a minute. "Sorry about him. He's running for my job next election, and… you know how kids are these days."

She rounded on him. "Why the fuck did you let him harass me like that, then? That fun for you?"

"How bad would it look if I started interferin' and protecting you? Besides, you took care of yourself awright."

Sanders was looking down the laneway toward the carriage house, which thankfully couldn't be seen from here. It was as if he knew something was hidden in the trees and thick scrub. She would need to get rid of Claudia's car soon but wouldn't rush. People who rushed weren't careful. People who rushed wanted to get caught. "Chester, what is it you want to say to me? I've had my fill of both of you for today."

"Just hold your horses. This affects the two of us now. Me 'n you." He pitched his voice lower but kept the smile on his face as if they were just shooting the shit about the weather and how the local hockey team was shaping up. "Sanders is starting to ask questions 'bout us. He's digging into shit that's been dead and buried for years."

"Why didn't you call me and tell me this before?"

He shrugged. "I'm telling ya now."

"Well, what questions? And who's he talking to?"

"I dunno for sure what questions, but he's talking to anyone he thinks might have information. Muriel Duckworth, for one. He don't think she's just a nut. And I heard from my friend Jim Clark down to the Hudson Auto Pick-A-Part that he was asking questions of Linnie Kitteridge over at the library and some of the old boys who breakfast together at the Classic Eats Diner on Route 9."

"Why them?"

"I dunno know why. That's what's got me worried."

Nan thought. As far as she knew, there wasn't anything these people could tell that could cause a problem. But Lambert was right. The simple fact that Sanders was nosing around meant trouble. "You've got to nip this in the bud then."

"How exactly am I supposed to do that? Can't fire 'im, can't shoot 'im. What's that leave?"

"I don't know, bury him in work or send him to training seminars out of state. Put him on some unsolvable cold case. How the hell should I know? Just *fix* it. That's your job."

"Maybe it is, maybe it ain't," Lambert said, and his face took on what, for him, passed as a clever look.

"There's no maybe about it. You made your choice. You took the money. It's part of the goddamn deal."

Sanders looked over at them in what appeared to be an idle way, but Nan knew it was anything but. He'd sensed a shift in the mood and had homed in on it. She calmed herself down and smiled, and she even touched the sheriff's arm in a friendly way. Sanders looked away, but he was still paying attention.

Lambert didn't seem to notice and instead plowed onward, oblivious. "Yeah, I took your money, but maybe this time I'm gonna need a little more compensation to get out my janitor's mop 'n bucket.

"Are you fucking serious?"

"Way I see it, you got a lot more to lose than I do." Lambert put on his campaigning smile and stared up into the blameless blue sky. "No one's gonna give a fart in a high wind if it comes to light I took money from the famous writer lady to keep my mouth shut. I'm at the end of my career, and the statute of limitations on most of the shit I done is up anyway. Vehicular manslaughter on the other hand... now that's maybe five years or so before the state just don't care no more, but rich as you are, and drunk as you *were*... prosecutor might just file capital charges against you. No statute on capital crimes."

"You piece of shit."

"Now I got some money saved up from before... maybe what you gave me back then didn't *all* go to paying off my debts. With a little more from you to add to my nest egg, I could just skedaddle on out of here, never to be heard from again. Down south to Florida, maybe, lay on the beach, drinking and workin on m'tan. Or even the Caribbean like... like where Ducky went. Right?"

It wasn't easy to surprise Nan, but Lambert just had. Sanders had always believed she'd played some part in Ducky's disappearance, but Lambert hadn't ever hinted one way or another what he thought about that subject. "I don't know what you're implying with that comment, but—"

A sound interrupted her. She cocked her head to the side and listened. A cell phone playing some stupid little ditty. The sound was coming from inside. It wasn't her phone; hers was in her pocket on silent, and even if it hadn't been, it didn't play an insipid tune. It just dinged twice. Which meant it could only be Claudia's.

Her interior temperature plummeted. *I turned it off.*

Maybe she had, and maybe she hadn't. It was hard to remember. Everything that had happened yesterday was a blur. Last night, when she'd gone to bed, she remembered sliding it into her bedside table drawer, *that* much she was certain of. But beyond that...

Sheriff Lambert didn't seem concerned by this disconnect in the slightest. Of course she was at a loss for words. He'd gotten her good! "We don't wanna take up any more of your day than we already did," he said. "If we need anything else… we'll be in touch." He looked at her pointedly. *I'll be in touch*, his eyes said.

He shuffled down the stone steps, letting his belly lead the way, and then he and Sanders got into the car and drove off. Nan watched after them, long after the sound of the engine had faded and the smell of leaking gas and burning oil was out of the air.

When she went inside to check Claudia's phone (it was indeed off, probably just hearing things) the house's atmosphere seemed to have changed, but just *how* Nan couldn't have said. It felt a little colder, maybe, and there was a slight smell that might have been Claudia or the chicken carcass from last night's dinner down in the garbage can. She went down to the root cellar and stood outside the door but couldn't detect any stench coming from behind it. Likewise, the kitchen trash. The chicken carcass still smelled of rosemary and lemon juice.

It's probably nothing, she told herself, just the shock of Sanders' accusations and Lambert's blackmail, both of which she would need to deal with soon. *Add it to the pile*, she thought.

It wasn't until much later that night, when she was in bed and terrified, that she would figure out what had unnerved her so upon reentering the house.

She hadn't been alone.

-2-

Christmas morning. The sun shone brightly off the thick crust of snow, and the sky was a brilliant, painful blue. Nan was down in the kitchen pouring coffee into two glittery mugs that said *Ho Ho Ho* in alternating red and green letters and hot chocolate into a smaller pink mug with a cartoon pig on it. It was the mug Lizzie used for damn near everything.

After flavoring the grown-up drinks with coffee liqueur, there was only a quarter of a bottle left, so Nan chugged it, wiped her chin and mouth, and tossed the empty into the recycling bin amongst the others.

Nick and Lizzie were waiting in the living room (formerly the billiard room), and she carried their drinks up on a battered wooden tray.

Lizzie sat on the floor beneath the monstrous pine (a fourteen-footer they'd trekked into the woods as a family to find and cut down), goggling at the mountain of presents beneath it. Nick sat on the sofa across the room, watching her. Sunlight angled through the windows, the Hudson winked and glittered, but there was something wrong with the light. Though she could clearly see the sun, the day seemed dark, as if she was looking at it through some strange tinted glass. Outside of this room and its cozy tableau the world felt gray and grainy, like an old black-and-white movie.

Because this already happened.

Nan shook her head as if hearing some late-season mosquito that had somehow survived the cold. "I've got Christmas morning drinks!" she announced in a singsong voice.

Lizzie, awake since about 4:30AM, had been just about bouncing off the walls all morning, begging to open her presents, but that wasn't their tradition. Tradition said no gifts until after coffee and cocoa, and most certainly not before 6:00AM.

Nick had started a cheery fire in the room's larger, more ornate fireplace, the one Nan and Lizzie had wrapped in fragrant evergreen garland and then hung their stockings from. There were four stockings total (one for Peanut too, Lizzie had insisted on that), which were all dangling low and full to bursting.

Nick sipped his coffee, arched an eyebrow, and set his cup

back on the tray. His eyebrow jittered for a moment at its apex like a caterpillar being electrocuted, and he slid down to the floor between the sofa and the coffee table.

That was weird.

Nan looked at him again, but everything appeared normal.

Lizzie took her cocoa and chugged it, her long brunette hair spilling down over her shoulders.

Was she brunette? She never had hair for very long.

Nan shook her head again. Damn mosquito. Her right eyelid quivered.

"Mommy, mine tastes funny," Lizzie said, frowning.

"I put some peppermint in there for you. To make it more Christmassy. I guess I should have asked you if you liked it first."

Nick's eyes clouded over, and his face darkled. Outside, a cloud scudded across the sky, briefly darkening the window. Then it was gone.

"No, I like it okay, I'll drink it."

The three of them sipped exaggeratedly in unison. It was usually a jolly sound, but now it sounded frightening as if something was shambling across the floor toward her, dragging some heavy, malformed part of its body.

A darkness, probably a shadow from another cloud, seemed to lurk near where Lizzie was sitting on the floor criss-cross-applesauce. She made a wet choking sound in her throat and asked, "Mommy, can I open my presents *now*?"

Nan shook her head again, and her eyelid twitched. "Finish your cocoa, then you can."

"You okay?" Nick asked, sliding over next to her and caressing her bare ankle beneath her robe.

"God, I resent you," she said, and Nick kissed her leg.

"I love you too, honey."

Lizzie continued sucking down her drink. It sounded like someone trying to pull air into punctured lungs that were filling with blood.

Another cloud across the sky. The Christmas tree lights flickered.

"I finished it. Now can I open?" Lizzie said, vomit dripping from her mouth in thick, foamy curds landing *plop* on the reddish wood floor.

"You may open one," Nan said and drank down her spiked coffee (which was really more spike than coffee). Soon, she would switch to something harder than coffee liqueur, but it was still a little too early. Maybe screwdrivers with breakfast. Or Bloody Marys. Her mouth watered.

Lizzie selected a large, ostentatiously colored box and dragged it across the floor to her chest. It left behind a trail of blood. "This one?" she asked.

"Okay, that one's safe," Nan said, but it didn't feel safe. Not safe at all. "I hate you, Lizzie. You ruined my life."

"I love you too, Mommy."

Lizzie grabbed the big red and purple bow and pulled it, turning the gift into something that wasn't a gift at all and the bow into a long black snake. Lizzie dropped it without noticing, and it darted beneath the tree, its arrow-shaped head a whispering corruption against the floor. The gift had become a large wooden chest, ancient and solid with rusting hinges, like something pulled up from the bottom of the riverbed. On the lid, a cruel yet familiar visage had been carved. Beneath this, scratched into the primordial wood, was a word written in a language that didn't exist, or if it did, did so on some plane no human had ever laid eyes on while still alive. Nan could read it all the same. It said **CANCER**. Below that, in smaller letters, was the word **CONTAMINATION**. Black sludge oozed from the corners of the box and mixed with the puddle of Lizzie's vomit on the floor.

Nick continued to run his hand up Nan's leg, oblivious to this, higher and higher. Her skin flushed there even though his fingers didn't feel soft and warm as they had in life, but like the twigs of a tree out in the winter cold.

Lizzie was watching them. "That's how I was made," she said, and smiled. When she did, the lower half of her face, from her nose on down, shredded and sloughed off as if it had been dragged across the freezing cold macadam of Little Church Road. Her teeth peeked through the torn remains, extending halfway up her skull like some vile creature imagined in the deepest depths of a nightmare. They grew larger and more misshapen as they marched up the side of her head toward her ear, which was a melted lump of candle wax.

"Yes, sweetie, it is," Nick told her, his twiggish hand exploring higher and higher still, pushing hard into Nan's flesh. It was an unpleasant feeling, like being prodded with a fork kept in the freezer, yet she responded with a moan and parted her legs slightly.

Nick looked up at her. His eyes were angry and accusatory and filling with blood. The left one became unfocused as if whatever normally kept it tethered in his head had snapped, causing it to float freely in its socket, and his mouth was a ragged flap of blackened skin. A fat termite skittered from beneath that skin, which hung like a torn curtain, and moved down his neck, disappearing beneath his shirt collar.

"No," Nan said and tried to bat his hand away. "Stop it. That part of our marriage is dead." In front of her was a half-empty bottle of scotch on the table with lipstick prints around the mouth. The table wasn't the coffee table anymore; it was the white and red enamel one from the kitchen.

"I said *yes*," Nick growled. His bony fingers turned into claws and bore down into her flesh, making her cry out in pain.

"No!" she said again, and the bottle of scotch was joined by another and another, all empty but for the last one, which was tipped over on its side and dripping death (*DECAY AND ROT!*) from the hole in its neck.

"Mommy, look!" Lizzie cried excitedly through her rapidly charring skin, which sizzled like a burnt marshmallow, while the Christmas lights twinkled merrily off the pale white bone of her skull. She held out both of her hands triumphantly. In the right one, she held a chemotherapy IV bag that was filled with curdled yellow pus, and in the left, her lower jaw. Bits of flesh fell to the floor and turned to maggots (*or termites? Hard to tell*) that wormed their way deep into the house through the cracks between the floorboards, down, down, down deep into the darkness.

Nan felt a wriggling sensation from beneath her robe and peered down at Nick. His face slid off to the side, then snapped back into place as if it had never moved. It all happened in the blink of an eye, but Nan had seen beneath his mask. It hid something foul and stinking.

She tried to stumble to her feet to get away from this imposter who clawed at her with its skeletal hands, holding her firmly in place. "No!" she screamed again in a voice starting to warp into someone else's.

"Yes, Mommy," Lizzie told her. "It's Christmas. This is what happens at Christmas." She selected a small, exquisitely wrapped box in gold foil paper and opened it. Bloody gravel spilled out onto the polished wood floor. "It's just what I wanted!" Lizzie cried, clapping and jumping, her voice now just as charred as her lips.

"Please. Please stop. I don't want to do this anymore," Nan said as fat tears rolled down her cheeks. "I need this to stop. This isn't how it happened."

This is how it happened.

"This is how it happened," Nick said. Three of his front teeth fell out and clattered into his coffee mug. He picked it up and drank it down, spitting his teeth back into the bottom when he was done.

Ho.

Ho.

Ho.

Lizzie picked up another box, a blue one with a lavender

ribbon tied around it. Nan remembered lavender was for cancer awareness.

You hated that color. Hated the ribbons and the chemo and the late-night vomiting and the fighting and the way people's eyes filled with pity around you. You hated her, resented her for turning your life into something it shouldn't have been. It could have been perfect and simple and beautiful.

"It's not true." Her voice was flat and emotionless.

"It is, Mommy. Me and Daddy knew all about it. He used to tell me about it when he tucked me in at night." She opened the blue package with the lavender ribbon and took a box of E-Rat-Icator from it. "It's just what I always wanted!" she said again and tossed it indifferently over her shoulder, grinning her ghoul's grin through the wet and smoldering remains of her face. The box burst in slow motion, scattering poison like snow over the remaining pile of gifts and the tree's bottom limbs. And still, Lizzie grabbed another package, coating her hands in rat poison, and tore into the paper. A blackened leg thudded out onto the floor like an overlarge charcoal briquette.

"Stop it, make her stop it," Nan said, turning to Nick, but he wasn't on the floor anymore. She peered down between her legs and saw his bloated purple feet with a thick growth of moss covering them. Dead feet. He had slid underneath her without her knowing, and she was sitting on his lap, which sagged beneath her like punkwood. Worst of all, she could somehow still feel his touch beneath her robe.

She tried to scream, but his cold hand with its spindly fingers clapped suddenly over her mouth, mashing her lips back into her teeth until she tasted blood.

"We're waiting," he whispered in her ear, but his voice was runny as if he were speaking through an unimaginably foul slurry of putrefying organs and maggots that had backed up his esophagus as his body liquified underground.

Lizzie whipped presents back over her head, not bothering

to open them and not looking back as they burst on the floor like infected boils spilling their nasty treasures: a broken taillight, a dented silver flask, a deflated eye, a tree branch, the length of which was slicked with dark, clotted blood, clattering teeth...

Nan squeezed her eyes shut as pain exploded over her left eye, accompanied by a dazzling flash of white light, and Nick's bony fingers bore down so hard it felt like they would punch through her skin.

The Christmas tree burst into flames. Decorations fell and shattered like drops of silvery rain, and the colored string of lights popped one by one down the line like popcorn.

"We're waiting for you down in the dark," Nick said, but it was Lizzie's voice that came from his mouth. When he spoke again, he sounded like Jeremiah Holt, full of cruel, childish mirth. "It's an awful, *stinking* place." Then his eyes were gone, replaced with gaping black sockets beneath his eyebrows, which writhed wetly like grubs.

The pressure beneath her robe intensified, becoming a pain that was simultaneously sharp, exquisite, and maddening... and then it was gone. Something large and wet fell from between her legs and landed on the floor with a smack. It made a mewling sound like a terrified newborn calf, and Nan could smell blood and shit and smoke.

Nick started shaking her back and forth, snapping her head hard first one way, then the other, and she opened her mouth to wail, but when she did, a river of scotch poured out onto the floor and drowned the squalling lump. The floor was no longer a floor but the slick, glistening macadam of the road, and she could smell gasoline and freshly sheared metal and tarry pine sap and see the flashing of red and blue lights as blackened ash drifted down from the (*sky*) ceiling and the world shook itself apart, color bleeding in through the grainy black and white even as the light dimmed more and everything became blacker and blacker and this was the dark place Nick had warned her of and she wanted to scream until she broke free of it, but the darkness just grew until it swallowed both her and her screams down its rancid gullet.

-3-

2:00AM. Nan sat bolt upright in bed, gasping for breath, her heart hammering painfully.

I'm having a heart attack.

All the years of drinking and eating fried food had finally come home to roost, just as she had known they always would. She tried to take a deep breath to help unclench the fist in her chest, but that only seemed to make her heart speed up. Then, as if that weren't enough, her skin started to prickle, and her hair stood on end. Waking from her dream, she somehow ended up in the middle of an ongoing situation that was, for the moment, incomprehensible, as if the dream was spilling out into reality. Listening to some instinctual voice that spoke without words, she craned her head to the left, absolutely certain that someone had just been leaning down over her and was now retreating silently. As they retreated, so did the prickling sensation, but the fear remained like the foam left behind by a receding wave. The scream which had been building throughout her nightmare finally exited her mouth but as a dry, frightened squeak. Peanut was beside her in the bed, staring blindly and growling low in his throat. The growl turned into a whimper.

Something glowed pale and blue beneath the bedroom door, accompanied by a sound that, for a split second, was so out of place that Nan had trouble recognizing it for what it was. A cellphone vibrating against wood.

Where's my phone?

She attempted to turn on the bedside lamp but ended up running her hand into the open drawer of her nightstand, knocking it from its hole and spilling its contents onto the floor.

I didn't leave that open.

Her fingers found the lamp and switched it on, but she didn't feel any better even with the bright circle of light shining around her. Her phone, which had been plugged in to charge on the dresser, was missing, and Claudia's phone, which had been in the drawer, was gone too. She switched on a few other lamps, throwing light into the murky corners of the room, cursing herself for not having Ducky put in a switched overhead light that would have dispelled the shadows with a single flick.

The room was empty.

That faint bluish light shone from beneath the bedroom door again, and with it came the *brrrrrrr* of a vibrating cellphone.

Nan's feet made hollow thuds as she vaulted across to the door and pulled it open. Outside of her room, it was dark and quiet. At the far end of the hall, moonlight filtered in through the window over the top of the stairs but didn't seem to brighten things any. She bent, picked up the phone (which was hers and not Claudia's, she could tell by the feel of the case), and started tapping the screen... but the phone was off.

"What?" she muttered, straightening. As she stood, she caught movement from the corner of her eye in front of the window, a sense of shifting darkness that was also straightening up to its full height. Her head moved in that direction, and her eyes watered even as her mind flickered briefly to the memory of the impossibly tall figure she had seen outside the library while cleaning up Claudia's blood. That figure had disappeared when her perspective changed; this vague, solid shape by the window did not.

Nan swallowed hard, coughed, then dragged in a shaky breath as her hands went to work, trying to turn her phone on. The figure appeared to be just watching her, yet there was something menacing about the way it stood, hunched just slightly at the shoulders to avoid knocking its head against the ceiling. Or maybe it was leaning forward greedily. It raised its hands to the ceiling and braced itself there. From where its face would be, Nan could sense it staring at her with eyes that never blinked, eyes that were so big they took up most of its face, just like the cartoon pig on Lizzie's favorite mug.

Finally, her phone turned on and threw a weak light into her face. She had the eerie sensation that whatever was at the far end of the hall watching was coming forward now that it could see her properly. It moved silently by gripping the exposed beams of the ceiling with hands that had somehow become adept at clutching, suspending it over the floor so it didn't make the wood creak or a groan, its feet dangling just low enough to produce sporadic scratching sounds.

And there... was that glint a reflection of her cellphone's light in its big wet eyes, or was it being bounced back off the window glass?

It felt as if the hall was filling with noxious gas, and Nan coughed again. When she tried to take a sip of air to reinflate her aching lungs, it tasted of peppermint liquor, and memories of her cruelty flooded in with it.

Shivering so badly her arms looked like a puppeteer with palsy was operating them, Nan threw herself backward into her room and raked the heavy wooden door closed. Barely a second later, something ran into it, producing a soft clicking thud, as if whatever had been rushing silently toward her had hit the wood and had used its long-nailed hands to slow its impact. The sound set terror loose in her body, and she staggered backward to her bed and collapsed onto it, legs numb even though they wouldn't stop shaking. The sound came again once, then a few seconds after that once more, like something was searching blindly for the doorknob.

It can't get in, her mind gibbered, trying to convince herself that she remembered turning the ancient brass lock. She tried to recall the distinct *clack* sound it made—and found she couldn't.

It doesn't matter if it's locked or not, though. In a second, that thing out there will start shrieking and beating at the door, trying to break in… but not down low where a normal person would. No, the sound will come from the tippy top of the door, way up high by the ceiling.

But it didn't. Silence filled the world. Time passed. Nothing happened.

It wasn't often Nan wished for another person in the house, but she wished for one now. Anyone at all. Her first thought was to call the sheriff's department and tell them there was an intruder but dismissed that idea before it was fully formed. Even if Lambert showed up instead of Sanders, he would insist on searching the house, and she couldn't risk having him stumble across the crypt accidentally (which, let's face it, is the only way he *could* find it). Claudia's body probably wasn't gone yet.

It was just fear making her jumpy and foolish. In the long years since Nick and Lizzie had died, Nan had relied only on herself for all matters not work-related. Involving other people only muddled things. She would take care of this in the same way.

When she was certain the thing in the hallway was gone, she looked beneath the bed, under the nightstand, and finally the under dresser for Claudia's phone, convinced she'd knocked it out of the drawer when she'd performed her impersonation of a mental patient. It wasn't anywhere. Trying to think of what might have happened to it was only getting her worked up again, so she decided to put that off until the sun was up high over the yardarm.

But that would be a long time coming. For the rest of the night, Nan stayed awake with all the bedroom lights burning, checking the camera feeds outside the house (nothing there, thank God), trying to read but not being able to concentrate, and finally switching on the TV to some bright and colorfully insipid show. None of it helped. Long after the sun had risen, splashing its golden brilliance across the surface of the Hudson, she finally closed her eyes and managed to grab a quick fifteen-minute nap. At 10:30 that morning, when the doorbell rang, she was showered and dressed and in the living room, drinking coffee with lots of sugar mixed in (even though it tasted saccharine and cloying), hoping it would help her stay awake. But all it did was make her feel sick to her stomach.

-4-

"Who's this little man standing on my doorstep?"

Trevor Potter, who looked like a tiny clone of his mother with the same chestnut hair and cool blue eyes, ran in and threw his arms around Nan's waist, knocking her back a step.

"Aunt Nanny!" he cried. He'd called her that the very first time they'd met about four years ago, and it had just stuck, as some things do. Lauren, who hadn't been working for Nan very long yet and hadn't known her well, had been mortified. "I don't know where he got that from," she'd said as Nan tried to hold in her laughter. "Trevor, you call her Mrs. Wickwyre like I told you to."

(Nan had still gone by Mrs., even after no longer technically being one.) But she waved that idea away immediately. "I'll tell you what, buddy. You can call me whatever you want to, okay?" She hunkered down so they were the same height. "Just so long as it's not a bad word... like *Republican*." Trevor giggled shyly despite not understanding what the word meant or why his mother laughed at it.

But he was a little older and a little wiser now. And even though he was only eight, he was nearly as tall as Lauren.

"Hey, Little Punk, why don't you help me carry this cooler and let your Aunt Nanny take a breath, huh?" In addition to the dark blue cooler, Lauren was laden with reusable shopping bags filled with picnic stuff.

"Okay, Big Punk," Trevor said. The cooler looked ridiculously oversized in his little arms, but he hefted it without complaint.

"Not so fast, little man," Nan said. "What's in the cooler, hmm? Is it money? Drugs? Did you become a gun runner when I wasn't looking?"

Trevor giggled helplessly. "No, it's sodas and sandwiches and stuff. What's a gun runner?"

"Nothing you have to worry about until you're older. It won't even be a viable career path until you're sixteen. Very well then, I suppose I can clear you for entry." Nan stepped aside so they could come in, then closed the door, throwing the foyer into gloom despite the bright fall sun.

"I'm going to take this down to the kitchen!" he called back over his shoulder as he ran for the stairs, the weight of the cooler causing him to list a bit to starboard, which made the ice inside clunk and chatter. It was a sound that reminded Nan of whatever had been outside her bedroom door last night, and she suppressed a shiver.

"Careful on those stairs, bud!" she called after him. Peanut, nearly apoplectic with excitement, chased after him, yarking in that high-pitched way he had and dancing around in circles.

"I am!" he called back. Both she and Lauren waited for the inevitable crash, followed by tears, but there was none.

"He was so excited to come here today. Thanks for making the time. I know you're busy."

"Nah, not too busy. You guys are welcome anytime, you know that. I needed a break anyway." Nan took a brown paper bag and one of the reusable shopping bags filled with towels from Lauren's hand, which allowed her to rebalance herself.

"Careful with that brown bag," she said. "It's got a surprise for you from Trevor."

"Ooh, can I peek?"

"Cupcakes. He decorated them for you special."

For just a moment, jealousy blossomed big and bright

within Nan. Lauren had a kid whose worst health concern was recurring ear infections. He was normal, healthy, and able to do things like decorate cupcakes and run down the stairs holding coolers full of ice and food. He would live a full, long life.

"Aww, that's sweet," she said. "You've got a good kid there, lady."

"I lucked out, that's for sure."

The two of them chatted down to the kitchen, where Trevor was sitting at the red and white enamel-topped table, kicking his feet. "Can I use this one for our picnic?" he asked. Sitting in front of him was Lizzie's pig mug with the big eyes. Seeing this mug so close on the heels of her dream made Nan's heart quake.

"Let's find you a different one, okay, buddy?"

He shrugged. "Okay." Nan took the mug, unsure where Trevor had even found it (she would have sworn it had been packed away with the rest of the things that were too hard to look at), and placed it in the cupboard over the stove.

The day before, Ava had made potato salad, a thermos full of lemonade, and a tray of from-scratch brownies for the picnic. Nan packed the food into a wicker basket along with some forks and napkins. She selected a coffee mug with a turkey on it that Nick had used to rinse his paint brushes back when he'd harbored delusions of being an artist. "How about this one?" she asked Trevor. "A turkey for a turkey."

He took it, laughed at the bird on the front, and chanted "*Turkey for turkey, turkey for turkey!*" at the top of his voice.

"Yes, okay, turkey, why don't you move your tail feathers outside before you shout the house down?" Lauren said, and Trevor went through the kitchen door onto the patio, still chanting, the grand marshal of his own little parade.

"We'd better get out there with him before he disappears on us," Nan said, still laughing. But watching Trevor march around in a circle on the patio, she didn't feel much like laughing. The fist in her chest she'd felt last night was starting to clench again, though she couldn't have said why. They stepped out into the unseasonably warm and sunny October day, but all Nan could think of was her dream; Nick and Lizzie and the profane Christmas.

Even on this incredible morning, a quintessential Hudson Valley sort of day, it felt like a bad omen.

-5-

Lunch was over: plastic wrap and used bags were collected, apple cores had been tossed into the woods to grow trees (or not), soda bottles were stuck back in the cooler for easy transport back up the path through the woods and dirty plates and forks were stowed safely in the basket.

When they'd headed out, Nan hadn't thought she would be able to eat anything at all. Her headache had been becoming more insistent, and her mind was preoccupied working on the dream, trying to suss out what about it was making her feel strange.

But after walking in the fresh air for a bit and then breathing in the brown, earthy smell of the Hudson as they laid out their picnic blanket, she found her appetite had returned. Even the headache plaguing her since yesterday morning had finally loosened its claws. One turkey and Swiss sub and two helpings of potato salad later, she found she was still hungry and proceeded to eat a few brownies and a bag of chips. Now, stuffed near to capacity, both she and Lauren watched Trevor as he played with Peanut on the rocky shingle of shoreline, the cliff face of Holt House leering down at them from above.

"Just be careful with him. He's an old dog, okay, Little Punk?"

"Aww, Mom, I know that I'm not a baby."

"I know, I know, you're a grown man and will be shaving

soon. I can see your mustache coming in from here. Just humor your old mom, okay?"

"Yes, Big Punk," Trevor said back and jumped around in circles laughing while Peanut barked.

"So, was Muriel up there today when you got here?" Nan asked, sipping a cup of Ava's freshly squeezed lemonade. It was tart and good. A little vodka would have made it perfect.

"Oh yeah. She's sitting in her folding chair with her notebook out, scribbling away, looking just as crazy as ever. I stopped and offered her a sandwich, but she declined, and not nicely."

Nan laughed. "Probably thinks it's full of arsenic."

"Probably. How have things been going with her?"

"Steady as she goes. She was gone for a little while, but she's been coming around more and more often. Boy, I wish Lyle Cooper would take back his offer to let her camp out there."

"Don't count on that. I think he's becoming as crazy as she is."

"Wonderful."

"Did you hear he pushed that man down the steps at the Classic Eats?"

Nan turned, shocked. "No, why on Earth would he do that?"

"Guy cut in front of him in line is what I heard. Trevor, not too far away now!"

"Jesus. Must be something in the water here. Everyone seems to be going nuts. I mean, who the hell would actually buy into Muriel's insanity?"

"I know what you mean. But people are. Smart people, too. Really makes you wonder."

A few seconds passed. The only sounds were the steady lapping of the water on the shore and Trevor singing a song to himself down the beach. Some late-season boater burred past, hitting the waves head-on, probably on their way to the marina in Poughkeepsie. There was snow in the forecast for tonight, so this would likely be their last hurrah for the season. "So, how are things, *really*?" Lauren asked.

Nan peered at her from the corner of her eye. "What's on your mind there, Potter?"

"No, I—" Lauren shifted and squirmed in her chair. "Look, don't take this wrong, but have you been getting enough sleep? Or are you maybe smoking too much lately?"

"Do I really look that bad?"

"No, I didn't mean it *that* way. You just seem... I don't know. Not yourself. You seem tired... I don't know. Just ignore me, I'm babbling."

"Calm down, I'm only picking on you," Nan said.

"It's just, first Claudia is a no-show, then Muriel pops back up, and *then* the cops show up and start grilling you..." She shrugged. "Probably made you feel like back when Ducky disappeared, and everyone was in your business. I just worry about you."

"I know you do, Mother." Lauren smiled at that. "You heard about the cops coming out?"

"Everyone in *town* has heard about that. Sanders gossips worse than a high schooler. He spread it all over the diner last night when he went in for supper." She slapped her knee. "God, it just makes me so mad. He shouldn't be able to talk about this stuff, right? Isn't it an ongoing investigation?"

Nan shrugged. "Try to prove it, though. You know Lambert will back him up."

"Piece of shit. He wouldn't try that if you were a man."

Nan shrugged again. People like Sanders did what they did and usually cared very little about the person they were fucking over, as long as they were fucking over *someone*. The good thing about people like him, she mused, was that they thought they were smarter than everyone else. You could blindfold them and drop them into a dark room full of other blindfolded people, and they'd still believe it. Luckily for her, people who thought like that were usually easily outsmarted.

She shook out a cigarette and arched her eyebrow at Lauren, who said, "Fine, only if you give me a hit off that. Just don't let Trevor see. They just learned about the dangers of smoking in school, and he'll read you the riot act if he catches you."

Trevor was still a little way down the rocky beach, squatting down digging a mud hole with a flattened soda bottle. Nan decided to get some proper beach toys for him for next time. It would be nice to make this a regular thing. Help to keep her mind off of everything else, anyway.

Peanut had most of his head down in the hole, right in Trevor's way, but Trevor didn't seem put out by this at all. Instead, he was petting Peanut, whose backend was rocketing side-to-side so fast if you put him in the water, he'd shoot across the river straight to Esopus.

Nan lit her cigarette, took a long drag, and handed it over to Lauren. She hadn't shared a cigarette since high school when she used to bum them from her best friend Becky-Jo Walser, and it made her feel like a kid again. "Did Tim say anything about the interview? Were they able to reschedule?" Lauren asked, exhaling smoke and smiling. "Oh, that's nice."

"Yeah, they're sending the other guy out sometime this week. I forget his name."

"Rufus Whitemarsh. How could you forget a name like that? Sounds made up, doesn't it?"

Nan laughed and nodded. "I bet his real name is Osvaldo Pudpuller or Cornelius Peckerwood or something."

Lauren laughed so hard that she started to cough and handed the cigarette back to Nan. Trevor perked his head up momentarily at the sound, but apparently finding nothing of interest, went back to his hole.

-6-

The best thing about coming to see Aunt Nanny, besides playing in the big yard (Trevor's yard back home was small and weedy, unlike this magical forested wonderland), was her dog, Peanut. His mom was allergic to dogs and cats and had told him she would probably never sleep again if there was a snake in her house, so he wasn't allowed to have a pet of his own. But Aunt Nanny had Peanut, and she always shared him, even though his mom warned him to be careful when playing with him every time. He wasn't a baby anymore. He knew the little dog was old and fragile, but grown-ups were always trying to tell kids things they already knew, and always with an exclamation point at the end of it:

Look both ways before crossing the street! Don't forget to brush your teeth! Wash your hands before coming to the dinner table! Don't talk to strangers! The list was almost endless. You'd think they'd have better things to do! But he wasn't yet at an age where he'd started to push back against it. Grown-ups were just weird sometimes.

So when his mom told him not to go too far down the beach, he'd listened and agreed with the same stoic resignation as always. But the seeds of discontent had been planted just the same.

I'm not a baby anymore. I can take care of myself. She doesn't need to say stuff like that and embarrass me, especially in front of Aunt Nanny.

But he didn't like the way these thoughts made him feel. He loved his mom. She was only trying to look out for him and keep him safe, any old bozo could see that, and those thoughts made him feel mean. Dancing and singing to himself didn't make that feeling go away, and neither did playing with Peanut, so he started digging a hole. There were no toys at Aunt Nanny's (once he'd found a little pink wheelbarrow and an orange bucket with a blue handle, but his mom had told him to hurry up and put them back where he'd found them with no explanation as to why. Grown-ups never needed to explain why, especially to kids. It wasn't fair).

His friend from school, Luis, had shown him how to flatten a water bottle and turn it into a scoop when they were playing in the sandbox on the playground, so that's what Trevor did instead of complaining. It didn't work the best, but it sure was better than digging with your bare hands and getting them all cut up by the sharp, flat rocks buried here.

Peanut kept sticking his head in the way, but he was happy, and that made Trevor happy. "You be careful now, Peanut, don't you go too far. The monsters might gobble you up." He laughed, but the laughter felt mean, too, so he abandoned it in favor of focusing on the rocks. Last summer, right before school started again, his mom took him to the Catskills, and they hunted fossils in one of the quarries there. He'd found a trilobite and some coral, and those were pretty neat. They sat in pride of place on his dresser, next to his plastic T-rex and his two-dollar bill. Just ordinary treasures, but treasures nonetheless.

A little while ago, he heard his mom and Aunt Nanny laughing about something, but that didn't interest him much. Grown-ups laughed at weird things, and it rarely made any sense. Maybe they were laughing about the smoke he could smell when the wind shifted. It was a bad smell but he liked it okay when his mom smelled like it when she would come back in from taking the garbage out. And it smelled good when he hugged Aunt Nanny, too. Even so, that was something else that vexed him. Grown-ups always were doing bad things and then telling *you* not to do them. It was all just confusing.

Trevor kept digging, so captivated by the perplexing tenets of adulthood he was turning over and over in his mind trying to make sense of (the way tumbling rocks polish them into beautiful new rocks) that he didn't notice the sun had gone away and the wind had picked up.

Something had changed.

He might have gone on digging away all night, but a sound broke through his Zen-like focus and activated some dormant lizard part of his brain. Peanut was growling. Never in his life had Trevor heard him do that before. The little dog was baring his teeth, and his hair stood up rigidly along his back in a stripe. Trevor looked up and, standing over him, closer than probable and impossibly tall, was Aunt Nanny.

Her eyes scared him. For a split second, they had looked almost black, like they were empty, but when she shifted them to look at the water, they were normal again.

Trevor looked down the beach to where his mom had been sitting in her lawn chair, but she was gone. The whole beach was empty down there, and the sky was turning gray and rainy.

"Your mom had to go to the house," Aunt Nanny said, and the way she spoke sent shivers up Trevor's spine. It was like more than one person was speaking from her mouth at the same time, their voices almost in sync with one another but not quite. It didn't sound like her at all. "Come with me, and I'll take you to her."

Peanut whimpered and started to growl again, backing away toward the water. Although he knew there was no reason for this, for a moment before rationality reasserted itself, Trevor wanted to do the same. "Hey, boy, what's wrong? You know Aunt Nanny. Don't be mad." He looked down at the little shaking dog, and when he looked back up, Aunt Nanny was already almost at the trees, standing still like a statue and staring at him. Her eyes seemed bigger than they should have been, almost like she was afraid of something. Maybe whatever Peanut was afraid of, he thought.

"Hey, wait for me!" he called, suddenly certain that there was some sort of monster in the water. His hair was all standing straight up and down, and he was scared. "Don't leave me here!" Chancing a look behind him, Trevor saw something in the distance scrabbling up the stony shore toward him, solid and gray and low to the ground, moving fast.

No. No, it couldn't be. It wasn't possible.

Yet somehow, it was.

His first thought was that he had somehow fallen asleep on the shore while digging for fossils, but the first cold drops of rain spitting down from the sky told him this was no dream.

Most of the things at Aunt Nanny's house were awesome. There was the beach, of course, and the old garden with the tall walls around it that looked like a secret place from olden times... and there was the playhouse in the woods where Aunt Nanny's little girl used to play before she got sick and died (that's what his mom told him, and he'd cried when he found out).

But there were some things that Trevor flat-out didn't like at all. The one he hated the most was the statue from the downstairs patio. The one over the front door looked sort of like a bulldog and was a little cute, so that was okay. And there were a few other statues near the driveway and the garden that all looked like women sitting on columns holding flowers, and, even though they weren't wearing clothes, they weren't scary. There was even one out by the playhouse that looked sort of like a long dragon (or maybe it was supposed to be a snake), swimming through water, but it was just a hunk of concrete.

But the one on the downstairs patio off the kitchen was something else entirely. It made his skin crawl and a hot ball of puke form in his stomach. It was this one that was moving in his direction now with the eerie speed and mannerisms of a predator, pulling itself along the beach with its solid stone arms, which stuck up and out to the side as it skittered along like a spider.

-7-

The nightmare he'd had after his first time seeing the statue had been super scary, but he couldn't remember it when he woke up. Only that something had been chasing him through the woods.

He'd cried and wet himself and called for his mommy as loudly as he could, feeling hot and ashamed because he was being a baby. But fear eclipsed his shame easily.

"Mommy, there's an argyle in my closet! I saw it go in there when I woke up, and it said it was gonna eat me! Don't let it eat me! Mommy, please, please, please!"

She'd held him and rocked him and told him everything was going to be okay. "It's not called an argyle. It's a *gargoyle*, Little Punk."

"Aunt Nanny said it was an argyle."

"No, it's just a statue, that's all. It's a piece of stone, just marble, that someone carved into that shape." She kept rocking.

"It's scary."

"Why is that one scary, huh? The one in the driveway and the one by the garden aren't scary, are they?" Trevor shook his head. "Then why is the one on the downstairs patio?"

"It *looks* scary."

His mom had been puzzled by that. "It's almost the same as the other ones. It's a bust of a woman who used to live in the house. The woman who owned it waaaay back when it was first built."

"What's a bust?"

"Well, that means just the top half. You know how the statue by the garden is the whole body? Well, a bust is just like from here up." She held her hand flat near the top of her stomach.

"She looks like a monster," Trevor whispered. "A monster someone trapped in the stone."

"That's just your dream, getting the real world all mixed up." His mom laughed and hugged him hard, and the fear faded as rationality bled back into the world. The nightmare was only scary pictures in his head.

But the statue was real. When he was a little bit older and a little bit braver, he decided to deal with his fear of it once and for all. So, while the grown-ups were busy in Aunt Nanny's office, Trevor crept down into the kitchen, holding the railing in both hands the way his mom had taught him to, and snuck up to the glass in the door to look out.

The statue was there, looking back at him. Before it had been facing the other way, out toward the water, but now it wasn't. That alone made him want to pee, but told himself not to be a baby. Big boys didn't pee when they were afraid.

Carefully, he turned the knob and tottered out onto the stone patio and, as bravely as he could, approached the hideous thing.

"You ugly old thing, you." Standing this close to it, the stone eyes seemed to be watching him even though the head was thrown back and the mouth distended down toward the thing's chest in a moue of agony. It looked enraged. "You don't scare me anymore, you know that? You're just a big old nothing. You're a piece of..." He turned his head cautiously one way, then the other, making sure his mom wasn't within earshot before he whispered, "... shit." That made him feel emboldened. "My mom said I can call you anything I want to. So your new name is Poop Head." He felt a little silly talking to the statue, but not as much as he should have. Despite his brave words, there was still something scary about it; the way it watched and listened made him want to run away and hug his mom.

Old Poop Head watched him as he approached.

"You're a mean old thing, and I hate you. You wanna see how brave I am?" Before he could change his mind, he balled up his hand into a little fist and thrust it into the statue's open mouth. Trevor's mind screamed in a panic because it was so easy to imagine Poop Head's mouth clamping down on his wrist, turning his forearm into jelly before starting to sluuuuurp him forward like it was sucking down spaghetti.

But that didn't happen.

He pulled his hand back. "That's what I *thought*." Then he did something his mom had told him *never* to do, but he was running on pure adrenaline, and it seemed like a good idea. He stuck up his middle finger and, just for good measure, said "shit," again, a little louder this time. Just to show old Poop Head he was a force to be reckoned with.

Still, it was prudent not to push his luck. Feeling better now and braver, too, he started back toward the house. The statue wouldn't be making any more appearances in his dreams. He was certain of that.

Then he heard something. Something like a voice whispering to him from deep down inside the statue's stone chest. He stopped dead, his skin cold.

"Are you talking?" he asked. Logically, he knew this wasn't possible. After all, his mom had explained what the statue actually was, but he heard it all the same.

What if it's wasps?

At the beginning of the summer, his mom had taken a huge nest out of the shed in the backyard that he used as a playhouse. The wasps had probably found a way inside sometime last fall, and had built a giant paper nest right between his dump truck and a wicker basket of misfit toys and blocks. His mom had set off a smoke bomb to knock them out. "This makes it so they can't sting me," she explained to Trevor, who was standing a safe distance away inside the zipped-up fly tent, but he hadn't been so sure. Even in their stuporous daze, he could still hear their angry humming as their home filled up with poison.

Trevor didn't like (or trust) wasps any more than he did Poop Head... yet he found himself taking a step forward anyway. The whispering noise was a *little* like the sound of wasps, but not exactly. He took another step.

Now, he could hear words, but they were too soft and far away to make out. He stretched his neck forward, bringing it within striking range if Poop Head decided to try and take a chunk out of him, and strained to hear.

You're not a baby anymore, he told himself when his legs started to shake. *That means being brave even when you're scared. There's nothing to that mean old Poop Head except stone and moss.*

He took a step closer and then no more. Suddenly, and with a swiftness that made him almost stagger, sanity returned. Had he known the word, he would have thought he'd been hypnotized by the soft sibilant sounds coming from Poop Head's mouth, but because he didn't, it just felt like his bravery had worn off.

He'd been brave enough for one day. The mean old statue hadn't been able to scare him away because his mom was right. It was stone and nothing more. Wasps, on the other hand, were nothing to be messed with.

Exhausted physically and mentally, Trevor turned and fled back into the house, though he hadn't thought of it as fleeing. More like a triumphant adrenaline-fueled victory jog. The statue hadn't gotten him that day. Just like in his bedtime stories, the brave knight stood up to and then defeated the monster, and all was right with the world.

-8-

But that was then, this was now, and he was scared. Aunt Nanny was gone. She had just been standing beneath the trees when Trevor looked back over his shoulder, but where she had been was only darkness now. He ran with Peanut at his heels, managing to bark and growl almost at the same time, listening to the growing sounds of solid stone hands slapping onto the flat rocks of the beach. No birds cried out from the trees like they had been when they'd come down for their picnic. It was like the whole world was holding its breath to see what would happen.

Beneath the trees, the path wound its way up to the house; gravel with little plants growing up through it and, in some places, just mud where the rains had washed the gravel away. It seemed oddly dark under here, like night was coming already, but it couldn't be. They'd arrived at Aunt Nanny's house before it was even lunchtime, and they had only been here a few hours. Dark was still a long ways off... and yet...

Aunt Nanny was far ahead of him. All he could see of her was the flicker of white from her sweater as she walked through the trees. She no longer looked too tall, but the weird, silent way she moved was frightening. Sort of like the videos of monkeys he'd seen online when they would pull themselves from branch to branch through the trees. And there was a bad smell in the air that hadn't been there before like she'd had an accident and needed to change her underwear. But even worse than that.

Trevor looked back and saw Peanut hunkered right down to the ground, shaking like a tiny paint mixer and whimpering. "Come on, boy, hurry!" he shouted, but the dog wouldn't budge. The thudding of the statue was getting closer now, and despite his great terror, Trevor stopped. If he went back to scoop Peanut up, he would definitely lose Aunt Nanny and be left alone in the woods. And what would Poop Head do to him when the foul thing finally caught up with him?

Hot urine splashed down Trevor's leg, but he didn't even notice. All of his focus was on Peanut. He didn't want to leave the poor dog behind to that fate, but... he called once more in vain and then, hating himself for the decision, turned away and started back up the path. "I'll tell them you're here, and we'll come and get you, I promise!" he shouted over his shoulder. "Don't be scared!"

As soon as Trevor was out of sight, Peanut turned and ran back toward the beach as fast as his sightless eyes and stumpy legs could carry him, barking as if his life depended on it.

Trevor heard him leaving. At the same time, he felt hot tears squirt from his eyes and start to run down his face. Never before had he been this scared; not when his mom took him to that haunted house hayride last Halloween, and they had that skeleton with a pitchfork sitting up by the driver, and not when he and Luis thought they'd found human bones in the backyard, crawling with ants, but they had turned out to be from a deer.

Something was moving parallel with him through the forest's underbrush off to the left, thundering through the dead trees and new saplings and last year's leaves. Trevor looked and saw a flash of gray stone.

How did it get up here so fast?

A strangled sob wrenched from his mouth as he ran, his tears blurring the world in front of him, turning tree roots into treacherous, grasping things that tried to trip him and pull him down to the ground. Down where he would be easy to gobble up.

Rain started to drive down hard, turning the world into something seen through a shifting silver curtain that mixed with Trevor's tears. His hair fell into his eyes, blinding him for a moment, and his sneakers kept threatening to slip out from under him as he skidded and stumbled through the mud where the gravel had washed off the path.

And then, suddenly, the statue was up ahead of him, moving faster than was possible, its stone hands pounding against the soft forest floor.

WhumpwhumpwhumpWHUMPWHUMP.

It sounded like some insane deer trying to run on its hind legs. Trevor squeezed his eyes shut for a second and skidded to a stop. If he kept going like this, he would run smack-dab into the statue, which was most certainly up ahead waiting for him to do just that.

He whined low in his throat just like the dog. There, right *there*, was the back patio of the house and the kitchen door, standing open, inviting him to run for it. If he could just get inside and close the door, he was certain he'd be safe. He was also just as certain that he'd never make it.

You have to try, he thought. It was getting darker by the minute, and if he stalled too much longer, it would be pitch-black. He couldn't stand the thought of being out in the woods at night while the statue hunted him.

It wasn't very far at all, about the same distance as it was from his bedroom to the bathroom at the opposite end of the hallway. At night, when his mind invented (or maybe not, considering what was happening) all sorts of creepy crawlies hiding in the dark corners, he was able, by the light of one little nightlight, to run down, pee, and run back without getting eaten. If he could do that, he could do this.

As he was gearing himself up for the last little dash to safety, hoping Aunt Nanny had made it inside already, the statue appeared from the forest at the side of the path. One long, gray arm thudded down onto the dirt, its fingers turning into claws as it did, burrowing into the forest floor for purchase, and then it dragged itself forward. The other arm thudded down after it and repeated the process until Poop Head was blocking the path, lying right in the middle with its torso propped up by its hands, staring at Trevor with a gaped alligator's mouth.

"Go away!" Trevor screamed at it. The mind can only handle so much terror before it just breaks, and Trevor was past his limit. He was exhausted, his poor little brain overloaded, and about to blow a fuse.

The statue opened its mouth wide—wider than it would have been able to even if it had been a real person—and then it snapped shut with the flat clap of stone against stone. Trevor wanted to scream, but his chest felt like someone had wrapped it tightly in elastic bands. He managed to pull in three or four quick, whistling gasps of air, but that was all.

The statue's mouth fell open again as if on a hinge, then clapped shut with enough force to send tiny shards of stone flying like shrapnel; hard enough to flatten a bone with one shot. And when it opened up the next time, Trevor saw that the smooth, shiny lips had turned into a jagged horror, a monster mouth full of biting teeth. And when they came back together, they made a sound like knives sliding slowly against a sharpening stone. Small puffs of stone dust floated out and were lost in the rain.

I can't let it catch me, or it'll eat me with that awful mouth, and no one will ever find me because there's nothing inside that thing but stone.

The thought of disappearing into the statue and becoming part of it was almost enough to get him moving again, but something buzzed past his head before he could. Whatever it was sounded *huge*, and the riffle of air against the side of his face made him think that it had been some kind of bird. But when he turned to see (making sure to keep one eye on Poop Head), it wasn't a bird at all. It was a gigantic wasp crawling sluggishly on the trunk of a nearby tree. The wasps his mom had taken out of the shed were big, about the size of cashews, all black and yellow. This one was black with a little bit of white on its face and was the size of Trevor's hand. Its body was plump, and the stinger that stuck out of its rear was as big as the needle the doctor had used to give him his shots. It dripped poison.

Another one flew past, and then another. Trevor watched as two more climbed listlessly out of the statue's open mouth and took off, beating their wings as fast as a hummingbird's to move through the driving rain. And then, all at once, there were hundreds. They *boiled* out of the statue's stone throat like a dark surge of vomit, and they all came after Trevor, who stood soft and immobile on the path.

When the first one stung his arm, he thought someone had hit him with a hammer. He shrieked as his arm twitched bonelessly up and away from his body, and he slapped at the wasp involuntarily. The feeling of its beating wings and alien, struggling thorax beneath his hand was disgusting, almost worse than the sting itself.

Almost. His slap hadn't damaged the wasp at all, and it flew at him again, angry now, and stung him in the hand, making it instantly numb.

And still, they clawed their way up out of Poop Head's mouth, their hard, shiny bodies clicking and clacking against one another. It was the sound of skeletons dancing.

Another wasp landed on his face, and in blind terror, Trevor slapped at it with a hand he could no longer feel, but it stung him near his eye just before he hit it and broke open its bloated body, spilling its revolting guts down the side of his face. His eye felt like it was on fire, and his skin was stretched tight as everything on that side of his head started to swell. He screamed and cried, and the tears burned.

The statue seemed to be grinning at him as a cloud of wasps circled its head, swirling like a tornado, buzzing so loudly he couldn't hear himself think. It was an awful, foreign sound, made so by its inability to be comprehended, like the electronic drone cicadas made that always reminded him of ray guns from his sci-fi cartoons. It was a sound that didn't belong to reality.

The vision in his right eye faded until all he could see was a world made of vague gray outlines and shadows. A wasp landed on his belly and stung him through his t-shirt, and he doubled over as if from a cramp, screaming again even though his voice was hoarse and his throat tasted like blood and felt like he'd eaten something scratchy, like steel wool.

I have to run, he thought. *If I stay here, those things will keep stinging me over and over again until...* He swiveled his head toward where the statue had been waiting, but it wasn't there anymore.

He thought it could be hiding off to the side in the woods, and when he staggered past half blind, it would leap out and grab him... or maybe it really was gone, back to whatever dark, evil place it had come from. With a child's easy gullibility, he desperately wanted to believe the latter.

But even if it was still there, just hidden in the late fall weeds, Trevor couldn't stay here any longer. Making it into the house was his only option. A few more stings and he wouldn't be able to move at all, and then Poop Head could drag itself over as slowly as it wanted to and start to devour him from the feet up while Trevor watched, immobile.

That image was enough to make him move. At first, he shuffle-shambled along like a zombie in that grown-up show he'd seen advertised on TV, the one that had given him bad dreams for a week. But as his muscles started to warm up and the poison worked its way deeper into him, he slowed from a shuffle-shamble to a crawl. Sweat dripped down his rain-soaked face, but he kept moving, bracing for when the next wasp would land on him or for the statue to snag his ankle in its impossibly strong grip and squeeze until the bone turned to dust.

Keeping these thoughts in the forefront of his mind, staying on his feet and motivated was easy. He slipped in the mud only once where the path went slightly uphill but managed to stay upright, which was a relief. (When he started to feel his feet sliding out from under him, something close by in the forest crashed through last year's fallen tree limbs even closer and then fell back when it saw he wouldn't go down so easily.)

One foot in front of the other, he sang to himself in his head, even as he keened like a kitten out loud and continued to sniffle and cry. *I'm going to be brave no matter what. I'm going to make sure Mom and Aunt Nanny are safe, and then we're going to go and get Peanut, and then all of us will be safe together.*

He was so lost in these thoughts that when he stumbled over the stone lip onto the downstairs patio, he just stared at it in stupid wonder. There was no way he could've made it here already, yet here he stood. Trevor raised his head and looked around the best he could.

It was true. Somehow he really *was* here. The kitchen door stood open still, and the sun was out, high and hot in the sky. Although Trevor was still soaked through from the cold October rainstorm, the patio wasn't even wet. And old Poop Head was perched in its customary place on the stone wall, looking out over the water just like it always had. There was nothing more menacing about it than there had been before, no sharp, shattered teeth, no wasps crawling over its face... it was just stone.

None of it made any sense to him, but he didn't care one little bit. He wiped his runny nose on his arm, dried his tears, and crossed the patio quickly toward the safety of the kitchen, all while keeping his good eye trained on the statue. It didn't move, not even once.

His hands closed over the wooden doorjamb, and he took a deep breath to calm himself in the familiar smells of Aunt Nanny's kitchen. However, the smells coming out of the room weren't good at all. It was that same stink he'd smelled while following her up the path in the woods. But the room was empty.

"Aunt Nanny?" he called tentatively. His voice was ragged and used up. There was no answer.

Suddenly, certain that the statue had tricked him, he whirled around and faced the patio. Poop Head would be right behind him, and it would reach up and take his arms in its powerful stone ones and yank him down where he'd be at the perfect biting height... but the statue was still affixed to the wall, staring out longingly at the water.

"Trevor!"

That sounded like his mom. Her voice was really quiet and far away, almost like she was back down on the beach, even though she *couldn't* be there. He'd looked. The beach had been empty. Even from this distance, Trevor could tell his mom was scared. Her voice sounded panicked, like it had been that time he'd wandered away at the mall.

"Mommy!" he yelled, his voice breaking, not caring who might overhear and call him a baby. He was too tired. Nothing at all that had happened since leaving the beach made any sense. His little eight-year-old brain was simply too overburdened, and he started to cry.

"Don't be sad, Little Punk."

It was his mom's voice, and it came from behind him.

He turned, looked into the kitchen which seemed too dark considering how bright the sun was, and saw her. She was standing in the doorway between the kitchen and the downstairs hall. He could tell it was her because those were the clothes she was wearing today: blue jeans and a sweatshirt for the local culinary school where she had gone for a year before deciding cooking just wasn't for her.

But her face was obscured by shadow. Something glinted from the gloom there. Points of light reflected off of something big and wet.

"Mommy?"

"Don't cry. It was just a game we were playing. Me and Aunt Nanny. Only a game, Little Punk." Her voice sounded a little like Aunt Nanny's had down by the water... almost like a cicada's, all buzzy underneath.

"I don't like this game. You're scaring me."

"But we're almost done. Do you want to help your mommy win?"

He shook his head and wiped his leaky nose with his forearm. "I wanna go home, Mommy. I'm scared. I wanna go to our house. I don't like it here anymore."

"You don't want to hurt your Aunt Nanny's feelings, do you?"

Trevor didn't think Aunt Nanny would really care one way

or the other, but he knew the answer his mom was looking for and gave it. "No."

"Okay then. Come over here. Come and take my hand, and we can finish the game. And when we win, I'll take you back home."

"You promise?"

"I promise."

And it was totally nuts, but he didn't believe her. She'd never lied to him before (not that he knew of, anyway), yet there was something about the way she spoke, her hidden face, and the stink that came from her direction like roadkill in the summer that made him want to turn and run away. But the statue was out there. He had just narrowly avoided becoming a meal for that horrible thing. He just couldn't go back out there and risk it again. This time around, he might not be so lucky.

"You really promise, Mommy? Cross your heart?" He took a shaky step forward.

"Hope to die, Little Punk."

He took another step, his knees wanting to buckle, but he wouldn't let them. His mom slowly extended her hand, and he could see the ring on her third finger, which had belonged to Gramma that Mommy had gotten when she died. Instead of looking like a magical red ruby like it usually did, it looked like runny blood.

"It's okay," she said. "Come along with me, and I'll show you a secret place not even Aunt Nanny knows about." Her voice sounded even less human now, but still he moved forward, wanting to believe in his deepest heart that this was his mommy, and she and Aunt Nanny *were* just playing some strange grown-up game.

But he knew better when he took her hand and looked up into the hidden face with the big wet eyes that didn't look at all like Mommy's (or any person's face ever).

Of course, by then, it was too late.

-9-

Nan and Lauren had finished the first cigarette and were just starting on their next when Peanut raced down the beach toward them as quickly as the blind old mutt could go, spinning and frothing and yapping, his eyes rolling terrified in his little skull.

"What the hell..." Nan started to say, but Lauren was on her feet before she could finish her thought, staring down toward where Trevor had been digging only moments ago.

"Where is he?"

Nan stood and scanned the water, looking for the splashes of a drowning child and then the tree line, thinking perhaps he had moved out of the hot sun and into the shade to play. The cigarette dropped from her fingers to the rocks and hissed out. "Okay, don't panic. He probably just wandered up the path, okay? Let's go look."

Lauren nodded, and half ran, half walked through the rocks that had turned treacherous and slippery beneath her sneakers, until she got to where Trevor's hole was. His flattened water bottle scoop was discarded on the beach beside it. "Oh my god," she said, scratching at her cheek. "Nan, where is he? Trevor! Trevor Liam Potter, you answer me right this second!"

A crow cawed indignantly in a nearby tree, bothered by the disturbance, and took flight with the heavy beating of wings. Other than that, it was quiet.

"Oh god, Nan, where did he go?"

"Come on, let's go up the path to the house. I'm sure he just had to go to the bathroom or something. You'll see, he's just fine." But fear was causing her heart to ram painfully in her chest even as she tried to comfort Lauren.

Because her headache was gone.

When it had started yesterday morning before Lambert and Sanders had shown up, she'd hadn't thought it was one of her *special* headaches, but now she wasn't so sure. Five minutes before Peanut raced down the beach barking his little heart out, her head had been beating sickly, and her teeth aching. Then, just like that, it had all gone away.

But I haven't heard a peep out of the voice in almost a year. The headache means nothing! It's just a coincidence!

Telling herself that didn't stop the panic, though.

Lauren, younger and fitter than Nan, was running as quickly as she could, screaming Trevor's name so often that even if he could hear her and answer, he wouldn't have the time. Nan followed her more slowly, looking at the ground for signs that the little boy had passed this way: a shoe print, a dropped toy, a chip bag, *anything*.

A few dark black objects on the path up ahead reflected the sun in a muted way. Lauren ran over the top of them without seeing them or slowing down, but Nan stopped and checked, hoping maybe they would be river rocks or something that Trevor had dropped.

They were wasps. At least, she thought they were. The bugs on the ground were enormous, something straight out of a horror movie, big black and white creatures with horribly cruel alien faces and stingers to match. They were curled into little commas, dead and broken. Nearby, she saw a small shoe print in the mud, even though the ground had been dry all day.

"Oh, Jesus."

Lauren's voice was becoming fainter, and Nan started to run, feeling the panic in her chest like a bat pummeling itself against window glass. Her shirt and pants were twitched by the prickers of dying wild raspberry bushes that felt like tiny fingers trying to stop her. Then, something big and heavy droned past her ear. She turned to look and saw a black and white smear and the blur of wings.

Putting on a burst of speed, cursing the cigarettes and junk food that made her breath whistle in and out of her lungs painfully, she leaped over a root that was arched up into a perfect tripping loop.

Lauren was wrestling with the locked kitchen door on the back patio when Nan puffed up beside her. Neither of them noticed the mud smeared on the hands belonging to the bust of Gretchen Holt, which were crossed demurely on the railing, or the fat black wasp that took flight from her stone face and flew off into the woods. "Why is this locked? Was it locked when we left?"

Nan didn't think it had been but said nothing except, "Move aside, I've got my keys." When the door banged open, Lauren ran into the house, screaming for Trevor in a blind panic, but she stopped after a few feet.

"Oh god, what's that *smell*?"

Nan noticed it the moment she stepped into the kitchen, and it chilled her blood. It wasn't Claudia, not this far into the house. It was the *other*, the owner of the voice. "I don't smell anything."

Lauren took another deep breath, looked puzzled, and frowned. "I guess I don't either. I thought I did for a second."

"It's okay, you're upset. Those kinds of things happen. Your brain just sort of... misfires." The back of her head was prickling with fear as bumps erupted down her neck and arms.

The two of them spent the next hour searching the house from the attic all the way down to the lower floor with no sign of Trevor as Lauren became more and more frantic. The derelict wing was still boarded over, and there were no signs he had gotten in there at all, but Nan gave it a cursory search, trying her damnedest not to go through a rotten floor or have a ceiling collapse in on her because she touched the wrong beam, while Lauren called the police. *This part of the house really should have been torn down years ago,* she thought while picking her way carefully from room to room, throwing halfhearted glances over the moldering furniture and rugs left behind while breathing the dust and mustiness of the years. By the time she returned to the kitchen, she was dirty and sweaty.

"They're on their way," Lauren said.

Nan nodded, preoccupied. Of course they would have to come out and search for the lost little boy, but that posed two significant problems. There was little risk of them finding the entrance to the crypt on their own; she had lived in the house for years before discovering it, but standing close to the old wine rack, you could catch just the tiniest whiff of corruption from Claudia's body as it festered down there in the dark. Lambert wouldn't notice this, but Sanders would.

The other problem was Claudia's car. Nan had meant to get rid of the damn thing, but there had been no time before Muriel came back and started documenting her movements once again. The sheriff's department was on its way, and before long, the entire local community would be tromping across her property, beating every bush, trying to find that little boy. A search party would almost certainly stumble across the carriage house, and then she would be in real hot water.

Her stomach churned uneasily. But what could she do about it? Nothing. Not right now, anyway.

Luck was with her that day, though. Sanders had been called out to a domestic disturbance on the other side of town just a few minutes before Lauren decided enough was enough and called the sheriff's department, so it was Lambert who showed up.

"No reason to worry yet," he said, poking his head into rooms and giving them the once-over with his fingers hooked into his belt. "Kids just do this sometimes. Go off and hide, or fall asleep and can't hear ya calling 'em. Prolly just off playing in the woods somewhere. My own son did that, Lord, I can't tell you how many times when he was young. Didn't ya say there's a little playhouse out there?"

Nan nodded. They hadn't checked that yet, mostly because she knew it would be empty.

"There ya go then. He's likely out there fast asleep."

Lauren's arms were crossed over her chest, and as she spoke, her voice rose. "He wouldn't do that. He knows better than to wander off. And he wouldn't just fall asleep in the middle of the day, either. He *never* sleeps during the day, not ever. Something happened to him, I know it, and you're just wandering along like some braindead moron telling me everything is going to be okay!" She was breathing hard. Nan shushed her and put her arms around her trembling body.

Lambert, not put out by any of this, opened a closet in the hallway, inventoried the boots and coats with his eyes, and closed the door. "He a good swimmer?"

"What? What are you talking about? What does that have to do with anything?"

Nan shifted uneasily while waiting for Lambert to answer the question, but he didn't. "He thinks maybe Trevor went into the water instead of coming up here," she said softly.

Lauren's body went rigid beneath Nan's hands. "Oh dear God and Jesus, no." She started to weep into Nan's shoulder, unable to keep it together any longer. "We came up here, and what if... what if he was trying..." She couldn't finish the thought, though. It was too horrible to even articulate. Nan knew what she was trying to say anyway. What if, while they raced up the hill to the house, Trevor was trying to keep his head above water? What if they'd picked the wrong direction to focus their attention?

"I saw his shoe print out there on the path, pointed this way," Nan told Lambert, who was making his way back down the stairs to the kitchen. He stopped and turned.

"Yup, might mean he came up this way," he said judiciously. "'Course, you don't know. He mighta turned around to look at something or other when you all were making your way down to the water for your picnic too, right?"

Lauren's shoulders hitched as she cried. "I guess that's true," Nan said. "But the kitchen door was locked, and neither one of us locked it before we left. He had to've come up this way."

Lambert nodded slowly. "Yup, maybe. But if you gals searched the place and came up empty, then where'd he get to?"

Nan knew where. Even as she tried to deny it to herself, she knew. Trevor was down in the dark under the house. And it was unlikely he was still alive.

It's because you buried that boy who came to shovel your driveway in Jeremiah Holt's casket. You made the voice angry when you denied it its treat, so it took another one. One that mattered more. As punishment.

It was all just so insane. Every bit of it from beginning to end, but in her gut, she knew it was true. She had assumed the voice was unable to provide for itself and needed her to take care of it, but thinking back on it now, maybe it had been capable all along. Maybe it just didn't like to be seen. It was all just a little too convenient, wasn't it? Whenever the headaches came, so did someone else: the victim of a wrong turn, two brats from Oregon no one would miss, a boy with a snow shovel who no one knew where he was... everyone she had taken to the crypt had come at just the right time and had been easy to disappear. Ten years' worth of people, and Nan had never thought about it before. How was that even possible?

"Come on, sweetie, just a few more steps," she told Lauren and helped her the rest of the way down into the hallway.

Lambert, already down below and headed back toward the kitchen door, stopped for a moment, his face wrinkled. "Peeyew! What under God is that smell? Stinks like a busted septic line or something."

Nan could feel the owner of the voice nearby, lurking and watching, devoid of all emotion. She turned in the direction she thought it was and saw something move farther back into the shadows.

"I don't smell anything. Lauren smelled something like that earlier, but I didn't. Maybe I have to get a plumber out here."

"Don't wait too long," Lambert said, then without giving it a second thought, went out onto the back patio, and together with Lauren and Nan, walked the path down to the water.

He stopped momentarily and looked at the shoe print Nan pointed out, surrounded by dead wasps of normal size and color, without much interest in it. Nan looked at those wasps for a long time before being able to move on.

They checked all along the stretch of beach where the three of them had picnicked and then the overgrown playhouse, which Nan didn't go into but waited outside of, looking back into the woods (wondering if something was following them), and then around the formal gardens, which Trevor always liked to play in. There was no trace of him except for the hole he had dug on the beach and that single shoe print.

Back in the driveway, Lambert took his hat off and fiddled with the brim for a bit, standing by the open door of his personal vehicle (Sander's had taken the sheriff's car for his domestic disturbance), looking perplexed.

"You got any cameras in the back of the house there?" he asked Nan, and she went rigid. Yesterday, when he and Sanders had come out, she had planned to dump all the footage of Claudia but had become sidetracked and forgotten to. She couldn't very well deny them access to the footage now that they thought Trevor's life could hang in the balance. Thankfully, she was quick on her feet.

"No, no cameras back there. Even if there were, it wouldn't do any good. The whole system was doing a software update this morning. It's been offline all day."

Lambert frowned and nodded as if he'd expected no different.

"But what if—" Lauren started to say.

Nan nodded. "I'll check anyway. I just don't want you to get your hopes up." She *would* check, too, she wasn't a monster, but there would be nothing there. And once this was confirmed, the footage would go to that great data dump in the sky.

"Awright, then," Lambert said. "Nan, you going to be home all night?"

"Of course. Where else would I go?"

Lambert's eyes twinkled as if he had a suggestion or two. "I wanna make sure someone's here in case the boy comes back, is all."

"What are you talking about? I'm not going *anywhere*," Lauren said, her voice edging toward hysterical. "You're going to have to drag me out of here kicking and screaming if you think I am, but I'm warning you right now, I'll fight you every step of the way." Her jaw was hardened and her eyes crazy with defiance.

"Easy now," Lambert said. "Come on down with me now to the sheriff's office and file an official missing person's report. Get me a pitcher of Trevor I can get circulating and other information I need, and then you can come right back here if that's what you want."

"Are you kidding me? What about a search party?" Lauren said. "He's only eight. He could be hurt!"

"If he was hurt, we'd hear 'im. There's a couple hundred acres here to search through, and it's startin' to get dark. On top of that, they're calling for up to six inches of snow tonight. High winds and ice, too. Now, I might be able to get a party of folks back here in a few hours... *maybe*, but we need some time to organize. I don't want people getting lost in the woods or snapping their damn legs in old woodchuck holes or anything like that. We gotta be smart about this. Most of the folks I can get on short notice like this'll be oldsters."

"Who cares about anyone else? My *little boy* could be lying out there hurt or worse, don't you understand that?" Lauren was shouting, her voice barely holding together. She looked around for someone else to take up her cause and talk some sense into this crazy man, but she seemed to have forgotten there was no one else there but Nan.

"If he's out there, we'll find 'im."

"What do you mean *if*? Where else would he be?"

Nan knew what Lambert was hinting at but (thankfully) had enough smarts not to say. Trevor could technically be anywhere. If he had come back up to the house, someone could have come down the driveway, grabbed him, and driven off. Or Trevor could have wandered out to the road and been picked up there. Regardless of what parents thought of their little angels, kids did stupid things and things they weren't supposed to all the time. Sometimes, for no other reason than they took a notion into their head to do it.

Daylight was burning and Nan knew she had to do something to ease this along, so she took Lauren by the arm and pulled the grieving mother into her shoulder. Lauren's tears were as hot as her breath. "Go on with Sheriff Lambert, all right? I've got my cell phone on me, I've got a big flashlight, I'm going right back out into those woods when you leave, and I'll look for him until you get back."

"I can't leave," Lauren sobbed. "I just *can't*. I have to be here. I *have* to."

"I know you want to be here now, but Trevor needs you to go with Lambert and fill out that report. We need to make sure all bases are covered."

"What bases? He's here somewhere, isn't he?" Her big eyes searched Nan's face, looking for hope and reassurance.

"Don't think about that right now. Focus on doing what you have to do to make sure everything's okay. I swear to you on my daughter, if I find him, I'll call you that *second*, and then I'll pack him into the car and bring him to you."

"How can I go?" Lauren whispered, too low for Lambert to hear.

Nan pulled Lauren's head up gently so they were eye to eye. "Because you're his mother, and that's what mothers do. They do the hard things. They make the tough decisions to make sure their kids are okay. This is the hardest thing you'll have to do *ever*, but you're not doing it alone. I'll look for him all night if I have to. So go and get it done, and come back as soon as you can."

Lauren nodded, her face red and sticky and covered in snot. At that moment, she looked eerily like Caleb Montgomery, the little boy in the snowsuit.

Nan walked her over to the passenger door of Lambert's car and got her settled in. Lauren didn't seem capable of releasing Nan's arm, so Nan pried her fingers off gently and set her shaking hand in her lap before the fresh gale of tears began. With that done, she closed the door before Lauren could change her mind, then walked around the front of the sedan to where Lambert was waiting.

"Take her home and have her get a few changes of clothes, too. A toothbrush, that kind of stuff, okay?"

Lambert nodded once curtly.

"What, Chester, what is it?"

He tilted his head to the side, looking off into the darkening trees, scowling. "This whole thing kinda stinks, don't it?"

"What whole thing?"

"First, the reporter lady goes missing. Now Lauren's kid. Cameras ain't working." He shrugged. "Makes you wonder."

"Wha—*what*? You think *I* had something to do with this?"

"Not what I said. Just said it made me wonder."

"Oh, bullshit, it's what you're implying, at least have the balls to say it. I was with her the whole time, you know. You can ask her; she'll tell you that."

"Maybe she will at that." He looked thoughtfully at the weeping woman in the passenger seat, clutching the seatbelt in her hand like it would somehow save her from all of this if she just squeezed it hard enough. "Just don't forget what we talked about yester'dy. Investigation like this one can go sideways real fast. Sometimes people get all caught up in 'em and have trouble getting out... even if they turn out to be innocent. You get my meaning?"

"You absolute piece of *shit*," she hissed under her breath.

"Don't got time for that right now. Just be thinking about what I said. Be ready to talk turkey."

The memory of Trevor shouting *turkey for turkey* this afternoon popped up in her head for just a split second.

The driver's side door screeched open, and the whole car dipped when Lambert dropped into the driver's seat. Nan watched as the car backed up, then sped up the driveway toward the road. She puffed up after it to close the gate. Muriel was nowhere to be seen, which was a small miracle. There was precious little time to waste.

-10-

The stink that assailed her nostrils when she opened the secret door to the crypt was unlike anything she'd ever experienced before; bags of meat left out in the hot sun for a week, turning green and black and swimming with maggots. She gagged, then vomited on the steps, narrowly missing her feet.

Claudia's body was still there, and the lime wasn't doing anything to help with the odor or the decomposition. She had to get it out of the house before Lauren and Lambert showed back up with a troop of volunteers to search the grounds.

Which meant getting rid of Claudia's car, too. Even though the carriage house was buried in the woods, it wouldn't be hard for someone to stumble upon it by pure dumb luck.

At first, the solution seemed simple. She could just set fire to the carriage house and let the damn thing burn to the ground and take the roadster with it. A few moments of consideration revealed how risky this was, though. The fire would only attract attention and wouldn't burn hot enough to destroy the vehicle's frame and metal components. Not being a car aficionado, there was no way to tell where the VIN would be, either. From research for her novel *Secondhand Car*, she knew they could be found in any number of places based on what type of vehicle you were dealing with, from the window glass to the wheel wells to the engine block. Without having the time or ability to look it up, that wouldn't work.

Burying it would have been a good option if there had been more time and she didn't have a group of armchair detectives about to descend on the property in a swarm, looking for any little disturbance in the dirt. Digging a grave that size by hand would take days anyway, especially given the condition she was in.

And driving it elsewhere and abandoning it wouldn't work because Muriel could pop back up at the end of the driveway anytime. For all Nan knew, she was up there right now, hiding in the weeds, watching. Besides, abandoning the car still left the problem of Claudia to deal with.

No, as far as she could see, there was only one viable option. It wasn't the best and certainly wasn't her first choice, but it would probably be okay if she carried it out intelligently. The Hudson River was almost sixty feet deep in front of Holt House. A vehicle with a body in the driver's seat *could* disappear for quite a while down there. Maybe even forever.

Thankfully, the car started up with only minimal futzing, and Nan was able to maneuver it back down the trail and onto the patio outside the kitchen door. The sky was steely gray and spitting down snow at a pretty steady pace, so she would have to move fast before the absurd roadster was unable to make it back up the wooded path, past the carriage house, to the top of the bluff. There was still half a tank of gas in it, so she left it running, just in case it didn't feel like starting up again.

But her resolve began to falter once on the other side of the wine rack surrounded by the reek of rot. The string of lights she'd hung dispelled much of the blackness, yet her fear descending the steps this time was greater than it had ever been before. She was in uncharted territory. Her job was to provide bodies. What happened to them afterward was anybody's guess. All Nan knew was that they always disappeared... until now.

Claudia's mangled corpse was still there, untouched. It didn't so much lie in repose on the plinth as the others had but rather rested the way an overinflated blowup doll might; barely touching the surface due to bloat and dangerously close to falling off. The body's arms (she had to think of it that way, as a *body*, not as Claudia) stuck out at strange puffed angles, straining at the clothes that restrained it, and the creases in the skin around the fingers were turning green and splitting from the pressure. A weird foamy-looking blood leaked from its nose and mouth. The corruption seemed too advanced for the amount of time it had been down here, but it didn't really matter. What did was getting it out of here and over the side of the bluff before anyone else showed up.

The flatbed dolly stood next to the plinth with a thick sheet of plastic covering it and ropes to secure the load once it was onboard. Maneuvering the corpse onto it would be the easy (though disgusting) part. Dragging it upstairs without spilling anything off would be the tricky bit.

Nan donned thick rubber kitchen gloves that Ava had left behind in the mop bucket last time, put on a medical mask smeared with mentholated chest rub, and fashioned an apron from some of the leftover plastic to protect her clothes from the worst of the clinging smells, which she cinched at the waist with a length of yellow braided rope. On her head, she wore a shower cap. The image she cut was ridiculous, but once dressed, she felt more confident.

Until it came time to actually *touch* Claudia's body.

She approached it timidly, trying to take deep enough breaths to calm her nerves, but not so deep the smell of decomposition could overpower the menthol.

Claudia's shoulders and upper torso were swelled like a

bodybuilder's. Nan positioned herself to grab the body's arms and sort of *roll* it over the side onto the dolly, but standing here looking into Claudia's upside-down eyes that resembled boiled eggs pressed into over-proofed bread dough, she faltered. It felt as if someone was watching her, and she thought there had been a sound, like a whisper. She turned, thinking the owner of the voice might be lurking in the shadows, but there was no one there. It was like living with a gigantic venomous spider that kept scuttling around when you weren't looking. You never knew where or when it would pop up and scare you to death.

"Are you there?" she said, her own voice shockingly loud. But only silence returned to her. And then: "Trevor?"

You don't have time to pussyfoot around. Grab the goddamn thing and move!

Shaking her head to dispel the creeping feeling that crawled over her skin, Nan grabbed the body's shoulders before fear could regain its foothold and, gagging, yanked the whole thing to the right. Part of Claudia stayed behind like burnt chicken skin in the bottom of a baking dish, having adhered to the stone plinth in the days it had been resting on it. Even though Nan's arms were strong, it took three powerful jerks before the corpse slid far enough to tip over the side and land with a low farting sound, followed by a pudding-like thud on the plastic sheet. The mask over her face did nothing for the reek that filled the room, and she had to run to the corner to vomit again. When she straightened back up, her stomach muscles felt sore and sprung.

Working quickly now by the yellow light of the string bulbs and feeling like she was a character in a Poe story, Nan dumped bleach over the plinth, unmindful of where it went, and then flipped the long end of the plastic sheet up and over the top of the body, covering it loosely. It did little for the smell, but not having to look at that strange dried apple doll face made things a little better. The sunken hole in the middle of it from the edge of the coffee table was especially heinous.

There was no way to actually seal the plastic short of melting the ends together, so she used duct tape to secure them as best she could and ensure that as few fluids leaked on the floor as possible. When that was done, she used the remainder of her yellow braided rope to lash the body down tight to the metal dolly. A subscriber to Murphy's Law, Nan knew if she didn't, the body would likely slip off when she got up to the top of the steps and tumble back down to the bottom, leaving pieces of itself behind the whole way. Tying it down took a little extra time, but it was worth it.

Speaking of time...

She checked her watch. Lauren and Lambert had been gone for just over twenty minutes. There had been no notifications from the camera app on her phone, which meant no one had tried to come down the driveway or to the front door, either. That was good. Lauren would be pushing to get back as soon as possible. Nan could ill afford to deal with some poorly timed pop-in from a neighbor or another fan who thought it was okay to ignore the gate.

The dolly rolled rough over the packed dirt floor, from which an unpleasantly damp smell rose, and then up the first few steps. It weighed a ton and was hard to control, but through sheer force of will, Nan managed to bully it upward and upward, even when it wanted to slip back down. From time to time, she held the cart with her legs and gave her arms a rest, but as the minutes dragged on, these rests became less frequent, even as her arms started to jitter from exhaustion. Tomorrow, she could stay in bed for the whole day if she wanted to, her body just had to make it through tonight.

Finally, after what felt like an hour but was only really about fifteen minutes, the dolly tipped up over the final step and was once again flat on solid ground. The body sloshed a little in its plastic shroud, but remained on the cart, and for a wonder, her duct-taped seams were holding the worst of the effluvium within.

Nan shoved it through the doorway into the root cellar and swung the wine rack door closed.

As she pulled the dolly as fast as she could toward the kitchen, where she could hear the beautiful sound of Claudia's idling car waiting to accept this heinous cargo, Nan was glad Ava had been here yesterday. It gave her time to get the house cleaned and aired out before the irritatingly perceptive old woman came back.

She had already slid the kitchen table and chairs out of the way to give the furniture dolly all the room it would need to get past, and now that she was on solid stone floors again instead of dirt, it sped along quickly.

Spinning the whole ersatz gurney around so the handle was facing the patio door, Nan slipped through into the fresh air and hauled it out after her.

Instead of gliding through the opening as it should have, the metal bed clanged into the doorframe, and the forward momentum transferred to the corpse as the dolly stuck tight like a stopper. Claudia's body shifted six inches forward, sloshing unspeakable effluent onto the patio stone, melting the snow that covered it like cotton candy.

"Fucking, *shit*," Nan said and dry heaved a few times. Had there been anything of the picnic left in her stomach, she would have thrown it up.

In the trunk of the roadster, she had placed a few items she thought could come in handy, one of which was Nick's old hunting knife. She pushed the dolly back into the kitchen so she could get around it and went to work as quickly as possible sawing through the ropes. The blade was dull and starting to rust, but it made quick work of them anyway, freeing the plastic-wrapped body from its metal frame. Without that cumbersome anchor holding her back, Nan was able to slide the body through the kitchen door without further incident and muscle it up into the passenger seat of the car. The plastic would stay on for now.

After returning the dolly to the crypt, where she could clean it at her leisure, Nan hopped into the roadster and gunned the gas a few times. The snow was coming down as if in a downpour, and there were two or three inches covering the ground already.

The car had summer tires on still, and there was no lever to put it into four-wheel drive, so she drove it along the trail slowly, avoiding the places with deep holes she hadn't gotten around to filling in yet. All of the windows were wide open because of the stench. It took only five minutes to get to the carriage house, which no longer caused her anxiety when she looked at it, and she turned to the left, down the trail that led to the little Holt Cemetery. Beyond its fence, which had been partially crushed by a falling tree at some point, the trail started to slope gently upward.

It would have been so much easier to take the car down the path she, Trevor, and Lauren had used today, but it was likely that when the boy wasn't located anywhere else, someone would get the notion to look in the water where he had last been seen. No, away from that spot was better, somewhere downriver where they wouldn't have any reason to look.

About halfway up to the top of the bluff, wet ice started to *tick tack* off the windshield, and the tires slipped and skidded. It was only a few hundred more feet. Her hands gripped the wheel as Claudia's body burbled and flumped in the passenger seat. Gases still pushed out of it into the makeshift plastic bag, announcing themselves with grotesque and somehow very human noises.

I'll have to burn these clothes. There's no way this smell will ever come out of them.

She was thinking this, trying to negotiate a sharp curve through the weeds and saplings that grew in close, when she heard a noise from the passenger seat that wasn't gases escaping. It started low and grew louder as the seconds ticked past.

Ignore it. Just keep going. You can't stop now.

Even if she could have, she wouldn't have. It sounded like the corpse was laughing; a putrefying, painful chuckle from dead vocal cords. And as it laughed, it's face had crept closer to Nan's. She could *feel* it. She glanced at Claudia surreptitiously and saw the bloated, dried apple face had turned toward her, but was no closer than it had been before. The mouth was obscured by the filmy plastic so there was no way to tell if it was grinning, but she thought she could see teeth.

It fell that way. It's this damn car sliding all over the place, that's all. As if underpinning this thought, the tires squealed and slipped on a patch of icy mud before catching and continuing to crawl ever upward.

The crinkling sound the plastic shroud had been making the whole trip now became especially disturbing. What had been so easy to dismiss before as the sounds of it shifting against the seat now sounded very much like searching hands trying to find the taped-up seams.

That's not what it is. Just watch what you're doing and ignore everything else. You've got maybe a hundred feet left if that. You can do this.

She pulled out the knob to turn on the headlights, but only the right one lit up. The left was as dark as Bobby Buckland's missing eye.

Claudia's left hand suddenly thumped onto the center console, and Nan screamed and jammed both feet on the brake pedal. The car slewed off to the side and then back, juddering dangerously close to the steep slope on the left, which would have dumped her unceremoniously into the Hudson. Luckily, she had reached a place where the ground leveled off, or there would have been no hope of getting it the damn thing moving again.

The windshield wipers flicked back and forth with little squeaks, trying desperately to keep up with the driving snow.

Claudia's body was in the same position as when she'd put it in the car—even the head was once more facing forward—but something was unsettling about it nonetheless. It made no sense. It was a bit like coming into a room that someone had recently vacated. There were signs, just little things that let you know a person had been there and wasn't anymore, but if pressed to point out exactly what those things were, you wouldn't be able to.

Had Claudia actually been here just now? It wasn't possible, and yet...

"There are more things in heaven and earth, Horatio," Nan said, wiping her lips with the back of her hand and swallowing thickly. She wanted a goddamned drink.

She was watching Claudia to see if she would move or laugh again (assuming she had done either of those things before), when a darkness swept past the car on the passenger side, moving silently with frightening speed. Nan blinked twice before her mind caught up to her eyes, and she jerked back against the driver's door, clanging her head against the window frame. It was too dark to really see what it had been, and the constant sheeting snow obscured it further, but it was tall whatever it was. Nan thought back to last night and the figure she'd seen in her hallway (maybe?), the one that had been as tall as the ceiling. Her hands started to shake.

When the revolting chuckling started again a moment later, something broke inside her. A person could not be expected to put up with constant terror like this. They just couldn't. She balled her hands into fists, and screamed.

She screamed it so loud and so long that her voice cracked, and she tasted blood, and dark spots bloomed like deadly flowers before her eyes. The world swam in and out of focus for a moment, and Nan closed her eyes and let it, ebbing and flowing with the pulsing darkness. When she swallowed, her throat was raw, as if someone had run it through with needles.

But overall, she felt better. A bit more in control.

And when she opened her eyes, everything was back to normal. Well, as normal as things could get. According to her phone, another ten minutes had slipped away while she had her little breakdown.

The roadster's engine was starting to sound choppy, so Nan goosed the gas pedal, making it growl, and then began climbing the last thirty feet to the top.

"And I'd better not hear one goddamn sound out of you," she told Claudia, who rode the remainder of the trip in silence.

By the time the car broke through the dark trees and onto the grassy knoll of the bluff overlooking the Hudson, everything felt sort of okay again. Nan parked the car, which was sounding sicker all the time, and rushed to the passenger side with only a cursory glance back at the trees to see if something waited there for her.

Claudia flopped out into the fresh snow, and the bag containing her finally broke open, spilling a steaming avalanche of what looked like chunky brown gravy. By now, Nan was so used to the intimate horrors of decay that she didn't gag or vomit but rolled her eyes with tired resignation, gathered up the body as best she could, and strapped it into the driver's side of the roadster.

"Don't forget *this*." She tossed the baggie of cocaine onto the dashboard, then slammed the door closed. There was a wonderful finality in that sound; the last nail being driven into a coffin, one might say. With the vehicle in neutral (and after collecting her tools from the trunk), she gave it a little nudge, and it was off, rattling down the hill toward the edge like a runaway toy, and then suddenly, *poof!* like magic, it disappeared.

Peering down over the cliff face, it was too dark to see anything below, but Nan could hear the distinct *blub, blub, blub* coming from the water as the car sank and, with it, the nosy reporter.

She held the plastic shroud aloft in the freshening wind until it filled with air, and let it go. It crinkled as it sucked out of her hands, and then it, too, was gone into the water. She did the same with her makeshift apron and the shower cap covering her hair. Someone may find these things someday, she thought, but by then, all evidence of her involvement would have been washed away.

Feeling looser now, *freer*, not even walking back through the dark woods bothered her. Whatever the thing had been that had rushed past the car, it was no longer on her radar. She'd had the foresight to bring along her big flashlight and used it to keep the imagined creepy-crawlies at bay.

Some days, things just seemed to click.

CHAPTER 5
HOUSEGUEST

"They spoke to me," *Maisy told Keaton.* "*The whole time I was unconscious, I could hear their voices, whispers coming from all around me. And even though I am fairly certain I am awake I can hear them still!*"

"*Only dreams, my dear. Dreams and a touch of hysteria. There are no spirits here.*" *Yet even as he said the words, Keaton wasn't certain. A week after Constable Bell had blundered his way into the cellar and Keaton had been forced to put a knife in his throat, he would have sworn he had seen the man standing out on the veranda, his face sunken, staring into the billiard room window. And he had seen Vincent, of that there was no doubt in his mind. Waking in the dark one night after hearing a noise, Keaton had looked down and seen two rotting hands sticking out from beneath the bed, grasping the braided rug Maisy had made him as a wedding gift. Vincent had laughed and called his name while Keaton hid beneath the coverlet with his eyes squinched shut. But these weren't things he could ever tell his wife.*

"*You're wrong, my love,*" *Maisy said, her voice quivering.* "*They're all around you even now. The constable and Vincent and so many others. We've filled this house with them, and now it*" *is full of spirits. They're starving things, and they've come to feast."*

-Nan Wickwyre, *Haunting Willow Hall*

-1-

Time felt very much like it had folded over on itself and was repeating what happened a decade before when Ducky disappeared. Now, as then, there were large coordinated searches, people linked arm in arm, marching through the woods and poking all the soft spots in the ground with sticks to see if anyone managed to spear a body. And then there were the missing person posters that went up everywhere all over town: the bank, the Red Sparrow bar out on East Market Street, the Classic Eats Diner on Route 9, and at the Route 9 Bowling Alley right next door. The front window at Cutler's Food and Pharmacy had been practically papered over with them, Trevor's small photocopied face staring sadly from each one.

And, of course, as with Ducky, rumors started to spread like herpes. The town was nearly evenly divided on whether or not Nan had been involved with the new disappearance, with Mulberry Lane and the other wealthier neighborhoods generally agreeing that the idea was foolish and everything south of Mill Road believing she'd probably drugged Lauren and distracted her so she could drown that poor boy. Rich or poor, though, it was almost unanimously agreed upon by the lifelong residents that Holt House had played some part. All those people who had gone missing within its walls over the years couldn't have been a coincidence.

As a result of the whispering and innuendo, Nan became even more of a recluse than she had been back when Ducky was the topic of discussion around the pickle barrel. She drove an hour into Danbury, Connecticut to do her shopping and errands now and was turning down all requests for interviews (of which there were many). Even her book tour had been postponed due to a "death in the family." Tim had nearly reached through the phone and strangled her when she told him, but there was little he could say to convince her. She'd stuck to her guns for once, ignoring his every wheedling suggestion, and when, exasperated, he threatened to drive out and kick her ass all the way up and down the Eastern Seaboard, she'd hung up on him and blocked his number. Her mother always told her she caused plenty of trouble on her own and didn't need to borrow any before it was time, so she decided to deal with him if and when that time came.

Lauren had stayed at Holt House with Nan for two weeks waiting for her little boy to return before her mother and father came up from South Carolina—where they'd retired to once the New York winters got too much—and took her home. She fought them as hard as she had fought Lambert the day Trevor went missing, but in the end, they had won.

Nan had stopped in every so often to reassure her that she was still searching every day (which, of course, she wasn't, no need to search when you knew what had happened), and to see how she was holding up.

"Sanders keeps calling," Lauren told her, speaking in a dead robotic voice. "He keeps asking if I remembered anything else that happened that day. Anything that could... could help. But I can't. He was so happy. Just my happy little boy."

All the visits ended in tears, so eventually, Nan stopped going. Not for her own good, she told herself, but because they were too hard for Lauren to endure. And she almost believed that.

Sanders and Lambert still popped around occasionally, ostensibly to check and see if there had been any changes but really to let her know they were watching. Sanders especially. He looked at her with bright, hateful eyes so intensely it was like he was trying to tell her telepathically exactly what he wanted to do to her. From time to time, Lambert and Sanders would organize a small group of volunteers to search the property again, but they never turned up anything. Of course, Nan knew these searches hadn't been about trying to find Trevor at all but about harassment. They wanted her to feel on edge and uncomfortable, each for their own reasons, and Trevor was a nice legal way to do it.

Lambert didn't mention blackmail again, though not out of the goodness of his heart or because he'd forgotten. Sanders seemed to be dogging his every step. He would eventually get around to it, but Lambert approached even extortion lazily as with everything else he did. At least they didn't have Claudia McKinnon to badger her with at the moment. The investigation had refocused on her ex-husband (and one-time dealer), who had no alibi for the window of time in which she'd gone missing. Nan hadn't heard any reports of strange things washing up downshore, either, and so put the whole sordid affair out of her mind.

The one and only bright point to Trevor disappearing (other than Muriel being driven back to whatever hole she lived in) was that Holt House had, once more, become a quiet and peaceful place. There were no strange shadows, bumps in the night, or movements caught from the corner of her eye. No voices or headaches, nightmares or apparitions in the woods. There were also no dreams—good, bad, or indifferent. And when, after Lauren had departed, Nan finished scrubbing the plinth and everything else Claudia had decomposed all over, she hadn't gone back down into the crypt at all. The compulsion that had driven her for ten years, that had been in the background of every decision she made and every thought she had, was just... gone. And she accepted this new change with stoic indifference.

It was because of this strange yet fortuitous disconnect in her mind she was able to resume a normal life once the previous chapter had been closed with THE END writ large beneath it in dark ink. She took long walks through the woods and along the river, cooked real meals for herself (things she'd never tried to make before like lasagna with béchamel sauce), rather than eating the junk food she had come to subsist on, and read anything and everything with a near voracious appetite for words. She was smoking more than normal, too.

But what she did most was write. Before, she had always felt at her most creative first thing in the morning after a cigarette, a few cups of coffee, and something sweet to help wash it all down. Now, she found herself thinking about writing all day long. *Return to Willow Hall* filled her thoughts but left no trace of itself behind. It was the *act*, not the story, that had become the new compulsion, much as drinking had once been. It was never about the booze, *per se* (although it sure was a bonus), but rather the ritual of drinking. While writing, everything else in the world fell away. She'd drop down in the middle of her precious Willow Hall, free to wander, explore, and chat with whoever might cross her path (or hide from those she was afraid of). Sometimes, when roused from this playground by hunger or thirst, tears were staining her cheeks. And sometimes, her body was all over goosebumps. Once, there had been blood on her keyboard from the fingernail wounds in her palms.

Even after Nick and Lizzie had died, writing hadn't been like this. Her daily output then had been maybe fifteen hundred words if things were flowing and feeling right. About six pages, give or take. Now, she was churning out over *eight thousand* words a day, an amount unheard of at any point in her career, adding over thirty pages to the unwieldy stack of manuscript on top of her printer every night.

Yet she knew not one thing of the story. With all of her other books, Nan had played Lot's wife, unable to stop herself from looking back at the Sodom and Gomorrah of her work before starting each day's session. But now when she sat down to write, the temptation wasn't there. Nor was the anxiety that usually sat down with her, whispering that it wasn't good enough, *she* wasn't good enough. Vito, with his heinous cigar breath and thrift store suits, had taken over, no longer requiring anything from her but to move her fingers over the right keys and to stay the fuck out of things. A deal that Nan found more than equitable.

It was, though unbeknownst to her on a conscious level, much the same deal she had made with the voice in the house. When it had required something of her (*DECAY AND ROT!*), she acquiesced by feeding the compulsion, and when the task was done, it was relegated to the back of her mind, not to be thought about or dwelt upon. She didn't investigate the crypt or her own motivations (beyond wanting to silence the migraines), nor did she allow the guilt to grow in her like a cancer. It was unfortunate that Trevor was gone, of course, but the act of creation occasionally demanded sacrifice. No less a luminary than God Himself had gifted *that* wisdom to the world. Besides, it wasn't as if she could change it even if she wanted to.

Everything was a thousand miles of smooth road, and she should have been out of her mind with joy, yet she wasn't. Something had entered her life that had never been there before on a surface level. Nan was afraid. Not all the time, but certainly more frequently than ever before; probably even more so than she had been when the voice first started to come to her. It was somehow woven into the very mundanity of life, the ease with which things happened and time flowed. She was scared while making her dinners, looking over her shoulder every so often for the person she felt watching her from a chair at the kitchen table. And she was scared while walking through the woods, hearing the occasional snap and crunch of whatever was following her down the path. She was even scared while writing, as if something nearby whispered the words to her while her mind was occupied. And even though that was ridiculous (she was alone in the room every time she checked, which she did often), it didn't silence the nagging fear.

But that was something she could live with. As long as Vito kept the spigot turned on and the story flowed, none of the rest of it mattered.

It was in this way, living just slightly east of Eden (but close enough to see its magnificently alien trees and breathtaking animals), that time passed. The air grew colder, the sky grew steely gray, and the days grew shorter.

-2-

It was a few weeks before Christmas. Ava was humming "Silent Night," not so silently, while scrubbing the downstairs toilet when someone rang the doorbell. A short, squat woman with short hair and short patience for being interrupted, she clucked her tongue and groaned as she straightened up.

Nan Wickwyre, as with all the wealthy muckety-mucks from away who had settled here along the water, thought herself pretty damn important. Early on, she had made Ava the offer to call her Nan, something which Ava just couldn't bring herself to do (whoever had said *familiarity breeds contempt* had spoken correctly in her opinion). Instead, she called her Mrs. Wickwyre or, simply, Missus. The muckety-mucks particularly enjoyed the latter. When she spoke of her employer to other lifers in town, however, Ava often referred to her as her Ladyship, which always brought laughter. Right now, her Ladyship was up in her attic room, making up lies to sell to the gullible masses, and was not to be disturbed under any circumstances. Although answering the door wasn't in her job description (she was a cleaning lady, and a damned good one, not a parlor maid at the lady of the house's beck and call for heaven's sake), Ava limped her way up the godforsaken steps to the front door.

"This had better be important," she grumbled to herself. "Hold your horses. I'm getting as quick's I can!"

The Potter woman was standing on the veranda wrapped in a blanket that was much too thin considering the temperature was hovering in the upper teens and the wind was howling to beat the band. Her hands were red and chapped, and she wore no expression.

Ava, who had known the girl's mother and father an age ago and neither liked nor disliked Lauren Potter, felt a twinge of motherly concern seeing her standing there, snow in her hair and snot on her upper lip.

"What in heaven's name are you doing all the way out here like that?" And when this question was met with only a blank stare, which showed no understanding or recognition, she added, "Did you walk all the way here?" There was no car in the driveway, just a single set of footprints staggering through the icy crust forming on the fresh snow. Still, Lauren said nothing. Ava stepped forward and touched her arm. "Where's your coat?" That's when she noticed Lauren was not wearing shoes or boots but house slippers that were soaked through with dirty water.

Lauren looked up, her eyes dead and empty, looking but not seeing. "My what? Coat?" Her voice was just like her eyes. The woman currently inhabiting this body was a mere shade of who she had once been. Everything was running on autopilot. She kept cutting her eyes to the side, looking down the sloping white wasteland of the lawn toward the river.

"Come on," Ava said and tugged Lauren's arm gently. Lauren allowed herself to be led into the house as though she was nothing more than a stuffed doll. Ava took her to the living room and sat her in a chair in front of the fireplace. The thin blanket she had worn on her walk over was stained gray by road salt, so Ava replaced it with a thick, wool one. Lauren sat there and let the blanket be draped over her shoulders like a shawl. Ava then peeled the sopping slippers and socks from Lauren's feet, which were almost neon red and as cold as death.

The large picture windows on the room's west side looked down at the stretch of forest through which Trevor had made his last, terrified scramble. If it had been summer or even early fall, the leaves would have blocked the view of the rocky beach down below where they had picnicked that day, but the trees were bare, and the river peeked through, gray and mottled looking, reflecting back the undersides of the clouds which held more snow in their bellies. Lauren's gaze kept creeping to the windows, drawn to them magnetically until Ava gently spun the chair around so it faced the other way.

"You don't need to be looking at that right now."

"That's where it happened. Where he went missing." She watched the fire. "I wasn't paying attention."

"Oh, child," Ava said. She took a seat beside Lauren and took her cold hands in her warm ones, which smelled faintly of bleach. Her skin was wrinkled from years of harsh chemical cleaners, yet was soft and comforting, like old leather. "Have you been blaming yourself all this time? Wasn't your fault. Wasn't his, either. Sometimes the good Lord does things that confuse and anger us, but He had His reasons."

"What are they?"

Ava shook her head. "Not for me to know or guess at. Nor you, hard as that may be to hear. You just need to trust in Him."

"I was smoking a cigarette. I was smoking and laughing and *gossiping* when he was taken from me. Why did I let him go down the beach by himself? Why would God have let that happen?"

Ava just shook her head again. As far as she was concerned, everyone in this life owed a debt of grief. Lord knew she'd paid on her own account over the years; you didn't live into your seventies without death creeping around like a thief in the night. But grief never seemed to travel alone. It brought along with it curiosity. *Why?* When someone died or lost a limb, or went missing, or lost a good job, it was what everyone always wanted to know. *Why?* The only thing Ava knew for certain was that there were no answers to be had, and most times, no accountability, either. "I don't know. That's a question for the ages."

Lauren looked down at her hands.

Ava sat a few moments more, her discomfort growing. Despite having participated in the search parties and despite her desire to help this poor grieving mother keep whatever hope alive she could, Ava did not believe Lauren's little boy was still alive.

Death bothered her. When her own sister, Frida, had passed a few years back, Ava had skipped the funeral, claiming stomach issues, and had gone bowling instead, something Frida had always loved to do. The truth was she couldn't stand the thought of walking into that chapel and looking at Frida in that box, which would soon and forever be six feet below the ground. "I'm going to get the Missus," she said, twisting her hands around one another like a war widow awaiting news of her husband. "You stay right here and warm up. I won't be a minute." Lauren gave no indication she had heard, but Ava didn't think she would be getting up and dancing the Watusi anytime soon.

The attic room was up two flights of stairs (*Bugger that woman for not installing an elevator!* Ava thought as she climbed), and with her bad knees, it took ten minutes to totter up and then another three or four to find her way to the little bolt-hole where the lady of the manor wrote. The upper floor of Holt House was a maze, and even though she'd been working here for over a decade, she still found herself getting lost and ending up in parts of the house she shouldn't have been able to get to. Some of these places she'd never seen before. Once, she wound up in the old, closed-off section and had to beat a hasty retreat. She'd felt watched. Why her Ladyship didn't just tear down that part of the house was beyond her; rich people thought differently than ordinary folk. The money rotted their brains.

She was scaring the bejabbers out of herself thinking about all manner of things best left unthought of. She knocked perfunctorily.

"I'm working, Ava! Do not disturb!"

It used to be if Ava had to interrupt her for anything, her Ladyship would take it in stride and use the manners God gave her. Recently, though, since about the time the Potter boy went missing, she had been getting shorter and shorter tempered. Ava wondered if maybe she was drinking again, though she would never have asked. A good Yankee woman knew when to keep her nose out of other peoples' business and when not to. This was one of those latter times. She'd known the Missus back when her poor husband and daughter were still alive, back when the liquor flowed freely, and there were some similarities in how she acted. Nothing conclusive mind, but it was interesting.

All of these thoughts were just so much useless clutter, though. Mercy, what was wrong with her? Usually, she was so much more focused, but today, she felt pulled in every direction at once. "There's no time for working now," she called sternly. "Lauren Potter is downstairs, and she's in a bad way." There was no response from the other side of the door, just the soft tippy-tapping of computer keys. Land *sakes*, what was wrong with that woman? Ava knocked again, a little more insistently. "She walked here, her feet are halfway to falling off, and when you talk to her, she just sits there looking right through you like she doesn't have the sense God gave a dickie bird."

Her Ladyship groaned but, finally, the tapping sounds stopped. Her chair squalled against the wood as she pushed back from her desk and stomped toward the door.

Well, cry me a river, why dontcha? Ava thought. *Not like this is my comp'ny dropping in, is it?* It was an uncharitable thought, but Ava had her own issues to deal with and couldn't stick around the house all night entertaining the near-comatose woman in the living room. Her husband, Marv, would need help getting to the bathroom before too much longer, and she would have to empty out his bedpan if he hadn't been able to wait. Then there was the changing of the bandages on the new wound that had appeared on his leg last week... from the time she got home to the time she finished up the dinner dishes, she'd be busier than a one-armed paper hanger. Probably beyond that, too, right on through to when she finally lay her head on her pillow tonight. And, if it was one of Marv's bad nights, there would be no rest at all. Being a charitable neighbor was important (it was how the good Lord worked through you, praise Him), but sometimes charity needed to start and end right at home.

The office door was yanked back from inside, and her Ladyship stood in the doorway, her hair a bit frizzy, her eyes frazzled. "For the love of God, what is it, Ava? I'm working. I told you not to bother me while I'm working!"

Under normal circumstances, Ava wouldn't have allowed anyone to speak to her like this, employer or not. Respect was paramount. But she hadn't even heard what her Ladyship had said, and if she had, it wouldn't have mattered. For the first time in her long life, Ava Bakker was struck dumb. The smell that had wafted out of the room for just a split second, more powerful than the smell of cigarette smoke, which also wafted out, was one of body rot. She'd started her career back in her youthful days as a nurse before deciding she'd seen enough death to last her a lifetime and then some. The smell of decomposition was one you never forgot. But that dissipated quickly and wasn't what had captured her attention.

It looked like somebody else was in the room, standing near the desk. But then maybe *somebody* was too generous a word. The figure she had seen for just a flash before it receded into the gloaming had been tall and thin as a reed and looked like a corpse with large, leaning teeth. Just like a monster straight out of one of her Ladyship's books.

Get ahold of yourself, old girl. Wasn't anything there a'tall. You've gone and given yourself the jimjams thinking on things you shouldn't've, that's all. Things what have no bearing on anything else. You ought to know better. You should be ashamed, a woman of your age acting a fool like that. But even this stern lecture wasn't enough to cut through the feeling of terror. And when her Ladyship pushed on her shoulder to get her attention, she nearly screamed, and wouldn't *that* have just been the icing on the cake.

"Come on, Ava, out with it. What the hell is going on?"

Ever the practical and hardheaded woman, Ava simply denied to herself that she had seen or smelled anything out of the ordinary, clenched her teeth, and resumed her holier-than-thou chastising. "I said Miss Potter is down in the living room, half out of her head. I set her in front of the fireplace, though she might need to be seen by a doctor. Looks in bad shape."

Incredibly, her Ladyship looked back over her shoulder longingly at the computer on her desk.

Ava knew what that look meant; could practically see the question forming and then worming its way through her Ladyship's mind. She shook her head. "I can't take her on right now. Got cleaning left to do, then Marv's got an appointment at six."

"Oh, for the love of... fine. *Fine.* Just come on, let's go. I've got things to do myself, you know. I was right in the middle of something important."

Ava's eyebrow arched, and she pursed her lips but didn't bother chiding the lady of the manor any further. It would do no good; she could see the faraway almost drugged-up look in her eyes she got when writing (*can anything that makes you look like that be a good thing?* she wondered). And anyway, the figure she *might've* seen in the office still took up most of her thoughts. It felt like it was watching her from the darkness near the window, its eyes gleaming with animal cunning.

It wasn't often Ava's mind worried about a topic after she'd ordered it to stop, and she wasn't quite sure how to deal with it. "I'm going back down to finish up the bathroom and then moving on to the kitchen," she said and started down the stairs, just glad to be putting some distance between her and whatever was watching her with those hungry eyes.

A moment later, her Ladyship followed, but only after shutting and locking the door to her office.

Curious, Ava thought, but by the time she'd reached the landing on the main floor, she had put the whole ordeal out of her mind.

-3-

"I'm sorry I stopped visiting," Nan said once she'd checked to make sure Lauren's feet wouldn't fall off. Sure, they were red and cold, but nowhere close to being frostbit, as the old-timers say. She didn't need a doctor, just a thick pair of socks. That Ava, always so damn dramatic.

"That's okay," Lauren said. She was much thinner than she had been the last time they'd seen one another as if she hadn't eaten a thing in the last month and a half. Her hair, usually soft and shiny, was a rat's nest of tangles.

Nan leaned forward, unsure what to do with her hands, so she clasped them together in her lap. "No, I really mean it. I wanted to. It just felt like it was doing more harm than good."

Lauren nodded slowly.

"I guess I was a little scared, too. I didn't really know what to say."

Another nod.

At the rate things were going, this conversation would wrap

up sometime around Juneteenth. Nan didn't have time for this. Being torn out of her story and away from Willow Hall was the worst kind of coitus interruptus. That was bad enough, but now she was expected to make tedious small talk with someone who wasn't even using words to communicate. Why had Ava answered the damn door anyway? Things had been going along so nicely before then.

It was time to fast-track this conversation and see if any of the afternoon could be salvaged. She left her chair, sat on the ottoman beside Lauren, and took her hand. It was like holding the limp hand of a corpse. And Nan would know. "Are your parents still staying up here with you?"

Lauren nodded, and her eyes leaked. "They're heading back down after Christmas."

"Okay, good. I'm going to call them and have them come here and pick you up."

Now, there was a reaction. Lauren's eyes popped wide, and she clutched Nan's arm with fingers hooked into claws like someone drowning. "No, please don't, don't make me go back yet! I can't go back there!" Nan soothed Lauren's fingers out. "I can't stand it. Everywhere I turn. *Everywhere.* His things. His art on the fridge, his clothes in the bathroom hamper, his school pictures all lined up on the mantle. Like he's just going to walk back in and pick up where he left off."

"I know."

"I dream about that sometimes," she said miserably. "I hear a noise in the kitchen, and I walk down the hall and he's sitting at the table eating a peanut butter sandwich and apple slices like he used to. He says 'Hi, Mom! Boy, I sure am hungry. I've been walking for a long time!' He waves, and there's peanut butter on his fingers and cheeks. I can see it *so* clearly.

"But that's when I figure out I'm dreaming, and none of it is real. I try to get to him and take him in my arms before I wake up, but I never get there in time. I know if I can just... just one time, actually *touch* him, when I wake up, he'll be there with me. Or I'll be with him. I don't care which way."

You might, Nan thought.

"You have to stop thinking that way."

"I don't think anymore. It's too scrambled up inside for that. These things just come to me. Even if I could stop it I wouldn't. It's the only way I'll ever see him again, isn't it?" Her voice broke.

"Lauren... I don't know what happened to him that day. So I can't say if you will."

"Don't bullshit me. He's dead. Isn't he?"

Nan sucked her lips back between her teeth, then said as softly as she knew how, "Maybe he is."

"Someone would have seen him if he was still alive. Someone, somewhere. It's like the earth just opened and swallowed him. Like he never existed. How can that happen?"

"I don't have answers for you. I wish I did."

"Was this what it was like for you? After Nick and Lizzie?"

"I don't like to talk about that."

Lauren's shoulders drooped. "Please. You're the only one I *can* talk to about this. Everyone says they understand, and they know what I'm going through, but they don't. Only you do."

Nan sighed. She remembered the empty platitudes people tried out on her during the funeral. *They're in a better place now. God never gives us more than we can handle. You'll be together again with them someday. It's all a part of God's plan.* She herself had been guilty of trotting a couple of those out in the past. They were meant to be comforting, but mostly, they felt smug. "It was the worst day of my life," she said. "The worst thing I've ever lived through, and I've lived through a lot. But I can't change it. Nothing will bring them back. I can't change it any more than you can change what happened to Trevor. Don't you see that? If we could, then nothing in the world would matter anymore. It would all be pointless."

"I don't care. I want him here with me, where he belongs,

even if the whole world has to burn. I didn't have the time with him I was supposed to get."

"I didn't, either. We're not guaranteed anything."

"I just want the hurting to *stop*. I want the pain to go away."

"You know what my grandma used to say about bad stuff like this?" Lauren shook her head. "It was one of her favorite sayings. She said it to me when I broke my arm falling out of the crabapple tree in her backyard when I was six, and she said it to me when my first agent dumped me before he could make a sale when I was twenty-six... and if she'd still been alive when Nick and Lizzie died she would have said it to me then, I've got no doubt. She used to say, 'This too shall pass.' And she was right. Even though it might not feel like it now, it will."

"It can't!" Lauren shouted, aghast. "It's all I've got left!"

"But it's not. Right now, you've got the pain, *and* you've got your memories. The pain is bigger, so it's taking over everything and blocking the memories out. But it *will* start to fade, I promise. When it does, you'll be able to see the memories again. And the shitty, unfair thing is *they'll* hurt at first, too. But then they won't as much. The pain won't ever go away fully. That'll be there in some form or another until the day you die, and maybe even past that. But it does lessen. And even though nothing will ever go back to normal again, things will eventually start to feel normal anyway."

Lauren wiped her face with her sleeve. It didn't look like this was the first time she had done that. "How did you live through the hurt?"

"I just did." It came off sounding a bit colder than she had intended, but it certainly wasn't something Nan was going to talk about.

"Is it because you think they're in Heaven?"

Nan hadn't been prepared for that question, and her mind flashed to the crypt below the house. "I don't know. I hope, for your sake and for mine, that what comes after is better than I think it is."

Lauren's eyes drooped, and she sniffled. "I'm so tired." She sounded like Lizzie after her first few rounds of chemo.

"Close your eyes. I'll have Ava make you something to eat."

"Not hungry." Her voice was fading fast. To an outside observer, it might look staged, but Nan knew how much thinking the thoughts Lauren was could wear a person down. Eventually, the body just shut down out of self-preservation.

"You've got to eat something."

"Can I stay here with you for a while?"

Nan froze with *absolutely not* on her lips, unspoken. To have someone staying with her, living in the house around the clock? Especially someone who needed as much attention and care as Lauren did right now? She'd never get any work done.

"Lauren..."

She sat up at the sound of her name. Nan thought the naked fear on her face was ugly to witness. *I hope I never looked like that after the accident. I hope I never looked like that*, period.

"Please, you have to say yes, you *have* to let me. I think I could handle it if I was here."

"I... I don't know if that's a good idea. It might make things worse."

"It won't, I swear!"

"And you should be with your own people now, anyway. Your mom and dad, your brother..."

"They don't understand," Lauren wailed. "They're so *infuriating* sometimes. They just don't get it! But you do. You understand what it's like. And I feel so close to Trevor here. Like I can still feel him nearby."

"Listen—"

"Please say yes! I'll stay out of your way, I-I'll do whatever you want me to, I'll pay you rent, I'll work for free for the rest of my life, just please, you have to say yes!" Lauren finished this pitiful plea by snorting back phlegm and wiping her eyes on her sleeve once again.

Nan pushed her slowly back into the recliner and pulled the

blanket up to her chin. "Lay down and rest for now. We'll talk later, okay?"

"Just... just please don't say no."

"Later," Nan said. Satisfied with the not-no she'd gotten, Lauren closed her eyes once more and took a deep, shuddering breath.

Before she left the room, Nan pulled the lever on the side of the chair and popped the footrest of the recliner up. Lauren's breathing started to even out.

"She finally close her eyes, did she?" Ava asked, setting a pot of tomato soup on the stovetop with a scowl. Nan didn't care what sort of faces the old woman wanted to make so long as she made some soup and a sandwich while she did it. She acted as though her day was the only one that had been fucked up by Lauren's unannounced visit.

"I think so. She's still pretty worked up." Nan shook a cigarette out of the pack, lit it, and sipped coffee. Tea just wasn't up to the task today.

"Yup. Has a right to be, I imagine. You know what that's like."

"Better than most. She asked to stay here with me for a while."

Ava turned the heat down to low. "And you said...?"

"I said we'd talk about it later."

Ava put her hands on her hips. "Don't know as that's the best idea. Might not be the worst, though. I read a story once of a woman who lost her husband young. Car crash while they were visiting California or some such place. Felt like she couldn't live in their home anymore and bought a place right down the road from where the accident happened so she could be close by." She shook her head at the baffling human condition. "Don't know what good it coulda done for her, but she seemed happy enough. Grief can do a number on a body."

"Uh-huh." Nan didn't really give a tinker's damn what Ava

had to say on the subject of loss and grief. Her own thoughts were more than enough for the moment.

The list of reasons why it was crazy to have Lauren stay with her was as long as her leg and twice as hairy, but she found herself considering it nonetheless. It wasn't because she thought Lauren would find the closure she was looking for here (she wouldn't), and it wasn't because it would stop the rumors flying around town; if anything, it would likely add to them. No, her justification for considering it was purely selfish. She thought, maybe, that she might not be so afraid with someone else in the house with her. The fear was something very new to her, and she found that she disliked it a great deal.

Oh sure, there was the concern that Willow Hall might be a bit harder to reach with Lauren here in the house, mucking up the general atmosphere of the place... and she was a bit troubled that in searching for any trace of Trevor, Lauren might stumble into the crypt by pure dumb luck and sheer determination, but her gut told her these were minor concerns. In fact, the best reason she could find to allow this to happen was that she felt the voice didn't want it to. Why it felt that way, Nan couldn't puzzle out, but with a few ground rules in place, it could be just the thing both of them needed right now.

When she looked up again, Ava was gone, and the soup was close to boiling over. Nan got up, turned off the heat, and finished putting the meal together.

Impossible woman, she thought.

-4-

Nan's bedroom was in the northwest corner of the house, above the living room, and just below her office. There was something comforting about being close to her manuscript pages, as if the secret entrance to Willow Hall was just above her head. The room she put Lauren in was kitty-corner from her own, at the top of the stairs. She would have liked to have put her in the attic, but the thought of hearing footsteps overhead at night made her uncomfortable. The southeast bedroom had the added bonus of being on the driveway side of the house, so Lauren couldn't just sit and stare out at the riverbank from her bedroom window all day.

It was late by the time they got back from Lauren's modest little ranch house on the other side of town, with a couple of suitcases of clothes for her and the T-rex figure from Trevor's dresser she had insisted on bringing. Lauren had crumbled almost immediately upon entering her house, so in the essence of time, her mother and Nan had done most of the packing. Her parents looked hurt when she told them the news, as only parents could, but in the end, they understood (and, Nan thought, looked a little relieved at being able to head back down south).

Now, back at Holt House, Lauren was calmer, almost like she had taken a sedative. She and Nan ate dinner together —Lauren managed half of the chicken and green beans on her plate, which was a good start—and then, because both of them were exhausted, they turned in at around eight o'clock.

But Nan didn't fall asleep right away. It was strange knowing someone else was in the house, some living breathing creature so near to where she now lay staring at the ceiling. In a way, it made her feel exposed. She hadn't really thought of it before, but she supposed in the years Nick and Lizzie had been gone, she'd gotten quite used to being alone in the big, rambling house. More than used to it, if you wanted to tell the truth. She'd grown to like her solitude.

A floorboard creaked in the hallway, and Nan sat up. There were a few timid, hollow-sounding footsteps. She squinted into the dark, waiting for her door to open or for someone to start pounding on it, but there was nothing more.

Just Lauren trying to find the bathroom. Nothing to worry about.

She lay back, but her guard was still up. Since agreeing to allow Lauren to stay, there had been this feeling inside her that something was starting to happen. None of the usual precursors to her headaches had appeared yet, thank God, so it wasn't that, but it felt similar. And, of course, there was still the problem with Sheriff Lambert looming on the horizon, but that was nothing new (and nothing she couldn't handle).

What she was sensing now was bigger than all of that. Like something old was coming to fruition. No, not old. Something *ancient.*

For one insane moment, she thought about throwing off the covers, running outside to the river, and just plunging into the water that had surged with the recent snow, letting the muddy brown serpent carry her off wherever it wanted to.

She strained her ears, listening. There were no more footsteps outside her door, so *that* was okay. Maybe now she could get some sleep. Yet when she closed her eyes, that creeping sense of dread remained. It was a long time before she could let that go long enough for sleep to sneak in like a parent with a pillow to hold over their child's face. But eventually, it did.

-5-

Outside in the real world, it was almost Christmas, but in her dream, it was Halloween, and she, Nick, and Lizzie were all in the dining room, pumpkins laid out on top of the newspaper that covered the tabletop. Time had slipped backward.

Well, of course it had. Looking down, she saw a tumbler of scotch in her hand with her lipstick along the rim. This wasn't her first glass. Who cared if this was only a dream? Her mouth was watering, and it wasn't like she would *actually* be falling off the wagon. Like sex, it didn't count as cheating if it happened in a dream.

She took a gulp, then gagged and sputtered, drooling it back into the glass as her gorge rose. It tasted like shit. Or, more appropriately, like death, as if someone had filled her glass with the liquid from the bottom of a casket. It was beyond foul and coated her tongue greasily.

It's not fair, goddamnit! Even in my dreams, I'm not allowed to do what I want! The desire to smash the glass on the floor grew within her, but what would be the point? Instead, she twirled it back and forth lazily between her palms, listening to her wedding ring clink against it.

Across the table, Lizzie was standing on a chair, leaning over a pumpkin almost as big as she was. Nick had sliced the top off it and helped her scoop out the guts into a big glass bowl. Later, they would separate the seeds from the meat and pulp and then roast them for a snack while they watched this year's spooky movie (*The House on Haunted Hill* with Vincent Price; Nan had chosen it, of course). Nick sipped a beer. *His first and probably only*, she thought, sneering.

Lizzie was bald again, looking not unlike a pumpkin herself. The lights overhead were shining off of her skull, which Nick had freshly shaved that afternoon so that they could apply the zombie makeup to it and make her look like her head was cracked open.

Nan sulked, watching the lights across the river through the big bay window. Halloween held no enjoyment for her anymore. As a kid Lizzie's age, it had been her favorite time of the year. Dressing up like something scary, walking a half mile down the street to the Lawson's farm, with her father holding her hand and breathing beer and cigar smoke down at her when he spoke (to tell ghost stories, naturally). Because they were their only neighbors and the only place Nan could trick-or-treat, the Lawsons always gave her tons of candy, which she ate most of after getting back home.

But she couldn't trick-or-treat with Lizzie. She wasn't *allowed* to. Even if she'd been healthy enough, Nick wouldn't have let them go, blaming it on the crazies. That's what he called the people who came out of the woodwork this time of year and magically found their way to Holt House. Mostly, the crazies would just gather at the gate at the end of the driveway as if they'd just made a pilgrimage to Medjugorje instead of the house of a fat, old horror writer.

Sometimes, they did more than that, though. The time that had finally made Nick put his foot down about the whole trick-or-treating business, a man wearing a long black slicker and a scary bird mask had jumped the fence and come up to the house. Luckily, Nick had seen him sneaking up the driveway and called the cops. Before the guy could disappear, Nick ran outside with the baseball bat he kept in the umbrella stand by the front door and held the guy against the garage wall with it until Lambert showed up. The bird mask wasn't the only scary thing he'd had on him either. Beneath his black slicker, he had concealed a length of rope, a handful of cable ties, and a knife. He claimed they were just a part of his costume, but no one bought that, and he'd been hauled off to jail. After this, Nick decreed trick-or-treating was just too dangerous given Nan's celebrity and the crazies that brought with it. So each year, on October 28th or so, they put up signs at the end of the driveway saying anyone caught trespassing would be prosecuted to the fullest extent of the law. Instead of going out on Halloween, they threw their own little parties, buying Lizzie all the candy she could want just like the Lawsons had done for Nan as a little girl.

Even though the bird man had been scary, people like him were in the minority, and Nan thought Nick's reaction was overcautious overparenting. But there was no point fighting with him about it. Fighting was all they seemed to do together anymore, and it was exhausting.

"Daddy, it's sticking to my hands and it's all stringy," Lizzie said. Nan rolled her eyes as she continued to roll the scotch glass between her hands.

"Here, princess, let me help."

"I'm a zombie, Daddy, not a princess."

"How about a zombie princess?"

Lizzie giggled, which turned into a coughing fit. Nick carefully pulled the stringy pulp from her fingers and threw it into the bowl on the table. When he did, the bowl changed. It no longer held pumpkin seeds and guts but wads of green meat and a slurry of unidentifiable organs. Flies buzzed somnolently around the lip and crawled over the surface. Nan's mouth flooded with the taste of decomposition again. She looked down at her glass and saw it was filled with the same festering putrescence as the pumpkin bowl.

Decay and rot, Little Punk, a voice croaked from inside the dumbwaiter. She watched the dark opening but could see nothing within. Neither Nick nor Lizzie seemed to hear anything at all.

"What if I... put some on your face." Nick shouted, and Lizzie squealed with delight as he dipped his finger into the nightmare bowl and wiped a black clot of blood on the end of her nose.

Nan blinked. The bowl was just cheerful orange pumpkin guts again, and the clot on Lizzie's nose was just a seed. She burped acid and raised the scotch to her lips before remembering and slamming the glass onto the table with frustration, slopping the coppery liquid up over the rim.

A sickening pulse started behind her eyes. She scrunched them closed, and when she opened them again, she was in a hospital room with bilious yellow walls and an underlying smell of industrial cleanser. Nick was sitting in a chair on the other side of the hospital bed, his hands clasped together beneath his chin. His eyes were worried.

Lizzie was in the bed between them, thin and frail beneath the flimsy sheet soaked with sweat. Her eyes were closed, the lids dusted lavender with fine blue threads of veins woven through.

"Would it be the worst thing in the world?" Nan knew this was the wrong thing to say but said it anyway. Part of her wanted to hurt Nick. The rest wanted this to stop hurting her. "She's in pain all the time. Would it be so terrible if she decided to just... let go?" Now that it was out in the open, a weight was lifted from her chest. The awful thought no parent should harbor, let alone give voice to, was out in the world, and there was no taking it back.

"You're a fucking *ghoul*," Nick said, his voice shaking. "Jesus Christ, how could you say that? How can you even think it? Don't you have a heart at all? She's our daughter. She hasn't even had a life yet!"

"What sort of life will it be for her? What sort of life will it be for *us*?"

Nick sat back, stunned. "Is that really what you're concerned with right now? That *you* don't get to have a life and travel and do whatever your heart desires when you want to?" His eyes brimmed with tears, but they didn't fall. "How fucking selfish are you?"

The hospital flickered out of focus like light from a malfunctioning florescent tube, and when it stabilized again, Nan found herself in the crypt beneath Holt House. Lizzie's hospital bed rested on the plinth, and Nick sat on the other side, his face unchanged. Bloated, blackened hands reached up all around them from the dirt, which was mounded up into a hill beneath them. They were searching for her, patting and writhing blindly in the glow of the one hospital room light overhead.

Then she was back in the hospital room, clean and antiseptic, but the sound of the searching hands remained. "*You're* the one who's being selfish," she told Nick. "Putting her through this every fucking time. Hooking her up to all these tubes and shit, force-feeding her when she's too sick to eat, letting her body die in painful little fucking increments because you can't let her go..."

"The doctor said there's a good chance she'll respond to this treatment!" he thundered, and when he did, the room darkened, as if his fury had taken physical form and blotted out the light. "This isn't the time we should be letting her go; this is the time we need to fight for her!"

"I'm so *fucking* tired!" Nan shouted back. People in the rooms around theirs could hear the fight, but she didn't care. Their shadows passed by on the other side of the room's window. There were a lot of them out there. "I'm so tired of worrying, of planning only to have it fall apart, of *hoping* that this time, *this fucking time* something will be different and she'll get better only to have this shit happen again, and again, *and again!*"

Lizzie groaned and frowned in her drugged sleep, but her eyes stayed closed.

"You think *I'm* not tired, too? When you're off doing your readings and signing and tours and whatever else you think is so damn important, who do you think is the one at home taking care of her, huh? Fucking magic fairies? No, it's me! I'm the one up with her all night long, rubbing her back and cleaning up vomit, changing her sheets when she has an accident, reading to her, and telling her everything's going to be okay! *ME!*"

"Where do you think the money for these treatments come from? You think your job as a math teacher would have paid for half the shit we've tried? She would have been dead *years* ago if it weren't for me! I'm not out having a grand time while you're home taking care of her. I'm doing my best to hold it together until I get back!"

"Then why don't you ever call when you're on the road?"

"Because you make me feel guilty about being gone, just like you are now!"

"Why not call Lizzie and check in then? You don't have to

talk to me if you don't want to, but I have to explain to her how busy you are every time she asks me why you don't call."

Nan shook her head and laughed humorlessly. "I swear to God, Nick, If I had known it would be like this…"

"You what? Would have gotten rid of her like you wanted to?"

"Well? Look what she's going through now. Look what she's had to endure every day of her life! And so what if it goes into remission? There's nothing saying it won't come back again like it has every other time. Her entire life from here on out is going to be dictated by this thing, cursed by it, *ruined* by the fact that one day that switch might just flip again, and that'll be the time she won't bounce back. So if she's going to die anyway, yeah, it would have been better if I had listened to my gut instead of letting you manipulate me into keeping her. At least then, we would have had a life together. When she dies, what's left for us now?" Her voice rang out and then fell silent. From the hallway came the sounds of shuffling feet and the low murmur of many voices conferring.

"I hate you," Nick said.

"I hate you, too."

Lizzie started to stir. Her eyes fluttered delicately, and then… Nick was gone. A second later, so was the hospital room and the bed with Lizzie in it, like a room in a stage play when the overhead light winks out, and the stagehands rush around in the dark rearranging everything so when the lights come back on…

Nan was sitting at the dining room table, a scotch in her hand, staring out across the river through the bay window at the pinpoints of light on the other side.

She sniffed, and her mouth watered. The scotch was really scotch this time. Before she could drink, movement from her right caused her to turn and see her daughter sitting across the table from her. What little of Lizzie's skin was left was brown and runny. She was grinning, not because she wanted to, but because there was no flesh around her mouth to prevent it. The surface of the road had peeled it away like the skin of a boiled tomato. Small pieces of asphalt were still visible, embedded in her neck, which boiled and undulated with (*termites*) maggots hidden below the surface.

Nan set the glass down carefully. Nick picked it up. He was sitting on her left in his accustomed seat, looking no better than Lizzie, and when he grabbed the drink, it squeezed the liquid from his palm (*corpse juice, like what I drank*, she thought), causing it to run like dirty rain down the side of the glass and onto the table. He drank her scotch, spilling some on the lapels of the suit she had buried him in. It was no worse for the wear, though. A greenish blue moss had spread along the fabric, which was dotted with gray and shriveled mushrooms that had somehow grown down there in the dark.

Lizzie slammed her palms flat onto the tabletop, making Nan jump. The little girl scrambled onto the table on her hands and knees and seemed to skitter across the surface like a bug.

"You would have gotten rid of her like you wanted to," she said in Nick's voice, watching Nan with eyes that drifted loosely in their sockets. They were red, as if she had been crying for a long time.

Nan retched. "Yes," she said. "Yes, I would have."

"The doctor said there's a good chance she'll respond to this round of treatments."

"You weren't going to. What happened was a blessing." A tear ran down her face.

"You never loved her."

"No!" Nan shouted immediately. "That's not true. I loved you so much. So, *so* much."

Lizzie opened her mouth, but no words came out this time. What did was a banshee shriek, something older than the stone that Holt House was built from; older than the planet and the universe that contained it.

Nan tried to cover her ears, but her arms wouldn't move, as if they were caged at her sides. Something hot trickled from her left nostril down over her lips, and she tasted copper and salt. "*I hate you!*" she roared, scrunching her eyes closed.

Something touched her lips that felt at first like wriggling bone worms. It took a moment for her to realize they were Lizzie's fingers brushing delicately against her skin, spongy, brown, and stinking. Then, with a sudden speed, Lizzie jabbed her fingers forward, trying to cram them into Nan's mouth. Nan clamped her lips down like a kid refusing a spoonful of bad-tasting medicine, but Lizzie kept pushing, and when that didn't work, she used her dirt-clotted nails to wrench Nan's lips apart, leaving bloody furrows behind. Nan cried out and when she did, Lizzie shoved her arm forward, stuffing her entire hand —a hand Nan had held and kissed when it was so small it could fit many times over in the palm of her own—into her mother's mouth, cutting off all of her breath. Nan's mouth flooded with the taste of death, and she tried to drag air into her lungs. Even the teensiest sip of it would feel ambrosial, but there was none to be had. Her heart thudded in the blackness of her chest, and her eyes flew open, and Nan found herself looking down into Lizzie's horrific open maw in which things squirmed and snaked in the darkness. Her jaws somehow creaked wider as she tried to scream with her dead daughter's hand blocking her airway, and Lizzie used this leverage to force her arm down all the way to her rotting wrist.

Thankfully, it was here the dream blew apart like a dandelion puffball in the breeze.

Nan was sitting up, her bedside lamp on and the drawer of her nightstand open. Claudia's phone was in it, covered with some foul-smelling liquid. She hadn't seen it since her dream the night before Trevor went missing. But that wasn't all that was in there. Sitting beside the phone was a small blue SD card, which Nan recognized at once. It was the same one she had taken from Claudia's camera after killing her. The one that *showed* her doing it. She stared into that drawer for a long time before slowly pushing it closed.

Getting out of bed as quietly as possible, Nan crept down the hallway, avoiding all the places she knew the floor squeaked and creaked, and put her ear to the door of Lauren's room. She was inside talking to someone, speaking quietly so her voice wouldn't carry.

Who the hell could she be talking to? Who indeed. There was no man in her life as far as Nan knew, and her parents said they were going to turn in early so they could catch their morning flight back to South Carolina.

Nan waited outside the door for a long while, trying to make out what Lauren was saying, but the words didn't sound like actual words to her, just muted gibberish. Eventually, deciding this was a fool's errand, she sneaked back to her own room and climbed into bed, but wasn't tired. So, instead, she propped herself into a seated position against her headboard and watched her door, waiting for it to open and for Lauren (or someone) to come sneaking in.

That was how she fell asleep.

-6-

The dream, or some variation of it, continued to come to Nan over the next few nights. Before Lauren came to Holt House and upset the balance, there had been no dreams (except for the Christmas one Nan barely remembered). Their resurgence had put Nan on edge. The logical part of her mind knew it wasn't Lauren's fault, but that part was shrinking by the day. The larger, nastier part was demanding she blame the one who had intruded on this very delicate ecosystem, imposing herself on Holt House and knocking everything out of whack.

To add insult to injury, Lauren had begun commenting on how tired Nan looked and asking her if everything was all right. Not that she could really blame her for saying anything. Nan knew how tired she looked. The morning after the dream, she saw the first emergence of purple bruises encircling both of her eyes. These had only deepened in the following days. It was as if having another person in close proximity once again had caused her to become more anxious. In fact, she felt like she had during her first days of rehab when the booze was still working itself out of her system. She wanted scotch when she woke up in the morning along with her cigarette, and again at midday while writing (which was also suffering some with her new house-guest). She wanted booze so often it would have been easier to say when the craving wasn't there. Her hands shook, her heart raced, and she had almost no appetite left. When she did eat, she became nauseated immediately afterward.

Perhaps worse than all of this was the fact that her insomnia had returned as well. So now she could sit up at night wishing for the numbing peace of cravingless sleep while feeling her body dying an inch at a time, knowing when sleep finally did come, it would be riddled with dream memories and visions of her decaying family.

At least she would be getting a few hours of peace today. One of the stipulations of Lauren's staying at Holt House was that she go and see a therapist to deal with her grief. Lauren had balked at first, which was a typical small-town reaction, where talking to someone was considered airing your dirty laundry in public, but Nan had insisted. Even though Lauren had thrown a monkey wrench into her life, Nan still liked the woman. This aside, her edict wasn't *strictly* an altruistic one. Taking care of someone (especially a *grieving* someone) wasn't really in her bailiwick anymore; looking after Lizzie had used up all of her give-a-shit as far as taking care of people was concerned. The tank had just run dry. Nobody's fault, really. And, if a therapist came with the added benefit that Nan would get the house to herself again for a few hours a week, where was the harm in that? It wasn't like she was sending Lauren out to score meth or anything. A quick internet search provided them with the name

Dr. Neema Stewart, a grief therapist in White Plains who had availability.

Lauren was sitting on the bench by the front door, staring catatonically across at the mirror hanging on the other side, clutching her purse in her lap.

"I'm nervous."

"You'll be okay."

"Are you sure you can't come with me?"

Nan had been prepared for this. It was no different than getting a child out the door on their first day of school. "I have to work today. You'll do just fine. And besides, getting out of the house will be good for you. Get some fresh air. You can stop and grab something to eat if you want. Make a day of it."

Lauren nodded, but Nan wasn't sure she was actually listening. She had seemed distracted the last couple of days. "I'm not really hungry."

"That's fine. Just go to your appointment, then. I guarantee it will help." Her phone chimed in her pocket, and she pulled it out. The app for the security cameras had been going off all morning, alerting her to motion disturbances from each of the five cameras, but when she looked, there was nothing there. She almost didn't look this time, but better safe than sorry.

The video started to play, showing the sheriff's car turning down her driveway, moving cautiously on the ice-slicked gravel.

Shit. What now?

There was no way of telling if it was Sanders or Lambert behind the wheel, but this wasn't good news either way. At least Ava was out of town to celebrate an early Christmas with her brother in Southern California. She'd be back in a few days to have a *real* Christmas, as she put it, with snow and cold and no fruity palm trees. Muriel wasn't posted up in her usual spot yet, either. Another stroke of luck.

"It's the sheriff coming up the driveway," she said, and Lauren perked up immediately.

"Do you think they found him? Did they find Trevor?"

"I don't know. Let's head out and see." If nothing else, at least it would get her off the bench without being dragged. "Don't get your hopes up too high, okay? Let's hear what he has to say."

Lauren wasn't listening. She was out on the porch, her purse forgotten on the floor where it had fallen from her lap. Nan scooped it up before heading out herself.

The weather was supposed to be clear and cold for the next few days, and the previous week's snow was still on the ground, crusty and turning dingy. The sheriff's car crunched to a stop, and Lambert got out. He was alone today. That could only mean one thing, Nan thought.

"Sheriff," she said, but this was lost in Lauren's babbling. She practically pawed at him as he tried to negotiate the slippery walk, not an especially easy task for the fat, graceless man.

"Is it Trevor? Did you find him? Is he okay?"

"No change," Lambert said in his usual tactless manner, and Lauren's face fell. "Still got the notice out, still gettin' tips and calls, but nothing's panned out yet. I'll keep ya posted if anything else comes along. T'day I'm here to chew the fat with this little lady."

He left her standing in the driveway and waddled up the stone steps.

"That's really charming, Sheriff."

"That's me. Charming as hell."

Nan took Lauren's purse to her and helped her into the car. "I'll try to see if he's got any more information, okay? Just don't worry about it now. Go on to your appointment and let me deal with him."

Lauren nodded and then sat behind the wheel for a full two minutes before seeming to remember where she was and what she was doing. She started the engine and backed awkwardly around the sheriff's car before disappearing up the driveway, the holey muffler making its presence known for a long time after she left.

"Probably shouldn't be behind the wheel," Lambert said, watching the bluish cloud of oil Lauren's sedan left in its wake. "Oh well."

"What do you want, Chester?"

Nan had left the front doors cracked a little, and Lambert pushed them all the way open with his meaty hands. The gargoyle over the door grinned down lecherously. "Invite me in, why dontcha, cold as a well digger's asshole out here."

"First, why don't you tell me where your shadow is. Will Sanders be joining us? Because if so, I'd rather just talk right out here."

"Nope. Just me n' you. You got any more of them cookies you had last time?" He was already in the foyer, moving down the hall toward the steps leading to the kitchen.

Nan rushed after him, grabbed his arm, and jerked him to a stop. "Cut the shit, Chester, I know why you're here. I'm not giving you any more money, so just get the hell out of my house."

She'd thought he would look frustrated or maybe angry, but he was amused. "Well, I thought you might take that attitude. I got some information you might wanna hear b'fore making up your mind. So why dontcha be neighborly and fix me some coffee."

"I don't care what you have to say! Get the fuck out, now!" Her voice echoed off the stone floor.

"Sanders is dead."

Nan's mouth fell open almost all the way to her chest "Dead? How?"

"Well, why don't me and you sit down all civilized like, and have us a cuppa coffee and a little chat? What do you say?"

"What does that have to do with anything?"

Without answering, he resumed his portly waddle to the stairs. As soon as her mind had caught up with the rest of her, Nan followed, turning the information over in her head, but by the time she got down to the kitchen, she was none the wiser about what impact this could possibly have on their arrangement.

Chester had made himself comfortable at the table, helping himself to what was left of Nan's bacon and eggs (which was most of it. After the dream in which her daughter tried to reach down her throat and perform a tonsillectomy on her, Nan had lost much of her appetite). She cleared the rest of the breakfast dishes and dumped them in the sink.

Chester's breath rushed loudly through his nose as he ate... although eating was a civilized act. This was more like attacking his mouth with food. She turned away and lit a cigarette, nauseated by what her mother would have deemed "feeding time at the zoo."

"Spit it out, Chester. What you came here to say, I mean, not the food. You seem to be doing just fine in that department."

He wiped his mouth demurely with the tablecloth, forcing a grimace onto Nan's face, and said, "Don't seem awful sad to hear about the good undersheriff's passing."

"I'm not. Tell me what's going on."

He shrugged. "Just one of those things, you know how it is. Got a call last night about a break-in out at the industrial park, one of those big warehouses, you know." He shoved more eggs into his already crowded mouth and talked through them. "Sanders musta surprised the guy 'cause whoever it was blew his face clean off with a shotgun, then skedaddled right on out of there nice as you please. Boys from state police forensics are going through the place with a fine-tooth comb, but they won't find nothing." The news certainly didn't seem to be impacting the sheriff's appetite. He snagged a piece of buttered toast from a plate on the counter nearby and sprayed its crumbs all over the table, too. "Sad damn thing. Hell of a nice guy. Least he didn't have no wife or kids."

Lambert couldn't be saying what she thought he was saying.

Could he? It sure as hell *sounded* like he was. "Where were you when the call came in?"

"Had a bit of an upset tummy last night, bad shellfish or something, you know how it goes, so I ran down to the drugstore there on Main to get some antacid. Just—"

"One of those things?"

Another shrug, another grin. "One of those things," he agreed.

Nan narrowed her eyes and watched Chester Lambert eat. "Looks like your tummy is just fine now."

"Twenty-four-hour bug musta been. Lots of those little buggers going around this winter. Should go and get your flu jab before there aren't any left. Wanna make sure you stay nice and healthy, don't we?"

It sounded like a threat because it *was* a threat.

After a few more minutes of listening to his lips smacking, Nan said, "Why are you telling me this, Chester? What's this got to do with me?"

"Well, now, I'm glad you asked." His plate was empty and he pushed it away with a soft belch. "Can I bum one o' them?" Nan handed him a cigarette, and he lit it and leaned back in his chair, his belt squeaking. "Before he met with his unfortunate accident, Sanders cornered me in the shitter down to the sheriff's department and spoke kinda mean to me. You know how mean he could be. Well, he tole me that he knew all about our little arrangement from way back and that he was going to take that information and go right to the press with it. Details News, that little peach, Claudia's station. Couldn't go to the state boys with it; he was afraid they'd just bury the whole thing. Maybe he was right about that. But a trial in the court of public opinion? Lot easier than proper channels, I imagine."

"How do you know he didn't already?"

"Dumb sonofabitch wanted me to drop outa the election so it would go to him. Said if I did, he'd make the whole thing go away.

Seen one too many TV shows, sounds like, but that's neither here nor there." He shook his head. "You believe that shit? Fight blackmail with blackmail. How do you like that? You gotta love his sense of irony." He tapped his ashes into the drying yolk on his plate. "After his accident, I found the file he made about us in his desk. Got most of the way toward figuring it all out, but I'll be damned if I know how. I didn't talk, and I know you didn't... right?"

The way he looked at her when he said that frightened her, though she didn't let on. It was like being looked at by some Mafia don who was deciding whether or not you could be trusted. All traces of the backwoods bumbling sheriff were gone. This man sitting across from her was one she hadn't met before, and she didn't like him one bit.

"I know how to keep my mouth shut, Chester."

"I'll just bet you do. Like about that Claudia McKinnon who went missing."

She stared at him but said nothing.

"No matter anyway. Here's what does. And listen up, this is the part that concerns you." He leaned forward, exhaling smoke into her face as he did. Up this close, she could see the broken blood vessels in his eyes and the tip of his nose and could smell more than bacon and eggs on his breath. The smell that wafted out of him was brown and disgusting, yet familiar. "You're gonna extend our arrangement in exchange for services rendered."

"Extend? What services?"

"Tack on a little interest to the principal, like. I still keep m'mouth shut about your drinking and driving accourse, that goes without saying, and I make sure you don't have nothing to worry about in the future. Not from Sanders, may he rest in peace... and not from Muriel Duckworth either."

Nan blinked and sat back. "Are you saying—"

"I'm not saying nothing at all. We're just talking here, right? Two old pals."

"And what if I don't want to go along with that? I had

nothing to do with Sanders, and you're just as guilty as I am for taking that bribe."

Lambert gave her a look that said, *come on, I thought you were smarter than this.* "You don't wanna play ball, that's your right, sure. But I think if that's the case, I might hafta pick Muriel up and ask her some questions about what you were doing last night when that tip for Sanders came into the office. She keeps such neat little notes in her book there."

"I was home. I can prove it. Lauren was here with me all night."

Lambert sat back again and folded his hands over his big belly, the last of the cigarette clamped between his teeth. He had to squint his eyes against the smoke, making him look like he was winking. "Here's an interesting little factoid. You ready for this? Did you know that in this town, there's still three functioning payphones?"

"What? I don't care, what does—"

"One down to the library that the kids use for selling dope still, just like back in my day when I was only knee-high to a grasshopper. Then there's another right out on Main Street by Pepperelli's Pizza, but that one's in a high-traffic area. Hard to make a call unnoticed from there, ain't it?" He grinned. "Any guess where the third is?"

She didn't have to guess. She knew. If you took a right out of her driveway onto Little Church Road and followed that down a couple of miles toward Route 9, you came to a place where Little Church intersected Fisher Rd. On the left sat a low-roofed, squat building with a big faded sign on the top that used to say CROSSROADS GAS. A falling tree from a storm a few winters back had knocked off the CRO, and some wit had spray painted an A, so it now read ASSROADS GAS, but it was a pretty well-known landmark. Those same dopers who liked to hang around outside the library also liked to skateboard and break bottles (and probably smoke some of that dope) out back of the Crossroads Gas Station. Right where the payphone was.

"Take you only a handful of minutes to get down there, call, and get back, I'd bet," Lambert said, tapping his chin. "Lauren goes off to bed, you zip out real quick... no cameras out there, neither. I seem to remember Sanders saying it sounded like a woman's voice on the line."

"Who'd you get to make the call? Muriel? What did you offer her? That I would get arrested for Ducky?"

"You know something? I bet you if I pulled the records for that phone, it would show a call made at the same time our robbery tip came in. What do you think about that? Willing to bet your life on it?"

"Enough." She held up her hands. "Just enough. I get the picture, okay? Stop with the fucking theatrics already. Just tell me what you want."

He hooked the pack of smokes with his finger and shook another out. "Way I figure it, having to lie to the state boys—if it comes to that, you understand—and make sure you're not bothered by nothing from here on out..." He exhaled a plume of smoke. "I'd say a million sounds fair."

"Jesus fucking *Christ*, Chester! A million dollars. You want a million dollars. You think I have a *million dollars* just lying around the house, squirreled under the mattress or buried in an old mayonnaise jar in the yard that I keep just in case of a rainy day?"

"Just un-wad your damn panties, all right? I didn't say I wanted it *now*, did I? God, you freaking women, I swear, you hear what you wanna hear. I'll give you a couple o' days to pull it together. Call it... let's say Christmas Eve. And before you even start spurting and sputtering that you can't, just shut up, awright? I know you can. I know how much you got and I know how much is liquid."

Nan clenched her jaw. She was having a little difficulty breathing but didn't want Lambert to know that. "Listen, you stupid cocksucker, I can't just get that much money in cash together in a couple of days. I don't have a checking account with a million dollars in it. It's all over the place."

"I got faith you'll figure it out. You seem to think you're awful smart. Well, here's your chance to prove it."

"How do I know once I give you the million, you won't come back for more, huh? Where's my guarantee?"

"Guarantees are a sucker's game, little lady. Short answer is, ya don't know. Guess you'll have to just trust good old Sheriff Lambert on that one." He patted his belly again, a strange gesture given the tenor of the conversation. "Speaking of trust, I want you to trust me when I say you'd better not be thinking of running outta town or going to the state boys and telling them what I said. I got more people keeping an eye on you than Muriel Duckworth."

"Like who?"

Lambert laughed and crushed his cigarette out in the runny yolk beside his first one. "You got a good head on your shoulders, Nan. Like Sanders does. Well, like he *useta* anyway. Be a shame for you to lose it. Real shame. But you know, sometimes things like that happen." He shrugged again and pooched out his lower lip as if saying *what can ya do? It's just one of those things.*

-7-

It was amazing how quickly the smell of Lauren's things had permeated the guest room upstairs. Nan stood in the middle of it, surveying the stuff that looked out of place amongst her own.

Just after Lambert finally moseyed out to his car with that stupid shit-kicker walk of his, Nan had been furious. More than furious. If she'd had access to the nuclear launch codes she would have used them without a moment's hesitation or regret, leaving the world a smoking crater.

But then she poured herself a tumblerful of calming brown scotch and sat rolling it between her hands, listening to the distinct lack of a clink where her wedding ring used to be, breathing deeply. Inhaling the fumes from her drink made her mouth water. Of course, that part of her dream where she drank from the glass of scotch and instead got a mouthful of coffin juice crossed her mind, but she ignored it. This was real life. There was only scotch in the glass and nothing more. If she drank it, it would go down like a fucking cloud. And so would the second and third and fourth.

Which was exactly why she dumped it down the sink drain. Chester *wanted* her to drink, was probably badgering her so she would. A drunk Nan would be off her game and much more likely to do something stupid. And while there were many times in her life she questioned her intelligence (how smart can you really be if you knew you were drinking yourself to death and didn't stop?), she wasn't *that* stupid.

I have to be more careful than I have been. I didn't give that roly-poly sheriff enough credit, and now he's blindsided me.

That was really the source of her current fury. It wasn't about the million dollars, it was that Sheriff Chester Lambert had snowed her for all these years. It was galling. The man didn't seem like he would be able to pick his nose if you shoved his finger up there for him and gave him instructions. And sure, there was still a little bit of that air of stupidity around him, but she wondered if all of it was an act meant to put her at ease and get her thinking she would be able to outsmart him. Even the number he asked for... a million dollars... it was like something out of a movie. He wouldn't know what to do with that much cash if he got it (which he wouldn't be; she had already made up her mind on that count). Was it all just subterfuge?

No, she told herself, lighting a cigarette. *He isn't some sort of criminal mastermind. You've just grown complacent and gotten sloppy. The old you would have seen this coming a mile away, but you were too preoccupied by stupid shit to see it.*

No matter how he was acting now, at heart, Chester was still the man who had driven over one of those chunks of concrete they use to divide parking spaces down at Cutler's Food and Pharmacy because he'd forgotten it was there. He was the man who had accidentally shot the side of someone's barn when he tripped getting out of his cruiser when responding to a call about a potential prowler.

He's the man who murdered Sanders in cold blood.

She paused. *That* one bothered her. Lambert had never claimed to like Sanders much, always thought he was a bit of a goody-goody and too rigid in his job, but wanting to kill him? No. That had come out of left field. He just didn't seem the type, not even for all that money.

And there was something else Lambert had said that was sticking in her craw. That thing about having more than Muriel Duckworth keeping tabs on her. What had that been about?

Luckily, her mind provided an answer. The night the dream first came to her, Nan had tiptoed down the hall, listened at Lauren's door, and heard her talking to someone. Not her parents and not a man, she recalled thinking at the time. So who? What if she had been talking to Lambert?

It was paranoid thinking, but that didn't change how absolutely right it felt. Would he have put her up to this whole thing? Sent her to Holt House to pretend to be inconsolable and beg to move in just so she could keep tabs on Nan from the inside?

No, it was totally nuts. Lauren never would have agreed to do that. Unless...

Grief was one hell of a bargaining chip, and God knows Lauren wasn't thinking the clearest right now. Maybe he had told her he was going to have to suspend the investigation unless she did him a favor. It all seemed so far-fetched, yet at the same time, unsettlingly plausible. Especially with this new face Lambert was wearing now, all in control and duplicitous.

Don't forget the phone and the SD card.

Yeah, and what about those? They just happened to show back up the exact day Lauren moved in? Delivered to her bedside table drawer as if by some sadistic Santa while Nan was asleep and Lauren was wide awake?

But where would she have gotten them from?

Maybe when they were looking for Trevor and Nan was in the old part of the house, Lauren had taken them from the drawer. Or better yet, once Lambert showed up, maybe he had seen them while searching and pocketed them, knowing he would need them for leverage down the road.

She shook her head. This was just blue skying. There was only one way she could think of to know for sure.

And so now here she stood in Lauren's room, listening to the gentle noises of the house settling and keeping her ears peeled for the sound of Lauren's rusted sedan returning. It made her feel strange being in here even though it was a room in her house; Lauren was only borrowing it temporarily.

Like a predator creeping into the lair of its prey. She grinned eerily in the winter silence.

Lauren had unpacked her clothes into the dresser and closet, and Nan went through these first, not expecting to find anything, and she wasn't disappointed. Lauren's big gray cardigan hung on a hanger on the back of the bedroom door. Nan took it and wrapped herself in it.

"Cloaked in the scent," she said, unsure of what that meant or why she said it.

Beneath the window was a stack of books, most of which had come from Nan's library, books she had mostly skimmed after Nick and Lizzie's accident: *Searching for the Metaphysical, Hauntings,* and *Divining the Spiritual World.* She flipped through them but found nothing.

Lauren's perfume (an acrid smelling one Trevor had given to her last Mother's Day), powder, lotions, and deodorant were arranged fastidiously on top of the nightstand next to a glass of room temperature water and a small framed photo of Trevor.

Nan recognized it as the same one used in the missing person report. In it he was smiling and showing his missing front teeth.

What exactly are you looking for? A secret communiqué written in code from Lambert? A telegram telling her to be careful behind enemy lines?

"Shut up," Nan said absently. There had to be *something* hinting that she and Lambert were working together, but all she found was melancholy and sadness everywhere she looked. The room was large, and even though Lauren's meager possessions didn't even fill a quarter of the space, Nan went through everything twice, even going so far as to check between the folded shirts and pants in the dresser. She slammed her fist into the wall, hurting her pinky. "There's got to be something, where the fuck is it?"

The sound of an engine slowing down stole her attention. She checked her phone and saw that forty minutes had passed. Forty minutes already! It was too soon for Lauren to be coming back from her appointment, but what if she had never made it? The way she had just sat behind the wheel of her car like a battery-operated toy some kid had forgotten to charge made this seem very plausible.

The car backfired twice, then sped on down the road. Nan wiped the sweat from her forehead onto the sleeve of Lauren's cardigan. That had been close. The room wasn't trashed or anything, but it had a picked-over look that Lauren would surely notice.

It was time to put things back to rights and get out of here, but she didn't like it. It left her feeling exposed. There was something she was missing, some simple thing she was overlooking.

Something slid out from beneath the bed, rasping against the floor. Nan screamed and whirled around. Lauren's suitcases, which had been stored away beneath the bed, were now sitting halfway out into the room. Someone underneath had pushed them. A big one, medium one, and a small one for cosmetics and toiletries. *Mama bear, Papa bear, and baby makes three.* Nan got down on her hands and knees and peered into the darkness below the bed.

"Who's there?"

A creak from the hallway behind her, then silence.

She reached for the closest suitcase slowly, as though it might come to life and bite her. It was the smallest of the bags, just some cheaply made thing that didn't look like it would be able to stand up to a menacing glare, let alone a flight.

It was empty.

The mid-sized one held only Lauren's diary, which unfortunately said nothing of interest; the last entry was about a week before the picnic. That just left Papa bear.

Nan dragged it to her, keeping a weather eye on the space under the bed, and opened it, certain this was what she had been waiting for. The smoking gun. But there was nothing inside this one, either. "What? No, *goddamn* you!" She slammed the flimsy lid closed, as much as a lid like that could slam, anyway. Something made a plasticy *tink* inside the big zippered pouch in the front that she had somehow neglected to search.

She pulled the zipper slowly with fingers that felt numb, flopped the lid to the compartment open, and peered inside. What she saw filled her with dread. Claudia's cell phone and the SD card from her video camera sat side by side, covered with the same foul brown streaks as when they had been in her bedside drawer, only now the brown stuff was dried. She touched it and it flaked off.

It's not possible, she thought. *It's got to be a different phone.* It wasn't, though. She recognized the stupid pink case. There was no way of knowing if the SD card was the one that showed Claudia's murder without plugging it into her computer and watching it... yet she did know.

Wearily, she plodded to her bedroom and opened the drawer in her nightstand, which was, of course, empty. *She came in here and took them. But why? Why did she leave them for me to see only to take them back again?*

There was no way of knowing this, just like there was no way of knowing if she had watched the footage on the card. Nan didn't think so. Lauren didn't seem frightened enough for that, but you never could tell. This woman she had thought was her friend, or at least friendly, had turned out to be just as big of a Janus-faced piece of shit as everyone else.

There was only one thing left to do that would ease her mind. She couldn't help if Lauren had seen the footage, that ship had sailed, but she could make sure Lambert never got his hands on the evidence. Then, at worst, it would be her word against Lauren's, and like most things in life, money helped to grease the wheels of credibility. All she had to do was ditch the phone and SD card. But where?

The river.

Someone said this aloud from beneath the bed, but Nan hadn't heard it. It was at that moment a brilliant idea popped into her head. *I'll throw it in the fucking river.* Claudia was in the river. Why not the rest of her shit?

"I think I'm losing it," she said. No one in the empty (?) room disagreed with her. "Just too much pressure. Scotch would help calm me down, I bet. I could kill a bottle right now just like I used to." Saliva squirted into her mouth, and she swallowed it. She didn't take a drink, though. Instead, she gathered up the SD card and cellphone and carried them outside in the pocket of Lauren's sweater and down to the river.

The Hudson was a deep, impossible blue in the graying day, charged with the runoff from the last snowmelt. The temperature had dipped low since this morning, but even though she was only wearing Lauren's cardigan and a pair of jeans, she didn't feel cold in the slightest. Nick's old winter boots were faux fur lined and warm and helped her trudge through the icy crust on the ground.

She pulled the phone from her pocket with reddening

hands, turned it over a few times checking for anything that might tie it to her, and then flung it sideways like a skipping stone into the water. It caught the gray light on its screen and flashed like a fishing lure before falling with a *bloop* and was swept away.

She took out the SD card next. *What if it's not the one from Claudia's camera?* But what else could it be? It was the same blue color and the same brand. What were the odds that it held footage from Lauren and Trevor's last Christmas together or a recording of Trevor's school play?

"A million to one seems right."

It didn't matter if it did anyway. The risk of not throwing it was just too great. *That's right. Just throw it into the water. Get rid of it.*

A strange feeling came over her. "Yup. Into the water," she said. "Right into the drink." A mangy seagull landed a few feet away and looked at her with its black tar eyes. She giggled an eerily childish sound. "Remember that?" she asked the bird. "They used to call rivers and lakes and stuff *the drink*. And oceans were big drinks. And someone who was attractive was a tall drink. People used to say, 'They're a tall drink that'll go down easy...' drink like a fish is another one. I bet they said that about me more than once. 'Nan drinks like a fish.' And I did, too. Or maybe it was the fish that drank like me."

She laughed that little kid laugh again. The bird cocked its head to the side and continued watching, a sort of human intelligence on its face. Nan turned back to the raging river, massaging the SD card between her fingers compulsively. "What about, 'Eat, drink, and be merry, for tomorrow we die'? That's from the Bible, I think. I bet the nuns who used to live here liked that one. I bet they drank their fill, too, all that sacramental wine. I wouldn't mind some of that right now. No, sir, I wouldn't mind that at all. No one could stop me. Lauren wouldn't like it, but I could just kick her out. Who *could* stop me anyway… you?" She turned back to the seagull, but it wasn't there.

Under her breath, Nan started to sing "Silent Night," softly and tonelessly. It had been stuck in her head lately for some reason.

In the woods, a tree cracked from the cold, startling her, and reality crept back like a beaten dog crawling on its belly. Thinking was difficult, though. Her neurons didn't seem to want to make the necessary connections to create coherence out of what was happening. She felt something in her hand and brought it up to her face to see what it was. An SD card.

I came down to get rid of that. And… something else… what was it? Oh! The phone, that's right. The phone had already gone into the (*drink*) river, the card was the last bit of unfinished business. No, that wasn't true. Lauren's room was still a mess that would have to be fixed. The sun was already down on the other side of the house, which meant time was getting short.

You're wearing her cardigan still. And her perfume.

She looked down, surprised, barely remembering putting it on.

Get a move on. Shake your tail feathers. She snapped the card in half, tossed both pieces into the river, and watched them disappear.

The bust of Gretchen Holt on the back patio railing seemed to scowl silently as Nan crossed the snowy lawn, her arms hugging the sweater to her chest. She could feel the cold now. It was good, clarifying, as if she'd had a fever before, and this was finally knocking it back down. She felt even better once she was back inside the house. It was safe here. Out there, everything was chaos and turmoil. But inside it all made sense again. She stripped off her boots and borrowed sweater and hurried around the house, putting things back where they belonged. As she worked, her mind considered the problem of Lambert and Lauren, trying to come up with a satisfying solution while she sang "Silent

Night," under her breath. She didn't quite see the answer yet, but that wasn't cause for concern. Eventually, she would figure it out. Whether contemplating a problem with her writing or engaging in her *other* compulsion, the answer always came.

-8-

Lauren stared at the cracks in the guest room ceiling, which looked as shitty as she felt. It was the sound of Nan's footsteps overhead that had awoken her. If it hadn't been that, it would have been the headaches before too long anyway. Never in her life had she suffered from migraines until moving into Holt House, where they had come on with such suddenness and intensity she would have been worried if she cared even a little bit about dying. They only really bothered her insofar as they kept her from searching for Trevor. It was unlikely there would be any trace of him at this late date (she wasn't delusional), but as her grandmother used to say, hope springs eternal.

The migraines weren't the sole reason she felt like shit. Christmas was just a week away, and Lauren was dreading it. Over the years, she and Trevor had created their own traditions for the holidays; things that were just for the two of them. They always made cookies together (molasses softies for her, butter cookies with gobs of frosting and sprinkles for him), and watched one Christmas movie each night, saving their favorites for Christmas Eve and Christmas Day. There was the usual milk and cookies left out for Santa, and carrots for the reindeer, but they also left out a piece of hard candy for Mrs. Claus (who had to watch her figure, Lauren told him), and a couple of dog poop bags so Santa could clean up after his reindeer. Trevor had been worried that people would get upset with Santa if there was reindeer poop all over their roofs, so this had been Lauren's suggestion. On Christmas Eve, they would exchange hand-made gifts with one another over big mugs of hot cocoa flavored by dissolved mini candy canes, and then stay awake watching movies as late as they could on the couch.

This would be the first year since he was old enough to walk that she wouldn't be doing any of them.

But even this, as awful as it was, wasn't the biggest reason she felt like shit. Since arriving at Holt House, her sleep had been plagued by dreams of Trevor. But maybe dreams wasn't the right word. They weren't quite nightmares, though, so she didn't know what to call them. All she knew was that when she awoke in the morning, usually with her head throbbing, her cheeks were wet.

Trevor had come to her every night since she'd moved into Holt House. At first, he hadn't said anything. He just stood in the corner by the closet, watching her with big, wet eyes that were off-kilter. On his first visit, she thought he looked scared, but when she tried to ask him if he was, he just smiled. She didn't remember anything after that, just a feeling of creeping dread. Dreams were like that sometimes. The mundane parts stuck in your head while the in-between parts fell to the bottom of the subconscious like silt settling to the bottom of a river.

The next night, he came a little closer to her and mumbled something, but she couldn't make it out. It sounded a little like *delay* something. Just her sleeping mind throwing out things her waking mind was too overwhelmed to deal with, she thought.

But last night the dream had changed a little. He'd finally crept close enough to take her hand in his (like chunks of ice, that's what his poor little fingers had felt like), and leaned down with his lips brushing the cusp of her ear while he whispered, *decay and rot*. The words sounded familiar, probably from some book or movie. And that was all the proof she really needed that the dreams meant nothing. Nothing beyond her body trying to process her grief, at least.

Lauren hadn't told Dr. Stewart about the dreams and

didn't know if she ever would. Partly because it was embarrassing and partly because it felt like she would be making too big a deal about nothing. All parents who had lost a child probably dreamed about them at some point. Maybe not every night, but so what?

But the real reason she wasn't telling Dr. Stewart was because, in the cold light of day, it became painfully clear that these dreams *weren't* dreams at all. They weren't hallucinations, either. They were real. Trevor was really in the room with her, holding her hand and talking to her while she lay with her head on her pillow, unable to move. Sure, his fingers were ice, and his voice was different, but it was definitely him. That was the thing that worried her most and made her think that she was really going crazy. Like bouncing-your-head-off-a-padded-wall-in-the-dark-while-pissing-in-your-pants, *crazy*. Dr. Stewart would probably readily agree. She would gently pat Lauren's hand with that look of pity and tell her that Trevor was likely dead and the dreams were nothing more than wish fulfillment. Well, Lauren didn't accept that.

Whether they were dreams or not, as a result of these night-time visits, Lauren wasn't getting much sleep. And neither was Nan by the looks of it. Lauren didn't know what was going on with her, but she'd been short-tempered lately and looked like she was losing weight. That made sense, she was eating less than before. Whenever Lauren asked her about it, Nan replied to the tune of, "I'm just not feeling well, I guess there's too much on my mind," while looking at Lauren in a mistrustful way. Like Nan thought she was up to something.

Lauren knew she was an imposition and tried to be as little of one as possible, but there were times when she just zoned out, when the pain and the grief got to be so big they overwhelmed her brain and shut it down entirely, and Nan had to take care of her. Maybe that was what the looks were about. Maybe it was just that Lauren's presence in the house reminded Nan that she had lost a child of her own. Or maybe Nan had been seeing things in the house, too. Lauren had almost worked up enough nerve to ask her about it a few days ago but had chickened out at the last second. How did you ask someone something like that without them thinking it was time to take you to the funny farm?

Since that botched attempt, Lauren had decided to just put it all out of her mind but found it was easier said than done. She kept returning to the idea of ghosts (or spirits or revenants or whatever the hell you wanted to call them) throughout the day the same way your tongue seemed to find that shred of popcorn kernel between your teeth and worried at it all on its own. The more she thought about it, the more convinced she was that the Trevor she saw and talked to at night was a real metaphysical representation of her son. If only he would say something besides *decay and rot*. It was nonsense, some bit of doggerel her mind had caught and latched onto like a dying man to a life preserver.

Lauren rolled onto her side, aware she had become fixated on the cracks in the ceiling, hypnotized by them. Ava would be downstairs in the kitchen by now, even though her flight from California had gotten in late last night. Not one to rest on her laurels, was Ava. There was even the slight hint of coffee and bacon in the air. Her stomach rumbled.

Eating was still a strange thing for her; wanting and enjoying food while Trevor was missing. Dr. Stewart had explained this was normal in her deep, oddly engaging voice. "The body craves comfort and normalcy," she said. "Food provides that. There is nothing to be ashamed of, or feel guilty about." Easy for her to say.

Lauren threw back the covers and dressed quickly, pulling on her jeans from yesterday (still clean enough, and even if they weren't, who cared?), and the gray cardigan Trevor had helped her pick out a few years back. It even smelled like the perfume he had gotten her.

Ava was scrubbing the slate sink down in the kitchen and looked up when Lauren entered the room. "Morning."

"Morning," Lauren said, pouring herself a cup of coffee. It was black and strong. Hi-test, Ava called it.

"The lady of the house back in her office?"

Lauren took a sip. "I heard her walking around up there, so I guess she is. How was your trip?"

"Bah. Bakersfield," Ava said, waving the dishcloth in her hand dismissively. "Can't figure why someone who grew up here, with all this beauty and green, would settle down in a place like that. Hot and dry, flat and boxy, everything looks the same. God's dumping ground after he finished designing the rest of the world and needed a place to put the odd bits n' bobs that were left over.

"Folks walking around with hardly enough clothes on, either, not the least bit ashamed of all that skin hanging out. Oh, you wouldn't believe it. And the way the kids wear their hair."

Lauren, who had walked around with her fair share of skin on display in college, with pink dyed hair to boot, didn't comment. "Was it nice seeing your brother, at least?"

"His wife's no prize. Can't cook, got a droopy eyelid, not that she can help that, mind, but you'd think it'd humble her a little. Nope, walks around the place like butter wouldn't melt in her mouth. But then Freddy wasn't ever much of a deep thinker. Match made in heaven, you ask me."

Lauren drank her coffee and tried not to enjoy it for Trevor's sake.

"Oh, but listen to me going on and on. How are you doing? Been getting on okay?"

"Yeah, okay. You know, considering."

Ava didn't seem fooled. She raised an eyebrow, threw the drying towel over her shoulder like a waitress, and shambled over to the table. Lauren poured a cup of coffee for her, and Ava lit a cigarette, knowing Nan wouldn't mind one bit. "Come on then, tell me what's on your mind that's got you looking like you just bit into a lemon."

"It's nothing. Just Trevor, you know."

"Yup. Not easy, that's for sure. You seeing a doctor, I heard?"

Lauren flushed. "Dr. Stewart in White Plains. Nan insisted. It's the only way she'd let me stay here."

"Seems a person ought to be able to make up their own minds about what's best for them, but I guess that's not any of my business."

"I don't think it's helping, really, but talking about him is nice. Makes him feel more... here. That probably sounds stupid."

Ava squirmed a little. "Not stupid. It's how grief works. We do what we do to get by."

"I don't know how to do that. Get by, I mean. It feels like this isn't ever going to get better." Lauren's voice was cracking, but she managed not to cry.

To her credit, Ava reached across the table and briefly covered Lauren's hand with her own. "But it will."

They drank their coffee in silence for a few minutes, Ava smoking and ashing into a chipped saucer Nan kept in the cupboard for just that purpose.

Lauren felt pressure building within her to ask Ava the question she had wanted to pose to Nan about seeing things in the house, and before she could stop herself, blurted out, "Do you mind if I ask you something?" It was ludicrous, Ava was so much more hardheaded than Nan and so much less forgiving of stupidity, but something told her she could trust this woman not to embarrass her or make her feel like a lunatic. Besides, Lauren knew she had to confide in someone about it or she would explode.

Ava frowned in a thinking sort of way. "I suppose. But I reserve the right not to answer."

Lauren's heart was hammering. Now that the moment was

here, she wasn't sure she wanted an answer, but there was no way she would chicken out twice. Something like this couldn't be attacked head-on, however, so she said, "What do you think happens when we die?"

Ava blinked. "Well... Bible tells us the good folks of the world go to Heaven, the bad folks to Hell, and those who are unbaptized or need to spend a little time thinking about what they did, wind up in Purgatory for a spell."

"Is that *all* you believe?"

"I don't go in for all that reincarnation malarky, just seems like New Age nonsense the hippies trotted out so they could do drugs and sleep around without guilt. And I don't believe we just wink out like a candle, either. There's too much evidence to the contrary for that. No, I suppose God made it pretty clear what happens when the party here is done."

"What about..." Lauren swallowed and then made herself continue. "What about spirits? Ghosts, I mean. Do you believe in them?" She expected the old woman's mouth to tick up at the corners and laughter to come boiling out, but Ava just made that thinking frown again. After a few moments of silence, during which her embarrassment grew rampantly, Lauren sputtered, "Never mind, just... just forget it, okay? I think I'm overtired. I haven't been sleeping."

Ava did smile then, but it wasn't cruel. "Just calm yourself. Isn't exactly a groundbreaking question you're posing to me here. You're not the first to wonder about this, and Lord knows you won't be the last. Just give me a moment to get my ducks in a row. It's not exactly what I thought you'd be asking me."

Lauren did, taking another sip of her coffee while Ava crushed out her cigarette and immediately lit another one, something she rarely did while working. "You're not starting to buy into that whole *Holt House curse* thing, I hope. That's pure foolishness through and through." Lauren shook her head. The idea of a curse was asinine. "Don't misunderstand me. This house has seen more than its share of human misery, that's true enough, but some houses are just like that. Has something to do with the people who live in 'em... and sort of infect them with their negativity, I think. It gets into the walls, like radiation, and can make you sick. Or maybe it's not the people but the places themselves. Some houses have radon, some have asbestos, some have misery."

She looked slightly embarrassed to be saying this but, in true Ava fashion, plowed ahead anyway, determined to have her say. "As far as ghosts go, or hauntings or whatever you want to call it... well, I suppose the best way to say it is like this; I'm of a divided mind on it, if you'll indulge the hemming and hawing for a minute. Book of Ecclesiastes basically says the dead don't have anything left to do here on Earth, so I guess that would mean any spirit or ghost we think we see wouldn't be a ghost at all, but rather some sort of... well, *demon*, I suppose would be the word. But then, on the other hand, there's the Holy Ghost, and *He* certainly isn't a demon, so there's that to consider."

"I'm not sure I'm following you."

Ava shrugged. "I suppose it means that what the Bible's got to say on that subject ought to be taken with a grain of salt. In situations like that, I tend to believe my own eyes and ears above all else. Probably some people who wouldn't like that, but they don't have to live with my choices. I do."

"Have you ever... seen anything that's made you think there could be something after? Something outside of Heaven, Hell, and Purgatory?"

Ava exhaled a cloud of smoke and looked into Lauren's eyes with a startling frankness. "Why are you asking me this?"

I've come this far, Lauren thought. *I may as well put it all out there.* But now that the moment to bring another person into this secret was here, she wasn't quite sure how to begin. So she just dived in.

"I've been seeing Trevor here. At night. I must be sleeping when I do, but it doesn't feel like I am. It feels real, like he's in the room with me. He touched my hand last night, and I *felt* it." She took a deep breath and waited. Now that it was out there, it didn't seem to have the same power it had before. And yet, she found it hard to meet Ava's gaze, choosing instead to stare at her hands. "So, what do you think? Am I crazy or what?"

Ava was pensive for a moment, then said, "I think if we're gonna have this conversation it might go easier with a bit of liquid courage, even so early in the morning. What do you say? I know where the Missus still keeps a bottle."

She hobbled her way over to the cupboard beside the refrigerator without waiting for an answer and grabbed the bottle of scotch from the back. It appeared emptier than it had been the last time she'd seen it, but so what if it was? That wasn't any of her business.

"Healthy slug will do it, I think. Just one apiece, no cause to get soused. That won't help anyone." Lauren thought the healthy slug Ava poured was more than enough to get her soused but took a sip anyway. It burned going down but in a good way. Ava took a gulp from her own cup, smacked her lips, and sighed. The hair on the old woman's arm was sticking straight up.

"What is it, Ava? Did you see something?"

"You sure you want to hear this? Might only upset you."

Lauren chewed her bottom lip. "I guess I have to. I need... I don't even know what I need anymore. I think I just have to figure out if I'm really nuts for thinking it could be him instead of being just a dream. If whatever you have to say could help me do that, I want to hear it."

"Fair enough." Ava took another gulp and puffed on her cigarette in a manic way that was totally unlike her. "You'll think I'm a foolish old woman, and hell, maybe I am at that, but I want to get this straight from the outset. I don't necessarily *believe* I saw what I think I did. I just can't think of any other explanation for what it was. You follow?"

"Okay."

"You remember, this was at least a year back, but there was that boy from town who went missing? During winter, young kid, six or seven, maybe. Went out to shovel driveways or some such and just vanished."

"Caleb Montgomery," Lauren said automatically. Children didn't often go missing this far from the city, so it was an easy name to recall, especially considering Lauren's circumstances.

"Yup, that's the one. I knew his mother in passing. She used to volunteer down to the church for the pancake breakfasts and what have you, before her boy disappeared. Nice lady. Now, this time I'm telling you about was probably two, three months after he went missing. I was here cleaning, waxing all the upstairs floors that week, don't know if you remember. Took forever and just about broke my back doing it, but that's what the Missus wanted so what can you do?

"Anyway, this was my last day waxing, I was working on the floor in the room you're staying in now, and I was almost done when I came over all funny, like. Get this feeling someone's watching me, you know?"

Lauren nodded. She'd had that feeling more than once since moving in.

"And not just anybody watching me, but a child. Sounds silly to make the distinction, but I had two little ones of my own, and there *is* a difference. A type of maternal ESP sort of. Like how you just know when they're gonna start puking in the middle of the night, and you're there with the bucket before it happens." Lauren knew this, too. She'd experienced it more than once. All mothers did. "I tried to just put the feeling out of my head and finish up my work. I remember thinking I was getting spooked because of the missing boy I saw on the news that morning. They'd just decided to call off the active search, as I recall, and it bothered me something rotten, knowing that poor mother wouldn't get any closure. I was also arguing with my own daughter at the time—just normal mother-daughter stuff—and figured I was overly emotional because of that. She's all grown up, but still my baby. You know how it is."

Ava seemed to realize what she had just said and became flustered, but Lauren wasn't about to let her stop there over a little slipup. "It's okay, go on."

"Well, like I said, I decided to put it out of my mind, but the work wasn't distracting me like I thought it would. Back of my head and neck got all itchy and tingly like, and I was starting to become certain that someone was gonna reach out and touch my back. I knew if that happened I would scream fit to burst, and the only way to make the feeling go away was to turn around and check behind me. It became this panicky sort of urge, like when you know you've turned off the stove, but there's that rankling thought telling you you definitely didn't. Only way to shut that thought up is to go on and check for yourself.

"I was still some scared, though. I knew I had to, but I couldn't seem to get my feet to listen to my brain. My hair was all standing up on end like a scared cat's, and my eyes were watering to beat the band... I was more scared than any other time in my life, except for maybe when my youngest, Joshua, had the croup, and I thought he was going to die on me in the middle of the night. I fancy myself a pretty tough customer, but I don't mind telling you now, that I didn't feel any braver than a newborn kitten. Because it wasn't only my fear, you see. It's like what we talked about a few minutes ago, a house being infected by a person's negativity and all that. This fear I was feeling was like someone else's radiating out of the air and into me, compounding my own.

"Finally, I got my body to cooperate and turn around, and I actually *did* see someone standing there. Was only for a split second—there, then gone—but I screamed and dropped my rag and fell backward onto the floor I'd just finished waxing. Thankfully, her Ladyship wasn't home at the time, or I never woulda lived it down.

"Don't know what happened then. There's a blank spot, like. Next thing I know, I'm downstairs in the foyer, my heart about leaping out of my throat, and I've got my purse in my hand and one foot out the door."

"It was that boy, Caleb you saw?"

"It was. And if it wasn't, I don't want to think of what else it mighta been. Could be he was just on my mind and I didn't really see anything at all, but was so expecting to that I manufactured him." Her voice got quieter. Resigned. "Don't think that's the case, though."

"You don't have to keep on if you don't want to," Lauren said.

"I mean to tell it through now that I've begun. Sick it up, and maybe then I'll stop thinking on it. You see, it's never really gone away."

Lauren understood this. If there were some way she could make it so she didn't have to think about Trevor all day, every day, she'd jump at the chance. Thinking so made her feel worse, though.

Ava was still living in her memory. She may have been looking at the kitchen, but she was seeing that little boy, Lauren would have bet on it. "Had this hat with a little puffball on top of it," Ava said. "Can't recall the color now, but I remember he was wearing it, all right. Eyes all sunken and purple, like he'd been up too late, the way kids get. Vomit all down his chin and the bib of his snowsuit, and I got this whiff of it... smelled like peppermint."

Lauren felt a chill work its way through her body. Just this morning, she had been thinking of how she and Trevor used to make Christmas cocoa with a candy cane melted in it.

"That wasn't the worst part, though, hard as that is to believe."

"What was? What was the worst part?" She spoke so softly that her voice was barely there.

"I think he was trying to talk to me. Maybe to tell me what

happened to him, beg for me to help him, I don't know. Christ above, it was horrible." She closed her eyes and drank down the last of her coffee, which was now more scotch than anything. She wiped her eyes, which had started to leak, and chuckled, embarrassed. "Quite a tall tale, I know, but I swear on a stack of Bibles it's true. Sometimes, like now, when I think about it... feels like the boy is still close by.

"I didn't leave the house then like I wanted to. I turned right around, marched myself back upstairs, collected my rags and buckets, and finished the floor. I wasn't about to leave them there in a pile for her nibs to stumble across and have a conniption over. But I don't mind telling you, going back up those stairs was the hardest thing I ever had to do. I was worried that I'd start to feel watched again, but I never did. I went back to work finishing up the floor, and when I got to the place where I'd seen the boy standing, I went right over it with wax. And I told myself that the finish on the wood hadn't worn away there in the shape of footprints."

She crushed her cigarette out, poured one more knock of scotch into her coffee cup, and tossed it back. She offered another to Lauren, who declined.

Ava brushed errant ash off the table and stood unsteadily. "I oughta get back to it," she said, but didn't leave.

"Is there something else?"

"Look, I'm an old woman who sometimes runs off at the mouth. I know that. And I didn't tell you any word of a lie here today, as hard as that might be to believe."

"I think I *do* believe it."

"Yup. Thought you might. Be that as it may—and I know it's not my place to say, you being a grown woman and all—but if you'd hear it, I'd like to offer a friendly bit of advice."

"Okay, what is it?"

"I think you oughta go back home and stay away from Holt House altogether. This isn't one of them dire warnings like in the horror pictures. Just common sense. Call it quits with this place from here on, and do what you can to move on with your life. I know it feels like you have to be here for your boy, but you don't."

Lauren shook her head sadly.

"Yup, thought you might say that, too," Ava told her. She squeezed Lauren's arm briefly, then put the scotch back in the cupboard where she had found it and left.

-9-

The trees were stark and bare against the deep blue sky, and although the temperature was dropping, the sun was warm on Lauren's face. There were only two or three measly inches of snow on the ground now, and dead leaves and branches poked through the white, making it look dirty. After Ava told her story, she had needed to get out of that house for a little while and into the fresh air, but it didn't seem to be helping much. Her head was still beating like a diseased heart, and even her teeth seemed to hurt.

She'd taken this path at least once a day since coming back to Holt House, looking for any trace of Trevor and never finding one (not that she really expected to). It was like a compulsion. There was no way she could sit on the couch and watch TV or read a book; she had to do *something* constructive, and this was the only thing she could think of.

When she stepped out of the trees and onto the beach, which had almost no snow on it, her eyes automatically went to where Trevor had been digging the hole the day he'd gone missing. So often, she thought when she broke through the tree line that he would be there, still digging, and come running over to her... but he never was.

"Trevor, where are you?" she said to the quiet. A twig snapped in the woods behind her, but there was no other sound. Usually, she brought Peanut out with her, but it was too cold for his tired old bones today, so she'd left him curled up in his basket in front of the living room fireplace. If he'd been with her, he would have started growling.

Yesterday, she'd gone to the left and headed down the beach southwest, so today, she chose right, moving slowly up the rocky shingle to the east, parallel with the trees, looking for anything the search parties might have missed a month ago. As she walked, she turned Ava's story over in her mind. It raised more questions than it answered, that was certain (why would the little boy, Caleb, have appeared to her here, at Holt House, and why had Ava smelled peppermint?), but Lauren truly did believe it. Seeing Trevor each night had a way of efficiently knocking down the walls of disbelief. But what did it mean? Nothing as far as she could tell.

Another twig snapped in the woods to her right, but she barely heard it.

Ava had admitted the boy had been on her mind when she saw him in the upstairs bedroom so that likely explained it. If it really had been him and not a hallucination, he may have just chosen her because she was thinking about him. That felt a bit like grasping at straws, but it wasn't as though there was some kind of handbook that explained how this stuff worked.

There was a path through the trees to her right she almost missed; any more overgrown and she *would* have. It wasn't one she'd taken before or had even seen, so she took it now, picking her way carefully through the brambles and pricker bushes, which still had a little bite in them even this late in the season.

A loud rumbling noise overhead made her stop, not because she didn't know what it was, but because it was so out of place. Thunder. The sky to the west was starting to cloud up. Lauren checked her watch and saw she'd only been out here for about fifteen minutes. The storm was creeping along by the looks of it, there would be time to see where this trail led and get back to the house before it reached her. As cold as it was, she wasn't worried about rain, but these winter thunderstorms tended to carry hail with them. She didn't love the idea of being pelted by chunks of ice the size of peaches. She started moving again but stopped just a moment later.

This time, it wasn't a twig that had snapped, but a branch, the crack so loud it echoed off the trees, making it sound like it was coming from all directions at once. Lauren stopped and whirled around, but all she saw were bare brown trees sticking out of the snow and her footprints leading up to... no, wait.

She squinted and took a tentative step back the way she had come. Perhaps fifteen feet behind her, maybe twenty, there were two sets of footprints in the snow. Hers continued on to where she stood now, breathing heavily, her skin all nubbly from goosebumps, and the other set just... stopped. They weren't small, either, as might be made by a child, but looked like they belonged to a full-grown adult.

Her mind turned to her son, as it always did, and she began to wonder if maybe these footprints belonged to the person who had taken him. A homeless man living in the woods, maybe, someone nobody else had noticed.

"Whoever's there better come out right this second," she said, trying to sound stern, but the way her voice quaked gave her away. Then she had another thought. "Muriel? Is that you?"

When the old woman with the puffy white hair didn't totter out onto the path, Lauren looked to the left and right, trying to catch sight of her amongst the trees, but could see nothing. The woods around her had gone quiet. Not a bird or squirrel dared make a sound. She felt eyes moving over her body.

If someone was hiding there, they blended in perfectly. Lauren breathed raggedly, sending irregular clouds of steam into the darkening air.

Ava's advice to leave Holt House came to her then, and she wished she'd heeded it, just gotten in her car and sped the hell away. She fumbled her phone out of her pocket, but there was no signal down here because of the trees and the bluff on which the house sat. Feeling foolish, yet not, she tried 911 anyway. Nothing.

Quietly, she started to make her way up the gentle slope, trying to keep her feet from crunching through the snow crust and failing. Every so often, she would turn back, hoping to catch sight of whoever was following her, but she didn't see anyone there, and (thank Christ), the footprints didn't resume. These were the longest ten minutes of her life, except for every ten-minute chunk of the day Trevor had gone missing, and each day thereafter.

Occasionally, she still heard cracking sounds from the forest (it could have just been the plummeting temperatures freezing the water in the branches, but she knew it wasn't), and the animals were still as silent as falling snow. The only other sound was the far-off mutter of approaching thunder.

Lauren scrambled as quickly as she dared, trying to keep ahead of the noise and the feeling of being watched, and when she finally broke through the trees on the upper side of the woods near the house, she felt a wave of relief. That relief was short-lived, though. What she had at first mistaken for the side of the house was another building she hadn't seen before. It was made of the same bluestone but had been partially consumed by the encroaching forest. There had at one time been intricate scrollwork along the roof, but this lay broken on the ground in front of her. It was probably the old carriage house, which she'd heard Nan mention in passing years ago.

In the front, a large begrimed, flyspecked window allowed her to peer through to the building's interior, but all she could see in the lowering light of the oncoming storm was what looked like furniture covered with canvas drop cloths.

Behind her, something thudded loudly, and she turned to look.

That wasn't a branch, she thought. It sounded like an

animal jumping down from a tree and landing heavily on the ground.

Movement caught her eye. To the left of the trail of footprints she had left behind, something willowy disappeared behind the trunk of a maple. *It's not real. I'm not really seeing what I think I am*, she told herself. But when a face eased out from behind the right side of the tree—the face of a living corpse with a sunken mouth and jutting teeth—it was harder to deny.

Her bowels felt hot and loose. It wasn't a person that had been following her. She had no idea *what* it was, only that she wanted to turn and run. Adrenaline dumped into her system, but instead of launching her forward like a jackrabbit, she froze to the spot and felt nauseated as her heart tripled in speed.

Don't pass out, she ordered herself, *don't you dare.*

A sound, like a very old person trying to gasp a breath into their lungs... then silence. Then, another gasping breath. Tears leaked from her eyes and blurred the world in a terrifying way.

The door to the building was close—ten feet, maybe less—and stood slightly ajar, leaking darkness from within. Lauren swiped her eyes clear, momentarily solidifying the world again, and then ran for the door without giving it a second thought. She didn't stop when she heard thudding footsteps rushing toward her from behind, each one sharp and separate from the next, as if whatever chased her ran on legs like bone pegs. And she didn't stop when that gasping breath came again, either. She didn't even stop when she thought she heard Trevor's voice call out from behind her, underscored by the raspy breathing. Lauren Potter ran like all the demons of Hell were after her until she slammed into the wooden door, pushing it further inward where it fetched up against the muddy ground. In one swift motion, she turned and slammed it shut.

A moment later, it pushed inward with a force beyond what a person could have mustered. It would have flown open if she had not been standing with her shoulder braced against it, waiting for just that to happen.

"Go away!" she screamed with what little breath she could manage.

The only response from the other side of the door was another of those gasping breaths that sounded like an old woman on hospice breathing her last.

The door thumped again, but without the same vigor as before, and then one final time where it barely moved.

Whatever was outside, she heard it stumble away with a groaning breath, moving down along the building. Lauren eyed the window; that single pane of glass that looked like a strong breeze would be enough to blow it out of its ancient frame and shatter it into a million pieces.

"Jesus Christ, no."

She wanted to open the door and run as fast and as far as possible, but running was tricky. She didn't know exactly where she was on the property or how far it was back to the house. Plus, there was ice and snow to contend with. What would happen if her feet slid out from under her? The thing out there was quick. *So* quick.

What about one of the drop cloths? she thought. There were three big piles of junk in the center bay and two more in the far bay covered by large canvas sheets that draped all the way down to the dirt. She could burrow under one and hide, just like in the furniture forts she used to make as a kid. The idea of being trapped under all that musty canvas while that *thing* tried to find her made her queasy, but it was better than being run down in the woods.

A shadow crossed the window, and she ducked down behind a large crate beside the door. At its base, she spied an old, rusted crowbar, probably forgotten there sometime before she was born. Even so, brandishing it in her hand made her feel slightly more protected.

The closest pile she could hide in was smack dab in the

center of the middle bay, probably no more than ten or twelve feet away, but getting to it meant crossing the open floor. Whatever was out there would be able to look right in and see her, which defeated the purpose of trying to hide.

This is crazy. This isn't happening! her mind threw out, as if by staging a sneak attack it would be able to startle her into agreeing with it. But it *was* happening. In defiance of all science of thought and reason, in contrast to everything she knew about the order of the world, it really was happening. Unless she had suffered a psychotic break, which she wasn't entirely ready to rule out.

Clouds scudded closer overhead, darkening the day, and thunder continued to growl. At least, she hoped it was thunder. The pitiful light from the window made it only about halfway across the floor, which threw the back wall into darkness. If she could get there and then inch herself along, she might be able to make it to a point directly behind the pile, hidden from the thing outside of the window. It was a flimsy plan but the only one she had, which made it the best.

Crouched over, Lauren ran as silently as she could along the soft dirt and didn't stop until she felt the stone wall. *There*, she thought, *that's the first step done. Not so bad.*

She couldn't see out the window from this angle, which was a blessing. She knew there was something horrible pressed up against it, its face mashed to the glass as it looked for her.

Taking a shaky breath, she started to move sideways, sliding her butt along the cold wall a little at a time so her coat wouldn't rasp too loudly against the stones. The window came sliding into view a few inches at a time, but all she could see through it was the bare tree limbs dancing and rattling in the freshening breeze. Straining, she tried to pick up the sound of that death rattle breathing, but the world was silent except for the approaching thunder and the weird clattering of branches.

Only a few more feet. Despite the cold, the crowbar felt

sweaty in her palm, and she gripped it harder so it wouldn't fall and ring out like a dinner bell. Five more feet now at most.

Now four.

Now three.

Lauren stopped and stared straight ahead. Through the filmy window, she saw something. Or, more appropriately, some*one*.

Trevor was standing outside. New snowflakes caught in his chestnut hair, and his little hands were pressed against the glass. If he had been a ghost, those handprints wouldn't be there, she told herself. He was really there. Only his eyes looked wrong. They were too big, too wet, and seemed to point off in opposite directions, but for some reason that didn't bother her at all.

She blinked, and for a split second, she thought she saw the corpse thing that had chased her in here, but it happened so quickly that it was easy to write off as nerves. Especially because that was her baby was there.

"Mommy?"

"Trevor, is that really you?" Terror and elation swept through her body, and she started to weep.

"Mommy let me inside." Trevor was crying too, the same way he had when he found out his goldfish, Hammie, that he'd won at the state fair, had died in the night; nose running, cheeks red and tired, dark circles beneath his eyes. "Mommy, I'm starving. I haven't had anything to eat since I got lost." His words were broken sobs. "Please, Mommy, please! I need to eat something! It hurts *so* bad!"

The crowbar slipped from her hand and clattered to the floor, where it might remain for another forty or fifty years. She stepped toward the window even though her brain was screaming at her that it wasn't Trevor out there. It just looked like him. The little boy flickered for another second, revealing something desiccated and shriveled underneath, and then he was back. Just a blink. Like he hadn't been gone at all. One

Her mouth was full of spit, and she wanted a drink. Instead, she finished off the warm, flat soda that had been sitting out on her desk. The sugar helped curb the craving, but not enough.

You could drink, you know. You still have the bottle down there in the cupboard. Just one little shot in celebration. For old times' sake. It's not like you need to get blind drunk or anything.

The more she thought of it, the more it felt like a good idea. Just a little nip of her anniversary scotch as a way to commemorate the moment.

Lauren was still around someplace, no doubt eager to report all of Nan's doings back to Lambert, and Ava's beater truck was still parked in the turnaround. Even if Lauren was living on Pluto, the old woman's eyes and ears were still as sharp as ever. Ordinarily, that would have made what Nan was thinking about doing a bad idea, but that same voice that had told her the book was ready to go out as is, told her everything would be okay now. She felt only excitement as she picked her way carefully down the stairs to the kitchen.

The bottle was right where she'd left it (or at least close enough for government work), although it looked a little emptier than before. She tried to remember the handful of times she'd poured some and then dumped it out at the last second, deciding sobriety was more important. Thinking of that made her stop and reconsider briefly. Was she really ready to do this?

Fuck yes, you are. You weren't celebrating then. That would have been sad drinking. This is happy *drinking. That should still be allowed, right? For Christ's sake, even doctors and nutritionists will tell people on a diet to occasionally eat the foods they crave because abstaining entirely makes you more likely to fail. Having a shot now would be like a cheat day, a way of maintaining your sobriety and making it stronger.*

Nick's turkey mug was upside-down on the drying mat, so she grabbed it and went back up to her office.

The darkness in here was soothing, the only light in the

room coming from her laptop screen. She poured scotch into the mug, no more than a dribble, and set the bottle uncapped on the desk. Taking the mug in her hands, she tossed it back quickly before she had time to change her mind and gasped when it hit her throat. It felt like rubbing alcohol on a wound.

"There," she said aloud to no one. "I had one. I'm just fine. The world didn't end."

You could hardly call that one. *It barely covered the bottom of the mug. That was more of a taste than anything.*

It hadn't been much, but then she hadn't *wanted* much, right?

"Right." Even as she said it, she took the bottle and poured a heavier shot. This one covered the bottom and a little more. Some to grow on, as Nick would have said. *This* was a proper celebration.

Her mouth was already watering when she brought the mug up (too fast, and clunked it against her front teeth), and drank it down in a single gulp.

There, now, doesn't that feel better?

It really did. After all these dry years, even so little seemed to make her giddy. She laughed once contentedly. Her hands went to work on their own, pouring more scotch, a little heavier this time. The lip of the bottle chattered against the mug. Only excitement, she told herself, licking her lips with anticipation. That's all. Just excitement.

Fifteen minutes later, she was well on her way to being drunk. Not blind stinking drunk, but as in horseshoes and hand grenades, close enough. She opened the draft of her novel and scrolled through it, loving how the words looked on the page. So perfect. In fact, there was no need to wait to send it to Tim. Call it an early Christmas present. He'd absolutely shit himself when he got it and then again when she suggested nailing down make-up tour dates for *Dead Stories.*

Even in this digital age, Nan never sent manuscripts through email—it was too easy for mishaps to occur, and she didn't entirely trust it—so she called the place she usually used in town to have it couriered to Tim. They told her to bring it in whenever.

With that done, there was really only one thing that required her attention.

"Well, let's just deal with that right now, why don't we?" she mumbled and pulled out her phone.

Lambert picked up on the second ring. No greeting, no pleasantries, just, "You got my money together that fast, huh?"

"Not quite yet. A few more days should do it." Her words were starting to slur together, which struck her as infinitely amusing for some reason, so she laughed quietly, hoping he wouldn't notice. "I think I should be ready to give it to you on Christmas Eve. How would that be, hmm? That enough time, Chester? Just in time to do your Christmas shopping, how do you like *that*?"

"I like it just fine," he said, sounding perplexed, but this was secondary to the greed bleeding through his confusion. She could practically hear him salivating. "You got all of it, right? I don't wanna show up and find out half of it is in Mexican pesos or autographed books or something."

"Nope, just good old American green folding money. Cashola, buddy boy." Had she been sober, she would have cringed at this, but had she been sober, she never would have said it in the first place. As it was, she could already hear her inner voice screaming to just shut up before she made it any worse, but that prim and proper little nag could take her own advice and stuff it. "How'sbout me 'n you meet up at the place we went the last time to conduct our business, hmm? The Classic Eats Diner would be like, poetry, you know? Full circle and all that shit."

Lambert was quiet for a second. "What's got into you? You sound drunk. You ain't drinking again, are ya?"

Shit. Shit, shit, shit.

"Why, Chester, you wound me. 'Course I'm not drinking

again. I'm just a little stressed out, as I'm sure you can imagine. Not to mention I just finished another book, right this moment."

He chuckled. It was a sound she couldn't quite read. "I hope for your sake it's a bestseller. Wouldn't hurt to have a big moneymaker right about now, would it?"

Her voice turned cold. She didn't want any part of her book in his disgusting mouth. It felt like an act of desecration. "Oh, it'll sell. So just shut up about it."

That same enigmatic chuckle again. "Well, now, that sounds like good news for both of us then, don't it?"

"Just be at the diner, Chester. Christmas Eve. Nine o'clock."

"Yup." He hung up, and she tossed her phone on the desk. There was still about a quarter bottle of scotch left, and for a second, she considered pouring the rest into her mug and just finishing it off but immediately wrote that off as a bad idea. Lambert had been suspicious almost from the word go, and her drunken stupidity hadn't helped matters. When Ava left for the day it would be best to just put the bottle back where she'd gotten it from and forget it was there. That would allow her time to work out what she had to do and ensure her idea was beyond reproach.

Nan pulled the cork and took a long swallow. The world swam away, then swam back, and seemed to shimmer at the edges. There, that was better. It was because of the way he had joked about her book. As if he had any right to comment on whatever he wished. "Uneducated piece of shit," she said.

Another long swallow followed by a contented sigh. *Goddamn*, she'd missed this. The bottle was almost empty now, no more than a few swallows left. A sense of panic, one which she used to be intimately acquainted with, rose from her belly into her chest. Being out of booze had, at one point, been one of the most stressful things in the world to her, and apparently, that feeling hadn't entirely disappeared.

It's okay, I can get another one, she thought. *Before I meet Lambert, I'll stop by the liquor store and pick one up. For the celebration afterward. But just one drink this time. For real.* "One real, proper drink," she said, lighting a cigarette without realizing she was doing it. *And then I can save all the rest of it. Only have it for special occasions. Like when the next book comes out. Just for really* big *things.*

There was no point in getting back into the daily drinking again. That had just been too demanding; trying to hide it from people, lying all the time, and the constant cravings at all hours (not to mention the shitty hangovers in the morning)... she didn't miss any of that. But doing it in a responsible way like a normal person, would alleviate the issues from last time. Honestly, it was crazy she hadn't thought of that until now.

She polished off the bottle, then set it back on the desk, wishing there had been twice as much in it. Not to drink all of it, God no, she only wanted one more *little* drink. A mouthful. A sip.

Just one fucking taste.

PART 3
STARVING THINGS
CHRISTMAS

2026

CHAPTER 6
A FEAST

Keaton stared in horror at the rock in his hands, as if he'd never seen it before. It was covered with Maisy's blood. She lay on the ground at his feet, her skull battered open like the piñata they'd seen children hitting with sticks while on honeymoon in Spain. The ground of the cellar was wet with her blood.

He dropped to his knees and gathered her poor, broken body up in his arms, and rocked it. "Oh, my darling. Oh, my love, what have I done to you?" She'd been hysterical and dangerous, a thing possessed, he'd had no choice. His face still bore the red furrows from her fingernails, and his bleeding lips were already beginning to puff. And yet, to see her like this, in such a state, made his heart ache with sadness. "My sweet little Maisy," he said, stroking the side of her head that was still largely intact. "Wait for me, my love. Give me but a few moments, and I will follow you soon. I won't leave you alone for long, this I swear."

With all the care of a father settling a child into its crib, Keaton laid Maisy's head on the befouled dirt and ran to his study to get his revolver. Perhaps, if he had known what was in store for him afterward, he would have walked instead. He just couldn't bear the thought of his poor Maisy alone and frightened.

He would hold her head in his lap and put the revolver in his mouth, and they would be found like that, together. And then they would know it had not been an act of hatred but one of love.

-Nan Wickwyre, *Haunting Willow Hall*

-1-

Tuesday. Christmas Eve. It was almost zero hour, and Nan was surprisingly calm. She'd checked and rechecked her plan and found it suitable each time, which was comforting. Barring some major catastrophe, it would go off without a hitch.

Well, without *another* hitch. Lauren had somehow managed to get her to agree to a Christmas Eve dinner together during a conversation Nan still didn't entirely remember. What she did recall was how strange Lauren had looked when she'd come back into the house from her daily walk through the woods. A bit distracted, eyes far-off and hollow. When she spoke, she did so in a clipped sort of way, starting and stopping frequently, as if someone was whispering the words into her ear and she was repeating them.

However it had happened, it was on the books, and it was better not to give her anything to report back to Lambert (even though that back channel would soon be closed). And anyway, not even the lie she had concocted about having a meeting in town at 9 with her agent was enough to get Lauren to cave. She'd simply suggested they eat later.

Nan checked her watch. Ten minutes to eight. She was early, but that was better. The local weather people were losing their minds about a nor'easter that was predicted to hit tonight, bringing with it more than two feet of fresh snow with a nice coating of ice for good measure. How funny would it be if she ended up getting caught because Lauren's car (which Nan had borrowed, unbeknownst to Lauren), got stuck where she'd parked it in the old Sears parking lot? She supposed it was very funny, in an existential sort of way, but nothing she wanted to experience.

Between the parking lot where she sat waiting and the Classic Eats Diner where she was meeting Lambert there was only scrubland. All that grew well there were fast food bags, plastic bottles, shopping bags, and cigarette butts. Right now, most of this was buried beneath a crust of old snow, making the place look nicer than it really was. As long as she could make it across on foot, Nan didn't care what it looked like. And thanks to the relatively snowless week, that would be easy as pie.

There were no other cars were in the parking lot, which was not so much a stroke of luck as by design. After the Sears moved across town, this location had sat vacant. It was used only during the summer months by teenagers looking for flat, empty pavement on which to board and bike, and camper-folks who needed to grab a few hours of safe shut-eye before moseying on down the road. During the winter, there was no one.

She cracked the seal around the neck of her new bottle of scotch that she'd just picked up from Davis Discount Liquor, pulled the cork, and sniffed. That was the other reason she had wanted to come early (and, of course, she'd had to drop off the new manuscript at the courier's, which she had done with a pang of sadness). And when her eyes rolled back, and her mouth began to water, she thought, *Not yet. Only after. To have any now could mess everything up.*

But maybe it would help. Her nerves were unsteady, as were her hands, and she would need both rock-solid for what she had to do. She took a small sip, then another, and then quickly recorked the bottle before she could talk herself into a third and, let's face it, a fourth and a fifth, too. The little nips of courage put her into a more confident mood, though she would have been lying if she'd said she was at ease. Anyone who was at a time like this was a sociopath.

She wondered if Lambert was getting close yet. When she'd driven past the diner earlier on her way into town, there had only been two cars there, neither one his. If he smelled a rat, he might show up early, so seeing that the old piece of shit he drove wasn't there had been a good sign. Probably. It was hard to say for sure. He'd been a little bit too cagey lately.

She checked her watch again. Twelve after. It was cold out there tonight. Waiting for him to arrive in the bushes would turn her into a popsicle before he got there, yet her gut told her time was running short. Better to be a little cold than to miss her opportunity.

The door squealed when she pushed it open, but no one was around to hear it. Even so, when she closed it, she did so quietly. It would be just her luck that someone passing by would turn and see her there and recognize her, rendering all of her preparations and precautions pointless. The keys she had left sandwiched between the driver's side visor and the roof liner for safekeeping, and the car she left unlocked just in case she needed to make a quick getaway.

At least the cold made the walk more pleasant; during summer, mosquitoes, midges, and deer flies would have eaten her alive. And the view overhead wasn't so bad, either. A glittering spray of stars against the velvety black sky.

But the stars weren't enough to hold her gaze for long. Inevitably, her eyes turned back to her watch. She saw the time and picked up the pace.

-2-

Sheriff Chester Lambert turned his POS-mobile into the parking lot of the Classic Eats Diner, parked in a handicap space near the front (so what? The place was empty), and killed the engine when the squealing from the belt started to rise in pitch.

He checked out the other cars. Two old beaters like his, neither of which belonged to the Grand Duchess of Holt House. Disgusting that one person could have so much money while the town sheriff had been forced to drive a piece of shit like this since Hector was a pup. And the indignities didn't stop there. He'd had to beg enough from the town each year to keep it barely limping along. Until now, anyway. After tonight, it would be the next guy's problem.

But that next guy wouldn't be Sanders. Lambert chuckled. Just about the whole damn town had turned out for his funeral, you'da thought some grand pooh-bah had kicked the bucket instead of some annoying undersheriff with a tendency to stick his beak into business that wasn't his. Lambert still didn't really remember much about that night (he tried not to think about what had happened), or even why he had decided to take such a drastic step against the little asshole, but it had worked out, by God. The staties were looking for the youth gang that they figured did the deed down toward the city, and Sanders was well out of his hair. Easy peasy. Still, it was a puzzler. Before then, he hadn't ever discharged his weapon at a *suspect*, yet using it on a man he had considered to be of a decent (if annoying) sort had come as naturally as breathing.

His breath now was coming out in fat clouds. Without the car running, the cold started to seep in, and he debated turning the engine back on for a bit. The cold actually felt kind of nice. Ever since that reporter lady went missing (dollars to donuts, she went off on a bender somewhere and just decided not to come back, and wasn't that just like a woman?) he'd not felt up to snuff. Little headaches now and again and strange feelings of being followed and watched. The feelings would go away for a while but never too far, then come roaring back at the worst times.

That's why he had to get the fuck out of this place. Go somewhere warm out West, maybe, where weed was legal, and he could live for a long time off of his savings. Not Commie-fornia, though. Vegas maybe.

He checked his watch and looked for the Wickwyre woman's car again, but it was still just the two old junkers that probably belonged to the poor unlucky bastards who drew the short straws and had to work tonight. He'd make it worth their while, he decided. Leave a whole twenty-dollar tip.

"A million fucking bucks," he said. It still blew his mind. He'd gotten a hundred grand off of her when she got hammered and killed her family, and that had been quite the windfall at the time. But a *million* bucks? It was almost unreal. And the total he'd be heading west with was probably closer to a million-five by the time all was said and done. He had his paltry pension that would add a bit to that, plus the house his father had willed to him when he died, which had seen a nice uptick in value ever since the yuppies and rich assholes from the city started spreading out farther like the disease they were.

Well, they could have the damn place. Chester wouldn't ever be coming back. His parents were dead, and he didn't talk to his son. From time to time, he stepped out with Glynis, who worked at the hardware store, but there was no way in holy hell he was coming back to visit her. She was five years older than him and had a bum hip. He was going to be a millionaire. He could have whatever sort of woman he wanted. And if the money started to peter out? Well, shit, he had his own drunken ATM out on Little Church Road, didn't he?

Tacky Christmas lights flashed inside the diner, bathing the front windows in pink, green, and silver. He thought it looked like something you'd see in one of those oceanfront hotels in Miami where all the queers flocked. The waitress was sitting at one of the tables eating a burger with a plate of fries, and Chester's stomach rumbled. Where the hell was Nan? If she weren't here in a few minutes, he'd head on in and order some food. And fuck the cholesterol, tonight was a celebration. And fuck the incipient heart disease his doctor was always warning him about, too. He'd take up walking when he got out to Vegas. *Yeah*, he thought and chuckled again. *From slot machine to slot machine, between courses of wagyu steak and bluefin tuna.* For tonight, though, one of those big Classic Eats burgers with fries and a chocolate shake would sure hit the spot. And if he could talk that high-toned bitch into climbing down out of her ivory wagon, maybe they could even hoist one last beer together.

Sheriff Lambert, not the kind of man to delay gratification if it could be helped (Glynis would have attested to that), said, "Fuck it," then shoved the door open. He had to use his foot to brace it so it wouldn't swing back and whack him before he could start to leverage his ass out of the divot it had worn in the seat over the years.

The stuck-up bitch is probably late on purpose, he thought. *Some kinda power play she read about in one of them women's magazines.*

His footsteps echoed as he plodded toward the door, but otherwise, the world was eerily silent. A fog rolled across the parking lot from the woods, probably a precursor to that storm all the weathermen were losing their tits over that would amount to nothing more than a dusting in the end, he thought. Seeing town this empty was weird, but most people were likely at home battening down the hatches or had already flown the coop for more exciting Christmas destinations.

Some pea-brained moron had dumped a scoop of salt on the stairs, which crunched beneath his poor, battered shoes, and made it slippery to walk without holding onto the railing. He was nearly at the top when, from his right, where the forest reached out and cupped the diner, Lambert heard a noise coming from a stand of juniper bushes. He stopped. At first, he thought it was a cat mewling and was about to leave it to its fate (which, on a cold, foggy night like this, was likely to be flat as a pancake out on Route 9), when he realized he was hearing words.

"Help me."

"Who's that, now?" he called. The last thing in the world he wanted to do tonight was more goddamned paperwork.

"Help... help me, please." The voice was soft and croaking, hardly a whisper. On any other night, he wouldn't have heard it over the roar of the traffic.

Inside the diner, the waitress (a pretty little thing, Lambert thought, except for the pink and green shit she'd painted onto her hair) waved to him desultorily, and he responded by holding up a beefy finger. *One second.* The waitress rolled her eyes and went back to her plate of fries.

"Whoever's back there, you just come on out into the light where I can see ya now," Lambert called. The sound was *definitely* coming from the clump of juniper, and he'd gone and left his flashlight in the car. He had his gun on his hip but wasn't even thinking about that.

When no one answered him, he started back down the steps, careful to hold the railing the whole way. It would be just his luck to wind up with a busted hip and be laid up in this shit-hole waiting for it to heal. He grumbled. All he'd wanted was a fuckin' burger. How hard was that?

"Listen to me back there," he said, raising his voice and imbuing it with all the years of authority he had in him. "This is Sheriff Lambert here. If you all need help, you'd best speak up, and if you're doing something you ain't supposed to, just clear the hell out, you hear? I don't want to hafta—"

Before he could say *take your dumb ass into jail on Christmas Eve*, a loud blast rang out, and the next thing he knew, he was on the pavement looking up at the sky, and there was a white-hot pain exploding in his right leg. He screamed, a high, squealing sound and tried to drag himself back to the steps using the bottom rung of the railing.

I'm fucking shot! he thought, astounded. *How the fuck did I get shot in this stupid shit-kicking goddamned town?* Following closely on the heels of this thought was another; just three words repeating like a musical beat in his brain. *Get your gun, get your gun, get your gun, get your gun…* If he didn't, he'd be a dead man.

A second shot rang out, and his right arm twitched painfully and went half-numb as if someone had grabbed it from behind and yanked it. The half that wasn't numb felt like it had been splashed with gasoline and lit on fire. He flopped onto his back again with his head propped up by the lowest step, and his scream raised an octave. He sounded like a woman, but at that moment, he didn't care. He'd made it through nearly thirty years of various law enforcement gigs and never once had even been shot *at*, and now here he was, plugged twice and bleeding like a stuck pig all over the pavement at a place where people got breakfast on Sundays after church.

Lambert wore his service pistol on his right hip (and his right hip pocket was where he'd shoved his cell phone, too), and tried to reach it with his left hand because the other one was just dangling there like a dead fish. He couldn't seem to get ahold of the thing, though. He struggled for a few seconds that felt like hours before finally feeling the grip slide into his palm. Never had anything felt so good in his hand (not even the parts of Glynis he liked best), but when he tugged, it stayed in the holster.

"Oh fucking Christ," he wheezed. "Fuckin' strap." In all the pain and chaos, he'd forgotten to unsnap the strap holding the weapon in place. Another shot exploded across the parking lot, but there was no accompanying pain to go with it. "Missed," he said through clenched teeth, his vision doubling then trebling because of the tears in his eyes.

Lambert leaned his head back while he fingered the strap and saw the waitress upside-down in the window behind him. She was no longer sitting there like a bump on a log but standing with her gape-mouthed face pressed almost through the window, just looking down at him.

"You fuckin' bitch, I'm shot! Call the cops!" The waitress

didn't move. The art deco Christmas lights flashed on and off like the lights of an ambulance, and Lambert started to weep.

Yet another gunshot in this never-ending night. Air moved past his face, but there was no punch and no pain. How many had that been? Three? Was it four? He wasn't sure anymore. Everything felt like it was on fire except for his left hand, which was still clawing at the strap of the holster. His index finger, more by pure dumb luck than anything else, snagged the strap, and hope bloomed in him briefly before being overridden by black pain, which swarmed him like a hive of hornets.

Yet his body continued to move and function, performing the tasks it had day in, day out for years. His left hand, moving as if through thick molasses (*molasses cookies, Christmas cookies, the ones Mama used to make for me every damn year because I loved them so, and she loved me so, and she's gone now, gone for years and years*), wrapped around the grip of his weapon, turned it to the side, and yanked it free from the leather which held it. He turned his head to the darkness of the juniper bushes and saw a flash of something low to the ground. *Muzzle flash*, he thought soupily. He heard the crack as the bullet flew but couldn't tell if it had hit its mark or not. His entire body was either numb or on fire. He couldn't even feel his fingers holding the gun.

Tears froze to his face as the temperature fell inside and out, and he leveled his weapon as best he could at the black patch of bushes.

Please, he thought. *Oh, please, let just one go where it's supposed to and end this fucking night.*

Three sharp cracks, *POW POW POW*, then his hand fell to the pavement with a metallic clatter as the gun spilled from it and skittered away. That was okay. The waitress had probably called someone by now, and they were on their way. The ambulance would get here soon. He thought he heard its shrieking siren, but maybe that was just the wind.

His leg was fucked, that much was easy to see. The material

of his pants was soaked and dark. Further up, there was a hole in his shirt near his bellybutton, which was pumping blood like that was its job. *When did I get shot there?* he wondered. He could taste blood in his mouth, and his vision started to close in from the sides, narrowing down as a black corona collapsed on itself.

I don't want to die, he thought. *It's Christmas Eve. I want to go home and get into bed, and wait for Santa. I'll sleep through until tomorrow when I smell bacon and pancakes cooking, and Mama will be there with all my presents 'cause Daddy has to work, just like every year. She knitted me mittens this year, and this time I won't lose 'em, or trade 'em to Tommy Delfinio down the block for bottle rockets. I'll keep 'em and treasure 'em, and they'll be my reminder of my Mama every time I see them. If I'd'a kept the ones Tommy took, I could be wearing them now, and I wish I had, cause my fingers are so cold.*

A shadow leaned down over him.

"Mama?" he said and smiled. She took his hands in hers and warmed them. They felt just the same as they always had, dry and soft. Even the bothersome pain hushed up because Mama knew how to make that better, too. She always did. "Can we go home, Mama? I'm so tired."

Mama said they could. And then they did.

-3-

One of the late Sheriff Chester Lambert's final three rounds had punched through the rear of the diner close to where Nan's head was concealed where she lay in the bushes. The second one had hit the frozen ground a few inches in front of her chest, sending a tiny explosion of dirt and rocks up into her face. A little higher, and it would have punched right through her breastbone and kept on trucking. The third had been the unluckiest of them all, but unfortunately for Lambert, not unlucky enough. It had grazed the back of her ankle, tearing her pants and digging an angry red trench in her skin that burned like the dickens and bled quite a lot but caused no lasting damage. She'd cried out once (it was this sound Lambert's dying brain had heard and mistaken for the siren of an approaching ambulance) but managed to stop herself from doing it a second time. The last thing she wanted was for someone inside the Classic Eats Diner to hear her and come out to try and be a hero.

I almost just died, she thought with amazement. *I would have if even one of those bullets had been slightly off track.* It made her want a drink, and when she got back to the car, she meant to have one.

Snow was starting to come down now in big fluffy flakes that melted when they touched the pavement. Soon, they would start to stick and accumulate. She had to get out of here before they did. Carefully, she dragged herself through the stand of bushes to the dark side of the diner and clambered to her feet. She tested her weight on her shot ankle and found it would hold her, but every time she moved, the skin there sizzled as it tore.

Getting back to Lauren's car was slow going, and although she couldn't see it in the darkness, she was certain there was a blood trail behind her. At least the snow would cover it handily enough.

By the time she felt the cold metal of the door handle in her hand, her leg was singing a high C, and the bottle of scotch was calling her name. That was for after, though. First, she had to fix her ankle, or she wouldn't be going anywhere.

Lauren kept a pump bottle of hand sanitizer in the pocket of the driver's door. Nan threw the gun Nick had bought after the botched attack on Halloween into the passenger seat to free her hands. It bounced and landed on the floor. Gingerly she pulled up her pant leg, which had already started to dry to the wound. Once the gash was exposed, she took a deep breath and slathered it in sanitizer. The pain was immediate. She had to bite the inside of her cheeks to keep from screaming.

In the center console, there was a roll of duct tape (which, judging by the car's exterior, appeared to be Lauren's favorite automotive repair tool), so Nan wrapped that around her ankle a few times as tightly as she could stand it. Only when that was done did she pick up the bottle, still in the passenger seat where she'd left it, now pleasantly chilled, and take three gulping mouthfuls. Its burn countered the burning in her ankle in the most wonderful way. She closed her eyes for a moment and relished it.

The sound of approaching sirens snapped her to attention again. They were still a little ways off but would get here in no time with how empty the roads were tonight. Luckily, the keys were right where she'd left them in the visor, and the car wheezed to life when she turned them in the starter. *None of that last-minute melodramatic panicky bullshit in my stories, no sir*, she thought and laughed like a lunatic. The scotch had begun working already. She affected her best British accent (which wasn't very good at all), and said, "Barely a proper drink and already squiffy. Ey, Jeeves?" She laughed again, rolled down the window so the cold air would help keep her alert, and had one more little nip from the bottle before pulling slowly onto Route 9, and pointing the car in the direction of Holt House.

Snow had made the roads slick already, even though there wasn't much of it yet, and the scotch had dulled her senses, so the trip back was slow going. She weaved a bit, but not badly, and had only one moment of panic when she thought she saw someone darting out toward the road, but it turned out to just be the headlights creating moving shadows in the trees.

Turning into her driveway, she scrubbed the side of the car along the gate's stone pillar on the left. "Whooops, didn't see ya there, buddy!" she said. She overcorrected and almost drove into an old maple tree on the right side before finally drifting toward the center of the gravel drive and straightening the car out. Just as she hadn't seen the stone pillar until it was too late, Nan also missed the puddle of partially frozen blood across the road where Muriel Duckworth usually sat taking notes.

"Home at last," she said and took another drink in celebration. Coming up over the rise in the driveway, the house came into view, magnificent and sprawling and lit up from stem to stern. Even the lights in the old section were on tonight. "Hold on," she said and, delayed, stamped both feet down on the brake. The car fishtailed a little and eventually stopped, the engine whining in protest. The lights were indeed on in the old section, and in each window was the silhouette of a person standing perfectly still looking out at her like they'd been expecting her. Except for the window closest to the front veranda. In that one, there were *two* silhouettes; a man, and a little girl.

Nan blinked slowly, sucked in a breath like she'd forgotten how to breathe, and huffed it back out.

There was no one there. She checked again with a drunken slewing of her head. The windows were all dark. No one sat in them watching her. She felt them, but the feeling was fading.

"Watchful windows," she muttered to herself. "Like eyes."

When she and Nick had looked at the house the first time, Nick said he'd felt like the house was watching them, and she hadn't really understood why; windows weren't eyes, they couldn't see.

She understood now.

No, I don't accept that. I'm drunk, she thought. *And I just went through something traumatic. That's all. There's no big mystery to it*. If only she believed that. For a single second in time, an interior voice she hadn't heard since moving into Holt House spoke up and told her to run. Run as far and as fast as she could. And then it was gone.

Slowly, she eased her feet off the brake and gently pushed on the accelerator, feeling a bit sobered. The car slid and skidded before catching and started crawling the last couple hundred feet down to the house.

She stashed the bottle of scotch in a planter to the left of the door to retrieve later (after a farewell slug, naturally), and crunched a handful of breath mints between her teeth. Mixed with the booze and the cold air, it made her mouth feel like it was on fire.

The window where she had seen the silhouettes of the man and the little girl was black and empty as far as she could tell. She eyed it mistrustfully as she opened the front door and stepped into the foyer, stomping the snow from her shoes, doing her left foot gingerly because of the bullet graze.

Beyond the foyer, the hall, which Ava had decked out a few days ago with fake holly and pine boughs, was lit with candles that ran its length. The flickering made it seem as if the walls themselves were moving.

"Lauren?" she called, unwinding the scarf from around her neck and hanging it on a peg. No response. Odd. She also couldn't smell anything cooking for the Christmas Eve meal that Lauren had made such a big fuss about, which was odder.

In the candlelight, Nan checked her leg. There was quite a bit more blood than she had expected, and it had seeped up above the edge of the tape. There would be no hiding this from Lauren, and try as she might, Nan couldn't think of one plausible explanation as to how it happened that didn't involve Sheriff Lambert and a gun. She would just have to sneak upstairs and change.

She had taken maybe half a dozen steps toward the staircase when she heard stockinged feet running toward her from the living room. She pivoted to see who it was when something slammed into the side of her face with the force of a train, shattering her cheekbone and bringing with it explosions of stars like fireworks across her blackened vision. Had she been sober, the blow may have killed her outright, which might have been a blessing. Being drunk with a relaxed body, though, she was awarded a few moments of awareness, during which her addled brain wondered if she had somehow hit her head on the wall, before collapsing to the floor like a sack of old clothes. After that, the lights winked out one by one until there was only darkness.

And in that darkness, she heard whispering.

-4-

Nick's baseball bat, which he used to keep in the umbrella stand by the front door and had once used to chase off a bird-masked home invader on Halloween, fell from Lauren's loosening grip and bounced end to end on the stone floor before falling silent. The shockwave it had produced when it connected with Nan's face had traveled up her arms to her shoulders, which were still thrumming like electric wires.

Trevor stood behind her in the doorway, mostly hidden in darkness despite the flickering candles and the pulsing of the Christmas tree lights at the far end of the room. "She's still alive."

"I think so. I think she's still breathing."

He seemed to float forward but not far enough to come into the light. All that could be seen of him were his large, wet eyes dancing in the candle flames. "You don't have much time then. She won't be unconscious for very long."

"I know." After what Trevor had told her, had *shown* her, and made her do to Muriel... she just wanted to get this over with. Her head thudded in time with her heart, and everything hurt. "You swear this will be the end of it?"

Trevor said nothing.

Lauren wanted to turn around and see her little boy to confirm who she was doing this for, but she couldn't quite bring herself to it. She was afraid he didn't look like himself just now.

Trevor spoke again, and from much closer, almost right behind her. There was an anger in his voice she didn't recognize. He had always been such a happy and easy child. "It's like my stomach rips itself apart. I'm so hungry."

Lauren saw a flash of images in her mind like the last few frames of a film before it spins off the reel with that *fwap, fwap, fwap* sound: a boy in a snowsuit. Nan digging up an old grave. And something so ancient and foul that her mind couldn't process it and short-circuited for a second.

"Go," Trevor said. Lauren did.

Nan was sprawled face down on the stone, her hair stained red with blood that had seeped from her cheek and pooled beneath her. There was bloody duct tape around her left ankle. Lauren started to wonder what it was doing there but decided it didn't matter. Her baby was *hungry*; he needed to eat, or he would die, and she wouldn't let that happen, not after the miraculous way she'd found him. She tied Nan's legs together quickly and efficiently with the rope she'd found on the bench in the foyer, using knots she learned from her father when the two of them would put up the tents on family camping trips when she was a girl. Next, she bound Nan's wrists, then attached to them a six-foot-long section of rope that smelled of engine oil. Nan was short but stocky, so this was the only way she could move her. Lauren seated the rope over the top of her shoulder, then started pulling Nan down the hall, leaving behind a slug trail of blood.

Once downstairs, she maneuvered the inert woman down to the root cellar and over to the built-in wine rack where Trevor had shown her the hidden latch. It shimmered deep down in the dark cubby. Just like the last time, Lauren reached inside until her fingers felt cold metal and pulled. The latch made a loud *clack* and the door swung inward, groaning.

Muriel's voice rose out of the darkness like a hoarsely

repeated incantation. When Lauren plugged in the string lights, Muriel started to shout, her voice cracking and breaking, rendering the words unrecognizable.

Ignore it, Lauren thought as she started down the steps, her breath forming icy clouds around her head. Nan's body rasped along the floor behind her like a snake. Trevor watched from the upper landing, nothing more than a small, black silhouette.

Muriel was on her back on the plinth, her hands bound tightly to the sides with rope. There was a nasty-looking gash on her forehead through which Lauren could see pale bone peeking. *I did that*, she thought, although the details were a bit hazy. It was a miracle the woman was conscious at all. Muriel flinched when Lauren stepped around the corner and blinked a few times. "Let me out, *now*. You don't understand what you're doing."

ROT! Trevor screeched. Both women turned (Muriel with some difficulty) at the sound of the voice, and a silence fell between them. Neither of them could see where he was in the dark.

Lauren dragged Nan over against the wall and dropped her on her back. She was still out like a light.

"Untie me," Muriel said. "Do it quickly. Before it—she—gets here."

Lauren pulled a sharp kitchen knife from her back pocket and looked around for Trevor. She couldn't see him. "Do I have to?" she asked him. He said nothing, and her eyes welled with tears. She didn't want to do what he said she must, but she couldn't let her baby starve to death. The way he had looked when they were out in the carriage house, all skin and bones, and how he pleaded with her for something to eat... the memory was unbearable.

"Yes, of course you do!" Muriel said, not realizing Lauren wasn't talking to her. "Do it now! She's watching."

Lauren's shoulders slumped. *It's for him*, she thought. *You can do it for him.*

The haft of the knife was slick in her hands, so she wiped her palms on her jeans and adjusted her grip.

"I can do this. I can *do* this."

"What are you babbling about, you stupid woman? Cut me loose, quickly. She's getting closer!"

"Do it," Lauren said. "Come on, just do it. Do it!"

She couldn't stand this any longer. Without giving it another moment's thought, she streaked forward and drove the knife down into Muriel's throat with all the force she could muster, so much so that the tip scraped the stone on the other side and snapped off. Hot blood pumped in spurts out over her hands, drenching them to the wrists, and she gasped.

Muriel's body went rigid, and her pleas stopped, which was a relief. Lauren wasn't sure how long she could have stood listening to them.

Around the blade of the knife, Muriel's breath whistled sharply, then gurgled as she pulled blood back down her windpipe. The noise it made was like water trying to flow through a plugged drain.

"I'm sorry," Lauren whispered. Muriel's furious eyes flew to the sound, and she tried to work her mouth, but the knife made it so no words would come. There was blood all over her teeth. "Oh, Jesus." Lauren turned away, dry heaving.

The gurgling sound went on for another couple of minutes, an interminable amount of time, before finally stopping. Lauren swallowed, took a shaky breath, and wiped away her tears.

"Lauren?"

Uttering a short, tired scream, she whipped toward the sound of the voice and saw Nan, eyes open (well, *eye*), staring right at her. "Lauren, what did you do? *Oh my god*, what did you do?"

-5-

Nan's entire world was pain. Pain from down below, which felt as if it had been wrapped in layers of thick wool—kind of soft and fuzzy around the edges—and a much sharper and more immediate pain coming from somewhere up top, close to where she was trying to think her thoughts.

Try as she might, though, she couldn't determine the cause of either. Her last reliable memory was no help; it was of her drinking scotch in the driver's seat of Lauren's car. That must have been part of a dream, she thought. Why else would it have been in Lauren's car? There was a flash of candles and stars, but that made even less sense. Probably just more dream flotsam. Unimportant.

Voices in the darkness. Muzzy and droning, overlaid by a high-pitched whine. Familiar, but not really. One whisper soft, the other verging on panic.

She tried to open her eyes—the right one cooperated, the left not so much—and even the low light sent stabbing pain through her head, so she closed them again fast. "What the fuck happened to my face?" she groaned. She couldn't open her jaws wide enough to form the words correctly, making her sound like she had a head cold.

She tried to call out again but instead hissed in pain. Christ, her mouth hurt. Talking only made it worse. Nan used her tongue to probe her teeth on the left side and found jagged stumps, a few holes, and something gritty. Her mouth flooded with saliva again, and she spit, sending tiny white pieces of tooth across the dirt floor. *Dirt?* she thought. *Where the fuck am I?*

She tried to order her thoughts as best she could (which, with a shattered cheekbone and maybe eye socket, too, was a painstaking process). Whatever had happened to her face, it had also done her the favor of fucking up something in her throat because it hurt when she swallowed... but that could just be a tooth lodged where one shouldn't be.

Before the puzzle pieces could begin to knit themselves into a picture, she heard someone grunt with exertion, followed by a sharp sound like a knife against a whetstone and then the telltale burbling of blood mixing with breath. Nan had heard *that* often enough to place it with little difficulty.

Both of the voices stopped. Slowly, mindful of what had happened the first time, Nan opened her right eye, and as consciousness continued to return, she was able to begin taking stock of what she saw. Dirt floor. Stone walls. Lights on a string hanging on pegs embedded in the wall. And there, in the middle of the room, a bit distorted and blurry, the stone plinth.

Am I dreaming? I have to be. There isn't any way I could be down here.

Then she saw a woman tied to the stone platform and what looked like the handle of her kitchen knife, the one Nick had bought when they visited New Orleans, sticking up out of her neck. Nan blinked to clear her vision, but it didn't work. Something in her mind was still addled by whatever had happened after she'd (maybe?) gotten drunk in Lauren's car.

Lauren. Holy God. It was her. The woman standing beside the plinth with her back to Nan and hands so bloody it looked like she was wearing red calfskin gloves was Lauren.

Rather than helping to cement the reality of the situation, it just made it seem all the more unreal. How could *she* be down here?

Nan tried to push herself up into a seated position and discovered that her hands were fixed firmly behind her back. Ditto her feet. That's when pain took a backseat, and panic climbed up front. She squirmed to the side and tried frantically to pull her arms apart, but the biting rope that lashed her in place had no give to it whatsoever.

Lauren turned toward her then, retching. Nan watched her until their eyes met, and what she saw there made Nan shake.

Lauren's eyes had drifted apart, neither one really focused on anything at all. She looked out of her mind. It was the same look Nan had seen on Bobby Buckland's face before he died and on her own, briefly, in the mirror when she'd gotten her first special headache.

"Lauren?" she said, trying to keep the quake out of her voice. "Lauren, what did you do? *Oh my god*, what did you do?"

"I had to. I'm sorry, but I had to. He's starving."

"Who is? What are you talking about?"

Lauren smiled through her tears. "Trevor. I found him. Oh, Nan, I really found him! He's back. But he's *so* hungry. If he doesn't eat soon, he'll die."

Nan's head swam. "Oh Jesus, Lauren, no, it's not Trevor. It isn't him."

She nodded sadly. "I know that. Except... sometimes it is."

"Did you hit me with something? My face is killing me."

"Nick's bat, the one he kept by the door. I... I tried to make it so you wouldn't suffer, like I did with Muriel, but it was easier with her. She was so much older. I'm so sorry."

Like I did with Muriel? She was *so much older*? From where Nan lay on the ground, she couldn't see much of the woman tied to the plinth with the kitchen knife sticking up out of her throat, but what she did see was a puff of white hair and a hand with red painted nails. Just like Muriel's.

"Lauren, untie me! Now, *now, right fucking now*!"

"I can't." Lauren cocked her head to the side like a puzzled puppy. "He says I'm not allowed."

"It's not him, *it's not him*, you know that!"

Lauren did that weird head cock again, nodded, and pressed her lips firmly together, sending a painfully clear message. *The time to talk is over.*

The hell it is! Nan started to babble like Muriel had at the end, but it did no good. Without looking back, Lauren ran up the stairs the same way Nan used to as a child when her mother sent her to the basement to get a jar of canned peaches, and she was so sure the monster beneath the steps would grab her.

"Get back here! *Get back here, you rotten cunt!*" Nan screamed. "You can't leave me down here like this! Don't leave me here to die!"

There was a long silence and then another sound with which Nan was intimately acquainted. The stuttering groan of the secret wine rack door, followed by the *clack* of the latch. She waited for the lights to go out, but they didn't. She couldn't decide if that was a blessing or a curse.

A moment later, she had made up her mind.

The plinth began sliding to the side as if on casters, exposing a dark hole underneath.

(*I rot in the well, Mr. Blackburn. I rot alone in the dark.*)

From the hole came the smell of decomposing flesh so strong and so old it made her eyes water.

The movement had caused Muriel Duckworth's blood to spill down over the edge and stain the side of the pedestal, then leak down into the newly opened trench beneath. Nan heard a sound like a dog lapping up water.

What she'd felt before hadn't been panic. *This* was panic. Without ramping up to it, her heart was going three hundred beats per second, and sweat broke out all over her body despite the cold seeping out of the dirt into her back. Breathing was starting to get difficult.

No, I don't want to see what it is. I don't want to know! she screamed in her head, too scared to say it out loud in case whatever was emerging from the hole heard her and decided it wanted something fresher than Muriel Duckworth's old carcass. She tried to quiet her breathing but couldn't. The faces of those she had left down here in the dark stuttered in an endless parade before her eyes.

In Nan's life, there were only a handful of moments when she had witnessed something so terrible that she had difficulty comprehending it until a long time after; like when her father had died. He'd gotten heatstroke and fallen from the hay mow onto the disc plow he'd parked down below to fix but hadn't gotten around to. Nan had been the one to find him. His eyes had been open and glazed and looked like stickers, and ants were crawling on his cheeks. And then, when she was a senior in high school, she saw Tim Armstrong, the resident class clown, darting back and forth across the road without looking, trying to get laughs but instead get creamed by an old man driving a car he wasn't able to stop in time. The blood on the pavement had looked wet and strange. Black almost.

But what dragged itself from the pit was worse than all the rest combined. It was too much for her to process all at once, so her mind separated it into pieces. On its base level, it resembled a human; it had two arms, two legs, a head, and ten fingers on its hands, but all similarities stopped there. It stood seven or eight feet tall, a corpse come to life, deformed by all of its years underground like a fungus growing deep in the darkness. Actually, there *were* fungi growing on it, she saw; pale, gray, and gelatinous, pushing up through the skin.

Its arms hung almost to its knees, capped with long fingered hands with too many joints, which were tipped by twisted and cruel-looking nails. The eyes took up most of the gaunt face, looking in different directions and shimmering wetly in the light. All of this was bad, but the mouth... Christ almighty, the mouth was the worst. The skin around the lips was pretty much gone, desiccated like a mummy's, leaving the rodent-like teeth to lean forward.

The legs were just bone, skinny and solid, and they made a thudding sound as they moved.

I'm getting used to my chicken feet, Nan thought. Bobby Buckland had said that right before he died.

A ring of stringy, dirt-clotted hair hung from a peeling skull. That, and the two sacs of deflated skin dangling from the chest, made Nan think this thing had been a woman at one point in life. The stink of rot and decay filled the room.

The woman (if such a monstrosity could still be considered as such), clattered from the hole, using long spidery fingers to drag herself up, then crawled up on top of the stone plinth to straddle Muriel's body. She leaned down, sniffed the knife, then carefully plucked it from Muriel's neck with the tips of her fingers and dropped it carelessly to the ground, where it stuck straight up and down. The woman screeched, a sound both human and animalistic as if warding others away from her meal, then lowered her mouth to Muriel's wound. Nan heard a sound that, if she closed her eyes, she might have been able to mistake for someone eating a chicken leg: stretching skin, tightening tendons, the wet slap of meat letting go. Her stomach lurched painfully, and she felt pressure at the base of her sternum. She was going to be sick, and nothing in the world could stop it.

The woman bent back down to her feast, latched that lamprey mouth onto Muriel's neck, and slurped out whatever she could get.

Nan tried to slow her breathing. She tried to think of something else, *anything* else, but in the end, nothing worked. Vomit surged up her throat, and with a series of wet belches, she emptied the contents of her stomach (which was mostly just scotch and the little bit of leftover mac 'n cheese she'd eaten for lunch) onto the dirt floor.

The woman on top of Muriel stopped ripping, tearing, and slurping and fell silent. She turned toward the new sounds which had invaded her space. Nan watched with growing terror as the rotting mushroom head swiveled and those gigantic alien eyes landed on her.

Scraps of Muriel Duckworth fell from the woman's mouth and landed with wet *paps* on the stone. Nan's breathing was ragged and fast, and she kept hoping she would pass out but stayed infuriatingly lucid.

The woman screamed a sound that was somehow both words and not words at all. Nan was reminded of her Christmas dream, in which a word had been scratched into the wood of the ancient chest Lizzie was opening in a language no one had ever read. If that language could be read aloud, this is what it would have sounded like. The woman slid with deceptive speed off of Muriel's body, landed on the floor, her bone-skinny legs punching down into the dirt. She took a moment to steady herself, then thudded over with shaky-jerky movements and stood looking down at Nan. She stood so for a moment and then, all at once, seemed to snap in half, bones cracking mutedly in what was left of her body as she bent at the waist. Her face (if you could call it that), came close to Nan's, and when she screeched, she exuded the odors of fresh blood and grave rot.

Nan closed her eyes and clamped her lips closed against another rising surge in her throat. *Please let it be quick. Please just let it be painless. Please, just let it happen soon.*

But the woman pulled back, straightening out to her full height. And, making a loopy sort of turn on her spindly Jack Sprat legs, she thumped over to Muriel again. She didn't climb back up on top of her, though. Instead, she placed one of her long-fingered hands on either side of Muriel's head, raised it up off the plinth, and drove it back down. The sound it made was like a walnut inside of a Christmas nutcracker. Nan belched again, but there was nothing left to come up but a thin trickle of bile.

The woman raised Muriel's head again, which looked decidedly flattened in the back, and drove it back down again like an otter trying to smash open a clamshell. This time, the crunch was more liquid.

The woman crowed contentedly and, peering down at the horrible ruin of Muriel Duckworth's head like a shopper trying to select the best piece of fruit at the supermarket, pinched something between the thumb and first finger of her many-jointed hand. She turned back to Nan, holding it.

In the low yellow light, it was faded pink and gray. A rill of blood oozed along it.

Those are Muriel's brains. Nan urked, and swallowed dryly.

The woman lurched back over, moving slowly now, and bent once again at the waist. She raised her fingers, pinching the slippery-looking muscle, and brought it to Nan's lips.

Nan drew her head back as far as she could against the wall and clamped her lips down so hard she tasted blood. It was like when she was a kid, and her mother had tried to force her to eat her broccoli, which to Nan had been the most disgusting thing in the world. There was now a new contender. "No," she said, opening her mouth as little as possible and shaking her head.

The woman hissed and squeezed Nan's face with her free hand. It hurt like hell, but that wasn't why Nan opened her mouth. It was the feeling of the woman's skin; cold and slimy, like drowned worms, yet strong enough to rip a person apart as if they were a well-cooked chicken. More than anything, Nan wanted those awful fingers off of her skin.

When her mouth popped open, the woman slipped the curd of brain inside. Nan tried to use her tongue to push it back out, but the woman placed her stinking palm over Nan's lips and nose and wrapped the rest of her fingers around the side of Nan's head. She recalled vividly the crunching sound Muriel's skull had made against the plinth and didn't wish to have the same thing happen to her.

Just swallow it! You'll probably throw it up in a second, anyway. Do it if it'll get that thing *away from you!*

It slid down her throat like it had a mind of its own. Thankfully, it didn't have much flavor; there was a salty, coppery taste of blood followed by a creamy sort of richness that was almost sweet (*unsalted butter*, her mind supplied, *if butter had a waxy consistency*), and then it was gone.

The woman wheezed and groaned. It almost sounded like words, as if she was saying *Good girl, you finished all of your veggies, now you can have some dessert!* and let go of Nan's face. Immediately, Nan started to hyperventilate, then to sob. The woman didn't seem to care about this at all. She climbed back up onto Muriel again with the painstaking slowness of an elderly woman climbing into bed and went back to her meal. The smacks, cracks, and crunches didn't seem so bad this time.

Nan closed her eyes and tried to throw up the wad of Muriel's brain that had gone down her throat, but she no longer felt like she could. It wasn't there *to* throw up anymore. Her body had already absorbed it.

After that, things got weirder.

-6-

Time is a strange and muddled thing.

-7-

Gretchen Holt was furious.

Nan was furious.

The two women were, in this place outside of time, one and the same. As Gretchen had done in the past, so Nan did now, the two of them moving together in an ageless dance, each one an echo of the other without knowing it. Gretchen Holt turned to regard the portrait that had been painted of her, and Nan saw it, her fury and dismay growing the longer she looked.

"Look at it, husband! Just look! She has painted my eyes to make me look like a fool! They point in opposite directions!"

"Gretchen, my love, they *are* in opposite directions. It does not diminish your beauty."

"It makes me look simple! As if I had been kicked by a horse as a child! I do not wish a portrait as unflattering as this to hang in my house. To be viewed by our children and all of our guests!" She took a long sip from her drink.

"I shall have it redone, then. Surely, the Cobb woman will retouch the eyes if you but ask her to."

"I do not wish for her to do anything! She has made a mockery of me with this."

"My love, how can you know she has done it on purpose? Perhaps she has only painted what she believed you wanted."

Gretchen folded her arms across her bodice, barely able to contain the rage within her body. Usually, the alcohol helped to soothe her fury, but it wasn't working. "She has been making a mockery of me all through the town, too. I have heard of it from Mr. Garrett, the grocer, and again from Mrs. Hartwell, the butcher's wife. She thinks my father ought to have put me down like a rabid dog! And all for the fact that my eyes do not line up with one another."

Percy Holt looked the portrait up and down. To his mind, it was fine, especially for being painted by a woman. Her technique would not soon rival Goya's but for the slightly mad wife of a farmer (and for what it was costing him) it was serviceable. "It is a cruel thing of her to say but not worth making yourself ill over. The Cobb woman is not right in the head—you know, she speaks the words that come to her mind without benefit of thought first. Besides, if you recall, I did admonish you to wear the patch over your eye when in public."

"The patch is no better than the eye itself!" Her voice rang out, causing the crystal to vibrate. Gretchen wanted to throw the fine crystal glass she held into the fireplace but didn't want her husband to see her that much out of temper. He might suggest she return to the sanitarium, and there was nothing Gretchen Holt wanted less in the world than that. Instead, she carefully set it on the marble topped highboy and poured more gin. (A thoroughly nervous creature, the damned maid had scampered off when the yelling started.) With the taste of gin fresh on her tongue, she felt able to continue. "The people of this town see me as a beast to be pitied or else as a mental defective. The patch does not hide my defect. It only serves to high-light it."

Percy Holt fetched a deep sigh. "What would you have me do, darling? Have her drawn and quartered? Have her dragged from her home and set afire in the town square? I have heard a rumor that she plays with dark magics. Perhaps that would be enough to persuade the rest of the town to have a witch burning."

"So you mock me now, too."

Percy stood and took her in his arms. "My love, I do not mock. I merely try to show you that your emotions have carried you away with them. Can you not see? The portrait can be easily amended, and we do not need to pay the Cobb woman for it. And I shall personally warn the town of her treachery and cruelty. By day's end, you shall have them all behind you, and the Cobb woman's trade will be ruined."

"You say it as though it were so easy. Do you not hear the whispers as we go through town? See the way the townsfolk point at us and speak of us when they think we cannot hear? We are not from here. They will not take my side, or even your side, husband, over that of a local woman."

"Then I pose to you the question again. What would you have me do? I can already see that your hand shakes, and your skin has gone as pale as cream. You will be ill and confined to your bed chamber again if you are not careful."

Gretchen swallowed the gin in her glass and set it aside. To take more now in front of Percy would no doubt result in him chastising her for overindulging and would only inflame her foul mood. She would take to her room with the bottle, and that would have to be enough. "I would be left alone now, husband," she said. "As always, you are right in taking your levelheaded approach to the matter. There is nothing to be done save for refusing to pay the thief, and with your leave, that is exactly what we will do."

Percy Holt kissed his wife's forehead gently and patted her

arms, as she herself did with her children to soothe them when megrims took them. "It will be done, my dearest. Think no more of this upsetting episode."

Gretchen bore his condescension as all women of her station did, yet could not resist adding: "And burn this miserable likeness of me. Were I to give it back, the old Cobb witch would likely use it to place a curse on me."

Reality grew as thin as smoke then, and the world seemed to reel before Gretchen/Nan. They closed their eyes against the vertigo, and when they opened them again, Gretchen looked down at her hands and saw a small blue vial of powder. Nan looked down at hers and saw the same. They blinked and were as one again. The day had changed, and so had the room.

It was raining outside, a hard, pounding rain that would be driving the farmers in from their fields all over town. Gretchen peered through the kitchen window and down the great lawn and saw the wide expanse of the Hudson River, a view unimpeded by trees. The sun was already beginning to break through the clouds on the opposite bank, where the relatively new town of Esopus sat hidden in the forest. If the rain cleared up this afternoon, she could ride to the Cobb farm tonight.

On the counter in front of her was a bowl filled with sweet batter for teacakes.

Do I truly mean to do this? she thought. Of course she did. The Cobb woman had been kicking up all sorts of trouble around town ever since Percy had refused to pay her for her so-called artwork. She haunted Gretchen wherever she went. The grocer, Mr. Garrett, had informed Gretchen that rumors and ill talk were circulating of her husband's inability to make payment, which was turning the tide of goodwill in the town against them.

"He can pay," Gretchen told him coldly. "He *chooses* not to." To have to explain her business to a man like Garrett was galling, yet the Cobb woman was proving to be more of a thorn in her side than she had anticipated. "Mrs. Cobb has done work of such a poor quality it does not warrant compensation, and I would thank you not to engage in such malicious and slanderous gossip, *Mister* Garrett."

Garrett had harrumphed and tied to backpedal, a crimson color rising into his thick cheeks.

Yes. I mean to do this. Gretchen upended the blue vial into the batter and gave it a good stir before recorking the bottle and slipping it into her apron pocket. Mr. Benson, the town chemist who had sold her the arsenic as a treatment for her frequent migraines, had assured her there was no taste to it. He'd also cautioned her to take a very small amount, as too much could lead to death.

The cook, whose name she had a devil of a time recalling, was clear across town visiting her mother, who had taken ill during the last cold snap, and Percy had taken the children to the city to take in a show and expose them to some culture (a thing which was sorely lacking this far out in the country). This meant Gretchen had the house to herself. There was no moment from the time she had thought up how to exact her revenge until now when she had second thoughts or doubts. All things being in convergence this day was itself a good omen, she thought.

While the teacakes baked, she whipped an icing together and added the remainder of the powder from the blue vial to them.

Gretchen wished she could be there to see the effects of the arsenic on Mrs. Cobb, to watch her gasp and struggle for every breath as the poison took over her body, but to know it was happening would have to suffice. The old woman would never again mock her and never again tell her fellow townspeople that Gretchen ought to have been drowned in the river as a babe like a dog that bites. The woman was a snake, and Gretchen meant to remove her head.

Once cooled and iced, the teacakes went into a wicker

basket and were covered with a clean but old rag from the pantry and—

The world reeled again. And again, for only a moment, the two women separated like solids and liquids in a centrifuge. Nan grew nauseated and lightheaded before the world re-solidified.

Gretchen sat in a chair in the drawing room, reading a book by Ellis Bell.

Nan sat in a chair in the same room (what would become her library, years and years in the future), holding the same book. Only the name on her copy was Emily Brontë.

There was a knock at the door. The maid, Elsie, hurried to get it, but Gretchen waved her off like an annoying fly and told her to help the cook lay out supper. When she was gone, Gretchen thoughtfully set her book on the table beside her chair and went to answer the door. This would be news of the Cobb woman's death, for there was nothing else it could be. It was all she could do to hide her excitement and not skip across the floor.

Muriel Cobb was standing on the bluestone veranda with a look of dark rage on her face. Her hair, which had been swept up that morning but had fallen on the ride over (along with her hat, which now rested somewhere on the forest floor), was a puffball around her head. She wore the same plain blue dress she had been wearing in town yesterday. The hem was stained with mud, and there were burrs stuck to the wool. As soon as Gretchen opened the door, Muriel flew at her, her hands rigid claws striking and slashing at Gretchen's surprised face.

"You murdered them!" Muriel screamed. Sweat rolled down her face, cutting through the powder she wore on her cheeks. "You have killed my husband and child with your poison treats!"

It was all Gretchen could do to hold off the rampaging woman who seemed to have the strength of ten men in her.

"You have lost your mind!" she shouted back. "I did not kill anyone!"

"You have! My child, my poor Alice! And my Franklin!"

Elsie tiptoed up the stairs, curious as to what the commotion could possibly be. A girl of only sixteen, she looked shocked and frightened to see the wife of farmer attacking a lady of society in her own foyer. Gretchen caught sight of her and screamed, "Fetch Mr. Barlow before she kills me!"

Muriel did not seem to have seen the girl. All of her attention was focused on Gretchen Holt, trying desperately to get her hands close enough to rip her lazy eye from its socket. After a moment, Elsie turned and ran with the strange rabbity hops she always used when frightened, to find the gardener.

"I would rip your throat out with my teeth, but it would still leave me unsatisfied!" Muriel Cobb screamed. "My child found your tainted food before I was able to spy it! She and my Franklin both ate of it before I could stop them and now lie cold and dead on the undertaker's table!"

It hadn't been Gretchen's intention to kill Muriel's child (in fact, she wasn't entirely certain Muriel even had one before leaving the teacakes on the farmhouse's kitchen doorstep), but it caused her no distress that Alice was dead. Nor the mad woman's husband, Franklin. They had not been the first people to land afoul of Gretchen's temper and would not be the last.

Muriel's hands broke free of Gretchen's grip and, with the speed of a striking adder, clamped upon Gretchen's throat and squeezed as hard as they could.

There was a cracking sound, felt by both Gretchen and Nan separately, and darkness bloomed before their vision, interrupted only by celestial swirls. Gretchen had a moment to be grateful that her son and daughters were down at the river with their governess and would not see their mother murdered in the foyer.

As if reading her mind, Muriel leaned down, her breath sour with anger, and hissed, "I would not kill you so quickly no matter the gratification it would give me. I would see you suffer for a long, *long* time and endure the same losses you have inflicted on me. I would see you turned on the outside into the very monster you are on the inside! Heed my words, for they will be made true. You will suffer, and I will be there to watch!"

From the pocket of her dress, Muriel Cobb took something small and shriveled that looked to Gretchen like the desiccated finger of a child and shoved it between Gretchen's lips. She then ate something herself before clamping her hand down over Gretchen's mouth and nose until the mysterious object had been swallowed (leaving behind an aftertaste of dirt and decay), and whispered something in a language with which Gretchen was unfamiliar.

A moment later, Mr. Barlow appeared. He wrapped his arms around Muriel Cobb's waist and, with an apology, hauled her backward. Gretchen expected Muriel to spit and fight like a cornered cat, but all the fight seemed to have drained out of her.

Gretchen sat holding her throat, trying to cough up whatever Muriel had fed her (certain that it must have been poisoned, surely it was), but could not get it out no matter what. "Get her out of here!" she screamed, but the sound was hardly a hoarse whisper. Whatever that crack in her throat had been, it had damaged something, rendering her voice useless. Gretchen coughed a few more times as Mr. Barlow dragged the inert Muriel Cobb to the front door and deposited her on her horse. Elsie tried to help the lady of the house to her feet, but Gretchen batted her away and, holding onto her throat, made her way to the doors.

Muriel turned in her saddle and glowered. "Your suffering will not end in your lifetime. Nor ten of them, nor a hundred. Your hunger will never be slaked, yet you'll eat. You'll live as death, trapped here in this foul house, while I merely live and exult in your pain. My life will be as long as yours, and I'll use it to watch your every torturous moment. And were you to come to me on bloodied knees and beg my mercy, I would spit in your face and send you back to your hell where you belong."

Ravings of a lunatic and nothing more. Muriel nudged her horse's side and it broke into a gallop, its eyes rolling as if terrified of the woman that sat astride it. After a moment, the thudding of its hooves was gone, and the world was once more silent.

Both Barlow and Elsie urged her to call for the doctor, but Gretchen sent them away. Her throat was not causing her any pain at all, and she was no longer worried that whatever Muriel had fed her had been poisoned. She had said *I would not kill you so quickly no matter the gratification it would give me.* Whatever the unhinged woman had stuffed down her throat was likely more disgusting than it was dangerous and, therefore, nothing Gretchen wished to think about further. She did attempt to sick it up a few more times, but it no longer felt present within her, as if her body had soaked it up somehow.

When Percy arrived home soon after, he had already been informed of the altercation. Either Elsie or Barlow (or both of them) had spoken the gossip to someone else, and now the whole town knew.

"Is it true?" he said to her, stripping his riding gloves and throwing them to the floor.

Gretchen had wrapped her throat with muslin smeared with a healing poultice. Her hand went to it as she croaked her answer. "She attacked me."

"Not that," Percy said, pink rising in his cheeks as he stalked toward her. "Is it *true*? Did you poison that poor woman's daughter and husband?"

"Why ever would you think that?" Not an answer, though not a lie, either. Percy grabbed her by the shoulders and shook her.

"Damn you, tell me the truth! I am your husband, and you will obey me! And do not lie! Did you do something to Mr. Cobb and that little girl? I had heard rumors of you before we were wed but took them to be lies crafted by a rival. And now this?"

Gretchen jerked backward out of his grip, leaving him stunned. "If I were in your place and believed that of me, I would be *much* more cautious of the words I chose. After all, if I could do something like that once, I could do it again, could I not?" A humorless smile crept onto her face when he didn't answer. "I will consider the matter closed then, and we will speak no more of it. Come now, the cook has put supper on the sideboard in the dining room, and I would eat. I am feeling hungry suddenly."

Percy didn't come to dinner that night. Nor did Jeremiah or Persephone. The baby, Cora, would not have dined with them anyway, staying instead in the nursery with the nanny, so Gretchen had the entirety of the meal to herself. The cook had prepared a roast with root vegetables, savory gravy, and home-made bread with fresh churned butter. There was even fresh cream and biscuits with honeycomb for dessert. Gretchen ate her fill of it all and could have continued to eat if it hadn't been for her upbringing, which told her she had already overindulged and was already in danger of becoming the topic of discussion amongst the cook and the maid this evening (and around town tomorrow). She hadn't been able to help herself, though. She had worked up a hunger that day.

Along with the hearty meal, Gretchen had also consumed multiple gins. Yet that evening, when she went to bed, her stomach churned and growled, and her sleep was broken.

And the world reeled once again.

When Nan and Gretchen came back together, it was weeks after the encounter with Muriel. Gretchen's skin was drawn and sallow, and her skull stood out starkly.

The joint Cobb funeral would be starting in about an hour, and all of the town had turned out for it. Percy Holt and his older children were in attendance, along with the governess to help keep an eye on them. Gretchen, of course, had stayed home. She had wanted to go, but Percy had put his foot down, telling her, "Muriel Cobb has been through enough. Leave her to her grief, and do not make the day all about you." Despite knowing the only reason Percy wanted to show his face there was to reclaim some of the town's good will, Gretchen had acquiesced. His business was starting to suffer, and he would not become a pauper because of his wife.

Unbeknownst to said wife, there was another reason. Too afraid to eat anything she had been left alone with, Percy and his children had resorted to filling themselves on apples and, when that wasn't enough, leftover bread that they had seen the cook eating from first. After the funeral, there would be a repast catered by some of the local women, and, therefore, a chance for the Holts to fill their bellies without worry.

Gretchen had taken to bed, feeling ill. Her hunger was a physical thing now, a presence she felt within her body. Every night she ate her fill at supper, and again every morning ate a hearty breakfast, yet there was no feeling of fullness that accompanied her feasting and no satisfaction in the flavor. As time passed, she could hardly taste the food, and when she smelled it being prepared in the kitchen, it turned her stomach. The only thing she subsisted on now was gin, consuming bottle after bottle despite her husband's disapproving looks.

Elsie the maid, Barlow the gardener, and whatshername the cook, had all been given leave by Percy to attend the funeral. The nanny, a Rubenesque woman with graying hair named Charlotte, had chosen to stay at Holt House with the baby, but Gretchen had sent her along as well, telling her to leave Cora behind. The plump woman had gone, not without reservation, leaving Gretchen and the babe alone in the big house.

At first, all Gretchen could do was clutch her stomach and moan, rolling in her sweat-filthy sheets, the pain in her guts so terrible that she wondered if perhaps Muriel *had* poisoned her after all. But she knew of no poisons which would have taken this long to kill.

Even as she starved, the thought of food was repulsive to her; fresh strawberries and cream would be like eating horse dung, and herbed and roasted chicken would be something fouler still. She worried that if she could no longer eat, death wouldn't be far behind.

Yet when their cat, Thomas, leaped onto the bed and deposited a dead mouse on the coverlet with a look of pride, Gretchen's stomach rumbled. Thomas preened and licked his paws, and when Gretchen reached for the little mouse, he tried to nab it back, but she swatted him away. She took the small white-bellied creature into her hands and stuffed it whole into her mouth. The very act should have reviled her, yet even as she chewed it, feeling the delicate bones crunch between her teeth like the skin of roasted pork, her hunger faded. What should have tasted revolting was instead subtly delicious and unlike anything else she'd ever eaten before. If it was what the cat tasted, it was no wonder it hunted as often as it did. As much of a delicacy as the mouse had been, it had not been enough, and her hunger, now whetted by the mere morsel she had tasted, roared to life, sending stabbing pains through her belly.

The baby cried from her bassinet in the nursery just down the hall. Gretchen turned toward the sound, salivating.

No! she thought with horror. *To do so would be the end of me!* Yet, there was something more powerful driving her from within. A compulsion. She found herself climbing from bed on legs which had become more stick-like over the last fortnight and tried to steady herself.

"Do not cry," she called to the babe, and her voice, though much repaired from Muriel's damage, was soft and predatory.

Looking down into the bassinet at the squalling thing within, Gretchen felt nothing. She thought perhaps there would be a wonderful smell, like that of suckling pig, veal, or lamb, but all she could smell was the fresh pink skin of the child.

It is because the child still breathes, a voice spoke. She turned in a circle to see to whom the voice belonged but was alone in the nursery. It had sounded like Muriel Cobb.

And yet... perhaps whoever had spoken was right. The tiny mouse had been freshly dead when she ate it, and the supernatural hunger that wracked her body had been momentarily sated. The child was much bigger than a mouse and so would likely drive the hunger away for much longer. Perhaps even for good. It was this last thought that decided her.

Before she could change her mind, Gretchen Holt took hold of the screaming babe by the legs and, with one swift motion, dashed Cora's head into the nursery wall, silencing her for good.

A wave of nausea swept through Nan's body, and it was enough to allow her to split from Gretchen for a moment and not have to witness what came after the act of infanticide. However, when the two women merged again, Nan no longer felt the clawing hunger.

After that, the visions (if visions they were) came more sporadically, all herky-jerky and in fits, where Nan embodied Gretchen for brief flickers of time and then not at all. Each new one was punctuated by that vertiginous reeling sensation of time turning around her.

A reel, then: Persephone and Jeremiah lay dead on the flagstone entryway of Holt House. Percy charged Gretchen, screaming nonsensical guttural sounds in a blind fury, only to be stopped with one swing of an already bloodied hatchet. The sound that emerged from his lips when the blade bit into his skin and parted his brow was unlike anything else in the world. Not just a scream but pure, unfiltered pain. Metal squelched against bone when Gretchen pulled it out.

A reel, then: Persephone's body, minus her right leg, dumped on the kitchen floor like the carcass of a butchered beast. The leg had been placed with carrots, onions, and potatoes in a roasting pan in the oven. Gretchen carefully removed the pan and saw herself reflected in its polished surface. She was even more emaciated than she had looked this morning, but the feeling of hunger was, for the nonce, gone. She sat down to her feast, eating every bite she was able to, and then threw up all of the vegetables.

A reel, then: Gretchen was smoothing Jeremiah's hair where he lay in the foyer, his body uneaten. Blood smeared her mouth, though, and it was then Nan saw the remains of Percy Holt off to the side, most of the meat picked from his bones. Gretchen had eaten him raw.

"I would not eat from you, my poor boy," she said as she stroked Jeremiah's hair. "You were my favorite of all of them, and I wish it had not come to this. But you will find peace in the next world. I will leave word to have you buried in a grand coffin, untouched, with a view of your beloved river." Yet even as Gretchen spoke, Nan could feel the raw hunger growing in her stomach. It seemed impossible that she might still be hungry, given the amount of meat picked from Percy's bones, yet the feeling was undeniable. How Jeremiah was left untouched was a mystery (as was where Percy's body had finally ended up), because that somewhat tender moment was followed by—

A reel, then: A nun moved down the upstairs hallway as if floating. She was tall, cloaked in a habit, with a curl of steel gray hair peeking from beneath her wimple. Her face said she would brook no argument, not even if God almighty Himself came down from on high and contradicted her, but her eyes pointed in two different directions. Behind her, she pulled a sack stained with blood. The house was quiet and empty, and the sun shone brightly through the windows. It would have been a beautiful day if not for the scene unfolding. Nan watched as the nun, Sister Anthony (this she knew intuitively, just as she knew the nun she dragged behind her was Sister Maria Francis, the last of the sect, but for one), took the body down the stairs and then through the secret door in the wine rack, which at this time was filled with bottles. Sister Anthony was tall and had to duck so as not to scrape the top of her wimple on the doorjamb as she went through.

She held a candle instead of a flashlight, which flickered uneasily in the crypt. With a strength she should not have had, Sister Anthony pushed open the top of a stone vault with a placard on the front that read **Sister Maria Francis, Rest With God in Peace** and deposited a crucifix, a bible, and a rosary into it. Exactly as she had done for all the rest of the nuns she had brought down here. The bodies themselves had, of course, been bound for the plinth.

Sister Anthony swung the bag up from her side (*seriously*, Nan thought, *the woman could have played football had she been born later*), and deposited it on the plinth. She then climbed up beside it and lay down, unmindful of the blood that seeped from it, said a Hail Mary, then blew her brains out.

A reel, then: A little boy in brown corduroy pants and a blue sweater running away from his mother along the downstairs corridor. He ran past a sign leaning against the wall amongst half-unpacked crates that read *Hotel on the Bluff*, done in old-fashioned lettering. It was the boy, Ricky, who had been killed here in the '60s, the one Claudia had mentioned during the interview. His mother chased him with a kitchen knife already slicked with blood, her hair wild and frizzy, her eyes pointing crazily in two directions.

"Daddy! *Daddy!*" Ricky screamed, but Daddy wasn't coming. The little boy cried and pushed through the door into the root cellar, and his mommy smiled. Nan could practically hear what the woman was thinking: *Perfect.*

Thankfully, time reeled again, speeding her along its continuum away from poor Ricky, who was many years dead by now, past the sight of a girl dressed in late 60s bellbottoms and a flowered shirt dead on her bed with her roommate standing over her holding a bloody letter opener, and past the sight of Bobby Buckland dropping, (minus one eye), to the floor in the dining room upstairs.

A reel, then: When time came to a stop this time, it was Christmas day. Nan stood in the kitchen in her robe fixing cocoa while Gretchen Holt, now a gangly and desiccated creature, stood nearby, waiting.

As Nan made drinks, she thought of Lizzie's long brunette hair. It had grown back over the last few years, but she would be losing it again soon. Doctor Osborne said the cancer had returned aggressively and that treatment needed to begin right away if there was to be any hope.

Nan had begged Nick and Doctor Osborne to wait until after the holiday to start, ostensibly to give her daughter one happy holiday memory, if nothing else. Neither one liked it, but both had agreed.

Nan poured scalded milk over the cocoa powder, then took a box of E-Rat-Icator from the cupboard and added some to each cup except for her own. To hers, she added a glut of vodka. Gretchen smiled, showing her rotted teeth, and nodded. Nan stirred the cocoa, then added a little peppermint liquor to Lizzie's and coffee liqueur to the other two and topped them all with whipped cream.

Ducky's crew was off for the week but had left their tools and materials littered throughout the house. Nan negotiated around these while Gretchen slouched behind her, following and whispering.

Lizzie was beneath the tree, shaking boxes while a Christmas movie played on the TV. "Mommy, can I open this one first?"

"Sure, go ahead." She set the drinks on the table. Nick took a tiny sip of his, then grimaced, and for a second, Nan thought she was caught.

"How drunk are you?" he asked *sotto voce* so Lizzie wouldn't hear.

"What? Why, what's wrong with it?" Her heart pounded.

He laughed. "You put peppermint *and* coffee liqueur in mine."

"I did?" Dammit, she probably had. Her mind was elsewhere this morning. Timing was crucial right now. She couldn't afford any fuckups. "I'll just make you another one quick." She stood to leave, but Nick took her arm and pulled her back down to the couch.

"I wasn't complaining, just calm down. It's Christmas. Look, I'll drink it." He took another sip, larger than the first, and grinned, resting his hand high up on her thigh.

"Lizzie, come drink your cocoa before it gets cold."

Lizzie walked over to the coffee table on her knees, dragging boxes behind her. She took her cup.

"Mommy, mine's minty."

Nan sighed heavily. "You *like* mint. What, so you want me to remake yours now, too?"

"No, Mommy, I'll drink it. Can I open my presents while I do?"

"Knock yourself out, kid. Live it up."

Nick's hand went higher up her thigh as he took another sip, and Nan batted it away. "Knock it off."

"Jesus, *sorry*."

"God, don't get huffy. I'm just not in the mood for that. We're opening gifts here. Just wait, all right?"

Nick pulled his hand back sulkily and coughed. Lizzie was coughing, too, unable to get a complete sentence out.

"Mommy," she paused, coughing. "Mommy, I—"

Nick was up and around the table at once, patting Lizzie on the back even as his own cough worsened. Nan watched this with fascination.

Lizzie opened her mouth again, and a freshet of blood and foamy vomit spewed out and covered the gifts at her feet.

"Oh Jesus, what the fuck?" Nick cried as blood burst from between his own lips, speckling the back of Lizzie's head. "What's happening?"

Nan sat there and absorbed Nick's fear. After all of his strength and the stalwart heroic man role he played for the doctors and nurses, and everyone else, his fear and lack of control were splendid to behold.

"What did you do?" he managed to choke out as his face went first red, then purple. Lizzie collapsed onto her back with a small but satisfying thud, and Nick reached out for her, but his perception was fucked now, and instead, he ended up collapsing on top of her. Their bodies convulsed as they retched and vomited. Lizzie tried to cry out, huge tears rolling down her cheeks.

Nan had given Nick more of the E-Rat-Icator to compensate for his height and weight, and he went first. Lizzie was only about a minute or so after, imitating the deep, wet, gurgling sound Nick had made as she aspirated.

Then, the house was quiet. A clock ticked. The tree lights flashed on and off. Nan sat there for thirty minutes, watching them. The phone rang twice (*Nick's mother, had to be*). She ignored it.

When she finally stood, the world seemed to (*reel*) swing strangely around her, a touch of vertigo, and she closed her eyes until it stopped.

She washed Nick and Lizzie's bodies in the downstairs guest bath, cleaning off the blood and vomit, then dressed them in the clothes she had laid out for them that morning; Nick in his blue suit with a white button-down shirt and red bowtie, and Lizzie in her white cotton dress with the Christmas tree embroidered on the front. With that done, she dragged them out to the car where it was freezing (*all the better to preserve you, my dear*), and buckled them into their seats. Then she went inside and cleaned up the mess in front of the tree. By the time she was finished, her back was spasming, and her arms were like rubber.

She set the first bottle of scotch on the coffee table and poured a large glass. For an instant, she felt as if someone was watching her, but wrote that off to simple paranoia.

She drank, and drank, and drank some more. She passed the day one glass at a time, with Christmas movies playing in the background and the tree lights flashing merrily until it was dark outside and the bottle was gone. It was time to leave for the dinner their friends were hosting. Nan stood unsteadily, grabbed her purse, and joined her family in the car.

Nick had slumped forward in the passenger seat a bit, so she pushed him back gently, tightened his seatbelt, and then checked on Lizzie. She was still upright, hands folded in her lap, pretty as a picture.

Nan buckled herself in and then sped up the driveway. She fishtailed her way out onto Little Church Road, then roared through the darkness that was broken only by the occasional front yard holiday light display. When she came around the last bend before Little Church connected to Route 9, she looked down at the Hudson that flowed like black blood, closed her eyes, and jerked the wheel, sending the car into the guardrail.

And the rest, as they say, is history.

There was no longer a solid thread of memory, just glitchy, bloody snapshots that ended when she opened her eyes and found herself sitting on the road with her back against the cold guardrail. Sheriff Lambert leaned down over her with a flashlight. Under her breath, she had been singing "Silent Night," along with the radio, but when she saw Lambert, she stopped. "Are they okay?" she asked, scotch fumes billowing from her mouth. She sat up a little straighter, wincing at the slight pain in her foot and wrist.

"Are they okay? *Oh God, what happened?*"

Her scream echoed.

And the world reeled.

-8-

Nan gasped and sobbed in the dirt as the scenes she had just witnessed played over and over in her mind. All those people. All those *years*. But especially Nick and Lizzie.

Gretchen Holt, or rather the creature Gretchen Holt had become, stood by the partially denuded body of Muriel on her bone legs, watching.

"Why?" Nan said. "Why did you let me do that to them if you weren't going to... to *use* them?" She couldn't quite bring herself to say eat. But as soon as the words were out of her mouth, she knew the answer. It was the same reason she'd been a drunk, and the same reason she'd been a killer. It was a compulsion. Rot and decay weren't the only things that provided sustenance. Pain, misery, and grief were all nourishing in their own ways. Whatever type of creature Gretchen Holt was now, whatever Muriel had done to her, it hadn't changed one fundamental thing about the woman she had been all those years ago. She was insane. And perhaps, worse than that, she was cruel. It was why she had not fed on Claudia McKinnon's body, forcing Nan to get rid of it herself, despite how painful it must have been to ignore such a tasty offering.

Nan had disobeyed her when she wouldn't allow Gretchen to have the boy in the snowsuit and so had to be punished. This compulsion Gretchen felt to feed on death might have deepened those qualities, but it hadn't created them within her. She'd always been this way. If Nan had known about Ava and Lauren's conversation about people infecting a place with misery, she would have thought it was spot on. Misery really loves company, so that's what Gretchen had spent her long life creating.

Maybe I've always been this way, too, she thought. *At least a little, deep down inside. I hated Nick, and I resented Lizzie and, in time, I grew to hate almost everyone else. And as much as I want to, as much as I deserve to, I don't think I can lay all of the blame for what I did to those people on this woman's shoulders.*

As if thinking about them had conjured them into existence, Nan saw standing around her, filling the crypt, all those who had been killed over Holt House's long and bloody history. Ricky in his blue sweater and corduroys with a slash through his mouth, extending his smile up the sides of his head, standing beside his father and horrified-looking mother. And there was Persephone, Jeremiah, and Cora Holt. Persephone held the baby while she and Jeremiah held hands like Hansel and Gretel lost in the woods. Percy looked on with shame because he could not stop Gretchen. There were others, so many of them, and somewhere in the back of the group, Nick and Lizzie. Their heads were bowed as if they couldn't bear to look.

What remained of these people was the human equivalent of the liquor bottles Nan used to sneak into the recycling bin every week. Just empty husks and guilt.

Gretchen struck out at them with her hand (which went right through the man from Ireland Nan had killed), and wobbled forward, clutching Muriel's half-gnawed arm. She dropped it to the ground beside Nan's head. "What are you doing?" Nan said, but Gretchen did not answer. She didn't really have to. The arm beside Nan could only mean one thing, but it was too horrible to even consider. She thought about Muriel shoving what looked like a child's mummified finger down Gretchen's throat, and then about Gretchen force-feeding her a squiggle of Muriel's brain in the same way. That groaning death rattle sound she had made after doing it may have been the very same words Muriel had spoken back in 1860; a curse, an incantation, or a recipe for hummus. It all amounted to the same in the end.

Gretchen made her way back to the plinth where Muriel's dregs lay, and she took hold of the arm that was still attached to Muriel's torso. Using it as a handle, she dragged the body down to the ground and then into the pit beside the plinth.

"Where are you going?" Nan called after her. "Don't leave me here like this! Untie me! Untie me! I won't do it, I can't!"

Gretchen Holt stopped and turned back. Her face broke out into what might have been a smile. The bloodstained flaps of skin that had once been lips pulled back, revealing those black, leaning teeth, which looked like they would be able to take off a person's head with one bite.

Decay and rot, Gretchen said, and then disappeared down into the hole. A moment later, the plinth ground across the floor back into place, leaving Nan alone.

She looked at the arm that had until recently belonged to Muriel Duckworth (née Cobb). Stringy meat and fat trailed from the ragged stump where Gretchen's teeth marks could still be seen.

I won't. I'd rather die.

But even as she thought this, she knew she would. Because if what she had seen during the nightmarish stroll down Gretchen's memory lane was true, Nan wouldn't be able to die. She would live a long, *long* life, and Gretchen, not Muriel, would be there watching and relishing in every horrible moment of pain and degradation. Because misery loved company and like calls to like.

And, of course, there was the other reason, too. A compulsion was a compulsion, simple as that.

Nan sniffed the arm. It reminded her a little of the Christmas ham her mother would make back on the farm, the one with the bacon gravy, fresh cracked pepper, and potatoes.

And her stomach rumbled.

And she ate.

Epilogue
One for the Road

-1-

The day after Christmas dawned bright and sunny in the Hudson Valley. The nor'easter, which had howled through town, had dumped about two and a half feet of sparkling white fluffy powder on the world and brought the power down for most of the town. Driving along the streets, creeping at a snail's pace so as not to crash his new car, Tim Rossiter could hear generators blatting unevenly. Some people were digging out, others using snowblowers, but almost everyone stopped and waved as he inched by in his big, black SUV.

"Hicks," he said under his breath and waved back. He didn't have time to waste with the small-town charm this morning. The courier had delivered Nan's manuscript late last night along with two other objects, which now rode in his briefcase in the passenger seat (properly sealed in bags, of course). Her manuscript, on the other hand, he'd left on his desk at home, held in place by a marble paperweight in the shape of a phallus that an old boyfriend had given him when he first broke into the biz.

His hands still shook as he gripped the wheel. Had, in fact, been shaking since he received the package last night and sat down to read the first pages of Nan's new book. And it was a whopper, too, over nine hundred manuscript pages. The title page read:

The Confession
By Nan Wickwyre

"Ka-ching," he'd said, taking it out of the box. Something else was rolling around in the bottom, so he'd upended it over the coffee table and dumped it out. A plastic sandwich bag with a cellphone bearing a pink case and what looked like an SD card fell onto the tabletop. There was something brown and sludgy on them that smelled kind of like roadkill (*Ugh, puke*), and they were damp even though the rest of the box was dry.

He'd checked for a note explaining what they were for, but there wasn't one, so instead, he poured a glass of red wine and started skimming through the pages.

Very quickly, he could tell something wasn't right. There was no story. It was just Nan writing as herself, claiming to have murdered at least twenty people, including that cokehead reporter the cops still hadn't found. He set down the manuscript and then took the phone out of the plastic bag and tried to get it to turn on. It wouldn't. Then he wiped the sludge off the SD card and plugged it into his computer, but the file was corrupted and wouldn't open. He ejected it and dropped it back into the baggie along with the phone.

He leafed through the rest of the manuscript until he got to the end (the snippets he read along the way certainly *sounded* like a Nan Wickwyre novel) and scanned the last few pages. This confession was different from the others. She wasn't confessing a murder that had happened, but one that *would* happen. The local sheriff, apparently. "Oh, come on," he said, gulping wine.

Tim read, doubting the plan would work—too far-fetched, in his opinion—then threw the massive brick of pages onto the table, where it landed with a *whump*. "Well, what the fuck was *that*, ladies and gentlemen?" he said. He glanced at the clock. If he left now, he would just have time to grab a little dinner before heading to the bar. It was always a goldmine there on Christmas Eve. Boys back home for the holidays who wanted a break from the family bullshit drama... yes, please. With any luck, he could pick up a couple of them for the night. Some nice Christmas packages to open under the tree. It practically took the sport out of the chase, but he wasn't one to complain.

He never made it to the bar, though. As he was getting ready, he turned the TV on to the news and saw something that made him stop dead and turn it up. The local sheriff, up where Nan lived, was found shot to death in a diner parking lot earlier that night.

"Whaaaat the fuck?" he said, collapsing into the recliner. He watched the whole news report (there hadn't been any more details, but he watched it anyway) and then reread the last chapter of Nan's manuscript. His hands started to shake and suddenly he didn't want company. He wanted to drink. And that's what he did. If what he was thinking was actually true, shit could be about to hit the fan for his biggest client. That was no bueno.

Tim turned the SUV onto Little Church Road, which hadn't yet been plowed, and inched along toward Holt House. He wasn't entirely sure what he would do when he got there. Ask Nan if she killed sheriff fatso? That seemed like an exceptionally stupid idea. And so what if she had? As long as she wasn't *caught*, it wasn't really a problem.

He could return the manuscript and tell her to burn it... that was getting a little bit closer to what he *should* do, but it still wasn't quite right. Her last book, *Dead Stories*, was selling fairly well, all things considered (and without the tour and signings to boot). He could keep the gravy train rolling a while longer if he could get her to get rid of the incriminating evidence (*if that's even what it is!* his mind insisted). Hell, if she just changed some of the names in her "confession," it would probably sell like hotcakes, a nice little follow-up to *Dead Stories*. Maybe torching it really was shortsighted.

By the time he turned into the driveway, he felt much better.

The SUV battled the snow fairly well, and he was able to get it most of the way down to the house before it refused to go any farther. Nan had all sorts of tractors and snow shit; she'd be able to get him out lickety-split. He saw her assistant's car (Lisa? Laura? Something like that anyway), buried most of the way under a mound of snow just starting to melt in the sunlight. He didn't know what she would be doing here the day after Christmas, but maybe Nan had a thing for young chicas. She wouldn't be the first old writer to wade into the dyke pool, God knew. It actually made him like her a bit more. And it certainly explained how she had gone ten years without a man since her husband died.

He knocked on the front doors and waited for someone to come. When no one did, he knocked again, harder. Eventually, the door opened.

"Lisa?" he said.

"Lauren. You're Tim, right?"

"Yeah, yeah. Listen, no offense or anything, but you look like shit. Are you okay?"

"Just tired," she said, smiling, then cocked her head to the side as if listening for something. It was kinda creepy.

"Hey, so is Nan around? I've got to talk to her about something sorta urgent. Nothing bad, so no worries."

Lauren's face was blank, her head still cocked, and she started to nod. "Yeah. Come on in."

Tim looked behind him, back up the driveway to where his car was stuck like a cork in a bottle, then stepped into the foyer. Lauren closed the door behind him, throwing the hallway into darkness.

"Come on down to the kitchen," she said, walking away without waiting for him to respond. "I'm just fixing a late breakfast." Nan's dog, the creepy little thing with the bulging white eyes, padded along at her side with its tongue lolling out.

Tim followed her down the freshly mopped hall, his briefcase clutched in his fingers, which, despite the cold, were starting to sweat. Something felt off, but he couldn't put his finger on just what it was. Lauren had lost a kid a while back, he knew. Maybe that's why she was acting sort of bonkers. And anyway, who really cared?

He sat at a red and white enamel-topped table (*kitschy*, he thought) and set his briefcase on the floor. "So where is Nan? She awake yet?"

Lauren took two mugs from the cupboard, one with a turkey on the front and one that said *Ho Ho Ho* in alternating red and green letters. "Coffee?"

"Can't, goes right through me. Got stuff for a Bloody Mary?"

"I think so. Or gin if you'd prefer."

"The Bloody Mary is fine. I'll take one for the road. I can't stay long, but it would sure hit the spot."

Lauren pulled an open bottle of vodka from the freezer, then mixed it with some tomato juice and a few other spices while he looked around the kitchen, trying to think of something nice to say about it and coming up short. When he looked back, she was stirring the concoction with a long-handled spoon. She set it in front of him.

He sipped, frowned, and then sipped again. *Probably the cheap stuff*, he thought. "Thanks. It's good."

"Sorry," Lauren said. Tim didn't know what she was apologizing for, so he ignored her. As he drank, his worries melted away, and after a few more big gulps, the drink didn't taste half bad either.

Down the hallway, a door opened, then a moment later closed.

"That'll be them, now," Lauren said.

"Them? Oh shit, Nan have company?"

Lauren didn't reply. She turned to the sink and started to wash last night's dishes as if making a point of not turning toward the door.

Tim glanced at the doorway, then at Lauren. "Who's she with?"

"A friend."

From the hall, Tim heard the sounds of two sets of feet moving slowly but deliberately toward the kitchen; one sounded like a slow, dry shuffle, like the *shhhh, shhhh* of slippered feet, and the other was a *thud thud* kind of noise, like peg legs moving on stone.

He took a gulp of his drink, thinking it would help hide his nerves, which had just come roaring back. *Why did I come here?* he thought. Then: *You're being stupid. Just calm the hell down. I'm sure there's an explanation for all of this.* He took another gulp. The more he drank, the better it tasted.

Shhh, shhh.

Thud, thud.

He wasn't able to calm down, though. His heart was racing, but he wasn't sure why. And thinking was getting very difficult. His throat hurt, too. Probably caught something trekking all the way out here to the unwashed asshole of New York.

He slugged more of his Bloody Mary down and started to cough. There was a taste of blood in the back of his throat. Sometimes, that happened in the winter, especially when he used his forced-air heat. It just dried everything out. But when he swallowed again, pain radiated from his gut up his throat like tiny shards of glass were being forced up and out, and there was quite a bit more blood accompanying it this time. He coughed it out across the table in a spray of fine droplets as his heart practically buzzed in his chest like the beating of a hummingbird's wings.

"Won't be long, now," Lauren said. She turned to face him (while still avoiding looking at the hallway door, he noticed), and Tim saw that her eyes were unfocused and pointing in two different directions, like the optic nerve in one had just snapped, sending it floating free.

Shhh, shhh.

Thud, thud.

A smell. That same one he had noticed on the phone and on the SD card Nan had sent him along with her manuscript. Tim squeezed his eyes shut and tried to muffle the sounds of his coughing with his elbow, not wanting to see what was about to stagger through the doorway any second, but he was having trouble breathing.

His eyes opened by reflex alone. Two shadows fell across the floor, one long, one a little shorter, both of them grotesque.

Rot, a voice from the hallway said. It was rough and creaking and old.

Decay, the other added. That one sounded like Nan. At least a little bit.

Tim opened his mouth to scream and to tell whoever (whatever?) was out there to just go away, he had to leave, had to get to a doctor, but the world started to go fuzzy around the edges.

He screamed anyway, a burbling sound, like screaming through a mouthful of gravy, as acidic vomit choked his throat.

And when the two things from the hallway came into the kitchen, he screamed again, louder and stronger.

And when the thing that looked like a walking corpse grabbed ahold of his arm with incredible strength and wrenched him from his chair down to the floor, he screamed a final time, high and ululating.

After that, mercifully, the world went dark. There was

nothing more than the very slight sensation of being pulled along the floor, so slight it could have been made by tiny bugs landing on his arm and then flying away.

In time (oh time, that strange and muddled thing), even that stopped.

-2-

Holt House stood tucked amongst the trees atop a stone precipice eighty feet above the Hudson River like a vulture looming over a dying creature; its sagging roof a pair of slumped, eager shoulders, its peaked arches staring eyes, the crack in the heavy stone wall made by a falling pine tree, a corrupt sneer. For a hundred and twenty years it had stood poised to strike, but now its time of waiting was over. Holt House was home to two starving things. And they hunted.

STARVING
THINGS
A NOVEL
ANDREW HEROLD

SHARE YOUR EXPERIENCE

Help *Starving Things* Reach More Readers

If you enjoyed the chills and thrills of *Starving Things*, please take a moment to share your thoughts with other readers. Your review not only supports Andrew Herold as a first-time author but also introduces *Starving Things* to others who might be hesitant to try a new writer.
Thank you immensely for your support!

ANDREW HEROLD

About the Author

Andrew Herold started writing at the age of ten, and quickly developed a love for all things scary; from haunted houses to psychological horror and everything in between. His writing reflects his dedication to character-driven, atmospheric horror.
He grew up in the Finger Lakes Region of New York, but has lived all over the country. A proud member of the LGBTQ+ community, he currently lives in Vermont with his husband, their dog, Bebe, and their cat, Shirley Jackson.

Visit his websites, andrewheroldbooks.com and starvingthings.com for a free short horror story, and for more information on his upcoming releases.
Starving Things is his debut novel.

amazon.com/author/andrewherold

instagram.com/andrewheroldbooks

threads.net/@andrewheroldbooks

ACKNOWLEDGMENTS

Writing a book is a solitary act. I like solitary acts. Interacting with people is draining to me; I crumple quickly under the pressure to be interesting and act "normal," (whatever the hell *that* is). The time it takes is, in my humble opinion, better spent rewatching *Heartstopper*, *The Sopranos*, and *Derry Girls*. I can quote all three extensively.

But life isn't a solitary act. If you're as lucky as I am, your path will cross with the right people at the right time, and you'll find your group; people who make you want to put down the remote and risk a foray into public just to spend time with them. Everyone here is incredible, kind, and outgoing, and has helped to make this book, and my life, the best it can be. I'd be lying if I said I understood how they looked at me and thought, "That's him. *That's* the socially awkward misanthropic curmudgeonly agoraphobe I need in my life," but I'm grateful every day that they did. And, honestly, a little baffled, too. But in situations like this it's best not to overanalyze things and just be glad the stars lined up the right way; stars are usually tricksy things. (And for those of you struggling to find your group, asking someone to read and provide feedback on your work is a crackerjack way of shanghaiing someone into being your friend...just sayin'.)

Having said that, any mistakes or liberties (such as with the geography of the beautiful city of Poughkeepsie, NY, or when there was a total eclipse in Maine) are mine. I'd like to further point out that this is by no means a complete list of those who have touched my life, so if your name doesn't appear here, fret not! There's always the next book.

There. Now that I've satisfied legal, I can get around to the actual thank yous. As my character Nan says, let's begin at the beginning. It is such a logical place to start, after all.

My fifth-grade teacher, Mrs. Shelansky, showed me the satisfaction that could be found in writing. She came into school early so I could use a computer to type my very first short story, which she had encouraged me to write as a class assignment. She's the first person who suggested I may have an affinity for the written word, and I'm grateful every day that she did. Writing is one of the greatest joys in my life; it's my lifeline to the world. I'm so thankful that she made sure I didn't miss out on it.

My husband, Mark, has supported me in every way possible. To list all he does would require a book the length you just read, so I hope he'll accept my blanket gratitude for everything. He made it so I was able to follow this dream. There aren't enough words–even for a writer–to express how important this is to me, so I'll just say thank you and I love you. (But then you knew that.)

Ann has read almost everything I've ever written, including this book three or four times...sometimes, I think she's immune to tedium. Her eagle-eyed observations and insightful recommendations always improve my work. I don't always take her suggestions like I should, but if there's something good on the page, she deserves the credit. She's my harshest critic, but one of my most ardent supporters. (*I'm getting used to my chicken feet* came from a dream of hers she generously bequeathed to me.) Thank you, Poodle.

My brother, David, has read and provided feedback on many stories for me, including this one. His enthusiasm for my work and his sense of humor has helped me to keep plugging away even when I don't feel like it.

My sister-in-law, Joanie, is one of my most eager literary

guinea pigs. No matter how many times I impose upon her to give me perspective on something I've written, she meets the challenge with excitement, which I find astounding. She's always ready with encouraging words, solid suggestions, and a chilled bottle (or three) of champagne to share. Which of these is the most influential to me changes daily.

Brigid is one of the best people I know. She's got a dry wit that is somehow full of love, drinks quality gin (like me), and sings all the best Irish songs. I owe her a great deal for introducing me to the gloominess and intelligence of Irish writers, for teaching me the phrase *caith siar é*, and for hoisting many a glass with me.

Anne-Claire and Antoine are two incredibly unique individuals. It's so rare nowadays to find someone who genuinely cares. They do. More than anyone I've ever met, I think. My day is always buoyed by their presence and laughter, and I thank the universe that I'm lucky enough to know them. Anne-Claire braved the horrors of *Starving Things* to help me craft it into a better tale, and Antoine designed (and designed, and designed) the cover to create something that is amazing and unsettlingly perfect. From the bottom of my heart, thank you both for this adventure we're on together. I never imagined I'd ever be here.

Geoff is always there for a late-night video chat to talk me down off of whatever ledge I've crawled up onto, with some of the most measured and grounded advice a person could ever want. He's also one of the funniest people on the planet. Getting drunk and ranting about horror movies with him is something everyone should experience at least once in life.

Stevie and Vic are both inexhaustibly generous people and I'm so lucky to know them. Stevie, thank you for all the wine, for your sense of humor, and for just getting me. I knew you understood exactly who I was when you gave me William Shatner's Christmas album as a gift. And Vic, thank you for the wine as well (I'm sensing a pattern, here...), your always engrossing conversation, and for the cooking and baking pointers.

I'd also like to extend a very special thank you to Sophia Cacciola, for taking time out of her busy schedule to read this book and write such a kind endorsement for it. We went to high school together once upon a time, and she was always so encouraging of my writing. Part of the reason I was able to show her this book is because she gave me the confidence to even try.

Finally, I would like to say to every member of the LGBTQ+ community and our allies, I see you and you are loved.